THE CHOSEN CHRONICLES

CHOSEN
A
LIFE

K.A. PARKINSON

For Brent, Rhett, and Tyge
I love you forever

Beneath the decaying soil of man's doubt and disbelief,
The seeds of truth behind all legend lay forgotten.
Tangled amongst tendrils of fairytales, fables, and falsehoods.

CHAPTER ONE

SECRETS IN THE DESERT

"IF I'M RIGHT, AND THIS IS ANOTHER NIGHT OF USELESS RECONNAISSANCE, we're getting real cheeseburgers tomorrow for dinner. Not squirrel meat on the crunchy crap you call a bun that you *think* passes for a cheeseburger." Macy paused in the middle of strapping her weapons belt around her waist to look at Bastian—her guardian and mentor—in the eye.

"I cannot believe you would drive one hundred miles for a slice of meat on bread. I do not see the point." Bastian leaned out the window of the parked '62 Ford to hand her a canteen.

She attached the canteen to the bottom of her small backpack and shook her head. "You're over a thousand years old and yet you still haven't learned to appreciate the genius behind a juicy cheeseburger."

Bastian sighed. "Some things are completely unnecessary."

She grinned as he tossed a pair of binoculars at her head, much harder than you would expect such an ancient-looking man to be able to. She caught them one handed and bit her lip to hold back a laugh.

Bastian ran a gnarled hand over his thick white beard. "Either way, you must succeed tonight and your chances do not look good." His strange sapphire-blue eyes, that on first glance would appear almost-human if it weren't for the color, were dilating and shifting, the black pupil growing and shrinking with each turn in his thoughts. He was *watching*.

"Hey, that's cheating! No looking ahead. You're not my Watcher right now, remember? You're supposed to be just some crazy old guy out for a drive in the middle of the Nevada desert."

Bastian shot her a glare for the sarcastic tone and she bit her lip. He wasn't in the mood to joke. She met his eyes, recognized the look, and turned her attention to her pack.

She started going over the contents aloud to keep him from bringing up what she knew was on his mind. "Three Glockshaw bombs, just in case. Small pouch of jerky—but I'm banking on that cheeseburger so I'm not eating it unless I get really hungry—"

"Macy." Bastian's tone twisted her insides so she talked louder.

"One canteen. Spare knife—"

"Macy." He opened the door to the truck and nearly fell in his attempt to get out.

She rushed over and helped him out, handing him his cane to use for balance instead of the rusty door. She kept her eyes down when he placed his hand on her shoulder.

"*LaUnahi.*" Her gut clenched when he called her that pet name, *my little bird.* He knew what it did to her resolve.

"Bastian, don't. Okay? I get it. I need to take this seriously. You're not always going to be around, blah, blah, blah. I don't see why we have to keep talking about it."

He reached a gnarled hand out and gently pulled her chin up until she looked at him. It was the last thing she should have done. To look into his aging face, to see the wrinkles, the thinning white hair, the ailing body, to hear his ragged breathing, it made the truth all too unavoidable.

Warmth started to flow through her fingertips as her Kuna, her *gift,* began to come to life. One of the side effects of being a Kunamin, or one who has the gift of wielding fire, was the constant emotions always battling so close to the surface. Macy felt herself losing control.

She took a deep breath and closed her eyes, ignoring his warm fingers on her chin. "You promised. You're not going anywhere until after I turn eighteen. You can't leave me to face my Transcendence alone!"

In less than two years, she would transcend and her human body would connect fully with her Kuna. She still hadn't gained as much control as she'd need before that happened. She forced down her frustration with her Watcher. Didn't he understand how much she still needed his guidance, his calming influence?

"Macy, you are stronger than you think. As much as I want to be there to help you through your Transcendence, I do not have control over my time. None of us do. No matter how powerful we may think we are."

She spoke through her teeth. "Fine. Let's just go over the mission, okay?" *I'm through discussing this!*

Bastian's eyes narrowed as he read the venom in her thoughts until she turned her focus to the mission ahead, hiding the pain until all she felt was the growing excitement she always experienced before a mission.

She heard Bastian's low sigh as she pushed him out of her head. She'd gotten good at controlling her thoughts over the years, but she'd never learned to stifle the guilt she felt for hiding things from her Watcher. Bastian loved her and only wanted what was best for her, but she didn't need to be coddled.

"You will be observing the group of Dark creatures I felt move into the area." Bastian followed her lead and turned the conversation to the job ahead. "Based on the slowing of their movements I expect they will have set up camp. The Guardians need us to discover what they are doing." He paused and met her eye. "Just watch, Macy. Do *not* destroy. We cannot let them know we are on to them. We need to be able to observe over a period of time. The Dark is up to something, something elusive."

"The Dark is always elusive, Bastian."

His eyes shifted. "This feels different."

Prickles rose on Macy's arms. "Okay, so stay hidden and observe. Don't kill anything. Shouldn't be too hard." *But boring.* "What am I watching?"

Bastian tilted his head and frowned.

"Oh, right. My mission. No help from you." She closed her eyes and placed her palms together to access her Kuna. The sensations she felt were familiar to her. Warmth flowed into her fingertips and calmed her. To find the answers she was looking for, she didn't need to actually create fire or endure the weakness it brought. Still, the gentle scent of eucalyptus and roses that accompanied her Kuna swirled in reassuring wisps around her head.

Bastian whispered softly, deepening her focus. "Feel for the malicious tremors of the Dark within the Balance, the world around you. Sense the way it affects your thoughts, your emotions, your instincts. It is this that you must rely on. Your eyes can deceive you. Your life force cannot."

Her breathing slowed, the crystal Radia shard that hung around her neck—the mark of her power and purpose—began to glow softly, and the sounds of crickets singing in the coming night disappeared. She could feel the subtle pulse and sway within the Balance that encased the world; the gentle, quiet warmth of the Light, the repulsive evil of the Dark, each repelling the other.

She spoke with her eyes still closed. "It feels like a small group…" She squeezed her eyes tighter. "Not small. Weak. Kreydawn miners?" She opened one eye to see Bastian nod approvingly and shut her eyes again. "One, maybe two Suppressor leaders."

She opened her eyes and held back a grin. She was right, she could tell by the satisfied smirk on Bastian's face.

"Very good." He leaned against the rusty blue fender and rubbed his temple with a shaky hand.

She bit her lip. There was something else she had sensed, something elusive as Bastian suggested, but she couldn't get a mark on it. "So, you know I was just kidding about not looking ahead right? And you were kidding about me not succeeding…right?" Macy tried for nonchalance but Bastian didn't have much of a sense of humor.

He looked at her and his sapphire eyes held no trace of humor. "I do not know. I can see you arrive. I can see you watching the movements of the enemy, but my vision stops there. You must be wary Macy. This is to be only a reconnaissance mission, but my heart tells me there is more to it. Be suspicious of hidden guards. I would not be surprised if they have Raksasha nearby just in case."

Macy snorted. "Bastian, I'm not afraid of Raksasha. I'll sense them a mile off."

"Not if you are preoccupied as the night falls or if they are being shielded somehow." He gazed over her shoulder, his eyes fixed on the horizon where the sun had nearly set. "Even courage can become fear if it is misused *LaUnahi*. Caution and respect for the enemy's knowledge is not fear, it is true courage and acceptance that we do not know everything. You may be far more powerful and intelligent than the Raksasha, but never underestimate the cleverness and tactics of the Dark."

He looked back into her eyes and the lines on his face softened. "Go now, while there is still a little light. You must reach the encampment before the sun sets and they awaken. I will stay here and *watch*. Come for me in the morning."

Macy nodded once, tugged her backpack over her shoulders, shoved a purple sucker in her mouth, and turned toward the horizon feeling Bastian's eyes on her until she descended the small hill into the thick, scrubby underbrush.

The air cooled considerably as the sun dropped lower and lower until nothing remained but a vibrant red line that slashed across the sky like smeared blood.

She shrugged off the morbid thought and focused on what she felt ahead. The vibes were getting stronger. She slowed her pace and lowered her stance. It was time to use her advantages. *"To' konsh'la,"* she whispered and the desert sounds became almost deafening. She could hear the beating of tiny wings of flies as they buzzed around her head. It was amazing how, once intensified, cricket song turned into a brutal crescendo of noise and the slither of scales over sand sounded like nails on a chalkboard—until you learned to tune it out and focus on the sounds that really mattered, like the low grunts and clanks she could hear about a half mile ahead.

The sun crept lower and the creatures that thrived in darkness began to stir. She belly crawled to the top of a long sandy knoll and peered over the edge. Below, encased in shadow cast by stone boulders and makeshift camouflaged lean-tos, her quarry started to awaken. It was a sickening sight.

Kreydawn, mindless slaves of the Dark, had no thoughts of their own. As far as she could figure the only thing they knew to do without being told was eat, but she even wondered about that. Suppressors pushed their thoughts into the Kreydawn's tiny brains and told them what to do.

Right now about twenty Kreydawn were scavenging, plucking scorpions and other insects from the sand and popping them in their mouths full of rotting teeth. Their chalky translucent skin, stretched tight over a human-like form, could be deceiving, until you saw their beady black eyes, dull and devoid of emotion, and the row of five stubby horns that stuck out of their forehead in a perfect line. The one nearest Macy had the tip broken off the horn above his right eye.

Only one Suppressor stalked among them, close to seven feet tall and bone thin. His black cowl hid his features, but Macy knew what lurked in the shadow. A pale mouthless face and single red eye. Every so often, he stepped on the fingers or toes of the Kreydawn, who didn't seem to notice. Slowly, one by one the Kreydawn stood and followed the Suppressor out of the camp. Macy shadowed them at a crouch along the top of the hill; about a hundred yards away from the camp they paused.

Macy found her vantage point in a thick, tall cluster of prickly sagebrush and shimmied her body lower in the sand, allowing it to cover most of her body. She pushed her pack into the brush, covered the edges with sand, and buried her sucker stick. At the base of the sage, she cleared a large enough gap to see everything the Kreydawn were doing.

Large wooden carts scattered the area, covered with heavy tarps. Stacks of shovels and picks rested beside tall piles of sand. One of the carts was exposed and it held what looked like large gray rocks.

She rolled her eyes. Looked like she was right. Nothing important. She was so getting that cheeseburger.

Her eyes followed the synchronized movements of the Kreydawn. Their arms lifted and dug at exactly the same pace. She blew out a low breath. Kreydawn were so easy to kill it was almost embarrassing. If only Suppressors could talk it would make this boring mission worthwhile. She could jump in, kill the Kreydawn, and force the Suppressor to talk, no need to watch. But Suppressor thoughts could only be retrieved by their Dark masters, as Bastian had said only darkness could understand darkness. So, unless she got lucky and a Dark captain just happened to show up and she was able to take *him* down, her tempting idea would never work anyway.

She sighed and propped her chin on her hand. It was going to be a long night.

Boredom was not welcome as a Chosen one. She *enjoyed* the fight against the Dark. She relished the adrenaline rush that flowed through her as she destroyed those creatures that thrived on death and carnage. Her gift of wielding fire thrilled and exhilarated her. Not everyone could create a firebomb in the palm of their hands and manipulate it to destroy a dozen creatures at once. She smirked at the memory of the first time she'd controlled her flame enough to melt through a wall of Raksasha. The demonic blood-trackers hadn't stood a chance.

She blew a strand of blond hair out of her eye. Too bad using her Kuna could be so physically draining. It was so freaking fun!

Boredom also caused other problems. Too much time to think. She glared at a lizard perched on the sand beside her arm. Bastian did it on purpose, he knew bringing up his impending demise right before her dull mission would make her think about it. He could be so sneaky.

She flicked sand at the lizard and watched it scamper away, wishing her thoughts would leave with it. Bastian had been with her for the last ten years, since her sixth birthday. As her Watcher, he could sense her thoughts, get glimpses of her future, and guide her in her destiny as a Chosen protector for mankind. But he was more than that, more than she wanted to admit aloud. She had few memories of her parents. She'd spent the last ten years suppressing painful thoughts of them and her human life viciously ripped away. Bastian was all she knew.

Bastian had taught her well. She even believed herself ready to face fighting the Dark on her own, especially after transcending to the height of her gifts. The idea of connecting to them fully, no longer being as drained by using her Kuna or enhancing her physical strength, was extremely appealing. She'd only brought it up to make him feel guilty. Bastian had taught her well, she didn't fear the Dark anymore.

The sun had set as a subtle breeze ruffled her hair and a chill she knew wasn't from the wind tried to force its way along her spine. There was still one creature of darkness she feared. One she never allowed herself to think about. One that hadn't been seen since the night she'd been chosen.

She squeezed her eyes shut and forced the thought from her mind. With her eyes closed, she became aware that she wasn't alone.

Crap! She'd gotten distracted just like Bastian said. She would never live it down.

She felt before she heard the approach of Raksasha. Their vibrations were intent. They'd caught her scent.

She twisted out of the sand, her knife already clutched in her fist. She would have to kill them silently, no Kuna. The Suppressor couldn't find out she was there or its masters would know a Chosen was in the area.

She felt at least two Raksasha flank her little hill. She couldn't feel any more, but as Bastian said, they could be masked. She'd have to be quick.

The top of the first Raksasha's head appeared and Macy readied her knife. "*Mig'nata,*" she whispered and felt strength surge to her arms. As soon as she saw his yellow eyes glowing deep within the sockets of his black, leathery, skull-like face, she snapped her wrist forward in one lithe movement, and after a brief whistle, her knife reappeared—lodged between the Raksasha's eyes. The creature fell back onto the sand with a soft thud.

Her feet barely shifted the sand as she ran nimbly forward, feeling for the direction of the other Raksasha. She'd just pulled her knife from the creature's skull when she felt the second jump up behind her.

Macy twisted in the air and tossed her knife the same moment the Raksasha threw his spear. It grazed her right arm just before her knife embedded in the center of his forehead. She ran over, pulled her knife out of the creature's head, and cleaned it in the sand.

She waited, crouched beside the dead Raksasha, for fifteen minutes before she was sure there were no more creatures surrounding the area. She quickly buried the Raksasha and went back to her hiding place to wrap her bleeding arm and finish out her watch for the night.

○○○

Hundreds of miles away a teenage boy bolted upright in his bed clutching his right arm.

CHAPTER TWO

GAMES

Tolen Parks stared at the sparkly popcorn ceiling in his room as the sun rose slowly outside his window. His right arm still tingled a little, just above the elbow, but the strange dream that had sent him flying awake in a cold sweat was trickling away like sand through his fingers. He squeezed his eyes shut and tried to remember, but it was gone. All he could recall was the intensity of the moment right before the pain shot through his arm.

He kneaded his forehead with his fingers. He was so sick of weird dreams. At least this one hadn't had the half-dead zombie guy in it. The creepy man had starred in his dreams all too frequently the past few months. He just wished he could have at least one night where he dreamed of something normal, or maybe didn't dream at all.

He heard his mother's rusty Honda start, the belt squealing loudly in protest. He glanced at his clock, 7:30, surprised that she was actually going to work. The Honda idled for a few minutes and died. She attempted it twice more, slammed the door shut, and then Tolen heard her walk back into the kitchen, pick up the phone, and call her boss.

He covered his face with the pillow so he didn't have to listen to her excuses. She was going to lose her job. He knew it was only a matter of time. Between their car constantly breaking down and the steady decline in her health, she'd missed more days than she'd worked in the past month.

A soft breeze moved the thin curtains covering his window as he climbed out of bed and pulled on a pair of shorts. The hot desert sun pushed its rays forcefully into the room. He sighed as he tugged on his sneakers and searched his closet for a shirt with the least amount of holes.

He'd been saving a little of his earnings from his job at the local grocery store in the hopes that he'd be able to buy a couple new shirts and some clothes for his mother, but he was beginning to think he'd barely have enough to help cover this month's rent, let alone buy them clothes.

He pinched the bridge of his nose as he thought about having to ask Mr. Grange for more hours. It was no secret that the freak Tolen Parks and his weird mother were the poorest family living in Green River—a tiny, nearly-abandoned town nestled near the base of the Book Cliff Mountains in southern Utah. This quiet place housed many destitute families, but Tolen and his mother surpassed them all. They lived in the oldest rental, on the oldest street, in the furthest, most forgotten part of town.

Mr. Grange would feel sorry for him and give him the extra hours. It was humiliating knowing they needed the sympathy if they were to survive.

He fought back the resentment he felt toward his mother. It wasn't her fault she was too ill to work. At least that's what he kept telling himself. He didn't like to think about her strange abilities that she would use to heal the smallest cut on his finger, or the tiniest sniffle, but for some reason couldn't use on herself.

The sound of his mother's bedroom door closing had him clenching his fists. She'd be spending another day in bed. He took a deep breath, grabbed the first shirt he touched, no longer caring about holes, and strode into the bathroom, his long legs carrying him across the cramped hall in two strides.

He closed the door softly, leaned against the cracked pink sink and stared at his reflection in the mirror. His wavy brown hair stuck out in every direction as if he'd just stuck his finger in a light socket. He turned on the water and dunked his head in the sink without waiting for it to warm up. The ice-cold stream distracted him from thoughts of his sick mother, responsibilities, and weird dreams.

Today was Saturday. A day off from school, from the outside life he pretended to live, and the people who, without always meaning to, made his life miserable. He didn't have to be to work until three and his best—and only—friend Dane had promised him a *The Lord of the Rings* video game marathon.

The idea of spending the day with Dane at his house in a video game coma, without having to think of anything other than how best to destroy Sauron, sounded like a slice of heaven.

He rubbed his hair dry with the ratty towel on the rack, and ran his fingers through the tangled locks until they finally lay semi-straight and shadowed his strange eyes. He didn't like to look at his reflection very long; it was just one more thing that kept him from fitting in. If he turned his head to the left, he looked normal. Brown hair, brown eye. Turn to the right however, and everything changed. He had the strangest blue eye he'd ever seen; so light it was almost translucent, with dark cobalt lines running out from a pupil that every so often would dilate and contract without the normal stimulant of light. Even weirder was what it showed him when it did this. It could pull in a bird in flight a half mile away. It could show him the sleek movements of the coyotes that hunted near his home in the dead of night.

He pulled out the box of brown contacts behind the mirror and popped one into the blue eye. It was uncomfortable. This eye, that so often seemed to think for itself, always itched behind the contact. Even though Dane had caught him without his contact once and understood that it was a rare birth defect, he couldn't take a chance that someone might see him as he walked to his friend's house and spread more rumors.

Suspicion made his mother do rash things, like pack their bags and move in the middle of the night. Tolen liked it here in this mediocre town better than anywhere else they'd lived in the last seventeen years, so he wore the stupid contact. He went to school and pretended to be like everyone else.

He waited for his eye to stop watering and pulled a blue shirt over his head. It clashed with his orange shorts, but he didn't care. He'd be coming home to change into his uniform before work anyway.

Not wanting to bother his mother, he tiptoed past her door and into the kitchen. He quickly scribbled a note reminding her where he would be before hurrying out the back door.

He sucked in a deep breath of warm summer air, appreciating the sweet smell of his mother's daylilies and rosebushes. The dirt crunched under his feet as he walked the half mile to Dane Smithy's, feeling the despair dissipate the closer he got to his friend's home. Dane, just by being himself, could make anyone forget his troubles.

"I still don't see why you would pick to be Legolas over Aragorn. He's the king, dude!" Dane stuck his thick fist into the bowl of popcorn between them, grabbed a handful, and shoved it in his mouth, shaking his head.

Tolen pointed to the TV screen. "Who else could use a bow and arrow, and double swords, and move the way Legolas does?" He took a bite of Dane's homemade jerky and titled his head. "Aragorn is good, but Legolas is awesome."

Dane rolled up onto his knees, his head barely as high as Tolen's shoulder where he lay propped up on one elbow. "Whatever." He looked in the bowl. "I'm going to make more popcorn. Do you want some more jerky?"

"Nah," Tolen shook his head. "I'm good."

Dane used Tolen's shoulder to lift his tiny frame off the floor.

Tolen flicked through Dane's pile of games on the floor deciding which to play next. *Guardians of Middle Earth* looked good. He opened the case and caught movement out of the corner of his eye. He looked toward the hall to see Hank, Dane's father, standing there staring at him, his dark eyes brooding and unfocused.

Tolen swallowed. "Hi Hank."

Hank's eyes narrowed and he grunted once before shuffling in the direction of the kitchen. Dane met him halfway and they shared a muffled conversation in their native tongue. Tolen always thought it sounded

German, but he didn't know German or any other foreign language enough to venture a real guess.

Dane sat back down and placed the now full popcorn bowl on the floor between them. He glanced over his shoulder. "Annoying old man."

"Is he mad? Were we being too loud?"

"No. He's out of booze. He wants me to run to town and get him more. Idiot forgets I'm underage." Dane shoved more popcorn in his mouth and spoke through full cheeks. "Like he needs more alcohol anyway."

Tolen held up the game. "One more round before I leave for work?"

Dane grinned. "You're on!"

ooo

Macy chewed slowly, savoring every bite of meat-loving goodness. "Mmm, perfection." She mumbled between bites.

"Completely unnecessary." Bastian shook his head as he watched her in disbelief. "Technically, you did not win. I am merely indulging your adolescent growth spurts."

Keeping one hand on the wheel, Macy wiped her mouth on a napkin before shoving a fry between her teeth. "Whatever. I'll take it." She swallowed. "But, I was right. Those Kreydawn weren't mining anything but a bunch of gray rocks. And those Raksasha deserved to die."

His eyes narrowed. She shifted uncomfortably against the worn material of her seat, and turned her attention back to the road and the mouth-watering scents wafting from the bag beside her. She popped another fry in her mouth and started humming to the static on the old radio, waiting for the lecture to begin. She counted to twenty in her head before he started.

"And you find nothing suspicious in their actions at all?"

Macy's fingers scrambled around the bottom of the bag searching for loose fries. "No, Bastian. I told you. I watched all freaking night. They dug up nothing but rocks."

"And the digging up of pointless rocks does not seem suspicious?"

She sighed. "Maybe?"

He dropped his chin.

She blew out a loud breath. "Fine. You bought me a burger so I'll admit it did seem a little weird. They kept putting the rocks in the carts, but there was no rhyme or reason to the type, shape, or color. I would have guessed they were looking for something else, but then why keep the useless rocks too?"

"Why indeed?"

Macy flashed a glance his way to see his eyes shifting. He couldn't see the future of the Kreydawn and discover anything more unless she was somehow directly involved. His Watcher gift only extended to as far as she was concerned. "Will we go back tonight?"

He closed his eyes and brief flash of pain crossed his face before he quickly covered it up. "No. Not tonight."

Macy's heart sped up as he leaned against the door with his eyes still closed and his hands started to shake. "Bastian?"

"I'm all right Macy. Just go home. W-we will resume our watch tomorrow." His chin dropped to his chest and he started to snore.

Macy's full stomach turned. He used to be able to go days without sleep, rarely needing to regenerate. Now, he seemed to drop off all the time, sometimes sleeping for days.

His time *was* short. And she was *not* ready.

Chapter Three

THE
WATCHER

Death approached in the wind. The Shadow Wraiths were hunting.

For two days Forrest Bastian had regenerated, unaware of the danger moving its way toward them. The elusive monster he had felt finally made its first move while he'd slept and left his ward unaware and unprotected.

He sat beside the dirty window, his translucent blue eyes dilating and contracting—focused on things only he could see stirring in the bleak May night. Flickers from the dying embers in the fireplace deepened the worry lines on his ancient face as an old carriage clock silently timed the advancing storm.

The battered radio on the coffee table cackled out another warning. Bastian sighed and glanced at the newspapers littering the floor, grateful that Macy never read the papers she scavenged for him, choosing rather to ignore her human connections.

Each headline debated the sudden rush of thunderstorms suddenly attacking the southwest. The icy temperatures and frigid winds were peculiar, especially in Nevada, but their journalistic guesses as to the *why* of them stood as far from the truth as the earth from the sun. The storms did not come from ordinary weather phenomena.

Shadow storms did not come from this world at all.

Thunder crashed. The Shadows were restless.

Bastian's thick white brows wrinkled in concern. The Shadows were not headed in this exact direction yet, but it was still too risky. The house was no longer safe. No matter how weak he might be, it was time to leave.

Macy would not be happy. This tiny shack had begun to feel like home to her, but he knew despite how far she'd come in her abilities, her past would render her powerless against the frightening effects of the Shadows. They would use her fear against her.

He grasped the crystal shard that hung from a strand of old leather around his neck. This gift from the dying Radia star allowed him to stay in sync with Macy's thoughts and emotions. It felt warm to the touch and glowed softly with the turn in his thoughts.

He glanced again out the window. Far in the distance, the black mists of the Shadow Wraiths writhed and twisted amongst the gray clouds. Even this far away, their evil pricked at his heart and mind.

Macy was feigning sleep in her tiny back bedroom. He wished he did not have to tell her what was coming. The Shadows had slept for centuries until they'd been released over ten years ago, specifically to find and destroy *her*. His hands trembled. If he'd reached her a second later than he had, they would have succeeded.

He balled his hands into fists. If he had gotten to her sooner—he shuddered at the memory—he could have saved them all. The image of her dying parents would haunt him forever.

The Shadows had disappeared right after. Not once since then had he felt their presence. Strange that they would give up so easily…until now. Why had they returned?

The clock chimed twelve low notes. Bastian slowly stood, leaned heavily on his cane, and shuffled to the window. His carpet slippers caught on the frayed rug and he stumbled into the window ledge. He took a steadying breath, rested his hand over the ache in his chest, and pushed aside the moth-eaten curtains. He leaned his wrinkled forehead on the cold glass and focused. The night seemed to squeeze into the room as he massaged his temple and allowed his Second Sight to search for any unseen danger.

He felt the shift in the Balance seconds before a small glowing orb appeared in the darkness. Before he could blink, it burst through the window. He threw his arms up to shield his face as flying glass sliced into every inch of exposed skin and his blood splashed onto the dirty floor.

Wind lashed into the room, extinguishing the last spark of light in the fire. Bastian's chair slammed into the wall of bookshelves and the table swirled into the fireplace. A cascade of bricks tumbled free and twisted up into the vortex. Tattered books flew from the shelves, as chunks of old plaster and faded wallpaper ripped loose from the walls and mixed in with the debris.

The Radia shard against his throat glowed brightest blue, a warning. Tremors shuddered through his body and he fell to the floor. The heavy mirror from above the fireplace shattered to the ground beside him. The fragments reflected the fear in his eyes as the wrinkles on his face smoothed, the liver spots disappeared, and the cuts on his arms healed. His gnarled knuckles softened, lengthening his fingers. His scalp began to tingle and the little bits of white hair he had left turned charcoal black. More hair grew in until it hung in thick waves that blew about his shocked face. His back aligned and his body filled out with ropes of thick muscle.

Strength surged through him and he slowly pulled himself to his knees. The wind continued to howl and pelt him with rubble, but he hardly noticed.

He raised his hands to his face in horror. Moments before it would have taken every ounce of power in his life force to make his ancient body run short distances, and then only if there was life-threatening motivation. Now he knew he could run miles without stopping, face a hundred Dark creatures, and still not need to regenerate afterwards.

This realization terrified him.

The glowing orb hovered just above his right shoulder, bringing a strange warmth with it. He lowered his hands from his face and the orb dropped into his open palms. The moment it touched his skin, the radiant mist surrounding it vanished, revealing another small, glowing, Radia shard.

It was the shard of the Ninth Chosen and the reason for his miraculous restoration of youth.

Bastian squeezed his eyes shut and image after frightening image flooded his mind.

Over the howl of the wind, he heard the high-pitched shriek of Raksasha and his eyes snapped open.

The Shadow Wraiths were coming.

ooo

The wall behind Macy's bed trembled, interrupting the relaxing sounds of the Rachmaninoff concerto. She jerked out her ear-buds and cocked her head to the side. The wind was always loud as it passed through the thin walls of this ancient house, but it had definitely gotten louder since she'd gone to bed. She shrugged. Maybe another dead tree had blown over. She was just about to push the buds back into in her ears when a second muffled thud shook the wall. This time she was certain it came from *inside* the house.

She rolled her eyes. "Jeez, Bastian. Chill out. You don't have to start throwing things." She'd promised him, the third time he'd come to check on her, that she'd really go to sleep. That had been over an hour ago. She punched her lumpy pillow into a more comfortable shape and started to lie down again.

A powerful gust of wind slammed into the house and an icy chill ran over her skin. Her eyes caught a sliver of movement beside the door and she paused with her head above the pillow. She twisted her old school MP3 player until the dim light cast from the tiny screen pointed at the doorframe. Dust swirled in strange spinning patterns through the crack beneath the door.

A boom of thunder resonated through the room, and pieces of plaster rained down from the rotted ceiling, sprinkling the top of her head. A familiar ominous feeling filled her body and her heart sped up, the Kuna within her reacting to the vibes of the Dark moving nearby—closer than they'd been just an hour ago.

She rolled off the bed in one swift movement and pulled her knife from a rip in the mattress.

"*To' konsh'la*," she whispered, and every sound around her intensified. She could hear the wind tossing the leaves in the trees outside, the brush of the tumbleweeds as they scattered across the dry desert floor, and the scurry of frightened animals.

She focused her hearing inside the house, searching for Bastian's familiar, wheezy, old-man breathing.

Instead, she heard strange whooshing, like wind through a tunnel, echoing from the direction of the living room…and moaning, soft, pitiful moaning…

Bastian softly called her name.

Her heart jumped to her throat and heat flooded her palms, but she willed the Kuna to stay inside her body.

Slow down. Gauge the threat first, Bastian's constant warning murmured in her head. *Save your strength.*

She clenched the knife in her fist, opened the door, and slipped silently to the end of the hall.

If this is some training exercise Bastian, or you fell again while fixing a midnight snack, I'm going to kill you. She edged along the wall, peeked around the corner, and her breath caught in her throat.

Books, papers, bricks, the remains of Bastian's favorite chair, and the coffee table were flying around and around in some sort of freak indoor tornado. A huge man knelt in its center, pale blue light issuing from his cupped hands. The odd light eerily accentuated his horrified face. He seemed completely oblivious to the remains of the living room furniture slamming into him.

He closed his fingers. The light and wind vanished, and the broken furniture crashed to the floor.

He gasped and fell forward, catching himself with one hand while the other remained in a tight fist by his side.

Macy's ears rang in the sudden silence.

"*To' inreedo,*" she whispered, and the man's frame came into perfect focus through the darkness. Even though she was certain she'd never seen the man in her life, there was something oddly familiar about him.

"Who are you?" She held her knife in front of her. The blade trembled in her fingers as her Kuna fought for release.

He didn't move. His eyes stayed riveted on his closed fist.

"What do you want?" She cast a quick glance around the room, but there was no sign of her ancient Watcher. "Bastian!"

The man finally looked up and turned toward her. Lightning flashed through the room and his eyes mirrored the glow—unnaturally bright, sapphire-blue, those eyes could belong to only one person.

Macy took a hesitant step back. "You can't be…"

The man stood up. He was *enormous*, well over six feet, and covered in thick muscle that bulged beneath his tight flannel shirt. His face held an expression she knew well—only on a different, much older face.

"Who *are* you?" Macy took another step back into the hall. The man's blood-splattered shirt looked exactly like the one Bastian had been wearing—the one with the missing front pocket.

She glanced down. Same faded jeans, same nasty old carpet slippers.

"Macy, I *am* Bastian."

She shook her head. "No, it's not possible."

"I promise to explain but we must leave, *now!* Go to your room, get your things." The voice was close to Bastian's tone, it held the same hurried finality he used when danger was near.

She didn't move.

If you really are Bastian—my Watcher—then you'll feel what I am thinking. She cast about in her mind for something only Bastian could know. The first thought that came seemed stupid, but it was the best she could do. *What did you give me for my sixteenth birthday?*

The man gave an exasperated sigh. "You do not allow gifts or even the acknowledgment of your birthday. This is ridiculous. Close your eyes. Look inside yourself. Your life force knows your Watcher."

Macy's hands shook. This guy appeared to be aware of her thoughts but that didn't mean it wasn't some trick of the Dark. "And my Watcher has drilled into me never to close my eyes when an enemy is looking right at me."

"I am not your enemy!" He threw his hands in the air. "Macy, there is no time for this! It is the will of the Balance. You have to trust me!"

That was definitely Bastian's matter-of-fact, annoyed voice.

With one last threatening look in his direction, she closed her eyes. A familiar quivering began in her heart and filled her whole body. Her life force *did* recognize the man standing in front of her, not because of the eyes or the familiar voice, but from the power that emanated from him. The evil did not come from him. It was outside, traveling to them swiftly from the northwest.

This man was her Watcher. It really was Bastian. This didn't make her feel better.

"Okay, fine. You're Bastian." She glared once in his direction before turning to run down the hall back to her bedroom. "The Balance has been known to do worse."

Her battered backpack sat propped against the wall. Her hands shook as she pulled a purple sucker from the front pocket and stuck it in her mouth. She rolled up her ragged blanket and tied it to the bottom of the pack.

Seconds later Bastian followed her in and waited in the doorway. His creepy new face a mask of impatience, his wavy hair tied back into a ponytail, his favorite carpet slippers swapped for hiking boots, his blood-spattered shirt traded for a clean one. No matter how hard she tried, she could never be as fast as Bastian.

"Feels like Raksasha." She spoke through her teeth as she rushed to tug knee-high leather boots over her jeans.

"Yes." Bastian glanced over his shoulder. "I sense at least four, but there could be more. They are moving as quickly as they can. They will be here in less than ten minutes." He held out her belt, and she stood and tied it around her waist. Her knife was back in the scabbard, and her survival pouches dangled beside it.

Macy lifted her eyebrow. "How did the Raksasha track us here? Do you think someone noticed me spying on the Kreydawn?" She thought back to the reconnaissance mission. She'd only noticed the mindless Kreydawn being controlled by one Suppressor. She'd killed the only two Raksasha guards that had been stationed outside their mining field…or so she thought. What had she missed?

Bastian didn't answer. His eyes remained focused out the window.

She knew when he purposely avoided an answer. She tried not to worry as she threw on her sleeveless jacket and pulled a hair band out of her pocket. Turning to the cracked mirror she quickly twisted her waist-length, dusty blonde hair into a haphazard ponytail. She met her wide green eyes in a scrutinizing stare for a split second before she looked down at the glowing face of her watch.

"Ready in less than thirty seconds." She smirked, tossing the pack over her shoulders.

"I suppose the complaints about having to sleep in traveling clothes will now stop." His voice was clipped and impatient and he left the room in a hurry, beckoning her to follow.

Whatever he was hiding couldn't be good. This wasn't the first time they'd "up and left" in the middle of the night, it was no less than to be expected, but Bastian was rarely this short tempered. Either the younger Bastian was more impatient or the situation was far worse than normal.

Her already nervous stomach tightened as she rushed after him.

Lightning lit the ripped floral wallpaper in the living room and a huge owl dropped from the ceiling, swooped low over their heads, and spiraled out the broken window.

Macy stopped.

Bastian squeezed his eyes shut.

The sucker fell out of her mouth and landed with a soft thud on the worn carpet. "That…that wasn't…a Ghost Owl?"

Bastian nodded, his eyes sympathetic.

"An omen from the Light?" Thunder cracked and she winced. The eerie cold she'd felt earlier once again brushed across her skin, raising goose bumps on her arms and the back of her neck, but this time she knew the chill wasn't caused by the weather.

"Yes." He took a step forward and held out his hand. She shook her head and stepped back. "Not a normal storm?" Bastian moved closer.

"The Shadows?" Her voice came out in a broken whisper. She could feel her throat constricting. Sweat beaded on her upper lip and along her forehead and her palms turned cold and clammy.

"They were released a few days ago, while I was regenerating. As far as I can guess by the stories in the newspapers, they were staying along the coast—"

"But now they're headed here." She could feel the blood drain from her face and colors started to swim before her eyes. She backed against the wall, tried to keep her legs steady beneath her, and reminded herself to breathe. "Why? What drew them?" *Why Shadows? Why now?* The questions she couldn't speak flowed from her thoughts.

"*LaUnahi*, we do not have the time to discuss it. They have shifted their direction toward us, but we can escape as long as the Raksasha do not slow us down." He put his hand on her shoulder. "Macy, we must hurry. The closer the Shadows get the more they will drain your strength."

She shook off his arm and gave him a nasty look. "I can handle it. Let's just get out of here."

As much as she fought it, terror twisted Macy's stomach into knots. She ran warily behind Bastian along the deep ditch that had once channeled water to the deserted ranch.

Raksasha she could handle. Crud, she'd take on any Dark creature. But why did it have to be Shadow Wraiths? The one kind of Dark she truly feared.

She closed her eyes briefly. The Shadows had killed her parents. It had been more than ten years, but whenever the memory of the Shadow Wraiths' attack forced its way to the surface, the remembered pain nearly incapacitated her.

Bastian slowed, held up his hand to stop her, and closed his eyes.

A muffled screech broke through the air and unbidden heat surged through her body.

Bastian shoved her ahead of him. "Go! Run! The Raksasha have caught our scent!"

"*Mig'nata!*" Macy pushed every ounce of life force strength she had to her legs, increasing her speed. Bushes and twigs scratched her face and arms as she pushed her way through the brush. The Ghost Owl appeared at the head of one of Bastian's concealed escape routes and she followed it without pausing to question, wanting only to be as far from the Shadows as possible.

The rusty International Scout seemed to grow out of a clump of tall sage. Macy ripped open the driver's side door, threw her pack in the back, jumped in the seat, and glanced around anxiously.

Where are you Bastian?

She leaned over and with fumbling fingers began to twist together the ignition wires dangling below the dash to start the truck, wishing briefly that the owl had led her back to the old Ford. The owl hooted, and she looked up to see two Raksasha clawing their way through the bushes.

Almost perfectly camouflaged by the darkness, the blood-trackers' black leathery skin clung to their bones, giving them the look of burned skeletons. Their ape-like arms swung by their sides, and their three-inch fingernails dripped ocher poison onto the hard ground. They paced the truck and sniffed at the air. The scent of a Chosen's blood this close to them filled their glowing yellow eyes with ravenous hunger.

Bastian, come on! Where are you?

She'd foolishly used up too much strength empowering her run and her nerves were too jittery to stay focused. She couldn't jump out and fight them hand to hand.

The Raksasha swayed closer. She had no choice but to call her Kuna. Hopefully she could keep it going long enough to distract them until Bastian caught up. She wouldn't think *if* he caught up. Not yet.

She rubbed her palms together quickly until they began to tingle and burn. The smell of eucalyptus and roses filled the truck, smoke rose from her fingertips, and she thrust her hands out the window.

"Mi'no ha!"

Two fireballs erupted from her palms. Shrieking, the Raksasha dove to the side and the fireballs disappeared in a shower of sparks and smoke.

The Raksasha resumed their pacing, eyeing her hands with contempt.

She gasped for air and tried to pull more heat to her palms, rubbing them together fiercely.

The creature on the left bared his black pointed teeth and lunged. Macy shot another burst of fire, this one much smaller than the last two.

The Raksasha sidestepped to avoid it and shrieked in triumph as the fire-ball slammed into the sage behind them, setting it ablaze.

Sweat poured down Macy's face, her chest constricted as she gasped for more air to feed the heat. One of the Raksasha sprang to the window and she scrambled backwards to the passenger side. Its fingernails were inches from the door when suddenly Bastian jumped through the burning brush, gripping his machete, covered in dirt and blood.

He swung, the blade flashed, and both Raksasha fell twitching to the ground, their heads rolling away from their bodies, black blood squirting from their necks onto the dry dirt.

Bastian jumped into the driver's seat, tossed the blood-covered blade into the back, and twisted the ignition...

Nothing happened.

Snakelike fingers crawling with maggots clawed their way up through the ground. The Night Demons had smelled the blood and were coming up to feed on the carcasses.

"Bastian..." Macy watched the slimy, scaly-white arm of a Night Demon followed by the tip of its emaciated shoulder break free of the dirt. "We *really* need to leave."

Bastian punched the dash. "I thought you fixed the truck?"

Macy reached over and twisted the wires dangling beneath the steering column. "And I usually drive."

He slammed the gas pedal to the floor and the engine caught and roared in a tortured sort of way.

He shot her a dirty look and she raised her eyebrows. "I've been telling you we needed a new ignition in the Scout. I would've taken the Ford, not this piece of crap, but this is where the Ghost led me."

Bastian shoved the shifter forward—grinding the gears—rocks and dust sprayed everywhere as he spun a one-eighty.

Three more Raksasha leapt toward the truck and Bastian flicked on the headlights. The creatures skidded to a halt and threw their hands over their eyes, momentarily blinded.

Their horrible screams rang in Macy's ears as the Scout barreled through the dirt and brush.

"Are you hurt?" Bastian glanced over once they'd reached the safety of the highway—the Scout carrying them away at its top speed of seventy-two miles per hour.

Macy clenched her teeth as a fire-truck passed by them, sirens blaring. "Nope, I'm *dandy*—just another wonderful day in the life of a chosen protector of the unsuspecting human race." She rolled her eyes angrily and pointed at the black and red blood spatters along his arms. "How are you?"

"Just a few scratches, nothing you cannot stitch up." He gave her a sideways grin that quickly turned to a frown at the look on her face. "Calm, Macy." His voice carried a warning.

Macy's breathing only increased, her arms trembled, and a thin stream of smoke curled from her palms. She turned in her seat to glare at him full on.

"Calm down? Calm down? What in the Sam-hill is going on? How in the name of Pete did they find us?" The weak smell of eucalyptus and roses once again seeped from her hands. "Bastian, come on! Shadow Wraiths? And what the *H* is going on with *you?*"

"Macy, getting angry and disrespectful is not going to help anything."

"I didn't cuss." She spoke through clenched teeth.

"If you think I do not know what you mean when you say Pete, Sam-hill, and *H*, you are insulting my intelligence."

"You're avoiding the question."

Bastian squeezed one of her smoking hands. "Focus. You need to regain your strength. The Shadows are far behind, but they are still following… I will not tell you anything until you show that you have control over yourself."

Macy gritted her teeth, shoved her hands under her legs, and started humming Beethoven's Moonlight Sonata double time. Five minutes later her heart slowed to a normal pace and the heat left her palms, but she remained too angry to speak calmly.

Bastian pointed to the glove box. She opened it and took a purple sucker from the bag stashed inside.

Sticking it between her teeth, she stared out at the passing landscape, allowing the sound of the music in her head to calm her temper and the sugar to help regenerate her life force.

Pink hues stained the horizon, a blood red sun peeked just over the rocky hilltops, and wisps of cloud streaked the brightening sky. The core of the Shadow storm trailed farther and farther behind them as Bastian sped along the deserted highway. They would be safe until tonight when the Raksasha came out to play again. They needed to be far away from here by then.

Slowly her body relaxed as the miles rolled behind them, but her thoughts continued to swirl with the night's events. Bastian had brought her to the deserted Nevada ranch a couple of years ago, saying the land had been forgotten by man and Hidden, preparing her all this time for him to *die*, and now he was all young and buff?

She glanced at the Watcher beside her. This man was a stranger…but not really. Whatever was happening, could it at least mean Bastian would not be dying anytime soon?

"I'm sorry Bastian, for my attitude and my actions. I should have known it was you immediately, and I should have had more control to pace myself. I shouldn't have taken all my strength to run." She paused and sucked in a slow breath. "It's so stupid! Those two Raksasha were nothing! The Shadows—"

He gave her hand a reassuring squeeze. "It is all right, Macy. You did the right thing by questioning me. I am sorry for losing patience with you. I know you understand the tools of the Dark. I will never think less of you because of what the Shadows' power does to you. Your past makes them more potent for you than they are for most everyone else—and they are very potent indeed."

An unwelcome lump formed in her throat and she dug her fingers into the tattered fabric on the edge of her seat.

"It is not a sign of weakness, *LaUnahi*." He touched her hand and she pulled away.

She took a slow breath. "Now that I'm calmer and we're safely away, will you tell me what just happened back there? And explain why you suddenly look like a twenty-year-old body builder?"

Bastian frowned, and his thick black brows drew together. "This will not be easy for you to take. I am still unclear on all of the details myself. I must get us someplace safe so I can focus and really *see* what is going on."

"What have you seen so far? What do you already know that you are doing everything you can to avoid telling me?" She swallowed. "Is it me? Are they after me again?" She tried to sound brave and irritated, but traces of worry leaked through in her voice.

Bastian stared at the road in front of them and the veins on the back of his hands stood out as he gripped the wheel. A muscle started twitching in his temple.

Panic started to rise in Macy's chest.

He glanced her way. "No, they were not sent after you. Not this time."

The panic lessened, but only slightly. "Then who? Why?"

"Macy…I…It is a dangerous omen when the Light uses the Balance to restore a Watcher. It would not do so if the circumstances were not dire."

"Okay, you're starting to freak me out. What's so bad that the Light is willing to mess with the Balance?"

Bastian took a deep breath and pinched the bridge of his nose. "The Ninth has been chosen."

Macy didn't realize she'd been holding her breath until it came out in a loud whoosh. The pain of betrayal seared through her heart. "What? No…No way. Tha—that's impossible. The Light wouldn't let the Balance do that. It *can't* do that. It wouldn't throw something like that out there without preparing us first—"

"You have been preparing, Macy!" Bastian tugged his ponytail in frustration. "We have all been preparing for this day—for centuries. The Light does not control the Balance, you know this. The Balance is affected by the choices and actions of both Hidden and human. It has decided that the time has come for the last Chosen."

Bastian lifted the necklace that held his Radia shard from beneath his shirt. Dangling beside it was a smaller crystal, similar to the one Macy wore, emitting a familiar faint bluish glow. "This shard belongs to the Ninth."

Macy shook her head. "That's totally backwards. Shards don't come to Watchers. Watchers are drawn to their shards." The urge to scream and throw something became almost overwhelming. Her palms tingled and she breathed deeply, knowing she had to stay calm or Bastian wouldn't tell her what she needed to know.

"It *is* the Ninth's shard. It drew the Shadows' attention and led the Raksasha to us. They were drawn by the power it exerted to find me."

"But…" Angry moisture burned the back of her eyes. She clenched her jaw and spoke through her teeth. "Watchers only protect those that hold the other half of their Radia shard. I have your other half—it found *me*. That shard is not part of yours." She pointed a trembling finger at the glowing crystal Bastian tucked back beneath his shirt. "It belongs to another Watcher. Why didn't the shard return to him?"

"At this point I do not understand any better than you do," he whispered gently. The frustration in his voice seemed directed internally, no longer at Macy. "There is more."

"What?"

"The Ninth is not human, he is Hidden kind."

The feeling of betrayal deepened and her eyes narrowed. First Bastian turned all young and freakishly huge, now the Ninth wasn't even human like the legends said—what else was the Light going to spring on them? She shredded the sucker stick between her fingers, taking slow deep breaths to keep from losing her temper. "But what does it mean? Why…what is it the Light wants from you? From us?"

"We must find the Ninth, before the Dark discovers he has been Chosen."

He? Great, the Ninth's a boy. She rolled her eyes. *Figures. I get to babysit some bratty little boy.* "What about the group of Kreydawn we're supposed to be watching? Who's going to figure out what they're up to while we're off searching for the Ninth?"

Bastian continued as if she hadn't spoken. "I am getting glimpses of the boy, but they are indistinct." He frowned and shook his head. "He seems to be a good child, humble and kind-hearted. My life force is pulling me towards him nearly as strongly as it did when the Light sent me for you." His eyes narrowed and his voice softened until it sounded almost paternal. "What course has changed to make it my destiny to *watch* for two?"

Bastian's tone brought the heat back to her palms. She bit her lip and willed her Kuna to stay inside her body.

The Ninth Chosen…?

This is bad. She shoved her hands back under her legs. *This is really, really bad.*

CHAPTER FOUR

THE NINTH

MACY GENERALLY HATED CHEAP MOTELS, BUT FOR ONCE, SHE'D ACTU-ally been glad to curl up on a lumpy, smelly mattress. She yawned as she peered between the dingy curtains into the faint morning light. Sleeping in the backseat of the Scout for the last two days as they zigzagged through three states to avoid Dark spies had not been comfortable—the ancient truck turned minor bumps in the asphalt into road hazards. When they'd pulled into the neglected motel in the middle of Nowhere-ville, Utah, she'd collapsed as soon as her head hit the yellowed pillow. She stifled another yawn as she spied Bastian entering the office, where he'd gone to check them out. The neon *No Vacancy* sign cast a sickly orange glow across the side of the building.

Macy had declined Bastian's invitation to accompany him to the motel office to check out and grab a free muffin. She'd wanted the time alone to think. Now she wasn't so sure that'd been a good idea. She stared through the grimy window, watching the sun slowly light the shabby parking lot without really seeing anything. Her thoughts and emotions tossed around in her head until they were nothing but a jumbled mess. Bastian was aware of it—of course he was—but he'd yet to offer advice. He was likely just as upset about their situation and too preoccupied with trying to figure out what to do about it to focus on how much it was affecting her.

She absently twisted a lock of hair around her pinky finger. She usually did a pretty good job of blocking the memories of the night she'd been Chosen. But ever since the moment Bastian had said they were going after the Ninth, the horrible details of that night, coupled with the last image she had of her parents had been creeping into her thoughts like a poisonous weed. She swallowed and closed her eyes as she felt them curl and twist through her mind, strangling her heart with painful memories.

The distant voice of Bastian explaining the legend seemed to echo through the years and fill the room. *The Ninth will be the last hope for the survival of the races… If the Ninth should fail, the Balance between good and evil will collapse, and evil will roam free…*

Her heart stuttered in her throat. Ten years ago she held her shard for the first time and from that moment she was able to actually see the horrifying hand of the Dark. It was then that she'd witnessed firsthand the cruelty of the demon Raksasha and felt the staggering power of the Shadow Wraiths. The idea of that kind of evil roaming free with no one to stop it…

She pushed her fists into her eyes. *Don't think about it!* But the darkness behind her eyelids only created the perfect backdrop. Black memories rushed in—the sounds and images as fresh as if she stood once again in their tiny kitchen.

The Raksasha jumped through the window, shrouded by the swirling mists of the Shadows… her mother screamed and her father pleaded uselessly for their lives…

Sick waves of fear crashed over her, her chest heated up and the Kuna tingled in her palms. *Breathe, just breathe… stay calm!*

But once the memories were free, they couldn't be stopped, and her fear had her cold. Horrible pictures of every monster she'd ever fought against for the ignorant human race filled her mind's eye. Crawling over the planet, unstoppable, killing ruthlessly, and not caring if the victims were innocent children or the elderly—until nothing remained but the Dark.

She forced her eyes open and focused on the hideous flowered bedspread, trying to stop the flood of terror. But the flowers turned into the weeping faces of the defenseless, curled into the disgusting, twisted features of Raksasha, and the writhing mists of the Shadows. The moldy, rotting smell of the stained carpet filled her lungs and became the smell of death and decay.

She folded her arms tightly over her stomach and rocked back and forth. Intense pain, worse than any physical injury, clouded her mind and crushed her heart. The Kuna burned in her palms and she knew she couldn't hold it back much longer.

Mom, Dad, I need you! She gasped for air; broken, tearless sobs forced their way free. *No, don't think about them!* She couldn't breathe…*Bastian!*

The door flew open. Bastian met her gaze for an agonizing second before he gathered her into his arms, and pulled her next to him.

She gagged. *The images…Bastian, please make them stop…the Kuna…I can't hold it back…*

Bastian wrapped her hands in his huge ones tenderly and she felt the heat lessen, but her mind was held fast. "Macy, *LaUnahi*, you are safe! I promise you are safe. All is well my little bird." He rubbed her back and began to sing, in a voice as soft as a whisper, the Soothing Song in the language of the Hidden. She didn't understand all the words, but slowly the peaceful calm only Bastian could bring, started at her toes and pushed the pain from her heart and the pictures from her mind, like sunlight piercing fog.

Bastian pushed a strand of hair off her sweaty forehead. "I am so sorry, *LaUnahi*. I have been far too preoccupied." He cradled her against his massive chest and wrapped his arms tightly around her shaking body. "Forgive me, my little bird. I promise I will no longer be distracted from your needs. You are, and always will be, my first priority."

Macy sat up, took a deep breath and leaned out of his arms, feeling embarrassment creep up her face. . She appreciated the soothing presence, but she hadn't needed coddling for years. Not since she was a small child trying to adjust to the loss of her parents and the grueling life of a Chosen.

She stood up and kept her eyes averted. "I just had a bad moment was all. The Ninth stuff caught me off guard." She rolled her shoulders, shoved her shaking hands into her pockets—silently cursing the tremble in her voice that would give her away—and focused on allowing the Soothing Song to finish its job clearing her thoughts. As the last dark memory faded back to where it could be locked away, she took another deep breath and met her Watcher's eyes. "I'm fine. It won't happen again."

Bastian sighed. "You are not fine, *LaUnahi*," He gave a sad smile and his eyes filled with something she couldn't quite pinpoint, it looked like regret. "But you will be."

She turned away and picked up her pack. "So are we going to adopt the Ninth today? I'm assuming the stop wasn't just so we could actually sleep in a bed. We're close, aren't we?" She cast him half a glance then wished she hadn't. Guilt washed over her at the disappointment on Bastian's face. She knew he missed the days when she told him everything she thought and felt, even though he already knew it. But she'd been a child then.

Bastian pulled a sucker from his pack and handed it to her, the disappointment on his face slowly fading into calculation. He wanted to keep her talking about her feelings, work through her fears, she could see it in his eyes, but he knew she wouldn't be a willing subject, and whether he wanted to admit it aloud or not, right now there were more important things to worry about. She unwrapped it and popped it in her mouth as he slung his bag over his shoulder, opened the door, and motioned her ahead.

"Yes, we are close." His tone implied the complexity of this truth. "I have discovered the exact location of the Ninth. He is about sixty miles southeast of us in an out-of-the-way town called Green River."

Macy tightened the belt of her jacket, making sure her weapons were completely covered. Her knees shook slightly as she stepped over a couple of crumbling muffins Bastian must have dropped in his rush to get back to the room. "What about spies? Is it safe to just show up at his house?"

"No. Things are very complicated with the Ninth. I am unsure of exactly how to approach him. The images of him come and go like bad reception. Sometimes he is so clear I can see his every move, feel his thoughts as I do with you…" he ran a hand over his face, "other times he very nearly disappears. I can still sense him, but my sight is blocked as if he is shrouded in a mist I cannot penetrate."

Macy glanced at him, surprised. Worry lines creased Bastian's forehead adding familiar wrinkles. "What does that mean?" she asked.

"I do not know." He frowned. "All I do know is that the time has come for extreme caution. We have evaded the Shadows for now, but we must be very careful. We do not want to alert the Dark to the boy's importance. If he already has spies watching him and they recognize us, it will not take them long to discover what we are after and why."

They reached the Scout and Bastian held open the passenger door.

Macy paused before getting in. "Are you sure you don't want me to drive?"

He looked at her with concern and warmth crept up her face. "I'm fine Bastian. Really. I can drive."

"Actually, I have found driving again quite enjoyable." He winked, and a slow grin spread across his face. "I have not put the metal to the pedal since you became tall enough to see over the dash."

"That's pedal to the metal, bud." She laughed as she buckled her seatbelt.

Bastian shrugged.

"You'd think after more than a thousand years you'd have the slang down a little better."

"Some things are completely unnecessary." He settled himself in the driver's seat and twisted the wires together with a tiny smile dancing on his face. "Well, since I dropped our muffins, shall we go somewhere decent for breakfast?"

"Sure." She couldn't help but smile in return. Underneath all the strange new muscle and hair, he was exactly the same Bastian. His simple kindness and poor attempts at humor were familiar and safe. As worrisome as the whole Ninth business was, she couldn't help but feel gratitude toward the Light for restoring her Watcher.

Several minutes later, they pulled into a run-down truck stop with a small restaurant. They walked past several men slouching wearily at the counter, their hands wrapped around steaming mugs.

Macy led the way to a corner booth and picked at a spot of dried food on the table while they waited for a waiter. Bastian stared out the window, his eyes dilating, *watching* again. She wondered whose future he was searching, hers, or the *Ninth's*. Macy turned her attention to the quiet conversation between two of the tired-looking men sitting at the counter.

"Sixty-miles-an-hour, that's what the news-anchor said. But I guarantee you Frank, it was more'n that." The older of the two, his thick scraggly gray hair stuffed under a grease covered blue ball-cap, whispered. "Nothing else could've relocated my old shed. That darn thing's solid wood, and been standin' there for more than a hundred years." He shook his hairy head. "And the cold… I ain't never felt cold like that out here before. 'Specially not this time o' year. Never been a day in June under seventy since I was in grade school."

"I believe ya, Jed," Frank whispered back, absently stroking his wiry black beard. "I lost six cows last week. Vet keeps tryin' to tell me it's some sickness or other, but I know it was that cold storm. They done froze to death. It ain't natural."

Macy shivered and looked away. If those guys knew the truth, that the storms—the craziness—was only going to get worse, they'd run away screaming. Too bad there wouldn't be anywhere for them to go.

"Eh'hm."

Macy opened her eyes to see a slightly overweight waitress with thick blonde curls.

"What can I get ya?" She smiled a little too widely for this early in the morning.

"Uh," Macy glanced at the menu. "We'll both have the Special and orange juice."

Bastian continued to stare out the window, the pupils in his sapphire eyes still dilating and contracting. The waitress watched him with a bemused look, whether because she'd noticed his odd eyes or because the teenager had ordered and not the adult, Macy was unsure, so she coughed to get the woman's attention.

The waitress jumped and Macy tried to offer a reassuring smile.

"Oh, um. I'll be right back with your juice." She cast one more furtive look at Bastian before hurrying off toward the kitchen.

"You know," Macy twisted the napkin around her fingers, "you could always say 'thank you', or even order and not look at them—it might make people less nervous."

"You are used to my voice and accent, humans are not. Besides it is impolite to not look someone in the eye when you are speaking to them."

So is ignoring them. She didn't say it aloud, but Bastian's eyebrow rose anyway.

"Your negative attitude concerns me."

"Huh?"

"There is hope for those men." He lifted his chin toward the men at the counter. "We *will* find the Ninth. The humans will be safe."

She chose not to answer and he resumed his stare out the window.

Fifteen minutes later the waitress returned with their food. After two bites of slightly crunchy pancake, Macy figured it was safe to start asking questions.

"So you never told me, how are we going to show ourselves to the Ninth?" She gave up on the pancakes and switched to the bacon. She lifted a piece to her mouth but stopped half way—bacon wasn't supposed to be stretchy. So much for a decent breakfast. Still, it beat trail food and Bastian's version of a home-cooked meal, which usually consisted of slightly stale bread and whatever animal he'd managed to kill that day. She was about to take a bite when Bastian's response made her forget all about breakfast.

"I am not sure yet. We will observe him at the high school first. That is where I seem to be able to *see* the clearest. Because this is the case, I am leery of approaching him elsewhere until I get a feel for the area."

Macy's head spun and her palms tingled. The bacon fell back to her plate in a puddle of syrup. "What? Wait. Did you just say high school? Why will the Ninth be at the high school?"

Bastian sighed and laid down his fork. "Because he is seventeen."

Not quite an hour later, they passed a sign declaring they were ten miles from Green River, and Macy finally felt calm enough to speak.

"I thought Chosen were picked when they were little. Train them when they're young and all that. How can the Ninth be seventeen? I mean, it's bad enough that I thought I'd be babysitting some bratty six year old—this guy's probably some stupid, know-it-all, wanna-be rock star."

"Yes, another teenager. Hmm." He glanced at her and shook his head. "You are passing judgment on someone you do not know based on teenagers you have seen on television. Macy, that is neither fair nor mature."

She resisted the urge to stick out her tongue.

Bastian's jaw flexed. "There are many strange anomalies with this situation. If he has been Chosen since he was a child, why was I never connected to his Watcher? If not, and he was just now selected, why would the Light do that? The logic behind such a decision is frightening to contemplate."

He meant it. Macy's stomach flipped—nothing frightened Bastian. "Why?"

"Because the only reason I can imagine the need for this sudden choice of the Ninth is that the situation with the Dark is worse than anyone has realized, and the Light could not wait for the Ninth to grow up and so selected an older child."

Macy started to wish she hadn't ordered the special. The crunchy pancakes were thinking about making a comeback. She pulled a pack of antacids from the glove box.

"Ah, there it is." Bastian pointed to a scattering of buildings in the distance as Macy stuffed the medicine into her mouth.

They passed three abandoned gas stations and she snorted. "This is a city? Don't blink Bastian, you might pass it."

Bastian's eyes scanned the barren desert. "This place is sad. Pity the dying, Macy. Do not scoff at them."

She mumbled an apology, and leaned her head back against the seat.

Bastian turned into a deserted motel, next to one of the empty gas stations, pulled around to the back, and hid the truck between two rusty, mammoth-sized dumpsters.

"The school is just over there." He pointed to a plain brick box sitting on the far side of a quarter-mile of dusty fields.

It was one of the smallest high schools she'd ever seen. Though she had to admit she hadn't seen many, let alone ever set foot inside one.

"So how long before the *Ninth* gets here?"

"Within the hour."

Tolen doodled on the chipped plastic tabletop instead of studying for the math final he'd be taking later that day. The aroma of toasting bread—held prisoner in the broken toaster by a spatula—mingled with the awful smell of the tea concoction simmering on the stove.

Sunlight spilled over the craggy Book Cliff Mountains, casting soft pinks and yellows across the dingy kitchen.

He caught his reflection in the outside window. His strange eyes stared back at him almost mockingly. He felt his blue eye dilate and focus in on a herd of antelope skipping across the base of the hills, miles in the distance. He rubbed his eye absently, trying to get it to stop, but he knew it wouldn't until it decided to. He sighed and resigned himself to watching the antelope until his eye decided to settle back to normal.

At least the Book Cliffs were a beautiful sight to look at. The town and its namesake were both a contradiction. The Green River wasn't green—it was murky and muddy as it passed through on its way to more inviting areas. The town wasn't green either, but flat desert, with a shrinking population. There were almost more abandoned buildings than occupied ones now, and the people who did stop here were either lost or passing through, like the river. Towns like this only served one purpose.

They were a good place to hide.

Three crows swooped across the back yard to land on the broken fence. Their beady eyes seemed to stare through the window right at him. He shuddered. He hated crows.

His mother shuffled into the kitchen still wearing her faded flannel pajamas. Her frayed bathrobe hung loose over her thin shoulders. Tendrils of her wavy auburn hair fell out of the bun at the base of her neck, the rich red in stark contrast to her pallid skin.

Areen Parks used to be beautiful, Tolen remembered. His heart clenched. Now, between the outfit, her sunken cheeks, and the dark circles under her eyes, she looked more like a junkie.

He bit his lip. She looked worse every day. She wouldn't be going to work…again. He hoped the extra shifts Mr. Grange promised would be enough to buy groceries as well as make up the difference in her lack of paycheck.

She slid onto the cracked vinyl chair across from him and pushed her briefcase to the side. A few sheets of paper stuck out—Tolen hoped they weren't important. She met his gaze and guilt washed over her face. She dropped her eyes to the doodles on the table.

"Would you like me to make you some breakfast?" she whispered hoarsely.

Tolen squeezed her icy fingers. "I ate some toast. I had to study for my Calculus final so I got up early. I made some toast for you, and I've got some tea on." He scrubbed out the doodles with an eraser and stood up.

He pulled the spatula free of the toaster and removed the slightly burned slices. Her eyes never left the table as he smeared jam over the bread, poured her tea, or placed her cold fingers around the mug. Her hands shook as she lifted it to her lips.

A little color came to her cheeks after a few sips. He had no idea why her strange tea always worked when nothing else did. The stuff smelled like dirt, but the way she drank it you'd think it was ambrosia from the gods.

Tolen started loading books into his backpack. If only she'd let him take her to a doctor—get her some real help—but she wouldn't.

"Will you be alright while I'm at school?" He struggled for a calm tone.

She nodded and started tracing the cracks in the table with her finger.

Tolen pulled on his backpack and turned towards the door.

"Principal Stoker called last night," she whispered.

He paused with his fingers on the handle.

She looked up with concern etched in every line of her face. "He's worried that Jeff Macro might try to retaliate. He thinks you shouldn't go anywhere alone for a while. Would you like to explain to me what he was talking about?"

Tolen groaned softly. "It's nothing. Jeff the jerk just loves any excuse to pick on people."

Her eyes narrowed and her cheeks flushed. Tolen could see her worry lines deepen and he gritted his teeth knowing he had to explain before she got all worked up. "Jeff and his buddies were calling me names when I was walking home from work the other day. A branch from the tree above them fell onto the jerk's big head. One little bump and a few stitches—it was no big deal. He was back to his normal obnoxious self two days later."

Her face paled. "Did you cause it?"

Tolen shifted his feet. "I don't know. Maybe."

"Tolen—"

"Mom, Jeff has no proof it was me and he'd sound like a freak if he tried to say it was. I wasn't anywhere *near* the tree. Besides, it happened over a week ago. If he was going to do something, I'm sure he would've before now. It's fine. I promise. Don't worry."

This wasn't entirely true. In fact, he kept overhearing how Jeff was biding his time until school got out for the summer so he could beat the crap out of Tolen and not have to worry about being suspended. Principal Stoker must have heard the rumors, hence the concerned phone call.

His fist clenched tighter on the door handle. This was the last thing he needed his mother to worry about.

Her lips tightened. She didn't buy his explanation, but she let it drop. "Would you like to do something to celebrate graduation?"

"Huh?"

"Since you don't want to go to the ceremony next week I thought maybe you'd like to do something else to—to celebrate."

He knew her pause had to be because of the look on his face. He worked at rearranging his expression as he bit back a remark. She sat there, weak and sick, yet she thought she would take him out and celebrate? Sometimes she made no sense. Pretend to be normal, but avoid everyone normal, while you try to blend in with normal—even if you're so sick, you can barely function.

"Dane and I talked about hitting a movie in Price. But we might just stay here and rent movies." It was scary enough leaving her to go to school or work. An hour away in Price he'd probably have a heart attack, worrying. "Well, I'd better go." He pushed open the screen door.

"Already?"

"Yeah, I need Dane to help me with the rest of the pretest."

She nodded slowly. "Okay."

Tolen swallowed hard, let the door close, and went back to hug his mother gently. "Make sure you eat something else today besides just toast and tea, okay? I put the leftover chicken in the fridge. Don't worry about the dishes. I'll take care of them after school."

She squeezed his fingers. "Have a good day, and don't forget your contact," she added as he walked away.

He stopped half-way outside. "I'll put it in before the bus shows up."

Her fingers tightened around the mug. "Okay."

She looked at him and smiled, but Tolen knew her fake smiles too well to be reassured.

He hurried out of the house, the screen door banging shut behind him. The smell of sage and dust swirled in the warm desert air. He took a deep breath and strode across the dry lawn.

There was so much he wanted to ask, but he couldn't and it infuriated him. His mother was too weak to handle any kind of confrontation and every time he asked about their crazy life that's what it became—a confrontation.

Tolen's shoulders relaxed as he pushed away the invading branches hiding Dane's shack of a house from view.

He tossed a handful of pebbles one by one at the tiny attic window, avoiding the front door for fear of the possibility that Hank was hungover again. Half a dozen stones later, a chubby hand pushed open the window and Dane poked his head out. His muddy brown eyes were puffy, but a huge grin filled his face.

"You're up early." He yawned.

Tolen smirked. "I need your expertise. I'm stuck on problem fifteen."

"Uh-huh, right. Just a sec." Dane's face disappeared.

Five minutes later, he hobbled out the back door—his usual strange breakfast of cold mashed potatoes on bread clenched in his thick fist—trying to juggle a backpack half his size in the opposite hand. Tolen reached down, took the pack, and tossed it over his own.

Dane craned his neck to look up at Tolen and mumbled, "Thanks," over a mouthful of potato.

Tolen chuckled. "No problem."

"Hey, slow down. What's the hurry?" Dane tugged on Tolen's arm. "You wake me up at the crack of dawn, and now you're practically running to the bus stop. You really that anxious for another day in the place you call high school hell?"

Tolen hadn't realized his agitation was making him hurry. He slowed his stride to match Dane's stubby legs. "Sorry. It's been one of those mornings." He rolled his eyes.

Dane nodded sympathetically. "Your mom's not getting any better I take it?"

Tolen shrugged.

Dane didn't push him for any details. "Did you have the nightmare about the half-dead zombie guy again?" he asked instead.

Tolen kicked at the ground, sending up puffs of dust. The tiny motes caught the first bits of light breaking through the trees. "Yep." He couldn't confide in Dane completely. He had to hide his weirdness from everyone, even his best friend. But they could talk about safe things. Things every other teenager had to deal with like crazy parents and freaky dreams.

"That's so bizarre. I mean it's not as if you watch a lot of horror movies. I thought you were gonna cry when we saw that Halloween show two years ago." Dane snickered.

Tolen pushed his arm. "If I remember right, you were the one who asked if we could leave early. I think you said you had a stomach ache."

"Hey, I ate too much popcorn." Dane paused, and his voice turned back to serious. "The dreams are coming more often, aren't they?"

Tolen gritted his teeth and nodded. "I wish there were some way to get him out of my head. Even when I wake up, it's as if a picture of his creepy face has been pasted to the back of my eyelids. Every time I blink I can still see him."

Worse was the fact that when he finally woke up, shaking and sweating, the pain and misery the man felt was Tolen's own pain. It took him hours to get back to sleep afterward. Dane waved a hand in Tolen's face. "Hey, you okay?"

"I'm fine," he lied.

They reached the slab of broken cement that served as their bus stop and sat down. Tolen pulled out his math. Dane did the same, occasionally offering help.

Several minutes later Tolen slammed his book shut and shoved it unceremoniously in his backpack. "I hate math!"

Dane grinned up at him, "It's not that bad; besides if you fail you won't graduate and you'll be stuck in summer school."

Tolen grunted, took his book back out and started writing. He could feel Dane watching him.

"Tolen, I know you're not okay."

Tolen kept his eyes on his book.

"You think you're good at hiding it, but I can tell how stressed you are. I understand if you don't want to talk about it, but you don't need to lie to me, okay?"

Tolen glanced at Dane's kind face and wished he really could talk to him, tell him everything. Even though Dane couldn't do anything to help, it would be nice to have someone to vent to. But that wasn't an option. He looked at the pencil in his hand and shrugged. "I'm just really worried about my mom. She's getting worse. I can hardly get her to eat. I want to take her to the doctor but she refuses and…" He sighed. "I'm just frustrated."

Dane patted Tolen's shoulder. "I'm sorry. I wish I knew how to help you, but look what I've got for a parent." He snorted. "Hey, there's at least one good thing you can look at. Nightmares can be better than reality, even if they are about freaky zombies. At least you get to wake up and it's over, right?"

Tolen laughed without humor, and pulled the case that held a single brown contact from his backpack. Leave it to Dane to try to find something positive. "Yeah, I get to wake up just in time to ride the bus back into another nightmare."

A cloud of dust rolled toward them, the outline of the school bus barely visible through the murk as Tolen popped the brown contact into his right eye.

ooo

"Finally." Macy jumped out of the Scout. She'd been thumping her foot against the dash, headphones in her ears, sweat rolling down her back, waiting for the bus to show up for what seemed like forever.

"He will be the second to the last to get off." Bastian spoke in a focused monotone.

Macy stood on the front tire, wiped the moisture off her forehead, and rested her elbows on the shaded part of the hood.

Bastian handed her a pair of binoculars. "Do not enhance your sight. Save your strength. I am not sure what we might encounter."

Macy held the binoculars to her eyes and watched the front of the school with an unfamiliar feeling of jealousy stirring in the pit of her stomach. She hadn't attended a real school since kindergarten.

Bastian leaned against the driver's side door, closed his eyes, and massaged his temples.

The bus emptied slowly. She tapped her foot impatiently against the tire.

When she finally saw him, a smirk touched her lips—it didn't take binoculars to see the Ninth was a total geek. Tall, probably right around six feet and lanky, his dark chocolate hair hung low hiding his eyes. He walked with hunched shoulders and his head down, as if trying to make himself invisible. But there was something about him that still managed to draw the eyes of those around him, especially the girls, no matter how hard he tried to avoid being noticed.

Macy focused in, trying to see what the girls were so fascinated by. Square jaw, sharp cheekbones. Broad shoulders that hinted of underdeveloped musculature. The girls stared, but kept their distance. Shy? Or something else? Could they sense he was different from them? He ran a thin hand through his hair and glanced toward the group of girls, who quickly looked away. *He intimidates them*, she realized.

Bastian huffed by her side. "You find him attractive." The humor in his tone brought warmth to her palms.

She tossed him a scathing look. "Bastian, he's a total dweeb."

Bastian's grin faded and she turned back to the binoculars.

The second the Ninth neared the front of the school, a group of sporty-looking guys walked over. A tall, buff redhead reached out and ripped the backpack off the Ninth's shoulder, guffawing stupidly as he walked away. The last kid to leave the bus, an extremely short boy, leaned down and helped the Ninth retrieve his books.

"Moron." Macy muttered. "He's the freakin' Ninth. He could totally annihilate those guys. Why doesn't he kick their butts?" She shook her head and looked down at Bastian.

Bastian's eyes snapped open and a strange look crossed his face. "Odd."

"What's odd?" When he didn't respond, Macy waved a hand in front of his eyes. "Hello? What's odd?"

"There is a strange energy surrounding the Ninth. Someone is trying to block him from my sight—but the power is weak, weakening every second in fact. And that small boy with the Ninth?"

"Yeah?"

Bastian pushed off from the truck and climbed back into the driver's seat. "He is no boy. He is a Doogar—at least eighty years old if my calculations are accurate, based on his features."

Macy jumped off the tire and stuck her head through the window. "A Doogar? Wait, aren't they those dudes who live underground and make stuff out of mud and metal?"

"Yes."

"Why would he be here?"

"That is a very good question."

Macy waited for him to elaborate, but he only continued to stare in the direction of the school where the Ninth and the Doogar guy had disappeared.

Prickles began to move up her arms. "Okay, so now what do we do?"

Bastian turned towards her—the serious look on his face brought on another wave of chills.

"You will wait, while I *watch*." He leaned his head back on the seat and closed his eyes.

ooo

Tolen held open his backpack by the now torn handles and passed his books onto the shelf in his locker, his heart still pounding from the short confrontation with Jeff. Man, he hated that guy.

"He's just jealous Tolen." Dane spoke from beside Tolen's elbow.

Tolen snorted.

"Seriously, he hates the fact that the girls stare at you."

Tolen rolled his eyes.

"Well, they do." A hint of jealousy leaked into Dane's tone.

"Because I'm the town freak, remember?" Tolen slammed his locker shut and turned to face his friend.

"They might not really think that. Why don't you ever talk to them?"

Tolen turned and started toward his first hour class. "I'm too busy." He avoided Dane's eyes.

Dane raised his voice. "You have days off you know."

"Yeah, and they're spent taking care of my sick mother." He walked into his English class without a glance back, not wanting to see the sympathy he knew would be on his friend's face. He didn't like being rude to Dane, who was a perpetually positive person, but he'd touched a nerve. Dane wouldn't understand how much it bothered him that no matter how much he wanted to, he *couldn't* be more like the kids around him.

He took his usual seat at the back of the class, opened his tattered copy of *The Silmarillion*, and pretended to read while his classmates laughed, joked, and flirted around him. He tried to focus on Tolkien's world while they discussed dates, the upcoming graduation party at the student body president's house, jobs, and college plans.

But his emotions were too chaotic to ignore the unfairness. He clenched his teeth as he listened to their carefree lives. What would it be like to laugh with them? To wonder which of the girls he would ask to the party? To care only about his next date, or where he would go to college?

His hands shook and he took a deep breath. No, instead he had to worry about putting food on the table, paying rent, and oh yeah, not suddenly losing control and showing everyone in this room how he could somehow get the trees outside the window to smash through the brick wall and squeeze the life out of any one of them.

Thankfully, before his emotions could send his abilities into uncontrolled action, the bell rang, the kids settled in their seats, and Mrs. Kay demanded their attention.

Tolen slouched lower in his seat as his heart regained its normal rhythm and he prepared himself for another day of pretending to fit in, wishing there was some way he actually could.

CHAPTER FIVE

FOUND

Three Days Later...

TOLEN CARRIED THE LAST CASE OF POTATO CHIPS INTO THE GROCERY store. "Where would you like this one Mr. Grange?"

"Just leave it by the door," his boss called from behind a stack of soup-cans. He walked out wiping his hands on his apron. "Thanks for the help, Tolen. I'll put them in the display tomorrow. You can go home now."

"Are you sure? I can stay and finish the inventory with you." Tolen pulled the rag off his shoulder and wiped the sweat from his face and neck.

Mr. Grange's eyebrows creased with concern. "You've already worked extra hours on all your shifts this week. You have school tomorrow."

Tolen didn't want his boss to know just how bad things were getting at home—it was hard enough to keep secrets in a town like this one, but they were in trouble. He cleared his throat and avoided the older man's eyes. "It's really no big deal, sir. I finished all my finals and we're just getting yearbooks tomorrow. They don't take attendance the last couple days of school. I can go late." No need to tell him he did not intend to even go, or get a yearbook. His picture wouldn't be in it. He was always absent on picture day, and he wouldn't have anyone but Dane to sign it anyway.

Mr. Grange raised an eyebrow and harrumphed.

Tolen dropped his eyes to his feet, shoved his fists into his pockets, and swallowed hard. "The truth is sir, the bank had to lay my mom off yesterday, she hasn't been feeling well, and…I was thinking that now that I'm done with school, maybe you c-could use me full-time?"

Tolen held his breath as Mr. Grange pulled a handkerchief from his shirt pocket and wiped his face. His deep-set brown eyes were sad. The folds of skin around his mouth jiggled as he spoke, like an old basset hound's. "Alright, you can stay and help me. Heaven knows your body can handle the lifting better than mine." He placed a fatherly hand on Tolen's shoulder. "You can start full time next week, but don't give up on college or finding a better future than working here, Tolen. You have a lot on your plate right now, but never stop trying for something bigger. You're a good kid. Don't let anyone ever tell you any different."

Tolen wished it were that simple. He forced a grateful smile and shook the old man's hand. "Thank you, sir."

At eleven o'clock they finally finished and Mr. Grange followed Tolen out the back door to lock up. "Would you like a ride home?"

"No thanks, sir. It's a nice night, I'll walk."

"Be careful."

"I will." Tolen waved goodbye and set off across the street.

A soft breeze cooled the sweat on his neck and swayed the rusty swings in the deserted park. Their ancient chains squeaked softly as he passed. He felt a lot better than he had that morning—he'd hardly slept last night after his mother tearfully confessed that she had been fired. With the extra hours Mr. Grange had allowed, he should have enough on his paycheck to cover the rest of next month's rent and buy some groceries. He was truly grateful to the old man for hiring him full-time. He didn't think it was a good idea for his mother to get a job until she got better. He just hoped she *would* get better…soon. A wave of panic rolled over him; she was nearly out of the herbs she used to make her tea—he didn't even want to think about how bad she might get without her tea. Maybe tomorrow he'd see if she was up for a trip to the health food store in Price.

"Hey Parks." Jeff Macro stepped from a clump of trees into Tolen's path, clutching a can of beer in his fist—apparently he'd decided to celebrate the end of the school year early. Six more of his flunkies circled around the two of them.

Tolen looked at their drunken faces and sighed. His mother was going to have a fit. She'd know he lied about Principal Stoker's warning.

"Thought you could get away with your little stunt, did you?" Jeff pushed a hand through his red hair and tossed his beer can to the ground, splattering Tolen's sneakers.

Tolen kicked the can aside, clenched his teeth, and fought to stay calm.

"Idiot thinks he's tough, Jeff. I say he needs to be taught where the real muscle is in this town." Someone shoved Tolen from behind.

"Yeah Jeff, punks like him don't got no business breathin' an s-stuff," another slurred. He shoved Tolen from the side.

"Shut up man, you're wasted!" Jeff scowled at him, momentarily distracted from the fight.

"Go on Jeff, put your anger where it should be man. Kick the loser's butt."

"Yeah, Jeff."

"Do it, man."

Jeff started to circle Tolen, hopping from foot to foot like a boxer in a ring.

He looked so stupid Tolen couldn't help but grin, despite what he knew was coming.

"What's so funny, loser?" Jeff sauntered forward until he stood nose to nose with Tolen.

Tolen's hands curled into fists but he kept them in his pockets. "I have a request before you beat me up."

"Oh yeah, what's that?"

Tolen pulled a pack of mints from his pocket. "Please? Your breath smells like sun baked road-kill."

Jeff's fist slammed into Tolen's nose snapping his neck back. Blood ran down his face and the back of his throat. His eyes watered and the air shifted—the trees were reacting.

No.... Tolen had no idea what the trees might do, or even how to stop them.

Someone grabbed Tolen's arms and yanked them behind his back. Jeff threw another punch to his stomach and Tolen doubled over gasping for air. He focused hard on controlling his temper as the beating continued.

He needed to move all conscious thought into the deepest, most quiet part of his mind, a place he had found by accident years ago. Once there, it seemed as if he floated outside his body. He was still aware of what went on around him, but he became detached, only an observer.

He focused on that place now and felt the pull. His body went limp. He knew someone held him up, but he could no longer feel any pain. He could see in his mind's eye the group surrounding him. Their intoxicated bellows were muffled, their fierce expressions almost comical. He started to wonder how long it would take Jeff to decide he'd had enough when the tenor of the conversation taking place around him sent him back into full consciousness with a jolt.

"Dude, you ever seen anything like that?" Someone asked.

"No way man…"

"What *is* he?"

What are they talking about? Tolen focused on coming back to his senses and every ache in his body hit him with force. A couple ribs had to be broken—each breath felt like knives stabbing through his chest.

He searched back through his thoughts for the incident that had brought on the confused shouting. The picture stayed hazy, but he could see that someone, he wasn't sure who, had lifted Tolen's right eyelid—probably checking to see if he was still conscious—and then jumped back, stumbling over his own feet.

Shocked back to the present Tolen blinked and felt his blue eye dilate. *The contact! Crap!*

"I don't know what you are freak, but I promise I'll knock whatever it is right out of you!" Jeff cocked his bloody fist back and Tolen quickly closed his eyes.

"NO!"

Dane? Tolen's head snapped up. Sure enough, Dane ran toward them as fast as his tiny legs could carry him.

"Dane, get out of here!" Tolen tried to shout, but the blood in his mouth muffled the sound.

"Well look-y what we got now boys. Two freaks for the price of one!" Jeff dropped his fist and the crowd parted to let Dane in beside Tolen.

Dane's face was covered with sweat and his small chest heaved. "Leave him alone. You stupid idiots need to find a new hobby."

Tolen struggled for breath. "Dane, just get out of here. I can handle this."

"Oh, would you listen to that." Jeff lifted a hand to his mouth, his voice dripping with sarcasm. "Parks is trying to protect his little freak. Don't worry Parks. We have special plans for your boyfriend. Wonder how fast those fat legs can run when they're dragged behind my truck?"

The crowd laughed again and Tolen's heart began to pound so hard it hurt.

"Or maybe we'll just try to give him a little face lift like the one you got tonight. Dude, he's so ugly I bet his father'c pay us for takin' him off his hands."

Fire seemed to rise from Tolen's toes and consume every part of his body. "Touch him and I'll kill you." The words left his mouth before he could think to stop them.

Blinding white light sheeted across his blue eye until he could see everything surrounding him as if it were midday instead of the middle of the night. His arms shook and his blood pulsed hard and fast through his veins.

The trees surrounding them began thrashing their branches so wildly that chunks of bark rained down on their heads.

Jeff and his friends started shouting all at once. A thick branch swept down knocking Jeff off his feet and his head hit the pavement with a sickening crack. Tolen's arms were released as the boy holding him was hoisted into the air by his ankles and lifted screaming into the trees. The rest of Jeff's cronies ran away yelling, tossing their beer cans behind them.

Tolen leaned over and tried to suck in air. His ribs burned and his lungs felt like they were in a garbage crusher. "Can't breathe…"

The guy fell out of the tree and landed with a thud.

"Tolen?" Dane grabbed Tolen's arm and everything went black.

"Tolen? Tolen, wake up."

Someone shook his shoulder. He wished they would stop.

"Come on man, you've been out for hours." Dane's desperate voice sounded far away.

Images flickered like the broken pieces of a dream before Tolen's eyes—he jerked upright and the room spun.

"Whoa buddy, take it easy." Dane's anxious face glimmered in the lamplight.

Tolen looked around. He was sitting on his bed. He rubbed his eyes with his fists and glanced at the clock on his nightstand. It was 2:00 a.m.

"Dane? What're you doing here? What happened? Did I…?" His voice drifted off as the memories came back. It felt like days since he'd left Grange Grocery.

"Did you get the crap kicked out of you by Jeff? Yeah. And did you annihilate them by calling the trees on them? Um…yeah, that too." Dane shifted on the edge of the bed, relief mingled with envy on his face.

Tolen's stomach twisted. "Did I…? How bad are they?"

"They'll live." Dane sounded disappointed, not at all shocked by what he'd witnessed. A grin worked its way onto his chubby face.

Tolen's suspicion rose. "Dane?"

Dane sighed. "Look, there's a lot we need to talk about."

"I'd say." More memories returned and Tolen realized he should be in agony. His heart started to thud in panic. "Dane, my mom saw you bring me home, didn't she?" Of course she did, she always knew when he lost control.

"Tolen, I—"

"Crap Dane! She can't take *any* stress right now!" It wasn't Dane's fault. It was his and he knew it. He started to get up but Dane put a restraining hand on his shoulder.

"Tolen, I tried to stop her. I know she's too weak to be using her gift, but she wouldn't listen. She wasn't about to let you die."

"Good grief, I wasn't about to die! Where is she? And how do you know about what she can do?" Anger trickled through his veins like poison.

"Tolen you've got to calm down. I promise to explain. Your mom's fine. She's resting on the couch. I made her some Lucid tea. She's been asleep almost as long as you have."

Tolen rubbed his temples and tried to push the anger deep before he lost control again and hurt his friend. "She's okay?"

Dane's head bobbed. "Healing you took a lot out of her, but she's one determined Sphere."

"Huh?" Tolen's head felt as if someone was beating a hammer against an anvil inside it.

"Nothing."

Tolen tried to remember what happened after the fight, but he couldn't. "How did you get me home?"

"You walked—you were incoherent, but you walked. Don't ask me how." Dane was grinning again.

Tolen looked into his friend's face. It was as if he were seeing Dane for the first time. He seemed…older, different. He no longer looked like the kid who loved video games, popcorn, and making Tolen laugh. Did he even know the real Dane? An uncomfortable lump formed in his throat. He swallowed hard, but the betrayal he felt was evident in his tone. "I'm going to check on my mom and then you and I are going to have that chat."

Dane's face fell as Tolen got up and left the bedroom.

His mom was sleeping on the couch, her skin dewy with sweat.

He touched her forehead—it felt like wet ice.

"Mom?" He shook her lightly. "Mom?"

"Hmm? Tolen?" Her eyes flashed to his face. "You're okay." She lifted her hand to weakly stroke his cheek.

"Mom…" He knelt by her side and each one of her ragged breaths cut into his guilty conscience. "Mom, I'm so sorry I lost control. You shouldn't have healed me. I would have been fine in a couple days."

She coughed. "You are my *son*. I won't see you suffer."

He clenched his teeth. "I wasn't suffering."

She placed an icy finger to his lips. "Uh-huh. How are you feeling now? I healed your cracked ribs and the deepest cuts on your face, but left the outside bruising for the witnesses. Dane said they were all so drunk it's unlikely they'll remember exactly what happened." She gave a half smile, but Tolen knew it didn't matter how he looked. There was no way they could stay here after what he'd done—drunken version or not, it would raise suspicion. Rumors traveled fast here in the middle of nowhere.

"I feel fine," he lied. "Are you going to be okay? Honestly?"

She put her clammy hand over his fingers. "Don't you worry about me, I'm—"

Someone banged on the front door.

Dane came scrambling into the room with his eyes wide. Tolen turned toward the door and his mother grabbed his arm.

"No, Tolen. Don't."

"Why not? You don't even know who it is…knocking on the door at two in the morning." His heart started beating faster and louder.

His mother threw a nervous glance at Dane and he nodded toward the window. "Tolen, see who it is—I doubt the bad guys would knock."

Tolen peeked through the curtain to see a huge police officer standing in the glow of the porch-light, his thick arms folded across his muscled chest. "It's a cop, but I don't recognize him. County Sheriff maybe? I don't see his car." He glanced back over his shoulder.

"Jeff probably called them," Dane whispered.

Tolen blanched. If they'd called in the sheriff, he was done for.

The cop knocked again. "Ms. Parks? Tolen? I need to speak with you about what happened tonight." His muffled voice sounded strange and unhappy.

"What should I do?" Tolen asked.

"Let me check his character."

"No, Mom, you're too weak."

Dane moved to stand beside Tolen's mother, his hand on her shoulder. "Tolen let him in. Areen, if it seems like the cop's suspicious I'll knock him out and we'll get out of here. But there's no sense drawing unnecessary attention by disobeying the law until we know more and there's no way you can run until you regenerate."

"How do we know he isn't a servant of the Dark?" She clutched Dane's arm with shaking fingers.

"Like I said, a bad guy wouldn't knock. You know how the Dark works." He gave Tolen the thumbs up, but his eyes were filled with worry.

Tolen's head spun with their strange conversation. They spoke of dark as if it were a thing, not what happens when the sun goes down or you turn out a light. And why was Dane suddenly giving orders?

He opened the door and his stomach seemed to drop to the bottom of his shoes. The police officer's bright sapphire eyes were frighteningly familiar. They were the same clear blue with dark cobalt lines stretching from the iris to the pupil as one of Tolen's eyes. The pupils were dilating and constricting just like Tolen's eye did.

This guy was not a normal cop.

"Hello, Tolen." The cop cast a fleeting look behind him and Tolen noticed his black hair was long and tied into a thick ponytail. "May I come in?"

Tolen's knees felt like rubber. His heart thumped painfully in his chest as, seemingly without his control, his muscles contracted and he opened the door wide enough for the man to enter. It felt as if something inside him, more powerful than his fear, recognized the guy and trusted him.

But as soon as the cop crossed the threshold, his mother sat up and screamed. Dane jumped in front of her in a protective crouch, and blindingly bright colors flashed across Tolen's blue eye as if he were spinning in a room with multi-colored walls.

"You!" His mother's face drained of all color. "Get out of my house!" She slumped back to the couch in a dead faint.

Tolen ran to her side but the weird cop made it there first.

"Tolen, get your mother's Lucid and wrap some of the dry tea in a wet rag. You, Doogar," he looked at Dane. "Your father is Handrak the known Doogar tracker is he not?"

Tolen shifted his gaze to his friend. *Hank's a what?*

Dane nodded, surprised.

"Bring him here."

Dane shifted his feet. "He's probably drunk. He doesn't like being above ground."

The cop gave a curt nod. "Go home and sober him up. My Chosen ward will come for you soon. I have much to inquire of you both. You know it would not be in your best interest to try to run from me. Go. Now."

Dane stood on his tiptoes and glared at the cop. "If you hurt either one of these two in any way, you will have me and all of my people to answer to."

The cop glanced up and the look on his face made Tolen take an involuntary step back. "You know I would never. Now, GO!"

Dane cast an apologetic look at Tolen and stumbled quickly out the door.

"Boy?"

Tolen jumped.

"Did you not hear me? Lucid, and the herb pack. Now."

Tolen tripped over his own feet as he ran for the kitchen—his blue eye still burning and dilating wildly.

What was going on? First Dane and his mother all cozy and familiar, now a cop whose eyes matched Tolen's blue one. Did that mean he was the same kind of different as Tolen? But his mother had seemed hysterical when she saw him. Whatever that meant it couldn't be good, but he *was* trying to help. And why would this stranger know of Dane's loser dad?

Tolen's stomach turned. This was a nightmare. It *had* to be a nightmare. Any minute, he would wake up shaking and sweating.

He poured tea from an already-brewed kettle into a mug. His hands shook so much he spilled more on the counter than he got in the cup. His head reeled, and he felt near passing out himself.

He'd nearly killed Jeff tonight—was that what had brought the guy with the weird eyes to his house? Had more people than just Dane known about him all this time and he'd been the only one left in the dark?

He sprinkled some dry tea on a wet rag, folded it over, and rushed back into the living room.

The cop knelt on the shag orange carpet, running his hands along Tolen's mother's face. He reached for the rag without looking up and wiped it across her cheeks, forehead, and neck. He used his finger to place a few drops of the tea onto her lips—all the while singing a low song under his breath in a language Tolen could not understand. He'd guess it to be Native American, but the cadences were different, mixed in a way that didn't fit anything he'd heard before.

Tolen stood back with his palms sweating, fighting the panic that threatened to overwhelm him. The questions running through his head demanded answers, but all he could do was look at his mother's ashen face, watch the slow rise and fall of her chest, and listen to her struggle for breath. She seemed so weak. Would this be the final thing to send her someplace where he would never see her again? Tears burned the back of his eyes as he tried to swallow the lump in his throat.

"She will be all right, Tolen." The cop's deep voice was oddly reassuring—he sounded so confident. The peaceful feeling radiating from him slowed Tolen's racing heart.

"How can you be sure?"

"Because I am."

The huge cop sat down on the floor by the couch, folded his legs beneath him, placed his elbows on his knees, and dropped his chin to his clasped hands. His eyes searched Tolen's face. "You will have to trust me. She will need to sleep for a while. I only hope we will be safe here while she regenerates."

"I have no idea what that means." *The cop knows what we are.* The words pounded through this head. *He knows more about my mother than I do.*

"You may call me Bastian. It is nicer to refer to someone by his or her name rather than a term. Don't you agree?" He tipped his head.

Tolen rubbed his blue eye as it began to burn again. "What?"

"It will be easier if you call me by my name, rather than continue to refer to me as 'the cop'."

Tolen shook his head. How did the cop...guy...Bastian...whatever...even know that was what Tolen was calling him in his head?

"I will explain it to you shortly."

Are you in my head?

"Not in the way you think."

Tolen stumbled backward, fell over the rocking chair, and landed with a thud on his side. He scrambled to his feet, fear clutching at his insides. "What are you? Who are you? How are you reading my mind?"

"I am not reading your mind. I am simply aware of your thoughts. Come back and sit down so I can explain. If I were here to hurt you, I would have done so already. You need to trust me."

Tolen edged toward the door, torn between the desire to get as far away from this strange man as possible and the need to stay and protect his mother. "Uh, I don't think so. I don't even know who or *what* you are."

"You wish to know who *you* really are—why you can do what you can do. I am someone who can tell you that."

Tolen's need for answers warred with his fear that the strange instinctual trust he felt was some sort of trick. Despite his doubts, he found himself slowly moving back to the chair.

The man, *Bastian*, had an odd accent. He didn't use conjunctions. His speech was measured, powerful. Rather than just hearing what Bastian said, his words seemed to move right through Tolen's ears into his heart and bones. It was freaky, and intriguing. Could he really tell Tolen all he'd wanted to know for so long? His heart began to pound in anticipation and he had to focus to reign in his eagerness.

"My mother recognized you. She wanted you to get out. That sort of implies that you can't be trusted." Tolen's weak knees knocked together as he collapsed into the chair. He slid it back a few inches so he had direct line of sight to the door and Bastian.

Bastian sighed. "Yes, your mother did recognize me. As for her reasons for not being happy to see me, well…I believe they go beyond me *personally,* to my race. You see, I am a Watcher."

"Watcher?"

Bastian's eyes narrowed, seeming almost surprised that Tolen didn't know what a Watcher was.

Tolen shrugged under the huge man's scrutiny. If he thought Tolen was clueless now, he was in for quite a shock.

Bastian cast a quick look at Tolen's mother and took a deep breath. "The duties of my race are quite disconcerting for some. Of course, we will not know your mother's exact reasons until she wakes up and I can question her for myself."

"Well, what's so bad about Watchers? What is it you do that she wouldn't like?"

"Watchers are a race of people who can sense with almost complete accuracy the thoughts and actions—past, present and future—of those individuals they are responsible for."

That didn't explain much. Tolen never thought he'd actually meet someone weirder than himself.

"As to the depth of my duties, I shall explain shortly." Bastian glanced out the window and Tolen followed his gaze. It was still dark out. Inky. Eerie.

Tolen shuddered and turned away from the window. "You told Dane someone would be coming for him. You're not alone?"

"No. My ward is with me. Right now she is double-checking the perimeter of the house."

"Oh." A very anti-climactic comeback, but Tolen felt at a complete loss for words. He rubbed his forehead, still half convinced he was dreaming the whole thing.

Bastian ran a huge hand across the stubble on his chin. "Tolen, how much do you know about who you are? Where you come from?"

Tolen gripped the arms of the rocking chair. "Nothing."

Bastian's eyes widened and his pupils dilated and contracted so fast it was dizzying to watch. "Nothing at all?"

"No." The festering resentment rang through the single word.

"Why …?" he glanced again at Tolen's mother.

"I tried to get her to tell me, but she always refused." The wood creaked beneath Tolen's fingers and he took a deep breath. "I had to stop asking when her health went down-hill. Confrontation always made it worse."

Bastian glanced at Tolen with a speculative expression.

"Who is your father?"

"His name was Daedal—"

The Watcher jumped to his feet so fast Tolen barely saw the movement. "Daedal Téloran?"

Tolen cringed back in his chair. "I-I don't remember him. He left us when I was a baby."

Bastian's eyes traveled over Tolen's face as if searching for something. "It cannot be." He turned, started to pace the tiny living room, glanced back at Tolen, and lifted his hand in the air. "I am sorry for frightening you. This information, it is…confusing."

Tolen swallowed and nodded, uncomfortable with the fact that Bastian knew he was scared, but more interested in what the man might know. "You…knew my father?"

Bastian's eyes flashed again to Tolen's face. "Possibly. Would you happen to have a picture?"

"My mom's got one. She doesn't know I know about it. Um, I'll be right back." Tolen jumped from the chair, his mind going a million miles an hour, and jogged to his mother's bedroom. He was sure his mother wouldn't be pleased with the conversation he was having with a man she had been clearly unhappy to see, but he couldn't stop the nervous excitement he felt to finally be getting some answers.

His heart thudded with anxiety as he lifted her mattress.

Underneath lay a faded photograph of Daedal staring down at a tiny baby in his arms. The caption on the back, written in his mother's hand, read:

Daedal and Tolen
July 15, 1996

Tolen had been just five days old. At one time, he'd wished that his father had been looking at the camera, wished to see a little of himself in the man there. Did he, too, have one blue eye and one brown? But as time went by, and Tolen never heard from the man, he stopped caring. He hadn't looked at the photo for years. Why should he bother with a father that had abandoned him?

His hands shook and the picture blurred.

He took a deep breath and left the bedroom. Bastian was still pacing back and forth when Tolen reached the living room. He held out his hand for the photograph, stared at it for a long uncomfortable moment, and dropped back to the floor with his head in his hands.

Tolen stuck the photo in his back pocket. "So, you do know him?"

Bastian kept his head down. "Yes. I know your father." He looked up with an expression that made Tolen's stomach squirm uncomfortably; he looked…angry. "There are not many of our kind who would not have at least heard of Daedal Téloran. I have only met him once, but now that I really look I can see him in your features."

Tolen clenched the back of the chair. The wood groaned beneath his fingers and started to splinter. "*Our* kind?"

Bastian's hard look softened to one of sadness. "You must understand Tolen, the world you have been brought up in is not what you think. Elves, fairies, mythical creatures, they all have a basis, a true counterpart. As does every myth, every legend you have ever heard, contain a seed of truth. Time and the philosophies of men have covered the seeds, cultivating them into the imaginary stories you read in fairy tales. But the truth still lies there beneath the imaginary. The race that began almost all legend is the race *you* belong to…They are called the Hidden. They have existed among humans, hiding their gifts and differences as necessary, since the beginning of time."

"So I'm—I'm not human?" Tolen glanced at his sleeping mother. No wonder she hadn't wanted to tell him. A government experiment, a weird twist of rare genes, an accident. All those things he'd tried to guess at weren't even close to the truth. *I'm not even human. I really am a freak.*

Bastian shook his head. "No, Tolen. It is not like that at all. Human is a relative word. All living things are connected, no matter their race or origin. One race is not superior to another. You are a Being, a gift of life with tremendous potential as all Beings are. Do not judge yourself based on a category that holds no value among the things that truly matter."

Tolen dropped back into the rocking chair and rubbed his pounding head.

Bastian sighed. "I am afraid there is not enough time for me to explain everything to you, to really help you to understand, but what I must tell you are the truths that are the most vital for you to know right now. You asked what my duties are. I am to find, train, and protect the Chosen ones…" He paused and tapped his chin; it was almost as if he was choosing his next words carefully. "Tolen, you have been selected by the Balance to be a member of this elite group of Light followers. It contains those with incredible gifts that are suited to protect this world from the servants of the Dark…."

No, not gifts. A curse. Tolen continued to massage his aching head. Balance, Light, Dark. It was all just a bunch of gibberish.

"They are gifts Tolen, I assure you." Bastian took a measured breath. He seemed nearly as irritated at Tolen's lack of knowledge as Tolen was. "With time I am certain you will see them as gifts as well. The Balance, the force that connects us all, sensed the Light, the goodness in you, and selected you as one of the Chosen. A pure-hearted soul who would not stand by and let the Dark, let evil, win. For centuries the gifted Chosen have kept the forces of darkness at bay—"

Tolen stood up and spun around, his back to Bastian. His breath came in large gulps and colors swam before his eyes. *He wants me to fight evil? This is nuts…This guy is nuts!*

"I am truly sorry Tolen. I do not know why your mother has kept the truth from you. I hope we can get to the bottom of it soon." Tolen felt Bastian stand up behind him, but he didn't turn around. "Go to bed. Rest. When it is safe for your mother to wake, I will come for you and maybe we can sort this out."

Tolen ran a shaky hand through his hair. "Like I'm going to be able to sleep after all this."

The front door opened and a tiny teenage girl—Tolen doubted she would reach his shoulder—stood in the doorway. Three dead crows dangled from her fist.

"Bastian, we've got a problem."

Bastian turned to face her. "Tolen, this is my ward, Macy. Macy, this is Tolen."

She dropped the crows beside the porch, dusted her feather-covered hands on her jeans, wiped her booted feet on the rug, and stomped into the room. A sucker stick poked from the side of her mouth. Her long blonde hair flowed down her back in messy waves and her wideset emerald eyes stood out, without the help of make-up.

She definitely didn't fit in with the standard, trendy girls he knew from school; yet there was something about her that made him want to look closer, stand nearer, find out more about her. She exuded a confidence that normal, self-conscious teens lacked. Power radiated from her, and something else…anger.

He stammered out a hello.

She lifted her chin in Tolen's direction and in the brief moment their eyes met, Tolen felt her anger directed at *him*, but he didn't have the faintest idea why. She turned her attention back to Bastian without a word of response.

"One of those crows was a Divinator. It saw what the *kid* did in the park."

Tolen cringed. Her tone conveyed the depth of her complete dislike. Annoyed, he directed his question to Bastian as well, completely ignoring her and all her intriguing, yet frustrating, attributes. "What's a Divinator?"

"Crows are often used by the Dark as spies." Bastian glanced at Macy with his eyebrow raised, before looking back at Tolen to explain. "Divinators are crows whose eyes have been replaced with Oracle stones. Whatever the Divinators see, their masters see. The problem here lies with whom these particular spies belong to, and just how far away they may be hiding. Divinators are rare and usually only the highest captains in the Dark have access to them. The fact that one was sent here to watch you is disturbing."

He turned back to the girl and sighed. "I had hoped to wait and give Tolen a few days to completely regenerate. Go and fetch the Doogar. It is time for a new plan."

Macy threw a parting glance in Tolen's direction—a look of pure disgust. Tolen watched her go, wanting to defend himself, but from what? He hadn't done anything to this strange girl.

Things just kept getting better and better.

CHAPTER SIX

SECRETS

Macy swung her legs from her perch on top of the kitchen counter and gnawed on a sucker stick, bored out of her mind. Two hours ago, the *Ninth* had conked out on the sofa and his mother had dragged them all into the kitchen to talk.

The uneventful hours had trudged slowly into late morning. The sun now shone bright above the mountains and the breeze coming through the window brushed too warm against her skin.

She drummed her fingers on the counter. Watching Bastian and the kid's mom argue had stopped being interesting after the first ten minutes.

It was ridiculous that they couldn't wake the precious Ninth from his beauty sleep no matter how many Dark creatures might be headed their way. For some reason Bastian refused to explain why he thought he needed answers from this crazy lady instead of just taking the kid and running for it.

A muscle started twitching in Bastian's jaw and he gripped the counter behind him with unnecessary force. Macy wondered idly how long it would be before he ripped out a hunk of Formica.

He shook his head toward the ceiling. "I cannot believe you have not at least told Tolen something about who he really is, even if you would not tell him his destiny. The boy had a right to know."

The kid's mother sat rigid in the kitchen chair, her previously pale cheeks flushed with irritation. "Don't you dare tell me how I should have raised my son!" she retorted in a furious whisper. "I didn't ask the Balance to choose him. The Light has no right to expect so much from one child."

Macy rolled her head and rubbed the back of her neck. Her muscles were getting sore from looking back and forth between the arguing adults.

Dane slept at the table with his head on his arms. Every once in a while a snore interrupted the disagreement. Macy wished she could be as lucky, but someone had to stay focused on what headed for them. She kept tabs on the argument with one part of her mind and felt for any Dark servants that might be nearby with another.

"You think that lying to him is a good idea?" Bastian pointed toward the living room. "He has no idea how to handle his gifts—gifts that are strengthening as we speak. You are insane if you think you can stop the will of the Balance!"

"Keep your voice down." She held her hand up. "I don't want to wake him up."

"No, you do not want him to hear. Let us be honest, Areen. You have to realize we need to find a way to protect the boy. Things are far more dangerous than I anticipated." He folded his arms. "A Chosen, unprepared, untaught, weak—if you will—is more a target than a threat to the Dark right now. You have made things far more precarious by hiding the truth from him. As your strength weakens, so does your energy field, which has veiled Tolen from the Dark. He cannot stay here after what happened at the park. Divinators are watching him." He stabbed a finger toward the window.

Macy followed the jab with her eyes, searching the sky outside for any crows. He was right—it wouldn't be long before more were sent in place of the ones she'd killed. They didn't have much time.

Areen flinched but her chin rose. "Speaking of the park, why weren't you there to stop him?"

Macy rolled her eyes and Bastian pinched the bridge of his nose.

"I would have tried to stop him but we were otherwise preoccupied as I have already told you." His teeth ground together.

Macy perked up. So he wasn't going to tell her about the Reconn they'd killed. *Huh, maybe he thinks she can't take it.*

Bastian's chin moved a fraction of an inch up and down in Macy's direction.

Yep. She rolled her eyes again. *If she thinks crows are bad…*

"Areen, your energy field blocked the majority of Tolen's power but the Dark will have felt the same shift in the Balance as I did as your strength waned. I knew I had to time our arrival in such a way that we did not tip off the Dark and call them in faster. I planned on sending you a message through the Doogar tomorrow, but Tolen's actions changed things."

Areen wrapped her arms around her chest and stared fixedly at the floor; her white lips pressed into a tight line. She definitely looked better than when Macy had first seen her, but the effort of arguing seemed to be depleting everything Bastian had done to help her regenerate.

Bastian took a deep breath. Macy knew the look. He was giving up the fight and going for the nice guy tactic.

"Areen, will you at least tell me…give me some sort of explanation for your actions?" He actually tried for a smile. "The Dark is after the boy. The Shadows have awakened. Your protection is weakening. You cannot hide him from his destiny forever. You know he must leave and you know I *must* take him with me. He is in far too much danger to remain with you. He is a ticking time bomb. All that anger he is trying to withhold is going to burst out—ooner than later, if you continue to lie to him. He needs to understand who he is." He sighed when she didn't take her eyes off the floor. "You cannot shield him forever."

Areen closed her eyes and a single tear trickled down her cheek.

Bastian's voice softened. "Where is Tolen's father? If he is who I believe he is, he should be with the Guardians."

Macy squirmed and the counter creaked beneath her. Dane's head snapped up.

"We were so happy." All the fight seemed to drain out of her with that single statement and the words started spilling from her mouth—her voice tinged with despair and something deeper. Agony?

Macy sat up straight.

Areen's wide brown eyes were fixed on the ceiling. "Daedal and I left our duties at the Citadel of Light. He renounced his oath as a Protector and I my oath as a Sentinel for the Guardians. We were exiled—our link to the citadel was severed forever. We would never be able to find it again, never be able to set foot on the sacred ground…ever." She took a deep breath and her voice caught. "We fell in love. We wanted to have a normal life, a family…Those precious things the humans take for granted. It is not right that the Guardians can forbid such things to those who serve at the citadel." Her eyes never left the ceiling as the tears trickled down her face and dropped off her chin. She made no move to wipe them away.

"Six days after Tolen was born a Radia shard showed up at our house," she continued. "We knew what it was. Why should our son be responsible for ungrateful, selfish humans?"

What?

Bastian shook his head slightly in Macy's direction, sensing the gist of her thoughts. He wanted information and an outburst from her wouldn't help. She had to bite the inside of her cheek to keep from speaking out.

Areen went on, unaware of the internal conversation between Watcher and ward. "Daedal told me to shield Tolen before a Watcher was sent for him. We knew *exactly* what it meant to be one of the Chosen and we would not allow that to be put on our child."

"Hang on." *To heck with this!* Macy jumped off the counter and threw her sucker stick on the floor. "First of all, it's a group of what you call 'ungrateful, selfish, humans' who sacrifice that blissful normal life you're raving about to help your scrawny butt, and secondly, how *freaking* crazy do you have to be to hide the Ninth for seventeen years? Don't you realize how much power the Dark has gained in that much time?"

"Macy—" Bastian reached toward her but she backed away from his hand, hot anger surging through her.

"Seventeen years he could have been training and now we get some kid who doesn't even know how much power he's got or how to use it. You do realize that without him the Dark's going to annihilate us all?" Her hands shook as the heat continued to build.

"Macy. That is enough." Bastian's eyes flashed; he pointed at the discarded sucker stick. "Pick that up."

Macy bent over and grabbed the stick with trembling fingers, tossed it angrily in the trash, and dropped into a chair. She ignored the faint smell of eucalyptus and roses and shoved her hands under her legs.

"Tolen is the *Ninth* Chosen?" Areen squeezed her eyes shut.

"Surely you knew?" Bastian turned to give the woman an exasperated face Macy knew well.

"I wondered, as his gifts multiplied, but I'd hoped to be wrong. His father is a mighty man—the strength of Tolen's gifts could have come from him." She added with a look that dared them to argue. "It doesn't matter now anyway."

Macy leapt to her feet again. "Doesn't matter! You really *are* insane!"

Bastian stomped over, put his hands on her shoulders and shoved her none too gently back into the chair.

"You have no idea what you are talking about, *child*." Areen's fierce, tear-filled eyes could have burned a hole in Macy's face. "You think you know everything about the Hidden, about the *Guardians*? About the way they do things? You think you know about evil creatures and the Dark? You're wrong. You put too much faith in your little group of Chosen children who have no clue about the real truth behind their selection." Her hands curled into fists by her side. "You are nothing but a naïve girl. If you actually knew the truth—the things *I* know, you would search for the deepest hole in the ground and bury yourself in it, begging for death, rather than face what is coming. So don't lecture me on things you know absolutely nothing about."

Dane reached over and patted Areen's arm. "It's okay Areen. She's young."

Macy's anger reached its peak. Who the crap did this woman think she was?

Sensing her rising anger, Bastian squeezed Macy's shoulders before moving back to lean against the counter. "Please forgive my Chosen. She still struggles with speaking out of turn. What happened then, Areen?" He shot a cautionary glance at Macy.

Macy ripped a sucker from her pocket, shoved it in her mouth, and started humming Rachmaninoff's sixth concerto under her breath, ignoring Dane's glare. Areen's accusations were spinning through her head like a hurricane, stirring up a pile of unwanted thoughts.

Areen turned her body completely away from Macy, directing her answer to Bastian alone. "Daedal left with the shard a week after Tolen was born. He said he would find a way to locate the citadel and force the Guardians to take it back. Daedal told me not to tell Tolen anything until he returned. I was to move around, hide, shield Tolen, and never let him develop the gifts that continued to come even though I didn't teach him how to use the strength of his life force. All the while I waited for word from my husband." She wiped her tears angrily with the back of her hand.

"When Tolen turned ten his life force grew so strong it took all I had to shield him. I no longer had the strength to continue to move us around. Tolen became depressed. He knew he was different and he didn't like hiding. His temper would flare and he'd lose control over his gifts."

"Green River is so small, and out of the way enough, that I knew it wouldn't take me long to know everybody, giving me the advantage if the Dark tried to send someone after us. I'd also heard rumor that deep in the mountains east of here, the ruins of a tribe of ancient Spheres lay hidden. The Doogar and Spheres have always been on good terms so shortly after we moved here I found the ruins and restored the communication link to the Binithan. I begged the Doogar Elders for aid. I didn't tell them any specifics about Tolen. I just said I was ill, alone, and in need of help with my young son. Two weeks later Dane and his father came. Hank was always so drunk I don't think he ever really thought much about Tolen and me, but it didn't take Dane long to discover Tolen was much more than the average Hidden kind, but he never told anyone, not even his father. He's been such a good friend. Tolen has done so much better since he arrived." She smiled tearfully at Dane and dropped her head in her hands.

Dane clumsily rubbed her back. "Tolen is one amazing kid. It's been an honor to have him as a friend."

Bastian took a deep breath and spoke softly. "I am sorry for your pain Areen. I thank you for sharing, it will help me better understand Tolen and his needs. Unfortunately, the knowledge also makes what I have to show you that much more difficult. You wanted to know what brought me here, why I was drawn to Tolen." Bastian lifted the Ninth's crystal from beneath his shirt. "Tolen's shard found me." Areen looked up and her face crumpled.

Macy twisted her hands in her lap and started chewing the sucker in her mouth.

"So Daedal *is* dead." Areen sniffed. "I—I've wondered for so long."

"We don't know that Areen." Dane squeezed her shoulders. "There's something you both should know. Tolen's Watcher's eye is also gaining strength. I think it might be showing him glimpses of his father. It's just a guess, but based on the descriptions he's given me, I can't help but wonder."

"What are you talking about?" Areen's voice trembled.

"I apologize. I never meant to keep things from you, but I wasn't certain, and with your declining health I feared to add one more worry to your mind."

"How did you come to this conclusion?" Bastian leaned forward, his eyes anxious.

Dane sighed. "Tolen has been telling me about a repeating nightmare showing him a sick-looking man lying on a floor of a dark room. The man calls out to him in the dream. Tolen hasn't said so aloud, but based on the emotions I can feel emanating from him as he tells of the nightmare, I would guess that he is not only dreaming about the man, but feeling what the man feels, seeing what he sees, just as a Watcher does. The nightmare plagues Tolen. It scares him."

Macy pulverized the sucker between her teeth. *Great, the kid's got Watcher abilities too?*

Bastian pushed off from the counter and started pacing. The stained floor squeaked beneath his boots.

"Where is he?" Areen's eyes were pleading as she tugged on Dane's arm. "Where's Daedal?"

Dane cleared his throat uncomfortably. Areen had grabbed his hand, squeezing so hard her knuckles turned white. "Well, from the description, it sounds like…"

"What? What?" She shook his arm.

"The Shadow Prison." Bastian spoke from the doorway.

Dane nodded slowly.

Macy's elbow slid off the table. All air and sound seemed sucked from the room.

"H-how can you know this?" Areen's voice broke.

Bastian resumed pacing and ran a hand over his face. "I have sensed the darkness of Tolen's dreams this past week, but I did not know for sure what they meant. Your shield kept the fullness of their content from me."

"So even if Daedal is alive he's as good as dead." Areen covered her mouth with her hand.

A heavy weight seemed to be crushing Macy into her chair. The Shadow Prison? *Do the Shadows know they have the Ninth's father?* Fear, irrational and horrifying, filled her mind.

Bastian walked back to Macy's side and laid a hand on her hair. Her breathing steadied.

He took a slow breath. "If Tolen is actually *seeing* as a Watcher sees, then the Light must, for one reason or another, desire him to find his father."

"No! Tolen *can't* go there!" Areen stood up still gripping Dane's arm.

Tolen suddenly stood in the doorway, his face drained of color. He ran past them and out the screen door.

Areen turned on Bastian. "You knew he was listening!"

He nodded guiltily.

"How long?"

"Just after I told you about his shard." Bastian stared at the door.

"So he doesn't know about the…the *Ninth*." She spit the last word.

"No. And I think it would be unwise to tell him until he comes to terms with what he has learned already."

"I hate you." Pure loathing seethed in Areen's eyes.

"I am sorry for that," he said softly.

A sob ripped from her throat and she dropped back to her chair.

Dane resumed rubbing her back as Bastian cupped his hand over Macy's cheek. "*LaUnahi*, it is okay."

"Okay?" *Okay? How is it okay?* Macy stared into Bastian's eyes allowing the thread of the thoughts she wanted to shout get louder and louder.

First I find out that the Shadows are on the hunt again, and now the Ninth's father is in the Shadow Prison! I know what you'll do, Bastian. If the kid's destiny involves saving his Dad, you as his Watcher will help him!

"Macy."

I can't do it Bastian, I can't face the Shadows. It's not just that I obviously don't want to—I can't! I can't go there! Her chest constricted.

"Macy we do not yet know the future."

"Yes, you do!"

"Not that far."

Dane watched their one-sided conversation with obvious confusion as he continued to rub Areen's back.

"*LaUnahi*, I do not know what is to come; so many factors still need to be sorted out. But I promise, I *will* protect you. Do you not trust me?"

Macy shuddered and took a deep breath. "I do trust you. I'm just—"

"Frightened." Bastian finished her thought and she felt her cheeks redden.

"You're not the only one," Dane mumbled.

Macy shook her head. She did trust Bastian to protect her, but—

"I need you to focus now." Bastian looked into her eyes until her breathing resumed a normal pace and relative calm filled her, clearing her thoughts.

She took a shaky breath.

Bastian smiled sadly. "Go and get Tolen—we *must* protect the Ninth. He has not gone far. Head south-east and you will find him."

"Why can't you go get him?" Macy's voice trembled and she clenched her fists.

Bastian raised an eyebrow.

"Fine." She turned and he grabbed her arm.

"Macy, try to be compassionate. You do not have to like him, but he has done nothing to deserve your animosity. Remember that."

Macy gritted her teeth and stalked out the door after the Ninth, her hands tingling.

She ran swiftly through the underbrush. The hot desert sun baked everything; heat waves rippled up from the ground. The dirt slowly gave way to clumps of sage, a thicket of willow trees appeared, and the rushing sound of the river met her ears.

She moved into the shade, closed her eyes, and pressed her palms together, focusing on locating Tolen's life force by the vibrations he unknowingly gave off.

Her eyes snapped open.

He was fifty feet down river. She turned and ran; the strength building in the air surrounding his life force had her worried.

When she broke through the trees, her knees locked and she skidded silently to a stop.

Tolen knelt in the dirt with his arms wrapped over his head, his body shaking. Occasionally a sob rose above the sound of the river. Suddenly, she no longer saw Tolen, the tall gangly teenager, but someone small and scared, someone like herself at six years old. She knew how it felt to have your life unexpectedly turned upside down; to discover that everything you believed to be real was actually a lie.

As much as she fought against it, a tiny glimmer of compassion rose in her heart and she stepped forward. *Bastian did say I didn't have to like him…You can feel sorry for someone without really liking him.*

She started to step forward, but paused when the tree beside Tolen dropped a thick branch and wrapped it around him in a sort of protective cocoon.

o o o

Tolen wiped the tears from his face in frustration and patted the branch. "Thank you Ardia." His mind rushed through what he'd heard and the anger seemed to be boiling his insides. Uncomfortable heat surrounded his heart, and his hands tingled so much it hurt. The trees surrounding him and Ardia swayed gently, but purposefully, as if only waiting for his command to hurt something or someone. He shivered. He had to control the anger. He had to calm down, but he was so confused! He'd wanted to stay and beg them to explain, but as his frustration grew so did the strange power within him, and he knew if he didn't run then something would happen and he'd end up hurting someone.

He looked at his palm wondering at the painful tingle. He turned it toward the tree in front of him and jumped when it shot a branch down and gripped his wrist.

"Could you stop doing things like that?" Macy stepped out from the trees with her hands on her hips.

As Tolen spun toward her the tree dropped his wrist and swung its branch around, pointing it menacingly at Macy. Ardia crossed two thick branches in front of him, blocking her approach.

"What are you doing here?" He spoke through his teeth, working to maintain his anger. He trusted Ardia, but he had no idea what the other tree might do.

She ignored the question. "You're leading the Dark right to us you know." She feinted to the side, but the branch stayed with her every move.

Tolen's resolve crumbled and the anger shot from his mouth. "No, I don't know that. I don't know anything!"

The branch swung and Macy barely dodged out of the way.

She stayed out of the tree's reach and held her hands up. "My heck dude! Could you call off the tree please? If I light a fire out here, Bastian'll kill me."

Rage rolled off Tolen's shoulders in heavy waves and suddenly every tree in the tiny thicket around them began to swat at Macy. For a moment, he felt vicious satisfaction seeing her jump around in shock. But then she began dodging every branch perfectly, almost as if she were dancing, and once again he felt that strange longing toward her. A need to get to know her that grew as he watched her move. Curiosity slowed the anger enough for him to think. He looked up into Ardia's vast branches. *Ardia, please tell the other trees to stop.*

Tolen, I do not trust this girl. She was enjoying the dance almost as much as Tolen.

He pinched the bridge of his nose as he tried to rein in his temper. *I don't either. Not yet, but killing her before I figure out what's going on won't help anything.*

Ardia swung a thick branch toward the other trees and they became perfectly still, their limbs barely moving in the slight breeze.

He glanced back at Macy to see awe mingled with resentment in her expression.

"If you can't stop doing that you're going to draw in any Dark servant within a mile of us." Her chest heaved, but there was satisfaction in her countenance. He'd bet anything she'd *enjoyed* showing off.

Macy pulled a sucker from her pocket and held it out to him. "Here. This'll help." She barely met his eyes and he was surprised at how green they were. Like emeralds framed with thick black lashes.

His teeth chattered as he pushed the anger deep and shifted his thoughts to menial things, like how weird it was to be actually talking to a girl. Although Macy was not a normal girl—standing there wearing cargo pants, boots, and a heavy belt loaded with pouches and a menacing looking knife. She was thin, but the muscles in her arms were hard and defined. Her long hair could use a good brushing, but the messy waves suited what he'd gleaned from her personality. Quick, no nonsense, slightly selfish, maybe even a little arrogant.

He realized his assessment had him staring too long when she cleared her throat uncomfortably. He reached out and took the sucker, barely brushing her fingers. A new kind of tingle ran through his hand, but a more pleasant one that muddled his thoughts, and he replied stupidly, "Help what? Give me cavities?"

She rolled her eyes. "You've been around humans too long."

The anger threatened and he opened his mouth to retort, but she interrupted him. "Chill dude, I just mean you react like a human. It's funny, I guess. I haven't been around humans for years. I forget." She shrugged, unconcerned with her insult.

Tolen continued to glare. She had no idea how close he was to losing control. How every sarcastic remark she made felt like fuel poured over his burning heart.

Her eyes flicked briefly to his again, she seemed to finally sense his frustration and tried to explain. "The sugar in the sucker helps your life force regenerate."

By the look on her face he knew his confusion was evident, but she didn't elaborate and Tolen added it to the list of questions he would demand be answered as soon as he knew he was calm enough to listen without hurting anyone.

"We need to head back. The Dark can track you by the power you give off." She started walking back and beckoned him to follow, but he couldn't move. He couldn't go back. Not yet.

He closed his eyes and let the need flow from his mouth without looking at her. "If I go back, I want the truth. All of it. No more secrets."

Macy's voice rose. "Excuse me? You don't get to make demands. We're here to save your stinking life!"

Tolen took a deep shuddering breath and clenched his fists. "Don't. Don't talk to me like that. I don't want to hurt you." He met her eyes and saw a shimmer of something. Pity, maybe, before she quickly looked away.

"Okay." She lowered her voice and took a few deep breaths of her own. "Sorry. I understand there's a lot you want to know and I promise— Bastian will tell you everything you need to know, but we really do have to get back, like *now*."

Tolen kicked a clump of sagebrush harder than he meant to and scared out a rabbit. It ran off without a backward glance. His heart slowed at the softness of her tone and the anger began to dissipate into embarrassed frustration. "'*Need to know*'—there's a classic phrase."

"Sorry." She mumbled. It wasn't much, but it was a start.

Tolen's shoulders sagged. "I'm used to secrets. Sick of them, but used to them." Though it was the last thing he wanted to do, he fell into step beside her.

Their shoes crunched in the hard dirt as they walked side by side in silence.

...even talk to this guy...weirdo is a legend and doesn't even know it.

"What?" Tolen looked over at Macy, certain she'd just insulted him under her breath.

She turned to him with surprise. "*What?*"

"Did you just...?"

She raised her eyebrow, but there was something in her eyes. She looked...guilty.

His eyes narrowed and he looked away. "Nothing."

Macy stopped walking and turned in a slow circle her eyes roving over the desert.

Tolen mimicked her, saw nothing, but a strange feeling began to come over him. Like they were being watched. "What?"

Her hands started to shake. "Do you feel that?" Goosebumps rose on her arms.

Tolen looked at her from the corner of his eye. Could she really feel it too? "Feel what exactly?"

"Come on." She took off at a dead run.

Macy beat him through the door, but only because he let her. The kitchen stood empty, but raised voices echoed from the living room. Tolen shadowed Macy's steps, grateful she seemed to be in as much of a hurry as he was to find out what was going on now.

When they turned the corner into the living room the first thing he saw was Bastian pacing—his agitated stride wearing a path in the thin carpet.

His mother sat on the couch holding a mug in her hands. If possible, she looked even worse. The tingle rolled back into his hands. No one even acknowledged him and Macy now in the room with them.

"What would you have us do then?" Dane stood at his full height, which still only reached Bastian's waist, his face determined and not at all intimidated.

"It is not a good idea." Bastian threw his hands up. "What if you are captured? What then? When you are under torture will you be able to keep Tolen's existence a secret?"

"You were ready to send Tolen in there!" Areen threw the mug across the room. Tolen jumped when it shattered against the far wall and thick brownish tea dripped onto the frayed carpet.

Bastian didn't flinch. "That is because it is the will of the Light. You cannot interfere with fate. Look what has happened already as a result of you trying to change his destiny. You may well have affected the outcome of the Final Battle. Do you not recognize what you have done, what you continue to do?"

Tolen stepped around Macy, no longer willing to be ignored. "What's going on?"

Bastian paused and met Macy's eyes. They were dilating and shifting like Tolen's did sometimes.

"We're not going to escape without a fight." Macy whispered.

Tolen glanced between the two, his heart hammering.

"No." Bastian met her stare with a worried expression.

"Someone please tell me what is going on." Tolen pushed the rocking chair out of the way and stalked over to his mother's side.

Macy ignored him, still focused only on Bastian. "The shift is strong…What *exactly* is coming?" Her hands trembled and she shoved them in her pockets.

Bastian closed his eyes and massaged his temple. "Everything."

CHAPTER SEVEN

RUN

Tolen rushed to the kitchen, his packed duffle dangling from his fist, the anger he'd felt earlier now buried beneath purpose. He still wanted answers, but the strange being-watched feeling was getting stronger, closer, and the seriousness he sensed from Bastian had him doing what he was told…for the moment.

His mother stood with her hands on her hips. "This is completely ridiculous!" The scorching afternoon sun beating through the open window couldn't compete with the heat of her anger. She wasn't an angry person by nature, unless she was really, really scared. Tolen could feel the fear coming off her in waves.

Macy wasn't responding to Areen's shouts, her movements were harried and her face tight with stress as she pulled out bags of herbs from their spice cupboard and stuffed them into a small leather satchel attached to her belt.

"What's going on?" Tolen asked, but Macy ignored him too.

"I'll tell you what's going on. These two," his mother gestured to Macy, and out the window where Bastian was pacing, "seem to think waiting for the Dark to catch up is a *good* idea!"

His own anger smoldered and he spoke without thinking. "Well, maybe if you would have told me what I am we wouldn't be in this mess."

His mother glanced up and the look in her eyes made him regret his words at once. He'd never seen so much pain on her face. Before he could take it back, she swept from the room, angry tears spilling from her eyes.

Macy paused in her search of the cabinets and cast a half glance over her shoulder, but before he could meet her eyes she went back to what she was doing.

Dane appeared at Tolen's elbow, making him jump.

"Should we take that out to the truck?" Dane pointed to Tolen's pack, his eyes pleading. Tolen could tell Dane wanted an excuse to talk alone in order to see where their friendship stood. He looked into Dane's earnest face and found no malice for his friend's deception. Dane may have kept things from Tolen, but he knew deep inside their friendship had been genuine. No matter what happened, Tolen would always be grateful for Dane's influence.

Tolen met Dane's eyes, nodded with a tiny smile, and followed him out the kitchen door.

Dane opened the truck door and Tolen threw his bag in the back. "What was my mom talking about? I thought we were in a hurry. We're not really waiting for the bad guys to catch up, are we?"

Dane took a deep breath. "It sounds like a nice idea, run as fast as we can, right?"

"Obviously."

"I thought so too, at first. High tail it out of here before the Dark shows up. That'd be great *if* there was only one group of Dark servants coming. But Bastian said there are *legions* moving in from every direction. We are literally being surrounded. No matter where we go, we will encounter something evil." Dane rubbed a hand over his eyes. "I just got back from talking to my father; he knows how to track the Dark. Bastian asked him to check our route and my father saw the evidence. Dark servants are everywhere.

"I'm sorry Tolen, but the Watcher is right, and whether your mom wants to admit it or not, our safest bet is to allow the weakest legion of creatures to almost catch up and lure them into a place that's to our advantage. If we escape them, we have a greater chance of getting ahead of the others."

Tolen looked over Dane's head at the horizon, trying to imagine what was coming, but failing. How could you be afraid of monsters when you'd been taught your whole life they weren't real? What exactly was the *Dark* anyway? He looked back at Dane. "What makes the group we're heading toward weaker?"

"They're mostly Reconns and Raksasha—scouts and blood-trackers. Raksasha are lethal but they're also stupid and easily outwitted. The Reconns will be more difficult because they are the ultimate chameleons. When they hold still they're literally invisible, but get them to move and they flicker, making them easier to pick off."

Tolen shook his head. "Okay, that made a lot of no sense." He rubbed his forehead. He'd given up the hope that he'd wake up from this nightmare in his own bed, but it still felt unreal, unbelievable.

He looked back at his home and felt the fear and doubt closing in until it seemed as suffocating as the dry desert air. It was so strange. This house, only days before, had felt safer to him than the world outside. Now they were leaving it and heading into an unknown he never could have imagined, and running from something far more sinister than he ever could have dreamed.

So many places they had packed up and left, but it had never felt like this.

The posters on the walls, the books on the shelves, his bedding—everything would stay behind. He wondered idly what the owners would think when they finally showed up and found their final rent check stuck to the fridge and the house full of furniture. What would the stories be? The corner of his mouth twitched. The whole town would love the scandal. It'd give them more entertainment than they'd seen in years; add in the story Jeff would likely come up with, and maybe they'd get some news coverage from a desperate local reporter.

His skin prickled. Deep down, he'd always known that whatever they were running from would eventually catch up to them, but he'd never imagined it'd be something like this. Evil had marked him, an evil that had already captured his father.

Dane coughed nervously and glanced around. "I'm sorry I couldn't be there for you as much as you needed me through all this Tolen. I had to follow your mother's wishes. I'm not allowed to interfere with Blood-Bonds."

Tolen caught a glimpse of his mother through the kitchen window, pulling food out of the cupboards and a muscle in his cheek twitched. He wasn't angry with Dane, but his mother? Yes. She'd betrayed him with her secrecy. He didn't want to hurt her, but how could she keep something this big from him?

"She kept everything from me. What I really am, the truth about my father, everything. I thought my dad was a worthless creep who wanted nothing to do with his family. You guessed that my nightmares were about him and yet, because of her, you couldn't tell me. I want to find him, but because of her I have no idea how, or even why he ended up in that prison in the first place. I've been so scared for her health, worrying every day that I might lose her, and all along if she would have told me what I am I could have learned how to protect us from whatever is out there." He leaned against his mother's rusty, broken down Honda and propped his feet on the Scout's bumper. He felt grateful he could finally vent his frustrations to his best friend, but knew he couldn't feed the anger.

He took a slow breath. "I'm supposed to be afraid of what's out there but I'm so frustrated I can't feel anything else. I can't get my head straight. I've always known I was different, no matter what I have or haven't been told, but this?" He shook his head and waved a hand through the air. "This is *nuts*. This is fantasy. You're some dwarf from a Tolkien book, and me? I'm supposed to be some sort of *Chosen* one that has to protect unsuspecting humans from monsters, when I'm nearly just as clueless as they are—"

"Technically I'm not a dwarf. I'm a Doogar—big difference. Very few humans ever get it right." Dane glanced at Tolen's clenched fists, seemed to sense his need for solid answers, and gave Tolen what he could. "Sorry, it's not a good time to joke. My people have been here since this world began. Some of us have Hidden gifts like you. Some of us are simply skilled with our hands. Most of my kind lives in underground settlements. We only come *above* when our services are needed. I guess that's where the dwarf comparisons come from."

Dane ran a chubby hand over his face. "I'm sorry, Tolen. I wish things could be different. I wish for your sake that you could go to sleep, wake up, and find all this really is another nightmare or just one of our video games. But you can't. Everything you've been told by Bastian is real. The sooner you start to believe it, the easier it'll get, not to mention it will help you with your gifts. Now that you no longer have to hold them back, they will be a great asset to you. The Chosen are held in very high regard by the Hidden. It's actually a great honor to be selected by the Light." He sighed. "It will get easier with time. I promise."

Tolen ran a hand through his hair. He didn't want to offend his friend, but at this moment he disagreed.

Macy rushed out of the house with a look of deep concentration on her face. Ignoring the two of them, she began scouring the overgrown weeds in their pitiful garden, occasionally pulling something up to stuff it in one of her many pockets and pouches.

A few seconds later, Bastian and Areen came out and started helping her.

Dane nudged Tolen's arm and nodded toward the others. "I know you're mad at your mom, but I really believe she was trying to protect you. She loves you so much she has given her life to keep you safe. To live in the Hidden world is dangerous. She was trying to do what she thought was best."

"And Bastian, well he's actually not so bad." Dane bobbed his head. "Macy's got a rotten attitude but she seems to be pretty skilled. Truthfully, if I had to pick who to run with, I don't think we've faired too badly. The guy's a Watcher so he's the best suited to protect you, and since Macy's a Chosen she will be able to help you learn your responsibilities."

Tolen blew out a loud breath. "Responsibilities I didn't ask for." He watched Macy force a rusty shovel into the hard dirt, dislodge a huge clump of something, toss it over her shoulder, reach down into the hole, rip out a bunch of stringy roots, and stuff them into the same satchel she'd put the herbs into. He shook his head. "I don't think I'll be asking Macy for lessons anytime soon. She'd probably strangle me like she did those crows, just for breathing wrong."

Dane sighed, "It does seem she doesn't like you much. Just jealous, if you ask me."

Bastian stood up, handed Macy something else for her bag and then the three of them walked over to Tolen and Dane. He tossed another duffle bag into the back. "We are nearly ready."

"Where will we go if we escape?" Tolen tried not to think about how everyone kept saying *if*.

Dane answered. "California, to the Binithan—my *real* home. The power of my people should shield us until we decide where to go from there."

Tolen glanced between Dane and Bastian. "If we'll be protected there, why not stay?"

"Um, lots of reasons." Dane wouldn't meet his eyes. "Bastian, my father has scouted the route. He said we should be able to draw the legion right to where you wanted as long as we get there before dusk. If we're later than that, they might head us off. They got pretty far last night."

Tolen glanced around. No one seemed to want to look directly at him. Bastian and Dane were facing each other. Macy stood behind them picking dirt out of her fingernails, a sucker sticking out of her mouth. His mother had her arms folded and stared at the ground. If not for the fact that no one would look right at him, he would believe she was just still offended by what he'd said. But that wasn't it at all. They were hiding something from him.

"I still think you guys are nuts." Macy pulled the sucker from her mouth with a loud pop. "We're not going to outrun the Dark with the kid's life force acting like a friggin' beacon the whole way."

Tolen clenched his teeth. "You know, I am right here."

Macy rolled her eyes but otherwise ignored him.

"We will break through the western line and head for the Binithan." Bastian gave Macy a hard look. "We will deal with whatever follows, accordingly." He looked at Tolen and his pale eyes dilated and contracted so fast it was dizzying. "Are your injuries bothering you at all?"

Tolen touched the bruise under his eye. He'd actually forgotten all about them. "No, I feel fine."

Bastian gave him another once over and turned to Tolen's mother. "He knows no combat skills, correct?"

"No."

Macy snorted.

Bastian put a hand on Macy's shoulder. "Make sure you have everything. We leave in five minutes."

Tolen looked at his mother. "So, I'm supposed to fight?"

Moisture gathered at the corners of his mother's eyes, but she kept her head down. "No, just stay behind us."

Frustration leaked into his tone. "And if something gets past you?"

"Nothing will." Dane twisted a small dagger in his hands. The strange blade glinted ominously in the sunlight.

Tolen bounced uncomfortably in the back of Bastian's ancient truck. Mashed in-between Macy and Dane, he felt like a sardine trapped in a tin being tossed around in a rock tumbler. Every stone in the road seemed to jump right through the seat and slam into his backside.

Bastian swerved to miss an antelope and Tolen's head knocked into Macy's.

"Ouch! Watch it kid!" She threw him an angry glare and rubbed the side of her head.

"Sorry," Tolen muttered.

"How much farther to the canyon, Bastian?" Macy continued to massage her head dramatically.

Bastian's eyes flashed in the rear view mirror. "Not long now. You know what to do."

Bouncing along the highway, Macy pulled various pouches from her belt.

"Here, make yourself useful. Hold these." She handed Tolen three small leather pouches blackened with age.

Tolen twisted the pouches with interest and Macy slapped his hand.

"Don't spill anything unless you want to lose your legs. TNT, get it?"

He held the strings at the top and let them dangle from his fist, fighting the urge to throw them back at her.

She set several flat squares of some sort of woven material on her legs. From each of the pouches she pulled out bits of multi-colored dirt and crushed leaves, and sprinkled them on top of the material. Then she removed one of his mother's herb bags from her satchel and added a pinch to the top of each pile.

He watched in resentful amazement as Macy worked. She moved her hands furiously fast, and yet they remained steady despite the constant rocking of the truck. She seemed to have good reason for her arrogance, but it didn't stop it from being annoying.

"Hold on." Bastian took a sharp turn at nearly sixty miles an hour. Tolen felt the side of the truck lift slightly. He looked down at Macy wondering if she was being serious about the stuff blowing his legs off, but the piles of dirt on her lap were gone. She held out her hand for the pouches.

"What were those things?" He watched her reattach the pouches to her belt.

She ignored him.

"They looked like Glockshaw." Dane clutched the window handle trying to stay in his seat. "Miniature bombs; Kunamin are famous for them. Very cool."

The side of Macy's mouth twitched.

Tolen only understood 'bombs' but right now he had a bigger concern. "Dane?" He cringed when they hit a bump that sent the springs smacking into his tailbone.

"Yeah?" Dane leaned into the door as they turned again.

"Where exactly in California is your home?" He asked wondering how long they'd be sandwiched in the back of this truck.

"The Lava Beds."

He looked at Dane in confusion. "Isn't that a National monument?"

"Yeah. You'd be surprised to find out how many colonies of Hidden use national parks, forests, and other protected lands as their homes throughout the world. They are some of the only places left that humans don't have full access to. It's a perfect setup if you think about it."

Tolen gripped the seat as Bastian slammed on the brakes, slowing from sixty down to thirty as they entered a small town.

"Macy, the first band will be on the left as soon as we enter the canyon." Bastian tapped his hands nervously on the steering wheel.

She nodded. "How many?"

"I am not sure yet."

"Why are we going into a canyon? Won't that box us in?" Tolen glanced at Dane. His mother glanced over her shoulder but didn't say anything. The look in her eyes sent shivers down his back. They were filled with fear.

"We don't really have a choice." Dane shrugged, trying to look unconcerned, but some of the same fear in his mother's eyes was mirrored in Dane's. "We need someplace we can use our gifts without drawing unwanted attention. Nine Mile Canyon rarely gets tourists this early in the season."

Tolen had been to Nine Mile Canyon several times. Its name was a ruse—its rocky dirt roads twisted and curved through the canyon until the total miles was more like fifty. Even driving as fast as they could, it would take over an hour to get out the other side.

"What about the people who live in there?"

Dane shifted in his seat. "Let's hope they're smart enough to stay inside tonight."

Just as the sun began to drop below the horizon, Bastian turned beside a sign declaring they were entering the canyon.

Tolen took a deep breath. Fifty miles of terror coming up…

Bastian clicked on the headlights as night settled over the desert. Tolen looked out the back window, wondering how far they would make it before they were attacked, when suddenly something slammed into the driver's side of the truck. Bastian swerved, skidded into the rocks and cranked the wheel, fishtailing back onto the road.

Bastian glanced in his side mirrors. "Macy, be ready."

His eyes flashed to Tolen in the rearview. "Tolen you need to remain as calm as possible. You will see things tonight that will be unlike anything you have ever imagined. Try not to let fear overtake you. Stay with one of us at all times and you will be fine."

Tolen had a hard time believing any of them were going to be fine as football sized rocks started flying in like a hailstorm, hitting the truck and crashing into the windshield, sending cracks spider-webbing across the glass surface.

"We're not going to make it much farther in the truck!" Dane shouted.

Macy rolled down her window and ducked. A rock the size of Tolen's fist sailed past her face and hit the back of Bastian's seat. She rubbed her hands together, breathed on one of the balls of dirt, and flung it out the window. A huge explosion shattered the air behind them and the rockstorm ceased for several minutes.

An enormous black something dropped right in front of them and Bastian veered sharply to miss slamming into it. The truck spun and teetered. Sure they were about to roll, Tolen gripped his seat and held on for all he was worth.

A wall of dirt appeared out of the darkness and the truck crashed sideways into it. The passenger side windows shattered, the truck's steel frame buckled and they were all shoved to one side in a tangle of arms and legs.

"Thanks." Macy muttered as she climbed off Tolen.

Dane rubbed his jaw. "Anytime."

"You did that? How?" Tolen's heart felt like it'd taken residence in his throat.

Dane shrugged then massaged his shoulder. "I asked. I didn't know if Earth would respond. But thankfully she did."

Tolen opened his mouth to ask what the black mass was that they'd swerved around, but Bastian began shouting and the panic in his voice drove the question out of his mind.

"Get out! Get OUT!"

They all scrambled trying to pry open the dented doors, but they wouldn't budge.

Bastian leaned into his door and pushed. With a loud grunt of metal, the door ripped from its hinges. "Everyone up here!"

They scrambled over the seats. Once Bastian made sure everyone got out, he grabbed Macy and Tolen by the back of their shirt collars and shoved them forward. "Run to that outcropping! Go!"

Seconds after Tolen started to run, an explosion behind them sent him flying forward to his hands and knees. He glanced back to see the remains of the black thing they'd swerved to miss shooting sparks and debris into the air. A second explosion and the truck ignited into a volcano of fire and metal.

CHAPTER EIGHT

CHANGE OF PLANS

"TOLEN, COME ON!" MACY GRABBED THE BACK OF HIS SHIRT AND wrenched him upright.

They stopped at the outcropping. Tolen leaned over with his hands on his knees searching the night, terrified for his mother and best friend. "Where's everyone else?"

Macy pointed towards the left of the smoking truck. "There. They couldn't get across before the truck exploded, so they jumped into the ditch."

"What do we do?" Tolen panted. Fear twisted through his gut. His body weak and shaky.

"First you gotta chill. Fear is a device of the Dark. Bastian wasn't joking about staying calm. If you let it get to you, you'll weaken and no matter what I do, you'll die."

"That calms me right down," he mumbled, trying to ignore that that was exactly what was happening. He could feel the fear literally taking strength from him, but he couldn't stop it.

"Shh. Get down!" Macy pushed on his back. "There are two Raksasha scouts at four o'clock. And I think a Reconn is nearing the ditch."

"What are you going to do?" Tolen whispered, struggling and failing in the fight against the powerful surge of fear that seemed to be a real monster bent on killing him.

Macy closed her eyes and rubbed her palms together. Tolen smelled something floral and minty and wondered fleetingly if she was smashing more herbs, but he hadn't seen her put anything in her hands.

She opened her eyes. "I think there are four more Raksasha running in behind the two over there." She pointed and he could swear he saw a tiny stream of smoke trailing from her finger. "I'm not positive though, Bastian's better at reading the Dark's vibes. If we can plan our attack with the others at the same time, we should be able to startle them enough to regroup."

"How's Bastian going to know to attack at the same time?"

"He's aware of our thoughts remember. Wait for my signal and then I want you to run back to the others, all right?"

Tolen nodded, noticing it was getting harder to breathe. "What's the signal?"

"When I take down the first two Raksasha."

"By yourself?"

"It's what I do." She closed her eyes once more, mumbled something under her breath, and then leapt from their hiding spot, soaring at least ten feet in the air before landing outside the circle of light cast by the burning truck.

Tolen couldn't see anything.

A muffled thump, a bone-chilling screech, and something rolled down the road in his direction. It looked like the blackened head of a skeleton with glowing yellow eyes.

He scrambled backwards until his back hit into the rock behind him. From the ditch he could hear more thuds and shrieks, but he couldn't see anything that direction either. Panic gripped his heart like a black dream. Sweat poured down his face and dripped into his eyes. He'd never been more scared in his life. How was he supposed to stay calm when he didn't even know if anyone was still alive?

He looked back to where Macy had disappeared. Why couldn't his weird abilities work when he wanted them to? He tried to see in the dark, get his eye to let in more light, but it wouldn't. He tried to search his mind for any trees nearby, but all he could feel was a growing sense of dread. His lips started to go numb.

How was he supposed to know when both Raksasha were dead if he couldn't see? He swallowed back bile, deciding that he was just going to run. What else could he possibly do?

Nothing.

He poised to run.

Macy appeared suddenly, struggling with what seemed to be some kind of man-sized skeletal black ape. It shrieked like a bat and clawed at the air. She danced just out of its reach, dodging its every move. The sight horrified him—worse than any of his nightmares. It was nearly as frightening to watch Macy as the monster. He hadn't been one to watch many real fights on TV, but even he could tell a master when he saw one.

Macy was lethal.

She twisted out of the way of the Raksasha's long, disgusting finger-nails and lunged. The creature began to fall forward and she ran up its back as it fell, launched herself from its shoulders, spun in the air, and came to land just in front of it. She reached down and pulled her knife from the back of its skull.

The two were dead. That was the signal, but now Tolen *couldn't* make his legs move; instead he leaned over and threw up.

Macy ran toward him, her knife dripping black blood. She jumped in the air and his first thought was *she's going to kill me*, but she soared over his head. He could hear her feet land on the rock above. Pebbles rained down from the edge, another shriek split the night, and a huge body fell at Tolen's feet.

The Raksasha's legs were still twitching. Macy jumped down and tugged her knife from between its eyes.

She shouted in Tolen's face and pulled on his arm, but he couldn't hear her, he couldn't hear anything but a strange buzzing sound. He felt the sensation of someone dragging him forward and then being flung over something moving—someone's shoulder? He was vaguely aware of his mother's voice. She kept asking him if he was okay, but a fog had started to settle over his brain.

"How the *H* are we supposed to outrun this legion if we have to carry Tolen the whole freakin' way?" Macy leaned against a pile of boulders with her hands on her knees. She used her life force to aid her eyes in the dark, but not to help her run—she needed all her strength for the Kuna.

Bastian lowered Tolen to the ground as they all tried to catch their breath, but it had to be a short breather. The Raksasha's shrieks were getting louder.

Macy could see hundreds of them through the darkness, crawling over the mountainside like an army of disgusting black ants. They would be here in minutes. The last firebomb she'd thrown into the mountainside hadn't slowed the creatures as much as she'd hoped.

Bastian opened his mouth, but Areen interrupted him from where she sat panting on the ground. "I will stay behind and distract them."

"I'll stay with you." Dane clutched his side—blood seeped between his fingers.

Macy rounded on them. "That's the stupidest idea I've ever heard." She turned to Bastian. "They're crazy! It's suicide!"

Bastian wasn't listening—the look on his face said he was considering their options—his eyes were dilating again. "Areen, I cannot tell if you will be able to get away after the three of us escape. You may both be captured or killed."

Areen's determined glare pierced the darkness. "That's a risk I'm willing to take to save my son."

"And I'll take to save my friend," Dane added with a grimace.

Areen struggled to her feet. "Can you see that you will escape?"

Bastian helped her stand and stepped back, his face reluctant. "Yes. The diversion will work. Ten Reconn and three Raksasha, will notice us and follow, but Macy will ensure our escape."

Macy raised her eyebrows. *I will?*

Areen's lips trembled as she leaned over to brush a strand of hair from Tolen's forehead. "We'll hold them off long enough for you to get out of the canyon. I should be able to shield Tolen at least that far. Then you'll be on your own."

This would likely be the last time Areen would ever see Tolen. Her final goodbye to her son, and he wasn't even awake to hear it. Macy looked at the woman's pale face. *No way.* This lady who looked like death twenty-four hours ago couldn't hold off an entire legion of Dark servants, even with the Doogar's help. But her jaw was set and her eyes held a look of determination that was all too familiar; Macy's father's face had worn the same look the last time she'd seen him—a look that haunted her to this day.

Macy clenched her teeth and balled her fists.

Dane bowed humbly to Bastian and turned to Macy. "Tolen is my best friend. Please help him learn the ways of the Chosen."

Macy shuffled her feet in the dirt, shoved her fists in her pockets, and nodded.

Areen touched Bastian's arm. "Please, please protect my son."

"With my life." Bastian ran his hand through the air above Areen's head. "By my blood and my oath, he will be safe in my care." He placed his hand over his heart.

Macy shook her head. *You're all insane.*

Bastian's eyes flashed in her direction and back to Dane. "Good luck Master Dane. I shall pass along your great acts to the Elders at the Binithan."

"*Liosladon,*" Dane whispered.

"*Liosladon.*" Bastian bowed his head briefly.

Areen nodded once in their direction as silent tears ran down her cheeks.

Once they were out of earshot, Macy looked up at him. "So, how exactly am I supposed to ensure our escape?"

Bastian hefted Tolen higher on his shoulder. "You are going to send fire to that location." He pointed to a high perch of rock, covered with dry brush and rocks, in front of Areen and Dane's hiding spot.

"It will startle the Raksasha and blind them to us. There are Reconn and Raksasha high enough above to notice us escape, but I can *see* that once

Areen and Dane engage the advancement they will be too distracted to hear the Reconn call the alert. You will send one bomb at them, enhanced with your Kuna. It will take them all out at the same time."

"That big an explosion is going to freak out any humans around, especially if they've already discovered the truck."

"We have no other choice. We can hope that they will not choose to investigate until dawn. By then, the Dark will have retreated."

"If I use that much of my Kuna, and we use our life forces to run the rest of the way out of here, I'll be too weak to move for days. They'll catch up." Already she could feel the drain.

"On the other side of that hill, the Bureau of Land Management has stashed a truck we can borrow." Bastian's brow furrowed as he stared into the darkness at things only he could see.

"I love the way you justify grand theft auto." Macy sighed. "Okay, tell me when to go." She rubbed her palms together until she could smell eucalyptus and roses, and pulled the last Glockshaw from her pocket. Smoke rose slowly from her fingertips.

"Now!" Bastian shouted.

Macy took aim. "*To' inreedo mig'nata!*" The other side of the canyon came into clear focus and strength surged down her arms. She threw the Glockshaw as hard as she could and marked it as it soared through the air.

Just before it hit the ledge, she thrust her hands toward it. "*Mi'no ha!*" Huge balls of fire shot from her hands. She twisted her fingers and the fireballs combined, forming into one gigantic flaming boulder. It slammed into the ledge with a deafening crash. White-hot flame burst into the air, lighting the canyon as if it were high noon. She bent over gasping for air.

"Good job, Macy." Bastian patted her on the back. "Now run!"

CHAPTER NINE

INTO SHADOW

NOT A FLICKER OF YELLOW LIGHT PIERCED THE HEAVY DARKNESS.

Something thick, black, and blood-like, trickled down the stone walls.

The Ookra shivered. The servants of the demons were not known for bravery. A single blue-flame candle, clutched in his clawed hands, barely revealed the way down the frigid passageway.

A loud wail, followed by a pain-filled scream, echoed through the blackness, and the Ookra shivered again.

The Tormentors were extracting.

A door opened on the left and the servant shuffled through it. Daemon, the Demon Master, stood in front of the stone fireplace, his massive figure filling most of the small room.

"Speak, slave." Daemon's deep, cold, voice reverberated through the room and the Ookra fell to his knees.

He gulped loudly from his supine position—the tips of Daemon's black boots were the only thing he could see. "They have escaped, Master."

"How?" Daemon circled the Ookra who began panting nervously.

"They split up. A diversion. We know which direction they are headed. We will catch them."

The room fell silent for several minutes. The Ookra chanced a look up. Daemon stared into the fireplace, his horrid face eerily lit by the strange blue flames.

"The prisoner?" He asked softly.

The servant's eyes moved back to the floor. "Weakening, Master. It will not be long before you have the information you seek."

Daemon circled again and his blood-red cloak swept across the Ookra's fingers.

"We do not have time to waste relying on the stupidity of the Raksasha, or the slow pace of the Shadows. The Watcher must be eliminated if we are to proceed. Release the DéHool."

His shadow, cast by the dim light of the ice blue flames, covered the Ookra like black fog.

CHAPTER TEN

REAL OR DREAM?

Tolen's eyelids fluttered and a girl's voice filtered into his ears.

"Hey, Bastian, the kid's waking up."

He knew this voice. Macy. Macy killed the Raksasha. He was supposed to run but he couldn't make his legs move. He'd lost his dinner all over the desert floor and…he couldn't remember what came next.

Where was he? He struggled to open his eyelids.

A loud motor rumbled beneath him and he realized they were moving—fast. Something hard and uncomfortable poked into his back; his legs were twisted at a painful angle. He wanted to sit up and find out what was going on, but his body felt so heavy.

"Tolen?" Bastian whispered.

He cringed at the sound of this voice. It scared him. *Why?*

He remembered now. His mom had been talking to him, wanting him to wake up, but he hadn't been able to get out of the fog. A little voice told him he could have if he'd chosen to, but what he'd really wanted was to stay there. There were no monsters in the fog. He was a coward. Guilt rushed over him as he realized they'd had to drag his unconscious body through the desert until they'd reached this vehicle. How much more danger had he put them in?

He slowly opened his eyes. "Mom?" He swallowed hard wanting to apologize, but not knowing what to say. It was dark; the only thing clearly visible were the outlines of two people and two sets of eyes, one blue, one green—both filled with worry. He was such an idiot.

He looked around for two more sets of eyes and realized he was squished in the cab of an unfamiliar truck. His long legs were half on the seat and half off, his big feet wedged against Macy's tiny ones. His head rested on the seat next to Bastian, who held a foul smelling rag on Tolen's forehead. There was no one else.

He swallowed again as his heart raced and dread crawled up his spine. "Where's my mother?" he licked his lips. "Where's Dane?"

Bastian glanced down from the road and shook his head sadly.

Tolen sat up so fast his head spun and he bumped into Macy. "Where are they?"

"Your mother and best friend stayed behind as a diversion. We could not have made it out without them. They saved our lives." Bastian's voice broke at the end.

Anger and remorse more powerful than anything he had ever felt flooded through Tolen's veins like a drug. He could feel the strength of his emotions building within him. The heat was back in his chest and his hands burned with power. "You're lying!"

"Tolen, I am not lying. Please, calm down." The Watcher spoke softly but there was an edge of nervousness in his tone.

Tolen shook his head as the heat rushed to his palms. "Go back."

"We cannot." His calm tone only enraged Tolen further.

"GO BACK! NOW!" The truck's engine stuttered and smoke billowed from beneath the hood.

"Stop it!" Macy screamed and grabbed Tolen's arm.

He twisted out of her grip and one part of his mind registered her gasp. "Pull over." To his surprise, Bastian did as he asked.

Once the truck rolled to a stop, Tolen reached past Macy and unlocked the door. "Move." He spoke through his teeth.

"Excuse me?" Macy huffed.

Tolen squeezed his eyes shut, feeling the build of heat that would release soon without his control. He didn't want to hurt her, but he would if she didn't get out of his way.

"Macy, let Tolen out." Bastian's voice was low and commanding. Macy slid back against the seat and pulled her knees to her chest.

Tolen pushed past her without looking at her face. He heard Bastian climb out and shut his door.

"Tolen, wait."

Tolen spun on his heel and looked at the strange man, feeling a hatred grow within him so powerfully it was as if a living monster had taken resident in his chest. *You made her STAY!* The voice that issued out of his mouth was not his own. It was low, like the growl of an animal, and in no way human.

"You are letting your subconscious take over—you are not accepting reality."

"They're *not* dead!" Tolen brought his hands up and flame shot out of them toward Bastian who ducked out of the way just in time. The burst of flame hit a spread of dry grass and it lit up at once.

Macy jumped out, twisted her hands in the air and the flame went out.

Tolen turned into the night and ran. He ran from the two people who should have stayed behind and protected his mother, and who refused to help him now. He ran from the possibility that the Watcher was telling the truth. He ran from his shame.

He would go back to the canyon. Retrace their steps. He would find the truth for himself. And if his mother and Dane were still alive, he would find them. If they were captured, he would save them. He ignored the voice in his head telling him he had no idea how.

The anger swelled within him and he felt the heat in his palms again. He raised his hands above his head and let the flame release toward the sky. He hadn't created flame in his hands since he was six and accidentally lit the neighbor's house on fire. He remembered the horror and guilt he'd felt as he'd watched their house burn while his mother packed their bags. He'd practiced hard to control this power, to never let it out again. He knew what the heat meant as his anger rose in the truck, but it had never been so hot, so impossible to contain.

His foot caught on something in the darkness and he fell forward on his face. He spit sand out of his mouth and turned his head to look behind him. He could just make out the truck's headlights, nearly a mile in the distance. How fast had he run?

While he stared, his eye shifted and he could see Macy standing on the front bumper bent under the hood as if she were fixing the truck. Bastian stood beside her holding a flashlight, but he was facing Tolen, his bright eyes fixated on Tolen's face as if he could see him perfectly.

Tolen didn't see his lips move, but he heard Bastian's voice as if he were standing beside him. *I am sorry.*

Tolen could feel the Watcher's sadness, but his own anger overruled. He stood up and looked back toward home. He took three steps and heard the Watcher's voice again.

Your mother is very gifted, as is Dane. Doogar have a very special alliance with the Earth. It is possible that they managed to escape.

Bastian was not convinced of this, it showed in his tone.

Even if you make it back there without something killing you, and they actually survived, you will never find them without my help.

The fury licked at Tolen's heart. For the first time in his life he wanted to use his curse to hurt someone. He wanted the Watcher to pay for leaving his mom and Dane behind. He wanted him to suffer the way Tolen suffered now.

Tolen, come back. Let me help you.

He'd never forgive this man for leaving his mother and best friend behind and he'd never forgive himself for choosing to stay unconscious. The two were connected. He knew it. And he'd never stop trying to find a way to make it right.

Tolen, it is not safe for you to be alone. Let us take you to the Binithan. Dane's people are expecting you. Come with us that far. I will do what I can to discover what happened to them. I will try to help you, but if you stay out here, you will die.

Get out of my head! Tolen's jaw clenched and he pushed venom into the thought, *I'll never forgive you.*

I will never expect you to… The Watcher's voice trailed off and Tolen felt his presence leave his mind.

His hands shook, his whole body felt weak, and his head spun. He hated the Watcher and his ward more than he'd ever hated anyone, even more than Jeff Macro and or any other bully he'd ever dealt with. But he knew he was being stupid if he thought he could walk all the way back to the canyon and try to go after his mother and Dane. After what he'd seen this night he knew he had no real idea what he was going up against. This rekindled the anger, but this time it only drained him. He'd lost and he knew it. For this single thing he needed their help. But once they reached the Doogar, he never wanted to see them again. If the Doogar people were as amazing as Dane was, *is*, then he would ask their help. His mother had trusted them and in that he knew that he could too.

He pulled the anger inside and buried it deep until the heat was completely gone and the facade he'd spent years creating fell over him. He could be with these two the same way he was with every other person he knew—aside from the two he truly cared about. He would treat them the same as the faceless people he went to school with, bagged groceries for, or walked past on the street. They meant nothing to him and he would control his anger by remembering that. They were merely a means to an end.

He ducked his head and turned back into the headlights, weak but determined.

○○○

"…other than the fact that it smells like dog fart under here we should be good until we reach the Jeep." Macy climbed out from under the hood to see Tolen standing beside Bastian, his chest heaving, sweat pouring down his face, but no longer angry. He looked so calm it was creepy, as if some other dude had taken his place. His eyes were guarded, but something still festered below the surface. He met her eyes briefly but not long enough for her to figure out what he was hiding. She shrugged. Whether the kid liked it or not, Bastian would know whatever he was thinking. She jumped off the bumper and Bastian closed and latched the hood.

"We have about another forty miles to the Jeep. You are certain we can make it?" Bastian asked.

Macy nodded. "As long as you keep it below sixty and watch the temp. He boiled all the water out of the motor, and there's a tiny crack in the block, but the water I added should get us there."

Tolen walked away and climbed in the cab. Macy tipped her head toward him. "Is he under control?"

Bastian whispered. "For now. Do *not* goad him Macy, I mean it. He is dangerous. Far more dangerous than even he realizes."

She wiped her hands on a rag from her back pocket. "I'll be good." Her eyes narrowed. "But if he pushes me like that again I can't make any guarantees."

Bastian shook his head and walked her to the passenger door. He waited until she was situated beside Tolen, as far away as the seat would allow, before climbing into the driver's seat and starting the engine.

Macy turned her head toward the window and pushed her headphones into her ears.

○○○

The sun rose too bright and cheery for Tolen as he stared out the window at the passing yellow lines of the highway. They reminded him of a swarm of angry bees: black, yellow, black, yellow, humming beneath the worn tires of the rusty Jeep they were now driving.

Dumping the conspicuous BLM truck had been their only stop in the last four hours. They'd left it on the side of the road near a storage unit where the Jeep *happened* to be hidden. Macy spent ten minutes under the hood and with two words from Bastian, "Get in," they were off again, without any explanations.

Tolen assumed the Watcher must have vehicles like this stashed all over the place.

Bastian had offered him some strange looking food for breakfast, but Tolen couldn't bring himself to eat anything. He could feel the urgency behind their movements, the speed at which they drove, and the overall tension that surrounded them, but he'd fallen into his own personal hell and couldn't bring himself to care as much as he knew he should.

The yellow lines seemed to be screaming their names. *Mom. Dane. Mom. Dane.* His last words to his mother had been in anger and he'd never told Dane how much he meant to him, how grateful he was for his friendship. He'd taken them both for granted, and he hated himself for it. He felt helpless, stupid, weak, angry, and ashamed all at the same time. He caught himself watching the road signs and counting the miles as they made their way toward California. His life was in the hands of these strangers for now, but once they reached the Binithan things would change. He'd make sure of it.

His throat tightened and his eyes burned.

"There is no shame in showing emotion." Bastian whispered from the driver's seat. "Emotion separates us from the Dark."

Tolen glanced uncomfortably over his shoulder at Macy, who thankfully still slept sprawled out in the backseat of the Jeep, before turning back to glare out the windshield. The Watcher reading his thoughts was annoying.

"Not read. It is the tenor, or the emotion behind the thought I sense. Thoughts are not words on a page. I can feel you blaming yourself. I feel your wrath and resentment toward me. You have every right to be angry with me. As your Watcher, I must do what is necessary to protect you, no matter the cost. I do not ask for, nor expect, your forgiveness. But blaming yourself serves no purpose and will not help."

Tolen clenched his hands in his lap, refusing to retort. Calm and aloof. This man meant nothing.

Bastian's eyes never left the road. Either he really was leaving Tolen's mind alone, or he was at least pretending to. He continued his one-sided conversation as if Tolen were actually interested. "It is not your fault you lose consciousness in sensitive situations. Your body feels something, and your life force reacts with your gifts. Because you have not been taught to use the power you feel, I believe that when you are particularly emotional in one form or another, you go into sensory overload. You have subconsciously figured out how to channel your anger to your most powerful gifts, which is why the trees will react and you cannot always hold back the flame, but your mind has no idea how to battle overwhelming fear or remorse. It goes into protection mode and shuts down."

"My most powerful gifts?" His voice was scratchy, but calm. He could do this.

The Watcher nodded. "Your first birthright is that of the Honitahai, the nature speakers. This is why it is so easy for you to hear the trees and speak to them. The gift of the Kunamin, the fire-wielders, is a very emotionally driven gift. Right now, because you have not been trained in your other gifts, this is your second strongest."

"What do you mean other gifts?" Tolen cast a swift look at Bastian, a sick knot forming in his stomach.

Bastian glanced over and his eyes were dilating again. Tolen's blue eye burned and he looked away. "What all can you do Tolen?"

Tolen shifted in his seat and stared out the window. He didn't want to tell this man any more about himself, not only because he didn't like him, but he didn't really know how. He'd always had to keep everything a secret. With time he'd even stopped telling his mother when he discovered something else he could do. But if he was going to follow through on his plan, then he needed to know, he needed to understand this creature, this Being that he was. His head flooded with questions and his hatred toward this man couldn't overrule his need for answers.

"I've never really tried to find out everything I can do. Sometimes things just happen. I can't remember a time when I couldn't feel something in the trees and that they understood me. I was six when I first created fire. I didn't mean to. The neighbor kids were really mean to me. One day I just lost it and lit their house on fire." He didn't look at Bastian to see what the man thought of this confession. Instead he went on, feeling for the first time a strange sense of relief letting it all out. "I am stronger than most people, and I can run really fast when my emotions are high—angry or even happy. Sometimes I feel things when I'm sitting on the ground, or in the wind. Almost as if they are trying to communicate with me, but I don't know how…" He trailed off and felt his face redden.

"Do not be embarrassed Tolen. You are not incorrect." He took a deep breath and scanned the horizon. "The histories and mysteries of the Hidden are many and they take a lifetime of lessons to learn, and even then I do not think one ever truly understands all until they pass to the other side and can view things from a grander perspective. I do not have time to tell you all the mysteries of the Hidden, but I think I can give you enough to help you understand, at least to a degree." He cleared his throat and shifted in his seat.

Tolen waited for him to continue, sensing the Watcher's discomfort only made him more curious.

"In the beginning, when this world was created, eight great Beings infused their gifts into the Balance. Honitahai, the nature speaker; Kunamin, the fire-wielder; Dicernan, the unseen; Lóklana, the light caller; Animashta, the animal listener; Arwah, the wind shifter; Leenwa, the water caller; and Télora, the earth mover. Because of who you are, you have been given the gift of each of these great Beings. With time you will learn how to speak to the earth, the wind, light, animals, the water, and use all your other gifts in the right way, at the right time, and for the right reasons."

Bastian took a deep breath. "You have also been born with a special gift that is yours alone. It is not elemental or physical. This is a gift of the heart. A gift of true empathy. There are some, such as the Spheres, that can use their gifts to sense the character of a person, but a gift of true and complete empathy is incredibly rare. You can sense the feelings of those around you, correct?"

Tolen nodded slowly. "My mother always said I was born with a thoughtful heart." A lump rose in his throat.

"This ability is one of your greatest gifts Tolen. It will guide you better than any compass, better than any map, better than any piece of advice or training you receive. I know that right now you cannot forgive me for what happened to Dane and your mother. As I said I do not expect you to, and I will never ask it of you. What I will ask however, is that you believe your *thoughtful heart* when it tells you I can be trusted and Macy can be trusted. Listen to it as you train, learn, and use it whenever it is time to make a hard decision and anger wants to overrule your good instincts."

The lump swelled in Tolen's throat and he didn't know how to respond. The horrible guilt he felt for his role in Dane and his mother's disappearance made it hard for him to listen to his heart when he wanted so badly to act. To seek vengeance against those who hurt his best friend and tore apart his family. But in the Watcher's words he felt the truth. His mother had always given him the same advice, *Follow your heart, Tolen. Whenever you aren't sure what to do, trust your thoughtful heart. It will not lead you astray.*

He kept his eyes out the window. "So Dane was a Télora then?"

Bastian nodded. "And Macy is a Kunamin."

"What else can they do?"

Bastian took a while to answer and Tolen looked over to see a tiny bead of sweat on his upper lip. "Not all of our kind can do all eight gifts."

Tolen's eyes narrowed. The Watcher was hiding something. As much as Tolen wanted to know what it was, he had learned enough from his mother to know when an adult didn't want to tell you something, no amount of prying would get it out of them. He switched gears to another topic that plagued him. "What did you mean when you said I was letting my subconscious take over?"

Bastian's eyes began dilating rapidly. Tolen rubbed his eye when it burned again.

"You were in a Dreamer's state." Bastian took a measured breath. "There are a group of individuals within the Hidden called the Dreamers. They have an unusual gift—the ability to use their subconscious in battle."

"What? How is that even possible?"

"There is a place where you go in your mind when you pass out, is there not?"

Tolen shifted in his seat. "I guess you could say that."

"Is it warm and bright? You feel safe and comfortable?"

Tolen nodded once but kept his eyes on the road.

"You have gone there when you are awake as well, have you not?"

He was reminded of his recent fight with Jeff. "Yeah, I have. But when I'm awake and I go there on purpose, I can still sense what is going on around me. I can watch it as if I am outside my body. It wasn't like that in the canyon."

Bastian nodded. "In the canyon your mind knew of this place and took you there to protect itself. A reaction based on learned behavior."

"But what is it? Where do I go?"

"To better understand, think of conscious and subconscious as two separate beings occupying the same space. Each has a job to do, but they cannot get in one another's way. So when the conscious must work, guiding the body through the avenues of cognizant thought and action, like tying your shoes, the subconscious is locked away. When the body must rest the conscious is locked away, while the subconscious is let out to travel the deeper regions of the mind, resolving problems, healing, dreaming. Do you understand?"

As convoluted as it sounded, it actually did make sense. "You can't tie your shoes while you're asleep and you can't dream while you're awake?"

"Precisely. The Dreamers' minds do not abide by the same rules. They can access either place, awake or asleep. Both conscious and subconscious can work at the same time, and the Dreamers are trained how to control each, to lock them away until they are needed in battle."

Tolen considered the Watcher. "What do you mean, in battle?"

"Remember the feeling you had when you left the truck and I tried to stop you, the voice that came from your mouth?"

Tolen swallowed, "Yeah. It was horrible, and powerful. I felt like I had no control…That was my subconscious mind?"

"Yes."

"I felt so strong…" It had been both frightening and enthralling, the power that had surged through him.

"In our dreams, we are not limited by logic. We can *be* super heroes. Because you are of the Hidden race, you have the ability to enhance your natural abilities—like running, hearing, and sight—but logic, the conscious mind, stops us from going too far."

Tolen regarded his reflection in the side window. What *was* he? "The Dreamers can become what they dream?"

"They can become as *powerful* as what they dream." Bastian corrected. "They cannot change their appearance."

"It took over. I didn't even know it was happening." He glanced at his hands. "How do I keep it from happening again?" No matter how fascinating the power had been, he did not like the way it had controlled him.

"Your conscious mind is naturally stronger than your subconscious. Now that you understand this ability, it will be easier to control it. Knowledge has already made your mind stronger. The next time you feel overwhelmed, you will stop yourself from going to the realm of the subconscious. It will be easier than you think." He paused and gave Tolen a searching look.

"As soon as we reach the Binithan, I will begin your training. The more you learn of your gifts, and your own strength, the less your body and mind will control you."

Tolen clenched his hands on the seat beneath him. Learning more about how to control his strange abilities was something he'd wanted forever, but could he handle being taught by a man he didn't like? Couldn't he have the Doogar teach him instead?

He peeked at the hard planes of Bastian's face—a man who did not look much older than himself. Bastian said he was Tolen's Watcher. Would he ever be out of his life? Did he even have a choice?

Bastian glanced in the rear-view mirror. "Macy?"

Tolen looked in the back to see her watching him with wide eyes.

He felt warmth crawl up his face. How long had she been awake? How much had she overheard?

"The sun is fully up." Bastian interrupted Tolen's musing. "The armies of the Dark have stopped their chase for now. I can see that our path will be mostly clear for the next hundred miles or so. Can you drive for a few hours while I regenerate?"

Macy nodded and Bastian pulled off the highway at a rest stop.

Bastian said it casually, but one word made Tolen's stomach clench.

Mostly…Their path would be *mostly* clear, not completely.

The angry bees were back and his head buzzed painfully.

The nightmare wasn't even close to over.

CHAPTER ELEVEN

STORIES

MACY GLANCED IN THE REARVIEW MIRROR AT BASTIAN. HE WAS REST-less—his legs kept twitching in his sleep.

It didn't help the state of her nerves.

Bastian was trying to keep the seriousness of their situation quiet so the kid wouldn't freak out, but she knew…Daylight or not, the Dark continued to move. Maybe not their armies, but servants *were* moving. It was subtle, but there. Every town they passed through she felt them stir, almost as if the presence of the Ninth awakened them.

Whether Bastian wanted to admit it or not, she'd been right. Tolen's life force was like a beacon, lighting the way for the Dark to follow.

She'd also become more sensitive to the specific vibes of the Shadows in the last few days. Their eerie, distant cold kept her Kuna tingling. She could feel their power gathering somewhere up ahead. Bastian hadn't mentioned this yet, and she knew why. She struggled enough with their predicament and he knew she'd put up a fight when he admitted that they were headed toward the Shadows, instead of running from them.

Two days ago, he would have been right. She would have taken off on her own if it meant she didn't have to deal with the Ninth and all the trouble that came with him. She'd loathed Tolen before she'd ever set eyes on him. It was childish, yes, but how she'd felt.

Now?

Watching him lose his mother and best friend had erased the irrational hatred she felt toward him and forced her to admit that she didn't know him well enough to hate him.

The truth? She let her breath out in irritation.

She envied him. And…she was afraid of him.

He had so much that she'd wished for; a home life with a mother who, even though she happened to be a little on the crazy side, adored him and was there for him every day. His father might be locked in the Shadow Prison, but at least he was alive and there was the chance he could survive. Yes, it was a horribly slim chance, but Tolen *could* be re-united with him one day. He had Dane, a really good friend, who'd been willing to die for him. He'd attended real school. He'd lived the human life Macy had been denied.

And now he had Bastian too.

However, stronger than her ridiculous envy lurked the dread of what his very existence meant. It was completely irrational, unfair, and downright stupid—he didn't choose his fate—but she resented him being born. The Legend of the Ninth Chosen had been told for centuries. Why did it have to come to pass in her lifetime?

She'd fought creatures that would scare the pants off the toughest grown men, but they'd all been small battles or preplanned reconnaissance missions to find out the movements of the Dark and send the information back to the Guardians.

The Final Battle stories also went by the name of Armageddon—the war to end all wars. Maybe Tolen's mother had been right. Maybe Macy *wasn't* strong enough for what was coming.

She glanced again in the mirror, making sure Bastian was still asleep and not focused on her thoughts.

She had a decision to make. Either she could accept the will of the Balance and help Bastian train the Ninth—which in turn would also, hopefully, help save the world—or she could continue to hate the kid, be scared and jealous of him, and make his life even more miserable than it already was.

But could she?

Could she face the Shadows again? Was she strong enough? Even if facing them ensured the success of the Ninth and could possibly save the world, she wasn't positive she'd be able to do it. The Shadows were miles ahead and yet the drain on her life force was already frightening, and it would only get worse. She knew the closer she got to them the weaker she would become.

She shook her head, squared her shoulders, and peeked at Tolen from her peripheral vision. Well it wasn't as if she really had much choice. Without the Ninth they were all doomed anyway. And Shadows or no Shadows, she was not going down without a fight. She might as well have the Ninth on her side when that happened. She made a face. Well, once he was actually trained how to fight.

She pictured the look on Bastian's face if he knew her current thoughts and scowled. He'd be grinning ear to ear.

Even if she did choose to do the right thing, she had no idea how to even talk to him. She'd never had to relate to someone her own age before—especially someone raised to be human. Jeez, *she* was the human and he knew more about being one than she did! She ran a hand across her eyes.

"Are you tired?" Tolen asked softly. "I can drive for a while if you tell me where to go."

He'd been so silent, leaning against the window, that she'd assumed he'd fallen back asleep. She shifted uncomfortably in her seat. "Um, no. I'm good."

Tolen pointed his thumb over his shoulder. "I was beginning to wonder if he ever slept." His tone was calm, measured, and she could tell, forced. Considering the fact that his mother had been so sick, and he'd been the one with the job, Macy figured he was used to being independent. He didn't like the fact that she and Bastian had seen him lose control, seen his weakness. Despite his quiet nature, he had an ego. Macy's lip twitched.

Tolen watched her expectantly, waiting for a response—he looked wary, like he was worried his effort to appear normal would blow up in his face. She bet his act did a good job of fooling normal humans, but he didn't fool her. She'd spent too many years fighting the Dark, the master of all deceptions, to believe his careful disguise.

She tapped the steering wheel. Bastian had told her not to provoke the kid. Well, if there was one thing she knew how to do well with humans, it was act. She had pretended enough around them that two could play at this game.

Here goes nothin'. She cleared her throat noisily and answered as casually as she could. "Yeah, Bastian…" She peeked at Tolen's eyes, wondering how *his* Watcher's eye worked. Obviously, he wasn't the same as Bastian, yet he could *see* some things. She realized she was staring and quickly looked back to the road. "Full-blooded Watchers don't need to sleep a whole lot. No one really knows why. Maybe it has something to do with the importance of their job." She shrugged and glanced in the mirror at Bastian. "It's been almost four days since he last crashed."

"Really?"

Macy nodded.

"Wow." He kept his eyes on the road, but every once in a while he glanced over at her.

It felt awkward, like he'd never really talked to a girl before. She wondered if it was true. After seeing all those girls stare at him, she assumed that at some point he had to have talked to them. Hadn't he? She mentally shook her head. Maybe that's not how it worked. It wasn't like she had any references in the romance department to go by. Bastian's stories were never romantic, almost always tragic, and not one included the proper way to flirt. Not that she wanted to flirt with the kid.

She cleared her throat again, quieter this time. "I know. It drove me nuts when I first joined him, but eventually I realized it comes in handy."

"Have you been with him a long time?" he picked at a spot on his jeans.

Macy tucked a strand of hair behind her ear, glanced in all the mirrors again, and licked her lips. "Ten years."

"Wow, you were young when you were Chosen." His eyes were on the road, barely interested, but she hesitated before she answered. These seemingly innocent questions could lead into dangerous territory.

"Six."

Tolen turned toward her, eyes wide. "It seems like a lot to put on a child."

She leaned her head back against the seat. "The Dark doesn't care about age."

"It doesn't seem fair."

Macy chuckled humorlessly. "Is life ever fair?"

The corner of his mouth lifted, but the smile was filled with too much pain to be genuine. "No. Life isn't fair."

The Jeep sputtered and Macy stepped on the gas pedal to rev the engine.

"Did Bastian teach you how to fix cars?"

"No." Her fists tightened on the wheel. She sensed what the next question would be before he asked it.

"Where'd you learn?"

She reminded herself that to him this was small talk, something to pass the time and take him away from the gravity of their situation. He wasn't really even paying attention to the answers. He had no idea what kind of memories the question would stir, what kind of horrors she had locked away. She tried to think of a simple answer that wouldn't lead to more uncomfortable questions, or even force her to lie, but she couldn't come up with anything.

She shrugged, trying for nonchalance. "My dad loved to tinker with cars. It was his hobby. When I was Chosen, Bastian said I needed a hobby—something to do between training and fighting. He would have liked it if I had picked something more girly, but my interest in auto-mechanic work has come in handy." She felt proud of herself for her calm tone; inside she was screaming.

"Do you still get to see him—your dad?" Tolen's tone held a hint of envy.

A horrible ache ripped through her chest and the words came out harsher than she intended. "My parents are dead."

She heard Tolen's sharp intake of breath and squeezed her eyes shut.

"I'm so sorry," he whispered. Chagrin and empathy laced the words, for a moment his careful facade slipped, and she realized that he knew exactly how she felt, not only because of his experience with his own parents, but because he was the *Ninth*. His Watcher's eye made him sensitive to the thoughts and emotions of everyone around him…everyone, because as the Ninth he was *responsible* for everyone.

She suddenly felt like a kid who just realized she'd showed up to school without her pants. All her thoughts were exposed to a guy she barely knew. It was one thing for Bastian to know, he was like her father, but Tolen? *Nuh, uh, no way. This is not cool!*

"I'm sorry…" He cast a cautious look her way before dropping his chin and pinching the bridge of his nose. In that moment she saw something else in his eyes, something under the anger. *Need.* He wanted to hate her and everything she stood for, but deep inside, this troubled kid needed acceptance from someone, *anyone* for what he was.

Her heart thudded in her chest and pity swelled in her heart. *Chill, just chill.* The kid didn't know what he was capable of. He didn't know he could sense thoughts yet.

She twisted her hair on her finger. "It's okay, Tolen. You didn't know."

"There's a lot I don't know," he mumbled.

He looked so broken. An unfamiliar wave of sympathy washed over her.

"Hey, in the glove box there's a bag of suckers. Wanna get a couple out for us?" She needed the sugar if she was going to go ahead with the thought that had taken root in her head.

Tolen pulled open the rusty glove box and took out a plastic bag filled with suckers. "Only purple ones?"

Macy shrugged. "I like purple."

He pulled the wrapper off hers and handed it to her before unwrapping his own. He stuck it in his cheek. "You said back at my house that they help regenerate your life force. I assume that's like code for 'gives you a sugar rush'?"

Macy snorted. "Sure. Sugar recharges our batteries—if you want to call the life force batteries. Whenever you use your gifts, it drains your physical body, which in turn, affects your life force. Sugar sort of helps get your energy back. Bastian loves Lucid with 'unrefined' sugar. I think it tastes like crap."

"Me too."

"Wait until you try one of his sweetened meat-cakes. You'll barf the first time, I promise."

Tolen laughed softly—a pleasant, comfortable sound. He was still protecting his real feelings, but she could feel him relaxing, allowing himself to settle into the conversation. "Thanks for the warning."

Macy glanced at him from the corner of her eye. He'd been through a lot. He was tougher than she'd given him credit for.

"The Dark is after me specifically. That's why my mom hid everything from me. I can feel it." He pulled the sucker out of his mouth and twisted the stick between his fingers.

It was random, way off subject, and Macy could tell he'd been thinking about it for a while. Her smile disappeared. She glanced at Bastian again, wishing he would wake up. Tolen was about to go onto ground she wasn't sure she could share.

"What am I?" His blue eye flashed, intensifying the frustration he obviously felt. He didn't look at her, as if he didn't expect her to answer, and was just throwing the question into the universe.

She clenched her teeth and turned her eyes back to the road, not sure whether she could, or even *should* respond.

They passed slowly through a small town with several squat derelict buildings. She felt the Balance shift and looked out her window. Something black and hairy hunched in the shadow between two buildings. Its red eyes gleamed threateningly from the edge of the shade. Grateful they still had half a tank of gas, she pushed harder on the pedal and the engine groaned.

She cast a quick glance at Tolen and then wished she hadn't. His hands were clenched into fists in his lap, his eyes hard. He was working to maintain the smokescreen, but it was thinning, his need for more truth was stronger than his desire to hide.

What was she supposed to say?

"That's a long story you should already know." She wished she could take it back when his face fell and he turned back to the window. "I'm sorry Tolen, I…"

"It's okay. You're right. If my mom had told me, I wouldn't be pestering you." He threw the remains of his sucker out the window and met her eyes for a brief moment. "I did try." He ran a barely trembling hand through his hair and the words tumbled from his mouth. "I tried to get my mom to tell me the truth. For years, I begged and pleaded. Then one day, my tenth birthday, I lost it. I'd finally gotten old enough that I could see how ridiculous her excuses were—and I came completely unglued. I wanted a birthday party, a real one with friends. I wanted to go to a fun park like the kids did on TV and play games. You know, all the good stuff." He chuckled cynically. "She told me we couldn't afford it. I thought it was a lie. I'd seen her taking cash from a box under her bed for years. Little did I know it was her life-savings and there really wasn't much left.

"I ran outside to the park behind our apartment complex. The one I'd only been allowed to play at late at night or early in the morning when it was deserted. I headed toward the tallest tree I could see."

Macy's palms started to sweat, slickening her grip on the wheel. She could feel where this was going and she wished he would stop talking, but he seemed to be speaking without really thinking, letting things out he'd obviously held in for years.

"She chased me, but I found the angrier I got, the faster I could run. Before she could catch me, I launched myself at the tree and it swept its branches down and lifted me high in the air, far away from my mother. I shouted 'I hate you!' down at her on the ground. Those three words sent the tree into a frenzy. It started swinging its branches at my mom. One of them slammed into her head and knocked her ten feet away…" his voice cracked. "I was horrified. The tree stopped moving and I climbed down and ran over to her. I can still see the blood gushing out of her head. I-I thought I'd killed her, but her eyes flew open and she looked around. People were rushing over, shouting and pointing. She reached up, put her hand over the gash, grabbed my arm with her other hand and started running. I don't remember much after that. We spent a few weeks hotel jumping before she finally took us to Green River." He sighed. "I never stopped wanting her to tell me the truth, but I could never let myself get that angry again."

He barely paused for breath. "Things were better in Green River. She tried to let me have a kind of normal life. Dane came along and even though I was awkward and shy and eventually got labeled the town freak, I was pretty satisfied with my life. All except for the part that I had no idea what sort of experiment went wrong to make me able to do what I could. As I got older, my mom got sicker. Every time I'd slip and ask a question or make a comment about our wacked out life, she'd get all pale and clammy and I remembered my tenth birthday, so I'd bite my tongue. I tried harder to control my anger…" His voice trailed off.

Macy swallowed, her eyes on the road. She was such a hypocrite. She didn't understand Tolen's life any more than he understood hers.

They were both misfits in their own ways.

She reached over and touched his arm, an action that surprised her almost as much as the reaction of her Kuna when her fingers met his skin. They tingled with heat—a pleasant heat. How strange.

He looked at her hand and then up into her eyes. The confusion on his face had to mirror hers. Did he feel it too? He held her gaze longer than should be comfortable. In that moment she felt something shift between them. He didn't hate her anymore, but in that he must have also seen what she saw. That sometimes hate was better than like. The people you liked had a lot more power to hurt you. She pulled her hand back and turned to the road, her face warm.

She cleared her throat to cover the awkward moment. "I guess we both have things in our past we'd like to forget."

He looked down and shrugged. "Yeah."

"Look, I'm really sorry for what I said earlier. I should have kept my mouth shut. Bastian always tells me I need to think before I speak. I just don't listen."

"It's okay." He gave her a tiny smile and turned back to the window.

"Wait., Tolen." He half glanced back her way. When the tiniest bit of light touched his eyes she made her decision without caring about the consequences. If the situation were reversed, she wouldn't be nearly as patient as Tolen was being. He was used to being in the dark, left to wonder. Maybe she could show him that not everyone wanted to keep secrets from him. She bit the side of her lip. Well, she'd still keep just one. "I'll tell you what I can," she paused. "But there are some things I'm not allowed to." His eyes narrowed. "Not yet," she clarified.

He looked up. "'Need to know' right?"

It reminded her of their conversation by the river. He'd said then that he was sick of secrets. It didn't help her feel better that he understood.

"Right. Sorry. Bastian has his reasons. He wants you to know, but he's a firm believer that timing is everything. He doesn't want you to know some things until he feels you're ready."

"Like what I am?"

"Well, I can tell you what you are. There are just some…details I'm not allowed to say."

His eyebrow rose slightly.

She looked his way and shrugged an apology. "I remember when I was Chosen. Six is young enough that I still believed anything an adult said." She gave him a crooked smile. "You're old enough to be skeptical, but I promise everything I'm about to tell you is the whole truth."

She looked at him from the corner of her eye again. His hands were clasped in his lap, his knuckles white. He held in a lot. He was way better at control than she was. She started to wonder if she would have better control if she had almost accidently killed one of her parents, and then shuddered away from the thought. "I'll start with the basics. The first things Bastian taught me."

He nodded. "Sounds fair."

His careful mask had never fully returned. He looked at her expectantly and she took a deep breath. Well, the cat was already out of the bag—or the Raksasha already had the scent, as Bastian would say. Now all she could do was run with it.

"The first thing you need to understand is the life force—or what humans call the soul."

"The life force is your soul?" He looked at her, his face skeptical.

"Yeah—don't look at me like that. You're thinking in human terms, humans don't understand the true strength of one's soul. The Hidden call a soul the life force for two reasons. Number one, it is the intelligence put into your physical body to give it *life*—it will still exist when your physical body dies. Number two, that intelligence was created with the immense energy to power and control the amazing machine of your physical body. Energy is the driving *force*, the strength needed to guide you. Make any sense?"

Tolen shrugged. "Why not? It'll take a while to throw out my human notions and start seeing things the Hidden way. So why is it so important to understand the life force?"

"Okay, this is where it's gonna get really weird." She twisted her pony-tail in her fingers. "Since we showed up, have you wondered why the Raksasha, and all those other Dark creatures, have never been seen by humans—why you haven't ever heard about their freakiness on the news?"

"Definitely."

Macy nodded in his direction and dropped her sucker stick in a hole in the door panel. "You ever study physics?"

"Are you kidding? I lived for physics. I was bound and determined to figure out the answers to my *issues*."

"Come up with anything?"

"Not really."

Macy nodded with a smirk. "Einstein and a few others came pretty close. I find the M-theory the most interesting."

"Dimensional theory?"

"Right."

"So…the Hidden is a different dimension?"

"Sort of."

Tolen tilted his head. "Sort of?"

"Dimensional theory only answers some of the questions."

He leaned back and stretched his arms above his head. "The likeli-hood being that the Dark are only visible to those that belong to that dimension—and since the Raksasha are obviously not from this dimen-sion, humans can't see them."

"That's my guess. When Bastian explains it, he uses all the Hidden terms and history that basically says things just are what they are and you have to accept it. I've always liked trying to see how humans explain things they don't understand. It's fun to put Hidden and human together. Like a puzzle."

He looked at her with an odd expression, like he was surprised she would be interested in studying. She started to feel defensive before he said, "I didn't think anyone else besides me liked to study the weird stuff."

She shrugged, ignoring the pleasure she felt over them having something in common. "There's a whole lot more to it than even I understand. I know that it wasn't always like this though, that's why it's only a theory."

"What do you mean?"

"Well, back in the early days of this world humans *could* actually see the Dark. I don't know how."

Tolen nodded his head, totally involved. "Bastian keeps talking about the Balance. What exactly is it?"

"I bet you can guess." She smiled.

Tolen looked out the window at the last remnants of the town and his eyes narrowed. "It must be the force that keeps the Hidden and human dimensions separate, yet capable of co-existing without destroying one another."

Her smile widened. "You're good. I think humans can see the members of the Hidden race that follow the Light because they're made up of particles from both dimensions. Humans can feel the Dark's effects when they are close by, but they can't see them." She snorted. "I never fully understood a child's instinctive fear of the dark until I learned of the *Dark*. Darkness is so much more than just the absence of light. The Dark thrives in the night because all forms of light drain their power, although natural light is the strongest."

"It makes sense," Tolen tapped his chin, lost in deep thought. "If you bring relativity into play, anyway, how our actions affect time and space. It explains how you knew the Dark was headed toward my house."

Macy nodded. "Exactly—you'll be able to sense it too, once you learn to recognize the different vibes in the Balance."

"But it doesn't explain how the eight gifts work."

"Sure it does. Think about it. We're all made up of molecules right? And so is everything around us. The eight had the ability to manipulate them. Once they imparted those gifts into the Balance, the Balance could select who to give those same abilities to."

"So we're actually just manipulating molecules…" He nodded to himself. "That's what Bastian meant when he said 'human' is a relative word. We're all interconnected as mass and energy, just different kinds."

Macy wasn't sure why his analogy made her uncomfortable. Maybe it had to do with the fact that she was human and he didn't know it.

Tolen went on, oblivious. "This is finally starting to make sense. Funny that being a physics nerd finally paid off." He gave her a sideways grin that turned quizzical when he saw her face.

She quickly rearranged her expression, nodded, and tapped her fingers on the steering wheel.

"So, why are there Chosen ones? Shouldn't all those with abilities be fighting against the Dark?" he asked.

"They are fighting, in a much bigger war on a much grander scale. You've only seen it from the human side so far."

He raised an eyebrow, the look on his face intrigued.

She glanced in the mirrors again. "The Chosen ones are needed because there aren't enough Hidden kind to protect themselves, as well as the *oblivious* humans." She could see he still didn't understand and took a deep breath. This was a legend she didn't care to re-tell, but he needed to hear. "It all began with your standard quest for dominance. In the beginning, there were Hidden who figured they were more powerful than humans for a reason. They wanted slaves. The Guardians, the group that leads the Hidden, freaked out and put a stop to it. But the idea was there and continued to grow.

"The Dark at the time was just matter in space; it seemed to be drawn to power, but it avoided the Light and all its attempts at contact. So the Hidden ignored it.

"Then the wars began over the freedom of the human race. The Guardians noticed the Dark matter seemed to be growing. They didn't realize it was feeding on the contention of the people until it was too late—like a parasite it attached itself to the Hidden dimension layer upon layer, coating the areas of the worst conflict, but staying away from the strongholds of the Light. They felt the creepy effects of the Dark strengthening, especially at night, and the Light cautioned against seeking it out. The Guardians even sent messengers into the enemy camps, warning them that the Dark seemed to be focusing on their fighters—they were afraid of what the strange power might be after. They begged the other side to come to an agreement, to make peace…" Macy chewed the side of her lip. "The freaks cut the heads off the messengers and sent them back to the Guardians in bags tied to their horses."

Tolen shuddered in her peripheral vision.

She plowed on grudgingly, knowing what she had to say next was so much worse. "The idiots ignored the warning and went out after the Dark. Something unconscionable was born."

She looked over to see goose bumps on Tolen's arms and lowered her voice. "The Dark took them over. Rather than winning a slave race for themselves, *they* became the slaves for the Dark. It literally mutated them—took all decency out of them. Without even the tiniest bit of kindness or charity left inside them, they became the demons that spawned legend and the horrors of the blackest nightmares. They no longer cared about making themselves a grander race. They only wanted power and the Dark's control of this world. They killed anyone—human or Hidden— that stood in the Dark's way.

"People were dying everywhere. The Guardians sent out their Protectors, and the Radia Warriors were formed, but the Dark continued to grow in power and numbers.

"According to legend, the Radia Revolution was the bloodiest battle this world has ever seen. The Light won, but barely. Hundreds of thousands of people died. The alliance between humans and Hidden evaporated."

Tolen blew out an exasperated breath. "Why?"

Macy sighed. "The humans figured it was the Hidden's fault that the Dark had come—they thought if they broke off the alliance with the Hidden, then the Dark would leave them alone. They were afraid—or just crazy." She shrugged. "They made this psychotic pact with the Guardians and a *Shroud* was created in the Balance, completely blocking humans from seeing the Dark from that day on." She shook her head. "But the

Guardians knew the Dark wanted to dominate all life, human included, and they didn't want to leave the humans unprotected.

"So they begged the Light for a solution. One day the Watchers showed up with weird news. The Radia shards they had spent their lives guarding had split in two. One half had disappeared, but they could feel the broken pieces sending for them. They could see images of children who held the shards. This was a huge deal because the shards had astonishing powers and up until then, the Watchers were the only ones capable of taming them.

"They eventually discovered that the Light, through the Radia shards, had shared the eight gifts with select humans—and—uh other Beings—whose duty it would be to exist among the humans, and unbeknownst to them, protect them from the Dark and work as spies for the Guardians. The Shards gave the human Chosen a single extra-sensory gift, as well as the ability to see the servants of the Dark. So, for obvious reasons, the Dark has been after the Chosen ever since." She trailed off, wondering if Tolen had noticed her blunder. The last thing she needed was to have Bastian bite her head off for letting slip to Tolen that he was the *only* member of the Chosen who wasn't human, but he was lost in thought, his eyes glazed over.

"That is definitely no fairy tale."

"Nope." She reached in front of him to the glove box and pulled out two more suckers—retelling creepy old legends was draining. He took the one she offered without really looking at it, ripped off the wrapper, and put it in his mouth.

"So what happens to a human Chosen if they lose their shard?"

Macy swallowed loudly. "They lose their gifts and are blind to the tactics of the Dark."

"Wow, scary."

"Yeah."

"Strange. This is the first time since I found out I wasn't human that I feel like it might actually be a good thing."

Before she had the chance to really think about the pain Tolen's words triggered in her, the Jeep lurched and sputtered again and she smacked the steering wheel instead. "Piece of crap."

"What's wrong?"

"This POS has been rusting in that garage for who knows how long. The carburetor isn't happy." She started to pull off at the next exit.

"Macy." Bastian spoke from the back and her and Tolen jumped.

She glanced in the mirror and swallowed guiltily. "Yeah?"

"We really do not have time for a pit stop." He was gazing ahead, *watching*.

"Bastian, if I don't get carburetor cleaner and some decent gas into this thing, we're going to be walking."

His eyes flashed. "Make it a fast stop." A muscle twitched in his jaw and his hands were gripping the seat as if it was taking all his self-control not to rip it to shreds.

Macy's hands tingled. *Is it that bad?*

Bastian gave an almost imperceptible nod and his eyes flashed to the back of Tolen's head.

He wouldn't tell her until Tolen wasn't within earshot. Goosebumps rose on the back of her neck. She glanced over to see that Tolen's hands were clasped tightly in his lap again.

ooo

Tolen's mind was running a million miles an hour as they pulled off the highway. He'd enjoyed the conversation with Macy, and for a moment had forgotten about the ache in his heart. He felt guilty, like he had again betrayed his mother and best friend by momentarily giving up his grief. He was also confused by the fact that he couldn't hate this girl—no matter how much he wanted to. Talking to her had brought out all the earlier curiosity he'd had about her and intensified it. As their conversation went on he felt the anger settle deeper and deeper until he could hardly feel it at all.

Yes, she was more than he'd originally thought. He still thought she seemed a little arrogant, but there was depth to her as well. She was kinder and more considerate than her rough attitude suggested, and she genuinely seemed to want to help him understand. He felt frustrated that Bastian had woken up and interrupted them. As soon as the Watcher spoke, the anger rushed back to just below the surface and he'd had to beat it back down again, hide it beneath his mask.

But when Macy finally let go and really talked to him, all he wanted was to know more about her. But why? What was it about her that could make him change his focus so easily?

Who was this girl?

CHAPTER TWELVE

A STORM IS COMING

THE TINY GAS STATION IN WINNEMUCCA, NEVADA, SMELLED FUNNY, LIKE wet wood and mold. Macy resisted the urge to plug her nose as she rummaged through the dusty cans and boxes in search of carburetor cleaner.

Tolen and Bastian raided the snack aisle beside her. Bastian tried not to look nervous, but his eyes told otherwise.

Tolen turned the corner, holding up a can of pears. The label looked ancient. "Do I even want to check the expiration date on this?" He lifted the can and grimaced at the numbers on the bottom.

Macy grinned. "It's probably best to just put it in the basket, dude."

"I thought there were laws against doing stuff like this."

Macy laughed, "You can't honestly tell me that they were good about it in that tiny little grocery store in Green River?"

Tolen smirked and lifted an eyebrow. "Actually, Mr. Grange was pretty good about staying at least within the year mark." His smile faded.

Macy gritted her teeth. Chalk up another 'stupid' for her. Here he was, trying so hard to appear normal and in control, and she had to go and bring up sad memories. Crud, she was terrible at small talk.

"No, you're not." Tolen put the can in her basket.

"Huh?"

"Didn't you just say—?"

"I didn't say anything."

"Oh. I could have sworn…" Tolen shook his head and shoved his hands into his pockets. "I guess I'm hearing things."

Bastian looked at her and they shared a worried look. Her earlier suspicions were on the mark. Tolen could sense her thoughts.

A bottle of motor oil slipped from her fingers and bounced off her toe. "Ow! Damage!"

"Macy." Bastian reproached quietly.

"What? I didn't cuss." She picked up the bottle and put it in the basket, instead of throwing it across the store like she wanted to.

"Close enough," Bastian murmured.

"Why do you do that?" Tolen asked, fighting a smile.

"What?" Macy snapped.

"Use alternative swear words. Is cussing against a Hidden law or something?"

Bastian ran a hand along the shelf, occasionally pulling something off and putting it in the basket. "In a way. Blasphemy is not allowed in the Guardian court. But, I have my own reasons for why I do not like to hear vulgarities spilling from Macy's mouth."

Macy flicked her hair behind her ear. "Bastian believes that profanity is the attempt of a weak mind trying to express itself. If you're so weak minded that you can't think of a better word to say, then it's better to keep your mouth shut."

Bastian smiled.

Macy held up a finger. "But…"

The smile faltered.

"…*I* happen to think that a well-formed and properly timed expletive is usually the best way to get the desired effect, *and* release built-up tension in a less harmful way than throwing something.

"Besides, I don't use normal, weak-minded profanity—I use my *intelligence* to come up with cleaner, less-offensive alternatives." Macy nodded her head with the air of a dignitary speaking before Congress.

Tolen coughed to hide a laugh.

"I rest my case." Macy grinned.

Bastian sighed and turned toward the checkout counter. "I think we have enough supplies to take to the Binithan."

"Is it alright if I use the restroom before we leave?" Tolen glanced to the back of the store and Bastian nodded.

As soon as he was out of earshot, Macy stepped in front of Bastian.

"Okay, he's gone. Spit it out, I can take it."

"It is nice to see you two getting along. He hates me, but his feelings are softening toward you."

"Yep. It's great. Stop stalling. What's up?"

Bastian sighed. "Something is not right.'

She rolled her eyes. "Nothing is ever 'right', Bastian."

He gave her one of his most exasperated looks. "Not long after we escaped the canyon I felt a double shift in the Balance. One is an energy that has followed us both day and night—it is gaining speed, but is not sinister, and does not cause me too much worry. The second shift was subtle enough that, had I not been so in tune, I may not have noticed."

"What is it?" Macy repeated, her pulse quickening.

Bastian's eyes narrowed. "A force I have not felt for hundreds of years."

"What?" she asked again, her Kuna heating.

"DéHool."

Macy rocked back on her heels. "Those demonic dogs that hunted the Watchers during the Revolution?" That particular story still managed to make her break into a cold sweat. "But they were all locked in Misery with Darsapean. Weren't they?"

"That is what we thought. Someone is working very hard to mask their presence, but I am certain that is what I can feel."

Macy's palms tingled, her Kuna building faster and faster. "Then what are we waiting for? Why didn't you say something earlier?"

He looked her in the eyes. "It is worse."

Panic swelled in her heart.

"I believe the Dark has discovered that Tolen is the Ninth."

"How?"

"They are summoning every monster known on this earth to try and intercept us. They would not do that for just any Chosen."

"Then let's go somewhere else. Hide somewhere else." Her voice rose, the clerk glanced over at them curiously.

"Shh, Macy. There is nowhere else close enough with the kind of power needed to shield Tolen until he learns to shield himself…" Bastian stopped talking when Tolen appeared beside them with a forced smile.

"Talking about me again? I seem to be a favorite subject. I had no idea I could be so interesting." His casual tone did not hide the frustration in his eyes.

Macy ignored him, more focused on keeping her Kuna under control, and followed Bastian to the counter where he paid for their items.

Tolen trailed behind as they walked back to the Jeep and stood off to the side as Macy popped the hood and poured oil into the motor; her hands shook so much she could barely hold the funnel still. Bastian followed her to the gas hatch and put his hand over hers as she dumped in the carburetor cleaner.

"Are you alright?"

"Seriously?" She shot him a glare.

"Um, Bastian?" Tolen walked toward them. "What's that?" He pointed across the street to a row of old shops.

"What is what?" Bastian lifted his hand to shade his eyes.

"Do you see that?"

"See what?" Bastian and Macy asked at the same time.

"That row of trees in front of those shops. They're swirling with color."

"You can see colors in the trees?" Bastian's jaw went rigid.

"Yeah, red and gold." Tolen curled his fingers into a fist and dropped his arm to his side.

Bastian and Macy both leaned forward. Macy couldn't see anything, but Bastian gripped the side-mirror. "They are sending you a warning."

"Uh, duh! Ya think?" Macy poked Bastian's back.

"Get in the Jeep. Now!" Bastian shouted but Tolen took off across the street.

"Tolen, what are you doing?" Bastian ran after him, Macy close behind.

Tolen stopped beside a small red-leaf maple tree, put his hand on the bark, and closed his eyes.

"It's Ardia! She's in a different tree, but it's her. I can hear her." His eyes snapped open.

Bastian circled the tree.

Macy's heart pounded. The tree from beside the river? "But that was a willow tree." She looked at Bastian.

"How is it possible?" Tolen ran his hand along the bark, a relieved, tender sort of smile on his face. The tree trembled under his fingers.

"The life forces of plant life are interconnected." Bastian watched the exchange with awe. "They can choose to leave the place of their birth, and flit to other plants that will allow them room. It is uncommon however, as once they do, their lives are considerably shortened."

"I can't believe it." Tolen whispered. "She says she's followed me since the day I was born." One of the small branches lowered to touch the top of his head.

Bastian turned to Macy. "Ardia is the good energy I felt following us. We need to get back on the road. Can you inform her of our situation? Perhaps she knows a better way to the Binithan."

Tolen closed his eyes and answered a few seconds later. "She says she knows the route, but it'll still be difficult. The Shadows are gathering in a huge coastal storm." He started back to the Jeep. "If you let me drive, Ardia can lead the way for me."

Bastian nodded and helped Macy into the front seat. "I will use the time to try and *see* ahead." He climbed in the back and put a hand on Macy's shoulder. "Will you be all right?"

She shrugged off his hand. She'd already guessed they were heading straight for the Shadows.

Bastian sighed and squeezed her hand. "I'll protect you."

Whatever. Macy avoided Bastian's eyes, not wanting to see how her attitude affected him. She hated being rude to him, but this was exactly what she'd been afraid would happen. Yeah, she wasn't about to go down without a fight, she'd just been hoping deep down that a fight with the Shadows wouldn't actually happen. Now it wasn't only Shadows, it was *DéHool*!

She glanced at Tolen. His strange eyes were focused on the road ahead, but every once in a while they would flick to the plant life outside the windows and Macy wondered fleetingly what it was that he saw. Whatever it was, she knew it was only going to lead them from bad to worse.

She leaned her head back on the seat and tried not to think about what was waiting for them in California.

○○○

Tolen watched Ardia's bright blue *life force* dart from tree to tree, his heart hammering so hard in his chest it felt like it was trying to leave his body. Macy's stories rushed through his head, filling him with dread. He was a Chosen and the Dark wanted him. Macy had neither confirmed nor denied that the Dark was after him specifically, which didn't give him any hope that he was wrong.

So, you trust the Watcher and his disrespectful ward? Ardia interrupted his thoughts. The harsh way she said *Watcher* reminded him of the way his mother first reacted to Bastian.

I don't know. I don't exactly have a lot of options. I need answers and I'm hoping Dane's people at the Binithan can help me. Is it Macy and Bastian you don't trust or just Watchers in general?

He felt a tremor of fear from her. *It's complicated.*

Why?

That is a story that will take too long to tell. For now, stay on your guard Tolen. I will watch them and help you whenever I can.

Thank you Ardia, for following me. It's nice not to be alone. Tolen wanted her to tell him the story that made her not trust Watchers, but right now there was something bigger worrying him.

Ardia, what are the Shadows?

Her soft voice filled his mind. *The Shadow Wraiths are a creature of the blackest kind. They are the most fearsome weapon of the Dark. Protected and hidden, they are only awakened when the risk of losing them is less important than their mission. They once belonged to the Whisperers; a noble race of wind creatures that spoke to the world through the wind. They sang such beautiful music. They called in the rain and beckoned in the sun…*

Until the Dark took them.

Now they are black as ash and just as filthy. Their music has changed from soft whispers on the wind into horrible gales that pierce the soul and deaden the heart. They magnify the Fear created by the Dark to the highest degree. When they cover you, you lose all that you are. You forget yourself, your purpose; all that matters to you disappears until you are lost in the black dreams of the Dark. Most do not return. Most dissolve into the mist that makes up the Shadow Storm.

But some, lost in a living nightmare, are taken…

Tolen swallowed. *Where Ardia? Where do they take you?*

Into their realm…to the Shadow Prison; where the Demon Masters use Tormentors to rob you of your gifts, your thoughts, your emotions, all that you are, until you become nothing more than a mindless slave to the Dark.

That was what had happened to his father. Tolen's hands tightened on the wheel. *How fast can the Shadows move?*

It depends on the strength of the storm they are controlling. The one headed for California…its wind speed is extremely fast.

Will we beat them to the Binithan?

I do not know. Ardia replied hesitantly.

Tolen pushed his foot down harder on the gas pedal. The engine whined in protest.

"You might not want to do that." Macy mumbled from beside him. She sat with her feet up on the seat, her chin on her knees. She looked smaller, almost weaker somehow.

Tolen eased up a little, and the speedometer dropped below eighty. "Sorry." His heart raced and he realized he not only needed to ease up on the Jeep, he needed to focus and stay calm.

"That's okay. If it was up to me, I would have stolen a jet to get away from the Shadows," she whispered.

"You can fly too?" His heart slowed as he listened to her voice.

Macy shook her head. "I wish. Bastian's not a fan of flying."

"Why?"

She shrugged and swallowed loudly.

"Are you okay?" Tolen glanced over. She was trembling. Her arms were wrapped tightly around her legs as if she was trying to hold herself together.

She nodded but didn't speak.

"Ardia told me about the Shadows." He looked out the windshield at the darkening horizon. "I thought the Raksasha were bad."

Macy leaned her head on the window and took a deep breath.

Tolen looked at her ashen face. "I take it you've dealt with them before."

"Just once." Her voice cracked.

Something unpleasant clicked in Tolen's brain. Macy said her parents were dead. Could the Shadows have had something to do with it? He looked in the rearview mirror to see Bastian staring at him; he gave a slight nod.

An uncomfortable lump formed in Tolen's throat. He reached over and laid his hand over Macy's clenched fist. Warmth surged up his arm and seemed to crash right into his heart.

She looked at him, her eyes unable to mask the anguish she obviously felt.

Tolen offered an understanding smile. The corner of her mouth lifted before she looked away, pulling her hand out from under his, and the warmth disappeared.

He took a deep breath and focused back on Ardia's life force, while a strange and overwhelming desire to protect Macy filled him, body and mind.

The stupid part of such a feeling was that he didn't have the faintest idea how.

CHAPTER THIRTEEN

INTO THE STORM

TOLEN'S BLUE EYE SHIFTED AND HE SAW ARDIA'S LIFE FORCE FLASH twenty miles ahead, from a half-dead Juniper tree. He felt *mostly* in control of his emotions. He couldn't feel a trace of anger. Instead he felt an odd combination of trepidation and excitement. He could feel the vibes of the Shadow's darkness ahead when he concentrated, just as Macy said he would figure out, and he understood that they caused the sense of foreboding he felt. He didn't like that it was his fault that Macy would be close to them, but he couldn't deny the tiny measure of excitement he felt to be going to a place where he could start to find out what had happened to his mother and best friend *and* more about his dad. Dane mentioned in Green River that they wouldn't be staying at the Binithan for long, but maybe because of what had happened they would decide to let him stay. Maybe then he wouldn't need the Watcher anymore.

A tiny spasm of regret followed this thought. If the Watcher left, so would Macy.

You're close. Ardia's voice echoed through his mind and pulled him back to the present.

And the Shadows?

Building…and gaining speed. Her tone turned urgent. *Tolen, I do not know if you will make it in time. You must hurry!*

We're going as fast as we can.

I am going into the park ahead of you. I want to check your path. Keep on your current course. Follow the road. I'll be back.

Tolen took a deep breath. *Okay.*

"She does not think we will make it in time?" Bastian leaned forward between the seats and Macy wrapped her arms tighter around her legs, her fingers leaving imprints in her skin.

Tolen squeezed the steering wheel and relayed what Ardia had said.

Macy's lips turned white. Tolen wanted to console her, but he had no idea how. How do you console someone when they are headed toward something that had taken all they loved most? He felt sick at his earlier excitement, and determined that this time he wouldn't be a danger to the others. He would do his best to fight any way he could. He glanced in the rearview mirror. Bastian was rubbing his temples with his eyes closed.

"Phantoms," Bastian whispered.

Macy gasped.

Tolen! Phantoms! Fear laced Ardia's scream.

"What are Phantoms?" Tolen shouted.

Bastian's reply came out in a nervous rush. "Demon spirits—as evil as Ardia is good. Dark servants put them into the skeletons of dead or dying trees and the Phantoms reanimate them."

Tolen remembered the strength of the trees in Green River, the ones that had been fighting for him in the battle with Jeff and his friends. He imagined that kind of power fighting *against* him, and his palms started to sweat.

Ardia, what are they doing?

They have been put into nearly every dead tree in the park Tolen. They're everywhere!

"What do we do?" Tolen asked aloud.

Bastian and Ardia both answered at the same time. *We fight.*

The clouds in the distance were flat black. They blocked the sunlight—it looked like evening instead of midday.

"Tolen, turn up the radio."

He did as Bastian asked and the long beep-beep-beep of the Emergency Broadcast System echoed through the jeep, followed by the computer-generated voice repeating the same warning. A radio announcer came on right after the warning, his voice muffled by the wind blowing in the background.

"A storm of record proportions is making its way along the California coast. Evacuations as far inland as Tule-lake continue. Even the Lava Bed National Monument has closed; all visitors have been escorted out. Meteorologists are unsure how long this storm will last and are telling residents to head to their basements or storm shelters, and stay away from windows—"

Bastian leaned forward and switched off the radio.

Tolen was grateful for the silence. Bastian said it should be easier for him to avoid that warm safe place in his mind, but as they neared the Shadows, the temptation to go there was stronger and harder to fight than he'd believed it would be. He clenched his teeth in frustration. He could do it.

Bastian started singing as soon as they passed the first sign indicating the remaining distance to the Lave Beds. His deep voice resonated through the interior of the Jeep, sending waves of calm calculation flooding through Tolen. His panicked heart slowed slightly and the fight to stay conscious got a lot easier.

Macy remained pale and sweaty beside him. The farther they went the weaker she seemed, but the look on her face now was resolute. She started to pull more stuff out of her belt. Not the dirt she used to make the Glockshaw, but what looked like small, softly glowing green rocks.

"Tolen, pull into that rest stop." Bastian pointed at a blue sign.

Tolen maneuvered the Jeep into the slow lane. "I thought we were in a hurry."

"We are not going to beat them there. We need to prepare."

Tolen's stomach clenched as he guided the Jeep into the empty lot and set the parking break.

Ardia echoed the Watcher's statement gravely. *He is right.*

Macy held two of the green rocks out to Tolen. "Serenity Stones," she answered his questioning look without emotion. "Put them in your ears." She waited for him to take them, handed two to Bastian and then put a pair in her own ears.

"The stones help counter the fear caused by the Shadows," Bastian explained. "However, the emotions they evoke are artificial and the stones will eventually dissolve."

Tolen pushed them into his ears. They weren't hard as he had expected. They seemed to mold themselves to the shape of the inside of his ears until he couldn't feel them at all. Instantly, a warm blanket of peacefulness fell over him and a desire to defend those around him intensified. It was strange having the two conflicting emotions— fear and serenity—swirling through his body. He could still hear every noise around him as if he had nothing in his ears.

Macy grabbed handfuls of what looked like tiny pieces of dried grass out of a bag he recognized as one she'd been filling in his garden, reached over, and sprinkled it all over him. "Camouflage," she mumbled.

It was oddly heavy and seemed to attach to his skin. He felt strangely giddy and his defenses climbed higher still. The clash of emotions was getting uncomfortable.

Macy covered herself and Bastian with the herbs as well.

Tolen sniffed his arm. "This smells familiar."

"Your mother has been mixing it in your soap and laundry detergent to help mask your scent, just in case." Bastian responded.

"Oh." Tolen ignored the pang at the mention of his mother. "Do all these emotions actually help against the power of the Shadows?" His voice came out stronger and louder than he intended.

"Yes." Bastian murmured. "The Shadows use fear and anxiety in order to weaken their prey. We must prepare for the assault that is to come. Emotional weapons are by far the most dangerous. The stones will help keep the Shadows from draining us at a distance and the Camouflage will mask the smell of our blood from the Raksasha—hopefully buying us some time. We should have an hour at least before the stones dissolve and we sweat off the Camouflage."

"What happens if they get close? How are we supposed to fight black clouds?"

From yet another pouch, Macy pulled three skinny rods, about three-inches long, covered in old leather, and handed them out.

"That is a Light spear, Tolen." Bastian laid one of his huge hands over Tolen's, stopping him from un-wrapping the rod. "It must be used as a last resort. Light spears are extremely powerful and will drain your life force quickly."

Tolen put the rod in his front pocket. "How do I use it?"

"Get back on the road and I will explain."

Tolen turned the Jeep back onto the nearly deserted highway. His arms trembled so much it was hard to steer.

Bastian spoke in a low voice. "The Shadow Wraiths are made up of a thick, black, oily mist. They darken the clouds to the nearly opaque black you see ahead. When they prepare to attack, they leave the storm and encircle their victim. Depending on their purpose, they either carry you in their black dreams to the Shadow Realm where they will imprison you, or they drain the life from you.

"If the Shadows get close enough that they begin to leave their storm and descend upon you and their dark Fear begins to fill your heart, you will open your spear and hold it above your head. The strength of the good inside of you is intensified by the power of the Light that is contained within the spear. It will cast a dome of protection over you, enabling you to run away. I only hope we will not have to use them until we are near the Binithan. If we use them too soon and we are not close enough to the entrance it could weaken us to the point of collapse—" He stopped when a soft whimper escaped Macy's throat.

Tolen looked at her, but she met his concerned gaze with defiance.

She bit her trembling lip and clenched her jaw. She didn't like pity.

Tolen looked away, but had to admire her strength as she determinedly went to face these demons of the sky that had taken so much from her. He clenched his teeth and focused on the road. He would not let anyone down this time.

∘∘∘

Macy's head spun. She only remembered feeling this sick once before; when she was five years old and had ridden the merry-go-round six times in a row on a dare.

For the past ten years she'd run from just the memory of the Shadows, and now she was running toward the real thing—and not just Shadows, but Phantom trees, Raksasha, DéHool, and who knew what else. The power of the stones in her ears fought with the thorns of dread that pierced her heart.

Bastian kept looking at her and squeezing her hand. She wished he'd stop. It only made her feel more weak and stupid. She wanted to tell him she'd be fine, be sarcastic, say she could handle this crap, but she knew he'd see right through it.

Tolen kept flashing concerned and apologetic looks at her as well. She knew from his earlier empathy that he was sensing her emotions. She squirmed in her seat. She didn't like him thinking she was weak. It was starting to tick her off.

That's it, focus on the anger. You can do this. You can do this! She focused on her anger, forcing it to cover her fear. Her fingers tingled and she held the Kuna there, letting it bring her a small measure of comfort. She didn't look at Bastian. She knew he didn't like her using anger to channel her Kuna, but right now she didn't care.

Tolen turned onto National Monument Road—obviously following Ardia more than the signs that pointed the way to the park. "Ardia says this is the direction we have to take. The Shadows are on the western border of the Lava Beds. Raksasha are hiding in some of the caves waiting for night. The Phantoms are everywhere. She said to assume all dead trees have one inside them, and be wary of the half dead ones as well."

"Does Ardia know where the door to the Binithan is located?"

"Yes. We need to go in through the north entrance. There's a parking lot there where we'll leave the Jeep. She'll guide us in from the Visitor's Center. She said we'd be safest if we travel above ground in the open. She's trying to get as many of the live trees to help guard us as she can. If we can stay away from any cave entrances and dead trees, she thinks we'll be okay. I can see the door in her thoughts though, and to me, it seems to be pretty far in. We might not make it before the sun goes down."

The wind howled outside the Jeep. Plastic bags, food wrappers, and other garbage whipped across the road. It was fast becoming a gale outside. The sky continued to darken the closer they got. Tolen turned on the headlights, but it didn't dispel the gloom. When the park entrance finally came into view, the sky swirled with black clouds, and the wind blew fiercely enough to rock the Jeep. Tolen pulled into the parking lot and stopped. Macy's heart thudded painfully in her throat. She could taste acid on her tongue.

Bastian's eyes were resigned; it made the Kuna move from her fingertips into her palms. Bastian looked at her and Tolen and nodded.

"Let it build."

"Let what build?" Tolen shook his head.

"Your gifts are reacting to your stress. That is the tingle you feel in your hands. Let it build, but stay focused. Do not let your emotions rule your judgment. Keep your head straight and your life force should be able to call your gifts as they are needed. Concentrate on recognizing the shift you will feel when your life force senses the presence of the Dark. It will guide you."

Macy wondered if Tolen had any clue what Bastian was referring to.

Bastian turned toward her. "Can you run?"

She spoke through clenched teeth. "Yes."

When she looked up, Tolen was watching her with concern. She fought the urge to roll her eyes, straightened her shoulders, and took a deep breath. "Alright, what's the plan? How far will we need to run? And will I need to pace my Kuna?"

Bastian twisted in his seat and handed everyone their packs. "We will let Ardia determine our speed." He looked at Tolen. "Remember your life force increases your natural abilities. When the need arises, say the word 'mig'nata'. It means 'the body', and it will tell your life force to increase your strength. When you feel the power build, concentrate on sending it to your legs. Do not do it unless absolutely necessary, it will drain you quickly." He looked back at Macy. "Do not call your Kuna unless you feel you have no choice. I cannot foresee as of yet if you will need it. Stay alert and focused. Trust your feelings."

Bastian handed Tolen a small bow. "Have you ever used a bow and arrow?"

"No, but I think I can figure it out." Tolen slung the bow and quiver of arrows across his back. He was trying to sound confident, but Macy could see the fear and uncertainty in his eyes.

"That is a Shupata. The arrows are drawn to the power of the Dark. If you at least aim in the general direction of the servant, then the arrow will do the rest. You only have five arrows, however, so use them sparingly."

"No guns?" Tolen's attempt at sarcasm sounded more like relief.

"Human weapons will not work on the Dark; only weapons forged in the Hidden way." Bastian jumped back to business. "The trees Ardia is asking for aid will be drawn to you as a Nature Speaker, but because you do not yet understand how to communicate with them you must rely on Ardia. Stay focused on her thoughts and listen to her warnings. Do *not* leave my side. Understood?"

Tolen swallowed loudly, nodded, and shut his eyes. Macy assumed he was calling to Ardia.

"How are we going to do this?" She tried to keep her voice calm and avoid being rude, but failed. The anger she was channeling overruled patience. "How are we going to fight off Raksasha, Phantoms, avoid the Shadows, and protect Tolen at the same time?"

Tolen's eyes snapped open and he shook his head. "I can take care of myself. I know how to fight. You just take care of you and let me worry about me, okay?" His hands twitched by his sides.

Macy shrugged angrily and pulled a sucker from her pocket.

Bastian sighed in frustration and motioned for them to get out of the Jeep. The wind slammed into the doors hard enough that the hinges groaned from the effort to open. Macy jumped out, looked at the gathering Dark and clenched her fists in her pockets. Tolen had no idea what he was talking about. He had no clue what they were headed into—what was going to happen to him as the Shadows moved in.

Bastian gave them both one last worried look and turned to lead the way into the depths of the storm.

CHAPTER FOURTEEN

BLACK AS NIGHT, DEATH BY LIGHT

THE STONES IN HIS EARS MIGHT HAVE BEEN HEIGHTENING TOLEN'S EMOtions, but even without them, he knew he'd still be furious with Macy. Just because he didn't know how to control his abilities didn't make him a complete waste of space. He diligently ignored her, concentrating instead on Ardia's life force as she moved briskly across the rocky terrain.

Tall Junipers coalesced in clumps so thick it was hard to see where one tree ended and the next one began. Ardia didn't like them—she kept calling them weeds and nuisances, but she managed to make friends with them despite her irritation. They listened to her requests and swayed their coarse branches over the three of them as they hurried across the park.

Bastian's head whipped around constantly and it made Tolen edgy. What did the Watcher see that he couldn't?

The wind picked up and turned icy. Not a single human remained in the entire park aside from them. Thick, ashen clouds completely hid the sun. Only an eerie gray light dimly illuminated the dismal terrain, casting strange shadows over the bizarre, volcanic landscape.

The hair on Tolen's neck prickled. It hadn't lain down since they'd left the Jeep. It was creepy how much he could now understand what Macy meant, about feeling the shift caused by something evil. As they walked farther and farther into the enemies' territory, he could feel something growing, something foul and dangerous. His entire being shied away from the feeling. The urge to flee was almost overwhelming.

Tolen! Hide! Ardia screamed.

"Under here! Hurry!" Tolen dove under the nearest tree and the other two followed without question. The tree spread its lowest branches over them just before the unwelcome squawk of a flock of crows met their ears.

Tolen shivered and the tree pushed its branches lower to cover them. The needles pricked into his skin but he didn't care.

Bastian mouthed, "Spies."

They waited, hardly daring to breathe, until the flock passed.

The tree lifted its branches and Tolen slid out from underneath. "I've always hated crows."

Bastian and Macy dusted off their clothing and cast frustrated looks at the sky. Tolen noticed Macy sway a little and Bastian reached over to steady her. She realized Tolen had seen and quickly shrugged out from beneath Bastian's hands.

Bastian sighed and motioned Tolen to lead the way again. "The Light and the Dark use different birds for different purposes." He seemed to be trying to cover the awkward moment. Tolen had to strain his ears to hear him over the rushing wind. "Birds can cover great distances quickly and have incredible eye-sight. The Dark uses crows—a daylight bird—because of their fearlessness and cunning. The Light uses owls—nocturnal—because they are bold, and wise."

Ardia shifted to a clump of Indian Paintbrush—drained of color in the gray light—and Tolen paused.

Ardia, how much farther?

Tolen, it is not the distance you have left that I fear. The door to the Binithan reads the hearts of those nearby, senses their intent and purpose. The Doogar will know the amount of evil that is swarming above them. They may have sealed the door.

It felt like someone had punched him in the gut. *What does that mean? They won't let us in?*

They may not even know you are trying to enter. If they sealed the entrance once they discovered the Shadow Storm was above them, their defenses will be set—the door will not open again until the threat has passed.

So we could end up stuck out here? He turned anxious eyes to Bastian, but the Watcher's eyes were focused on the black horizon.

A light sheen of sweat covered Macy's forehead and upper-lip. She had a wild look in her eyes. "Bastian—they're coming. I can feel them." Her hands started to shake. Tolen could smell the strange minty, floral scent coming from her again.

Bastian ducked until his eyes leveled with hers. He placed one hand on her arm and the other on Tolen's shoulder. "Yes they are coming, but you and Tolen are stronger than the Dark. We will get to the door. I am certain Handrak was able to get word to the elders. They are expecting us. They will keep the door unsealed."

Tolen wanted to believe Bastian's words, but the horror of their situation was settling in, despite the stones in his ears. Gut-wrenching dread made his heart beat faster as his hands started to shake. Ardia paused up ahead and he could feel her concern.

We will die if we don't make it to the Binithan in time. Won't we?

Ardia flitted back to a closer tree. *Tolen, I fear the outcome for you would be much worse than death.*

Bastian looked around them. "Tolen, I can sense a band of Raksasha, likely they are hiding in a cave nearby. Ask Ardia if there is a side route we can take. We need to avoid being seen as long as possible. They may be able to sense your life force, but if they cannot see or smell us it should take them longer to discover our exact location."

Tolen tried not to think about the fact that his life force was the reason their trek was so dangerous and asked Ardia if she saw what Bastian needed. He pointed in the direction she showed him in his mind. "There." It was a rocky fissure carved deep in the ground. "It's narrow and steep, but it will hide us from view of the Raksasha. She'll show us where to climb back out. Some stumps of burned trees that stand along the top edges concern her. They're not the best houses for Phantoms, but if they are close enough to sense me…"

Bastian nodded. "We will be ready for anything."

Tolen shivered. The wind whined through the cracks of the fissure, causing unnatural, hair-raising echoes. Thin chinks of gray light seeped through narrow openings, throwing strange flickers along their path. But it wasn't the strange tricks of the light or the creepy wind that was giving him chills, it was the fear that pressed in on him with every step he took.

He'd been afraid before, of both silly and serious things, but this was different. It felt as if they were moving toward a living, breathing monster of despair. The poisonous tentacles reached out to him, assaulting every cell in his body. The farther they walked, the more that panic and terror threatened to overtake him.

The Shadows were very, very close.

He could hear Macy's ragged breathing and Bastian's soft footfalls behind him. Ardia's blue life force occasionally dropped down to flit through the grasses that poked here and there from the walls. She kept him putting one foot in front of the other.

Fifteen minutes later the temperature suddenly dropped and the gray light dimmed even more.

Sunset.

A loud shriek ripped through the wind from somewhere above them and Tolen stopped. Bastian moved to his side. Macy leaned over with her hands on her knees, her whole body trembling.

"The Raksasha are above us." Bastian whispered.

Ardia?

A group of ten, maybe more. They are spreading out, searching, but in random formations. The Camouflage must be working. They know you're here, I'm certain they can sense you, but they don't seem to know your exact location yet.

"Ardia says they haven't discovered us." Tolen glanced at Macy. "How close *are* we to the Shadows?"

"They are still miles away."

Tolen ran a hand through his hair. Miles away and it felt this bad? He hated to think how he'd feel without the Serenity Stones. He checked to make sure they were still molded in his ears.

Bastian's jaw flexed and he lifted Macy's arm. She tried to pull away from him but her strength seemed to be draining every step they moved closer to the Shadows. "Keep moving," he said through his teeth.

Tolen duck! Ardia shouted.

Tolen dropped and yelled, "Duck!"

A barrage of black spears slammed into the fissure wall where seconds ago their heads had been.

Unearthly screeches ripped through the night air, and before Tolen could get back to his feet, at least thirty Raksasha jumped into the fissure with them.

Bastian ran in front of Tolen to protect him and began swinging his machete. Black Raksasha blood saturated the rocks. Macy twisted and curled between the creatures, brandishing her knife, shooting fireballs, launching herself off the walls to kill at least half, but Tolen could see she was weakening—fast. She wouldn't be able to continue much longer. The Shadows' effects were too strong.

He had to do something! *Ardia! Help!*

Roots shot through the side of the fissure and wrapped around the Raksasha, crushing the life from them.

"Run!" Bastian shouted as more Raksasha lined up at the top, ready to jump.

They barely made it a few feet when a thick black root shot through the side of the fissure and knocked Bastian into the opposite wall. Macy threw her hands out and shot a burst of flame at the tree, but as the fire ate up the dead wood, the tree wrapped its blazing branches around her waist and dragged her up and out.

"Macy!" Tolen screamed.

"No!" Bastian began clawing his way up the rocky ledge, blood running thickly down the side of his head.

Tolen scrambled after him as fast as he could.

As soon as he reached the top, Raksasha surrounded them and a monstrous skeletal tree stood formidable at their head, gripping an unconscious Macy in one of its vast branches. Its trunk swirled with black and purple energy. Bright orange flames licked from its roots and snaked their way farther and farther up the tree.

A Phantom.

"Tolen! The Shupata!" Bastian ran forward swinging his machete at everything in sight—black heads and arms flew through the air, black blood splattered the ground. Tolen tried to lift his arm and take off the Shupata, but he couldn't. He stood frozen to the spot, his eyes locked on Macy's limp body being thrashed around as the Phantom tree swatted at Bastian.

Tolen could feel the Raksasha closing in. He could feel the Shadows' blanket of fear getting heavier. The pull of the Dreamers pressed in on him, more powerfully than ever. But he couldn't give in. He wouldn't!

"Macy!" Bastian's anguished cry carried in the howling wind and broke Tolen's stupor.

His eye burned as if someone had shoved a branding iron into it. Colors flashed blindingly bright across his vision and he saw several seconds into the future. Into *Macy's* future.

"No!" The image of her broken and lifeless body, crushed by the Phantom, sent waves of agony through him. "NO! Macy!" The Shupata fell from his hands as he ran forward without a thought of what he was doing. He only knew he couldn't allow what he'd just seen to happen.

Out of nowhere six different trees, life forces burning red and gold, roots lifting and curling through the hard ground, converged on the black tree.

Tolen's only thought was to get to Macy. Black streaks flew beside him as he blew through the army of Raksasha battling with Bastian. He felt the heat build in his palms as he had many times before, but this time he realized what was coming and held his hands in front of him. Great bursts of fire shot from his palms toward the Raksasha, melting them where they stood, burning him a direct path to the black tree.

Five more Phantom trees had moved in to fight the red trees and blocked his path to Macy. The rage that surged through him fed the heat to boiling point, his entire body felt as if it were on fire. He slid to a stop and held his hands in front of him, as if grasping an invisible beach ball, but he could feel the heat there, even if he could not see it. It built stronger and stronger.

The black branches lowered to grab him, "*Mi'no ha!*" The words burst form his mouth as he threw the ball of heat. His thoughts focused on the black trees nearest, the ball surged forward, split into five, and collided with the Phantoms.

A flash of brightest orange and the Phantoms dissolved to ash. The sixth tree, still clutching Macy, its side burning from her fireball, was fifty feet in front of him, swinging angrily. Its roots twisted and curled away from him as if trying to run away. He rushed forward and a golden branch appeared beside him. He ran up it without thinking and launched himself forward. More red and gold branches whipped towards him, creating a path as he flew through the air. He jumped from limb to limb until he was on the Phantom tree. Acting on instinct, he drew his fist back and slammed it into the bark as hard as he could.

The wood cracked beneath his fist. His knuckles shattered as the strength of the punch carried his entire arm to the heart of the tree.

Something snake-like and ice-cold twisted around his arm. As it furled along his skin, a weaker version of the Shadows' power pushed against his heart and mind. Macy's face flashed across his vision again and he pulled his arm back, dragging the Phantom through the heart of the tree. It fought against him, tugging backward and squeezing tighter around his arm. Pain seared through Tolen's broken hand, splinters from the tree lodged into his skin, but still he pulled harder and harder until his arm broke free of the tree.

A familiar word rushed into his mind, one he couldn't remember ever learning, but knew now was the moment to use it. *"Radi'non!"* He shouted, and a blinding flash of light filled the air in front of him. As soon as the light touched the coiling black form of the Phantom, it screeched in agony, dissipated into a thin mist, and blew away in the wind.

The tree changed from swirling energy to a deadened gray-brown and became completely still, aside from the remainder of Macy's fire that continued to burn through the dead wood.

Macy? Where was she?

Horror coursed through him.

Tolen, I have her. Ardia's voice was worried.

Tolen looked over to see Ardia's life force glowing from one of the red and gold trees. Macy lay cradled in one of her lower branches. Momentary relief coursed through him, and he looked around for the Watcher, expecting him to be tending to her injuries.

But Bastian still fought the Raksasha.

Save him. Tolen called, hoping the other trees could still hear him. They did, and swarmed over the Raksasha.

Bastian broke free of the throng and ran over. Tolen climbed down the side of the tree not yet engulfed in flames and dropped to the ground. His hand throbbed and blood ran steadily down his fingers, but he only had eyes for Macy's limp and broken body.

Ardia lowered Macy into Bastian's waiting arms.

Ardia, is she…? Tolen swallowed a lump in his throat.

She is alive, Tolen. But hurt badly. You must hurry. The Shadows know where you are. They are sending an army to keep you busy until they can reach you. If you are stalled again they will reach you before you make it.

"Bastian, we need to go."

Bastian ran his fingers down Macy's cheek and wiped at a trickle of blood running from her lip down her chin. "I cannot run with her. She will die from the pain. She is broken in so many places. Macy, I am so sorry. I have failed you." He turned tear-filled eyes on Tolen. "Heal her… *Please.*"

"What?"

"Heal her. You have the ability. Please."

Guilt washed over Tolen. "I don't know how!"

"You just saved us without knowing how. Focus, ask your life force to heal her."

Tolen, you must hurry!

"Please. I beg you. The word is *lon'adras*. Please, Tolen, just say it, please!" Bastian's voice broke and tears leaked from the corners of both eyes.

Tolen ran a hand over his face and tried to imagine what he needed to do. Why had he never asked his mother how she did it? He took a deep breath and lifted his unbroken hand to Macy's face. He pictured it not the way it was now but when it was filled with one of her sarcastic smiles, her green eyes dancing. *Please, please let this work.*

"*Lon'adras.*" He whispered and the feeling of fire in his veins returned and surged toward his fingertips. He closed his eyes and his hands seemed to move of their own accord; tracing the contours of Macy's face, burning hotter where the injuries were the worst. They trailed along her side and he cringed as the broken bones shifted back into their proper place. She moaned softly and Tolen opened his eyes.

"I think that's the best I can do."

Bastian nodded with gratitude, his face filled with pain. "Which way?"

Tolen pointed. "Ardia says there—through the Catacombs. The Raksasha are everywhere." He glanced at Macy. "Follow me." He turned and started to run. "*Mig'* what?" He called back to Bastian.

"*Mig'nata.*"

"*Mig'nata!*" Strength surged through Tolen's body and he concentrated on pushing it to his legs. He felt the increase of power flow through his muscles and his speed increased until everything around him became a blur. Bastian met him stride for stride, with Macy in his arms. The crashing sounds of the advancing Phantoms and Raksasha grew louder and louder behind them.

A sick wave of fear washed over Tolen and he stumbled. He glanced up—the Shadows were nearly over them.

"Tolen, the spear! Use it now!" Bastian pulled his own spear from his pocket, which grew to three feet in his hand. White light covered him and Macy and, amazingly, his speed increased. Tolen un-wrapped the spear. As it grew in his hands, he instantly felt the despair pushed away, but also felt the drain of the spear's power. He pushed his legs as fast as they would go. Brush, trees, and other living things moved from their path as he led the way to where Ardia was waiting.

Brilliant gold light streamed from the entrance to the Catacombs. Raksasha screamed and howled as Tolen, followed closely by Bastian and Macy, dashed inside its protection.

CHAPTER FIFTEEN

THE BINITHAN

THE LIGHT INSIDE THE BINITHAN SEEMED TO COME FROM THE WALLS themselves. They pulsated with the same kind of energy Tolen could feel from the trees. The Binithan, though made of volcanic rock, had a life force.

It was alive.

The Raksasha shrieked right outside the entrance. Tolen could see their shadows rushing closer. "Bastian?"

Before Bastian could reply, an opening appeared behind them in the cave wall, spilling more light into the cavern. They charged inside and behind them, the rock began to reform into solid wall.

Suddenly a horde of black arms reached through the gap, clawing at the stone, but it was closing too fast, severing several of the Raksashas' arms. Their shrieks resonated through the rock.

The walls shook, pebbles rained down on their heads, and an unearthly howl echoed beyond the sealed door. Waves of terror washed over Tolen. The dread and horror wrapped itself like a living thing around his heart and he sank to his knees. The spear in his hand vibrated and split in two. He dropped the pieces to the ground beside him and waited for death to come.

"Unastrah...Con...Diadras." Bastian's deep voice seemed to move through the walls, forming a barrier between them and the force outside.

The cold dread in Tolen's heart disappeared. "What did you just do?" He asked between deep breaths.

"I told the Dark it is not welcome here. The Binithan did the rest." Bastian gently lowered Macy to the floor of the cave. She was still unconscious. The golden light showed her injuries better than the dismal gray outside. Tolen felt horrible. It didn't look as if his healing efforts had done much.

"You did very well, Tolen. She will be all right. The Doogar will be here soon, they will look after her." Bastian slid down the wall and sat on the floor beside Macy. He looked exhausted. The blood from his head wound was dried on his face and congealed in his long hair. The black blood of the Raksasha covered his clothes. Deep cuts up and down his arms oozed blood and what looked like yellow pus. The skin beneath the pus twitched slightly.

"Is that—"

"Poison?" Bastian looked down at his arms. "Yes."

"Are you going to—"

"Die? No. Raksasha poison is slow. Its purpose is mainly to cause enough pain to incapacitate their prey. I am fine, Tolen. Do not worry about me." He glanced at Macy then nodded toward Tolen's hand.

"Are you in a lot of pain?"

Tolen looked at his broken hand and the scratches on his arm—splinters stuck out of his skin here and there. *Huh, I forgot all about it.*

Bastian nodded and closed his eyes. "The pain will catch up to you later, when your adrenaline wears off. Do not be surprised if you sleep straight through the next several hours or even days. That was quite a show of power out there."

Tolen slid down beside Bastian but averted his eyes from Macy, because when he did look at her, his pulse raced and the overpowering urge to go back out and kill every creature that had caused her harm nearly overwhelmed his common sense. "What do we do now?"

"The Doogar know we are here. They will come. We will wait." Bastian's head dropped to his chest and he was silent except for his deep breathing.

Tolen looked at the poison on the Watcher's arms and hoped he'd been telling the truth. His eyes followed the scratches up to the Watcher's face. Even in sleep the worry lines between his eyes and in his forehead were prevalent, making him look older. This huge man cared deeply for Macy, like a father for his child. He had felt Bastian's anguish as he'd looked at Macy's broken body. He felt it as if it were his own as Bastian had begged him to heal her. Could he honestly hate this man who could love so deeply? Did he honestly believe that Bastian had left his mother and Dane behind out of selfish cruelty?

Tolen remembered what Bastian had told him. *As your Watcher, I must do what is necessary to protect you, no matter the cost.*

He turned away, wrapped his arms around his knees, and stared down the narrow passageway into the cave, unwilling to think about it anymore. He was not ready to forgive Bastian, no matter what he'd felt or witnessed. Maybe he couldn't hate him, but he doubted he would ever forgive him. He still believed that this giant of a man could have found a way to save Dane and his mother if he'd really wanted to.

The next thing he knew he was being poked awake with a long, knobby stick.

He looked up to see a very old man, who could only be three-feet tall at most. His small stature reminded him painfully of Dane. A Doogar?

"Up. Get up, boy." The old man had a squeaky voice and his thousand tiny wrinkles quivered as he spoke. His bushy eyebrows nearly covered his huge black eyes, and his white hair and beard trailed to the ground. He wore a strange floor-length green tunic over a thick brown woven pant-suit, with tall black boots that hit just beneath his knees. A wide belt filled with an array of strange objects peeked from beneath his tangle of beard.

The old man poked Tolen again. "Come on boy—to the Infirmary. Hander say nasty business you're up to, yes. Very nasty indeed." He shook his hairy head side to side. "Tis' dark times, these. Dark times indeed."

Tolen stood up and groaned. "Who is Hander?"

The old man rapped him on the leg with his stick. "I is Hander, dummy."

"Sorry." Pain rippled across Tolen's entire body. His arm felt as if he'd shoved it into a bonfire and his legs felt like he'd run a hundred miles. "I'm Tolen." He held out his good hand.

"I already knows who you are." Hander clicked his tongue. "Come on." He started forward and Tolen looked ahead to see Bastian stumbling along carrying Macy. Six more Doogar, ranging in age, walked beside him, their arms up as if ready to catch them if Bastian collapsed.

Tolen trudged slowly behind the assembly, trying to ignore the pain. The old Doogar walked beside him, occasionally looking up with concern.

"You are all right, yes?" He asked every few minutes.

Tolen answered verbally the first several times, but as the pain intensified, he switched to quick nods. Finally, after what felt like hours of walking, the Doogar led them through a doorway into a circular room lined with tiny beds, ornately carved end tables, and dressers. The golden light inside was brighter, like daylight. Tolen squinted as he followed them inside.

Beautiful carvings of every mythical creature imaginable adorned the walls and worked up and across a ceiling that rose barely a foot above his head.

Someone tugged on his arm and he looked down to see a tiny woman in a long emerald dress with wavy floor-length hair the color of burnished copper. "You are very big, ya." Her black eyes twinkled when she smiled up at him. "No beds to fit you here, no." She held onto his good hand and led him toward the other side of the room. Hander stayed with Bastian. "Come this way. I am Helga. I will see you right, ya."

Macy was small enough to fit on the Doogar's tiny beds and they were arranging blankets and pillows on the floor beside her for Bastian. He gave Tolen a reassuring nod before layers of gauzy curtains were drawn around Macy's bed, hiding them from sight.

The woman led Tolen to the opposite side where they had pushed together three of their small beds. "This will be alright, ya?" She pulled Tolen forward and pushed on his knees to get him to sit on the bed. When he did, she shoved her tiny hands on his chest. "You will lie down, ya. We will fix you up." Two more women in similar deep green dresses came over, walked around him in circles, looking him up and down.

"You will take this, ya?" Helga held out a small, steaming cup. "It will help you sleep. So you will feel no pain, ya." She waited patiently for Tolen to swallow the bitter liquid—which he barely managed to do without gagging—and then smiled as his eyelids began to droop.

His last thought was a shiver of dread at the idea of what would have happened had they not reached the door in time, if they had been left there. Left, like his mother and Dane. Shimmers of warmth from the drink fought the pangs of grief spreading through his body, dulling the pain, and slowing his thoughts until finally he drifted into a welcome, dreamless slumber.

ooo

Bastian twisted the wooden cup in his hands. The Doogar Elders sat at the far end of the table whispering and occasionally sending him a covert glance or frown.

He sipped the root tea and looked over the bandages on his arms as he waited. The little Doogar Healers had cleaned most of the Raksasha poison from his wounds—he felt hardly any pain.

He tapped his thumb on the side of the mug. It would not do well to demand anything from the Doogar, but it was very hard to maintain a calm facade with so much at stake.

Tolen and Macy had slept soundly for the last twelve hours, and the Doogar Elders had been in council nearly the entire time. An hour ago, they had finally invited Bastian to join them. He hoped they had decided to help. The Doogar with their many caves beneath the earth would be a great asset.

In that hour, Bastion had explained recent events, informing them that though it was not yet time for him to know it, Tolen truly was the Ninth. As he finished, the Elder's looked at him blankly before Hander quietly spoke.

"We's will help you. Our Sphere will be shielding the boy until the girl heals. You's must teach him to shield himself. Then we will lead you to the camp. The boy is too powerful to be staying here long term. It is not the safest idea, but the Dark makes nothing safe right now."

Bastian lowered his head. "I am truly grateful for your sacrifice. While Tolen is here, I was hoping you could help me train him. He has much to learn and your people are very skilled. For far too long he has thought of his gifts as a curse and has sought to subdue them. When he feels an overwhelming emotion, his gifts burst free and he has no idea how to control them. Every minute his gifts grow in strength. I do not want to waste a single moment that he could be taught."

The elders shared a long look before Hander looked back to Bastian with a grave nod. "This request is justified. Helping the Ninth we help us all."

"I am forever indebted." He paused "I have one final favor to ask, even though it is not fair of me, since you have already promised so much."

Hander's bushy eyebrows rose and several of the other elders started shaking their heads at his nerve. Bastian plowed forward, knowing he had no choice. The hazy future concerned him.

Bastian rubbed the back of his neck and leaned forward. "This is a bit more complicated. For centuries, the Dark has been mostly quiet, but for the last several years, I have watched the signs, and felt the growth of evil shift from slow to alarmingly fast. Too fast. In the last ten years alone we have seen the Shadows released twice, crow patrols have increased, and Raksasha and other vile creatures' numbers have swelled, keeping the Chosen and their Watchers too busy to notice…"

"Notice what?"

Bastian ran a hand over his eyes. "The Guardians put my ward and me on a special reconnaissance mission. We were to stalk a group of Kreydawn in the deserts of Nevada. They were mining something, but whatever it was, they were keeping it well hidden. Disguising their actions. Before we were able to discover what they were doing, Tolen's shard arrived, the Balance restored me, and we left to find him. I have not been able to get word to my contact with the Guardians—"

Hander waved his hand in the air. "I's will pass the word along and inform them what has taken place. What are you's really getting at?"

Bastian took a deep breath. "When we arrived at Tolen's house, my ward killed a Divinator."

A collective gasp passed through the elders. "But they's hasn't been seen since the dark days." A red-bearded elder spoke from Bastian's left.

"No. Not since Daemon was in this realm." Bastian said softly.

Hander leaned back. "You's are thinking he is back?"

Bastian shook his head. "I do not know, but the evidence is worrisome." He spread his hands on the table and started ticking things off the mental list he had been compiling since Tolen's shard landed in his hand. "Kreydawn and their Suppressors have been in this realm forever, but are usually easily outwitted, but the Suppressor in Nevada was different. Whatever Dark captain was controlling that Suppressor was smarter than usual. I think it is the same captain who had Divinators watching Tolen."

The elders surveyed him with wide eyes as he continued.

"Not long after we took Tolen from Green River I noticed something else. Something that only deepens my suspicions. The DéHool have been released."

Hander laughed in disbelief. "This is not true. We's would have felt it!"

Bastian shook his head. "Whoever let them out is shielding their presence very well. I have only been able to feel glimpses of their power, but I would know it anywhere."

Hander went back to stroking his beard, his dark eyes bright. He turned to the others and they began whispering again. Bastian leaned back in his seat to wait. It was a full ten minutes before they addressed him again.

"You's are suggesting that Daemon, highest captain in the Dark—second only to Darsapean, the ruler of the Dark himself—is back and up to's something." Hander leaned toward Bastian, while the others stayed back in their chairs, their faces troubled and suspicious.

Bastian raised his hands in front of him. "If he is not in this realm, he is somehow managing to exercise a lot of power from within the Shadow Realm. Either possibility should be a cause for concern."

"And what's is it you be wanting *us* to do about it?" Redbeard asked.

Bastian met the eyes of the elders one by one. "Get word out, not only to the Guardians, but to every Hidden colony you can, to start preparing."

Hander twisted his beard nervously. "Preparing for what?"

"War."

○○○

Tolen had been awake for the last fifteen minutes, sitting on the tiny bed, knees drawn up to his chest, tapping his fingers in a restless rhythm on the bedspread, trying to decide what to do. The little women were gone and the curtains were still closed around Macy's bed. He wanted to know how she was doing, but he didn't want to disturb her rest. He wanted to learn what had happened while he'd slept, and he was anxious to talk to someone who could help him find out about his mother and Dane, but he was miles underground and if he took a wrong turn, he presumed he'd end up lost down here forever.

He'd slept for fourteen hours according to his watch. It was 10:00 a.m. He'd been on the run for two days. His mother had been missing for more than twenty-four hours. He had to talk to someone, anyone. He couldn't keep waiting.

He stood up and was about to leave the infirmary, despite the possibility of getting lost, when Helga walked through the door. She noticed he was awake, gave a clap of glee, turned, and left.

He moved to follow her, but she reappeared seconds later carrying a tray of food and a water jug.

"You are hungry, yes?" Her dark eyes were kind.

Tolen's stomach rumbled. "Yes, but—"

"No, but. Sit. Eat." She smiled as she pushed him back toward the bed, placed the tray carefully on his lap and sat the jug on the bedside table.

"Thank you." He looked at the tray and picked up a piece of what looked like black bread. "I was wondering—"

"Eat." Helga pointed to the plate and waited with her finger raised. Maybe if he started eating she'd let him ask her some questions.

He bit off a chunk of bread. It was grainy and tasteless, but his empty stomach didn't care one bit. He took a swallow from the jug of water. "Um, are Bastian and Macy awake?"

She sighed and pointed to the plate again. "Macy is healing. The Watcher in council."

Tolen swallowed a spoonful of stew. It was unlike anything he'd ever had before, but not terrible, sort of like flavorless, thick, chicken noodle soup. "So, I um…I was wondering…do you-do you know Dane?"

Her gaze fell to her lap. "Dane was good friend."

Tolen's stomach dropped. "*Was?*"

She raised her head and met his gaze with fierce eyes. He'd offended her with his question. "I say no more. You eat, now. *No* talk."

Tolen felt an additional pang of guilt for upsetting the kind woman and went back to eating his meal in silence.

Helga waited until he ate every last crumb of bread and drank every drop of soggy stew. She took the tray and turned to leave.

"Wait. Can I talk to someone in charge?" Asking her had been a bad idea, but surely he could talk to someone.

"No."

"Hander!" Tolen remembered the little man who'd led him here. He'd seemed important. "Can I talk to Hander?"

"No." She repeated. "Sleep. Heal." She tilted her head, gave him a searching look, and left quickly the way she'd come.

Tolen jumped up, determined to try to follow, but when he stepped out of the same door she'd left, he found himself in a small antechamber with four golden hallways, each leading in different directions. He had no idea which direction Helga would have gone. He scratched his head, then turned and trudged back to the infirmary. He dropped back onto his bed, leaned against the wall, and rubbed his eyes with his fists. He didn't like being alone with his thoughts, which were torturing. How long would he be stuck in this room? What would he have to do to get someone to help him? Or even talk to him? He stretched his arms above his head, popping his joints.

He jumped off the beds and did a few sit-ups, trying to wake up his body. His broken hand burned a little and his muscles were stiff and sore. Other than that, he had no proof of all that had happened in the Lava Beds. It felt like a dream—or rather a nightmare—the things he'd been able to do without even knowing how or why. He knew it wasn't his subconscious taking over. He hadn't necessarily been in control, but the power he felt hadn't scared him the way it did when his subconscious took over. This had seemed more like instinct. As if somewhere buried deep inside, he already knew how to do everything. He simply needed to *remember.*

He stood up and started to jog in place. Five minutes later, Bastian walked into the infirmary. He peeked in at Macy before making his way to Tolen's side.

Tolen cleared his throat, feeling awkward and unsure how to act. So much had happened since their last conversation. Even though he'd decided he didn't hate Bastian, he still didn't necessarily like him. It was uncomfortable talking to someone you didn't like. "How is she?"

Bastian smiled, but his eyes were wary. He looked exhausted. "She is much better today. How are you?"

Tolen shrugged. "My body feels weak and rubbery, but I'm wide awake."

"That is normal. It takes your physical body longer to regenerate after such an experience than it does your life force. Give it time. Do not push too hard. You need to let your body rest."

Tolen sat back on the beds and took a long drink of water. He could feel the truth of the Watcher's words, but he didn't like it. His eyes wandered to Macy's side of the room. He wanted to see for himself that she was okay. All the anger he'd felt toward her when they'd entered the Lava Beds had completely evaporated. "She's not like I thought she was when I first met her."

Bastian sat down on a low stool beside the bed, rested his elbows on his knees, and dropped his chin onto his clasped hands. "No, she is much more than a snotty teenager." He chuckled once then added seriously. "You saved her life."

Tolen put the jug on the table, keeping his eyes off the Watcher's face. It was easier to talk to him that way. "How bad was she? I couldn't really tell as I healed her."

"You will be able to recognize more with practice." Bastian took a slow breath. "Most of Macy's ribs were shattered by the Phantom tree; her left arm and leg were broken in several places. She had some internal bleeding as well, from where the ribs had pierced her lungs. If you had not healed her, she would have been dead by the time we reached the door." Bastian's voice broke. "I owe you so much."

Tolen shook his head and glanced at Bastian. "You don't owe me anything." He didn't like to see the Watcher weak. It made him feel pity he didn't want to feel.

Bastian's strange eyes raked over Tolen's face. "You are much more than I expected you to be as well, especially given your circumstances."

Tolen sighed. "Am I supposed to know what you mean by that?"

Bastian shrugged a shoulder. "I suppose not."

Tolen stared back at Macy's curtains. "How did I do it? How did I heal her?"

"You have your mother's gift of healing, Tolen. Your gifts are part of you, even if you do not recognize them. You were right in your thoughts earlier. You do know your gifts; you just have to be taught to recognize them, and how to use them. The words I have taught you, the word you remembered out there with the Phantom, they are all part of our world, part of you. You were able to call on them in your time of need."

"Why did the Phantom disappear when I pulled it out of the tree?"

"Phantoms are made up of darkness itself. Where the light is, darkness cannot be. '*Radi'non*' means 'light come forth'. The sun heard you, sent a ray of its light to you in one quick burst, and killed the Phantom."

Tolen tugged on the bottom of his shirt. "Where the light is, darkness cannot be." A shiver ran along his shoulders.

"Yes."

"It's deeper than that, isn't it?"

Bastian leaned back against the wall and folded his arms across his chest. He looked so tired. Tolen wondered if he'd slept at all since they'd got here.

"So much deeper. Light is knowledge and truth. It is love and compassion. It is what bonds families and gives a person something worth fighting for, worth dying for. Dark is the exact opposite. It is hatred and cruelty, malice and anger. It is revenge and bloodlust, greed and selfishness."

An uncomfortable sensation moved into Tolen's stomach. The Dark embodied all those feelings he had toward the Watcher in this moment.

Hatred, anger, and selfish need. He cleared his throat and pushed the guilt away. This was different. He was justified in his anger; anyone could see that.

Bastian's countenance fell and Tolen remembered he would know his thoughts. He squirmed, but Bastian went on as if he'd heard nothing and Tolen turned his focus to the Watcher's next words. "The Light shows you its goodness and invites you to follow, whereas Dark enslaves, chains you to it, and then uses you for its own selfish means."

Tolen leaned forward. "You talk like they're people."

"They are."

"Huh?"

"Light and Dark are forces that have existed before the earth, before this universe. Light creates. Dark is drawn toward creations who have turned their hearts to evil and destroys them. You see, their strength comes from the people who choose one over the other. In recent years, the Dark has become more devious in its tactics; it is gaining strength at an alarming rate. So many people have fallen into the Dark's foul clutches without even realizing it. As more people become slaves to the Dark, our work as followers and defenders of the Light becomes more and more difficult. It will not be long before a full scale war will be upon us."

"Another war?"

"We are already at war, Tolen. It is just that the war up until now has taken place outside the knowledge or awareness of humans."

Tolen thought about the Shadows, the Raksasha, and the Phantoms, just a small number of creatures of darkness. Yes, they were definitely already at war. "I'm finally starting to understand why my mother was always afraid of thunder storms, and hated night." He swallowed back the memory. "Is it always like this for the Chosen? Are you constantly running from, or fighting the Dark?"

Bastian looked uncomfortable. "It is usually not to such an extreme degree, no."

Tolen lifted his eyebrow. "Will you ever tell me whatever it is you're hiding from me?"

"Yes, Tolen. When I believe you are ready to know, I will tell you."

Bastian held Tolen's gaze and something passed silently between them.

Bastian knew Tolen wouldn't forgive him, and didn't like him, but he also knew how desperate Tolen was for answers. Tolen realized that even though Bastian was here and determined to be Tolen's Watcher, he too had misgivings about his new ward. He didn't believe Tolen ready to hear the whole truth. But he did know things, things the Doogar wouldn't be able to answer. If Tolen could prove himself to him, Bastian would eventually tell him everything.

They were at an impasse. One of them would have to give in and Tolen knew who it would need to be if he wanted to get what he was after.

Bastian did too. He took a deep breath and settled lower on the stool. He didn't look smug or relieved at his minor victory. Only determined. "Ask your questions, Tolen."

"But will you answer honestly?"

The Watcher nodded. "I may choose not to answer, but I will not lie. If I feel you are not ready to hear something I will tell you why. I do not believe in secrets. I believe in timing." He gave Tolen a long look. "You will also have a chance to talk to a Doogar leader, but they will not give you audience just yet. Doogar are a very traditional people and you must wait until they have finished their preparations."

"Preparations?"

"For our stay."

"How long will I be here?"

"Until Macy finishes healing and you learn to shield yourself from the Dark."

Tolen met the Watcher's eyes and his blue eye burned again. He rubbed it with his fist. "And you're going to teach me to do that?"

Bastian nodded.

"And you'll answer my questions…as much as you choose to anyway?" He added with slight irritation.

He nodded again.

"And I will get to talk to a Doogar leader?"

Bastian ran his fingers through his beard. "Yes, but Tolen, I am aware of your plan and there is one thing you should know before you ask them to help you find your mother and Dane."

Tolen's heart pounded with unease.

"Dane's connection with the earth has been lost." His voice was grave.

"What does that mean?" Tolen felt he knew exactly what it meant, but he wanted Bastian to confirm it, or by some slim chance, deny it.

"The Télora are connected to one another through their connection to the earth. The other Télora here cannot feel him anymore. Handrak—or Hank as you call him—has also been to the canyon, studied the evidence himself, and sent word here. I am sorry, Tolen. He is gone."

It felt like someone kicked him in the stomach. He gazed at the floor as a loud buzzing started in his ears. "My mom?" He looked up at Bastian to see his expression.

The Watcher's eyes were guarded, but it was clear he was telling the truth when he answered softly. "They are uncertain. They have never been able to sense her, unless she initiated the connection, but her chances are not good. As I said, Handrak studied the evidence and he does not believe they took her captive."

Tolen's hands trembled and he squeezed them in his lap. "But that doesn't mean they didn't."

"No. It does not."

"So there's still a chance."

Bastian sighed. "A very slim one. Yes." He leveled his gaze on Tolen's eyes. "But, I beg you Tolen, wait to put your plan into action. Ask the Doogar what you will, but give me a chance to train you and help you get stronger. If you go after the Dark too soon, they will defeat you." It was not said coldly, but Tolen still bristled.

"Fine. Tell me about my dad."

Chapter Sixteen

Watchers and Wards

Tolen looked at the Watcher's face, fighting against the part of him that said he should let the man rest. Give him time to *regenerate* or whatever, but Tolen had to do something to feel like he was at least trying to help his parents, or the guilt would eat him alive. He swallowed and tried to soften the question. "*Will* you tell me about him?"

Bastian sat up a little taller on the stool and took a deep breath. "I will tell you what I know, or have been told in the legends."

Tolen moved to the edge of the bed. His dad was a legend?

"Daedal Téloran was one of the most revered Protectors—that is the title given to the greatest warriors for the Light—of all time. He led the Radia Warriors in the victory against the Dark during the Radia Revolution. He was instrumental in the imprisonment of Darsapean, the leader of the Dark, *and* in the banishment of Daemon, Demon Master and High Captain, to the Shadow Realm."

"Macy said the revolution took place over a thousand years ago. Are you saying my father is over a thousand years old?"

"Your father is two years my senior."

"You're over a thousand years old?" Tolen looked at the dark haired, muscular man, dwarfing the stool he sat on, in disbelief. The Watcher looked barely a day over twenty.

"Hidden age slower than humans and some may be restored to a younger state by the Balance, if necessary."

"How old is my mom then?" It hurt to ask about her, but she was beginning to feel as much a stranger to him as his father.

"That I do not know. I had never heard of, nor seen, your mother before." He reached out as if to pat Tolen's arm, but pulled back and folded his arms again. "When you first told me your father's name it surprised me. Protectors are bound to their oath. They cannot marry. Your mother told me later that they both served at the Citadel of Light—home of the Guardians."

"What did my mom do there?"

"Your mother belongs to the race of Spheres. They have the ability to manipulate the Balance surrounding other people in order to hide their life force from detection. They can also manipulate the cells in the mortal body, ask them to return to their state of wholeness—it is how they heal. Her duty would have been to help shield the Guardians and care for those who came to the citadel in need of healing."

Tolen thought about his conversation with Macy about particles and scientific theory. It wasn't too hard to imagine how his mother's gifts might work. It's what he'd felt when he'd tried to heal Macy. Almost as if he could tell the cells wanted to move, they just needed help getting back to where they belonged. "So they met and fell in love at the citadel?"

"I do not know if that is where they first met. I only know the stories of your father from the revolution, and I met him but one time, not long after the war, when he was at the citadel and I was there being set apart in my duties as a Watcher. According to your mother, they ran away from their duties and married. I do not know how long ago that was, or how long they were married before they had you. A miracle in itself."

"A miracle, how?"

"Our laws cannot be broken without serious consequences. Your parents' marriage broke the oaths they made with the Guardians—it should have rendered them unable to procreate. Your birth is legendary in many ways. There is a change happening, a change that goes deeper than any of us can imagine."

Tolen didn't like the idea that his birth was legendary. "If my father was such a legend, how did he get captured, and why do the Shadows want him?"

"Those are good questions. A man of his ability should have been strong enough to avoid capture. As to why the Shadows want him, the Dark wants control of every powerful being. They want to try and turn your father."

"So, he's there now. In the Shadow Realm? With Daemon and all those evil creatures torturing him?" Tolen swallowed. What if that was where his mother was now? What if they were torturing her too? His stomach turned and he started to wish he hadn't eaten.

"Yes. That is where your father is." Bastian didn't say anything about if Tolen's mother was there too. He didn't know, so why speculate aloud on something so horrible?

Tolen had to do something. Something to help them. He had failed his best friend, but if his mother was still alive he would find out, and if they were both in the Shadow Prison he would find a way to save them. Bastian himself had said back in Green River that the Light wanted Tolen to go after his father!

Bastian leaned forward and put a hand on Tolen's shoulder. "I did say that Tolen, and I do believe you are meant to try. But, as I said before, you are not ready. Let the Doogar train you. Let me train you. Trust me enough to believe that I will do all I can to help you."

Tolen looked into the Watcher's face and knew he was telling the truth. He didn't have to forgive the man for what happened in order to trust him, right?

He closed his eyes, pretending for a moment he did not have an audience, and tried to look beneath the guilt to the real emotion. At the truth he needed to see, and grasp onto. "I have one question before I decide to trust you and wait to put my plan into action." He spoke with his eyes closed.

"All right."

Tolen licked his lips and opened his eyes to see the Watcher regarding him thoughtfully. "If the Light is so powerful, so loving, so *perfect*, as you describe, how could they let the Dark hurt so many people and not stop them?" He clutched the blanket beneath him in his fists. "How can they ask me to fight for them when they did nothing to protect my parents?"

Bastian tilted his head and crossed his feet in front of him. "That is a deep question Tolen, without a simple answer. Do you remember what I told you about the Light and the Dark?"

"Light beckons. Dark enslaves."

"Yes. And in that lies your answer in all its complexity. The Light and the Dark are complete opposites. Light is choice and freedom. Dark is forcefulness and domination. The Light can give us aid when, and only when, we ask for it. The Dark will force its evil upon us every chance it gets. The Light cannot change a course of actions set in motion by our own choices, but it can give us aid, and help us through our afflictions when we ask for its help, and then choose to listen and accept it. It cannot force its help upon us or it would not be the Light. Do you understand?"

Tolen folded his leg beneath him and tried to grasp what the Watcher meant. "The Light couldn't change what happened in the canyon because it was our choices that led us there?"

Bastian nodded. "But it was there helping us Tolen. Not a day of my life has gone by when I have not asked the Light for its help and guidance. Macy holds a gift of the Light and she was there doing all she could to protect you, your mother, and Dane. Dane used his gift to help us by his own choice. The Light was with us all that night, Tolen. It could not change the events, but it never left us alone as we fought the darkness that sought to take all our lives. It was your mother's and Dane's choice to stay behind and save the rest of us. Theirs was a sacrifice, not a punishment, or abandonment."

This concept felt true, but it was hard to accept. He still wanted to feel angry and abandoned and he wanted to feel justified in that anger. He understood right and wrong, so it made sense in that way, but the Light and Dark were a lot bigger than just right and wrong. His mother had taught him the difference between good choices and bad ones, and it had never been in his nature to seek after anything that felt evil or wrong.

"Okay, what will I be learning first?"

Bastian tapped his chin. "Well, unfortunately, Macy was right about one thing. Your life force is immensely powerful and the Dark can sense the shift it causes in the Balance, so they will always know where you are. First and foremost, we must teach you to shield the power of your life force in order to keep it from affecting the Balance. You have to learn to contain its strength within your physical body. It is extremely difficult to do, but extremely necessary if we are to ever leave here without being captured."

"Why can't we stay here and train, if it's safe?"

"For one thing, the Dark knows you are here. We cannot, in good conscience, allow the Doogar to risk their home for us indefinitely. Eventually, the Dark would find a way in and destroy this place."

Tolen shuddered. No, he wouldn't stay here and do that to Dane's people. Not after all they'd done. Not after everything Dane had done for him.

Bastian nodded. "Exactly."

"Once I learn how to shield myself, where will we go?" A small degree of excitement began to build in Tolen and he started tapping his fingers on the bed. Now that there was a plan, he wanted to get moving.

"You need advanced training that I cannot give. The Radia Warriors have camps all over the world where they train their forces. Hander knows of one concealed not too far from here, in the Klamath National Forest. Once you are ready, and Macy has healed, they will lead us there."

Something Bastian said earlier suddenly clicked in Tolen's brain. "That's why my mother was sick. It was because she was shielding me all those years, and it was weakening her, wasn't it?"

"Yes. Spheres are the only Beings capable of shielding a life force besides their own, and it takes a lot of power. That is why there are so many who serve at the citadel, so they can share the burden. Do not let her choice cause you any guilt. If your mother had brought you to the Guardians or allowed you to have a Watcher, you could have learned to shield yourself."

Tolen planted both feet on the floor and bit back the defensive remark he wanted to say. Instead he asked the question that would hopefully make it make sense. "*Why* didn't she take me to the Guardians and let me have a Watcher. Was it because they'd broken the law? Would they have taken me away from her?"

Bastian took a deep breath. "You would have been placed in the care of your Watcher, yes. I do not know what her punishment would have been, but the biggest reason your parents did not do as they should have concerning you, is *Fear*." He lifted his hand up. "Do not misunderstand. I am speaking about more than simply being afraid of something. I am speaking of an *unnatural* fear, something that is in and of itself. It is what you felt as we approached the Shadows—the overpowering feeling that dropped you to your knees when the door closed on the Binithan."

"Ardia said the Shadows magnify Fear to the highest degree. I didn't realize it was an actual thing."

"The Dark created a weapon more powerful than our kind knew how to combat. When Fear first reared its ugly head, we had no idea how to fight it. Many who heeded its cunning subtleties were destroyed.

"Fear is not simply an emotional response to something frightening— although it may begin that way. When you dwell on that fear, focus on it until it affects your thoughts and actions, it weakens you until the Dark can sense your distress as it affects the Balance. At that point, they send in their creations.

"This unnatural fear seeks you out and pulls you down to the Dark without you even realizing it. When it takes you, it affects your thoughts; it makes you do things that are neither rational nor ethical. Fear, used as a tool of the Dark, poisons the soul, making its way deeper and deeper into the individual until it takes over that person's heart and mind. You are not evil—just lost in doubt and anxiety, making you a much easier target. I believe this is what happened to your mother. Fear weakened her. Only her superior gifts as a Sphere managed to keep the Dark from finding you both. As you grew stronger, so did her fear for you. There were moments when her shield weakened and the Dark sensed you briefly, which is why crows were watching you even before Macy and I found you."

Tolen looked at his hands—if only he'd known. He didn't want to be angry with his mother, but some of the earlier resentment that he'd felt back before they'd left home was still there. If he'd known about himself, and how to use his abilities, he could have helped her. He could have protected them. He ran a hand through his hair and turned his attention back to Bastian.

"When you were born, your parents were hiding from the world of the Hidden, trying to be something they were not, making them vulnerable to the tactics of the Dark. When you were Chosen, they knew this would take you into that Hidden world. Their fear of losing you drove your father to try something impossible." Bastian looked at Tolen with sadness. "He tried to interfere with the Balance; he tried to change your destiny."

"My destiny? How?"

Bastian lifted a necklace from his shirt. Two shining crystals dangled from it. Bastian slid the smaller of the two off the necklace, pulled a piece of cord from his pocket, and laced it around the crystal. "This is yours."

"Is that what Macy called a Radia Shard?" Tolen's mouth went dry.

"Yes. When the Balance selected you, it came to your home. Your father took it and tried to find the Guardians to persuade them to take it back." He shook his head. "But the shift in the Balance had already occurred. Fate was already in motion. The Balance read your heart and knew that your life force contained everything the Chosen would need…" He opened his mouth as if to go on, shook his head once more, and looked at the necklace in his hand before holding it out to Tolen.

Tolen took the shard. It glowed brighter once it touched his skin. It was warm and throbbed like a tiny heart.

"I do not know how long after your father left you that he was captured." He nodded toward the shard. "But your shard only found me a few days ago. It led me to you."

Tolen thought of the image of the zombie-like man who haunted his dreams. "I've been dreaming about my father for weeks. Is he going to die in that prison?"

Bastian shook his head. "I do not know. To my knowledge, no one has ever left the Shadow Prison alive, but your father was a very formidable Protector. I am sure that is why he has survived this long."

"What if he dies before I learn how to use my abilities and can try to save him?" He squeezed the shard in his hand until the sharp edges dug into his skin.

"Then that would be his fate." It was a cold sentence, but Bastian said it with so much regret that Tolen couldn't be angry with him.

"Put it around your neck, Tolen, and never take it off. It will link you to me and to the other Chosen. Guard it with your life. It must never fall into the hands of the Dark. With time, it will share with you more of its powers and purposes."

Tolen pulled the shard over his neck. It felt warm as it rested against his throat. "Macy said that if human Chosen lose their shard then their power leaves. What happens if I lose mine?"

Bastian pointed at Tolen's chest where the shard lay. "Being Hidden kind, your gifts were born with you. The possession of a Radia Shard is an added bonus. As I said, it will eventually show you more of its purposes and powers once you have earned its allegiance. For now, it can enhance your powers as you learn to tap into it, and keep you connected to me and the other Chosen."

Tolen lifted the small shard from his neck and twisted it in his fingers. "I have no choice but to *be* a member of the Chosen, because the Balance selected me. Even though I have no idea if I even can, or *want* to?"

"Tolen, fate and destiny are more than what you have been taught to understand. There is choice in everything, and with every choice there is a consequence, good or bad." He glanced up at the low ceiling. "Although much of fate is already determined by actions put into place eons ago, whatever you choose now will still affect your destiny. All in all, *you* control the outcome of your life.

"It does not matter how much it might seem that your path is decided for you, choice will always play a role—help determine the outcome. When it comes right down to it, you *do* choose your path. No matter what the Balance decides, you choose where you will go, what you will do, and how you will deal with it."

"But you said that the Balance had already shifted, fate was already in motion." He put his hand over the shard. "Doesn't that imply I'm kinda stuck?"

"No, Tolen, you are not stuck. Things that were put into action years ago by the choices of others cannot be stopped, that chain of events is already in motion. But every choice you make from here on out will affect your final destiny in unfathomable ways. There are events in this world that must happen—it is the law of survival—but the way in which things come about changes day by day, choice by choice."

Tolen put a hand behind his head and leaned back against the wall. "So, that means that my father couldn't interfere with my destiny because it was *my* destiny. Only my choices can affect the Balance as it relates to my own fate. The choices of others can affect my circumstances, but my destiny remains solid unless I choose otherwise?"

"Yes."

"So I *can* choose whether or not to join the Chosen?"

Bastian rubbed a hand over his chin while his other hand curled into a fist on his lap. "Yes." There was fear in his voice.

He's afraid of what I might choose. Tolen thought of the graduation ceremony that he wouldn't be attending tomorrow, all the kids he'd spent the last few years with walking down the line and getting their diplomas. Did they, too, have choices before them that were almost impossible to fathom? Or were their lives easy and uncomplicated?

Worrying about money for rent or food and dealing with Jeff Macro seemed so simple compared to the new worries that plagued him. He'd wanted to know everything about who he really was for as long as he could remember, but now, the more he learned, the more he wondered if ignorance hadn't been better.

His mind sifted painfully through all he'd been witness to in the last few days; the Raksasha trying to kill them, his mother and best friend gone, and seeing Macy nearly crushed to death by the Phantom.

His hands trembled. Could he really sit back and hide while creatures like that continued to destroy innocent life? Especially now that he knew he'd been *Chosen* to stop them?

All these abilities really did have a purpose, a greater purpose. His life was no longer a four-walled prison. It had become a long, winding road of twists and turns and he had no idea where it might lead.

As long as the Dark continued to thrive, the world would never truly be free. *Tolen* would never truly be free.

He sat forward again and gripped the blanket beneath him. Being trained as a Chosen, learning how to use his abilities in combat would give him one more weapon in his quest to save his parents. Tolen took a deep breath and looked Bastian squarely in the eyes.

"I want to be a Chosen. When can I start training?" The shard pulsed with an energy that coursed through his body. It felt as if he were wearing a living thing around his neck. He could feel emotion flowing through it, and from it, into him. It was *happy* with his choice.

"A Doogar will be here shortly to take you to your first phase of training." Bastian seemed relieved, if not still a little wary.

Tolen nodded and leaned his head back against the wall.

Bastian opened his mouth as if he wanted to say more, but instead only squeezed Tolen's shoulder and stood up. "I need some time to regenerate. Enjoy your training." He disappeared behind Macy's curtains, leaving Tolen to wait impatiently for his first chance to train.

CHAPTER SEVENTEEN

FRIENDS?

Tolen's breath came out in a loud whoosh; he wiped the sweat off his face with his good hand, and dropped into the tiny chair.

"I can't do it."

"You are making it more difficult than it should be." Kiad circled around Tolen, his steps agitated. He didn't have the same accent as the other Doogar down here; he had obviously spent time among humans. From his brisk, no-nonsense attitude and shaved head, Tolen had to wonder if his human friends had been drill sergeants.

"I'm trying."

Kiad stopped in front of him, put his hands on his hips, and stared up into Tolen's face. Kiad's eyes weren't the shiny black of Helga or Hander, they were the same muddy brown as Dane's.

Tolen swallowed loudly.

"We need a different tactic, something smaller, less difficult…" Kiad tapped his temple. "Heal your hand."

Tolen looked at his bandaged hand and back to the little man. "Um, that's not easy."

Kiad thumped him on the thigh. "Yes it is. Do you remember the word?"

"*Lon'adras?*"

"Yes! What do you feel?"

"Nothing." There was no burn in his fingertips, nothing compared to what he'd felt when he healed Macy.

Kiad scratched his head. "Each gifted Being has to learn to connect to their life force on the conscious level. You are not finding the connection. You found it out there while you were fighting, when you healed the girl, when you asked the trees to stop the bullies. You must look deeper. Your trigger is there. Find it."

Tolen clenched his jaw and resisted the urge to roll his eyes. Why *couldn't* he do it? It had just come to him those other times—like instinct, so simple. He hadn't *had* to do anything. But now, concentrating as hard as he could it wouldn't come. He closed his eyes and rubbed the bridge of his nose, thinking back.

When Jeff was threatening Dane, Tolen had only felt a strong desire to keep Jeff from beating up his friend and the trees had reacted. He hadn't *asked* them to do anything. Whether Kiad believed him or not, that hadn't been him. With Macy, it was different, in his mind he'd been screaming, begging anyone to come and help. He'd felt Ardia and called to her, he'd felt the other trees and called to them, he'd called to everything he could feel out there, and then it just happened.

The physical pain caused by the image of her broken and lifeless body had nearly dropped him to the ground. His only thought after that had been to get to her. He couldn't remember anything else.

Kiad walked away to talk to a younger female who came in. Bits of their conversation filtered back to him. It seemed they were talking about Macy.

A tiny bit of warmth zinged through his fingers. He looked down at his hands. *What?*

"…she's not healing as quickly as we hoped." He heard the woman say, and the warmth in his fingers increased.

The more they talked about Macy's healing the more heat surged into his fingers. It seemed that empathy was his trigger, which kind of made sense.

He focused on his concern for Macy. His hopes that she would make a full recovery. She'd been fun to talk to and she knew a lot. She'd be a good help to him as he trained.

The growth of the warmth was slower than when he'd been terrified for Macy's life. It took quite a while for it to feel like it would actually do anything. He felt his eye dilate behind his closed lid. His heart seemed to swell with inexplicable peace and then it trickled down to his fingertips. He lifted his good hand and ran it over his injured arm.

"*Lon'adras*," he whispered, and he felt the skin knitting itself back together beneath the bandage. It was painful, but the strange, peaceful warmth kept it from being excruciating as it moved along the broken lines of the bones in his hand, shifting them back into place. The Doogar had set it as best they could, but it had not been perfect. It was now.

The warmth slowly faded as the healing finished. Tolen pulled off the bandage—there wasn't a single indication of his injury. Not even the hint of a scar.

Kiad slapped Tolen on the shoulder and he jumped. He hadn't noticed the little man's return. "Good job. Don't stop. Focus on what you felt. The power. Sense it as it surrounds and moves out from your body. Call it back in and hold it there."

Tolen put his head into his shaking hands. He was so tired. And it wasn't power, it was warmth. There was no other way to describe it. He focused on bringing the warmth he could feel surrounding him back inside. He could feel it pulling against him, like it wanted to be free—like it was too big to be contained in his body.

"Yes! Yes! Like that!" Kiad exclaimed.

Tolen fell out of his chair, the breath whooshed out of his lungs, and lights danced in front of his eyes.

"Good job!" Kiad knelt on the ground beside him. "Take a few deep breaths. You figured out how to pull it in, now you have to work on keeping it there. With much practice it won't be so hard. Wait here. I'll bring you something to help."

Kiad left the room and Tolen rubbed his eyes with his fists.

Six hours later, Tolen was back in the infirmary absentmindedly rummaging through his pack. He was tired from working with Kiad, but felt restless. They'd told him his dinner would be brought to the infirmary where he would be more comfortable, and so he was stuck here again. Waiting. He shuffled through his meager possessions and pulled out his only other set of clothes. Kiad had promised him a chance to clean up after dinner.

His hand brushed across something stiff and he lifted out the picture of his father holding him. His hands trembled and he shoved the picture back in his bag. He dropped back onto the row of beds and lifted the shard in his fingers. It was a beautiful thing, really. The light from the Binithan danced off its surface, giving it a golden hue, but just beneath, it glowed softest blue. He felt a kinship toward the shard—not long ago it had been in his father's hands.

A strange tugging sensation in Tolen's stomach seemed to draw his attention to the opposite side of the room where Macy and Bastian slept.

Bastian's head appeared out of the curtains. He peeked back at Macy before walking over to take the stool he'd only recently vacated.

"You had enough sleep?" Tolen asked.

Bastian nodded and his cheek lifted in a half smile. He pointed to the shard in Tolen's fingers. "You are feeling the link that binds you and Macy together as Chosen. It will become less noticeable the longer you wear the shard. After a time you will have to concentrate to feel the pull. But it will guide you to me or any member of the Chosen that you seek to find."

Tolen dropped the shard beneath his shirt. "You said I should never take it off. Does that mean like, ever?" He pictured having to wear it all the time. He really wasn't much of a jewelry fan, not to mention it would get in the way in the shower.

"A Radia Shard is a very valuable gift Tolen; one that should never be taken lightly. If it were to fall into the wrong hands, the consequences would be dire."

Tolen looked back at Bastian. "Dire, how?"

Bastian's smile faded and he cleared his throat. "Within every Being lies the potential for greatness. But that greatness remains latent until the individual discovers their own possibilities, talents, and gifts through their experiences. A Radia shard can see the potential within its bearer before the bearers sees it within themselves. It takes that potential and magnifies it beyond imagining. Watchers were given the job of protecting and taming the shards because of our abilities to sense with such accuracy the variations in the Balance. We always know when something sinister is after the shards."

Bastian lifted his own larger shard from beneath his shirt and twisted it in his fingers. "You see, Tolen, the shard only senses greatness, it does not determine between good and evil. It is an object of power that can be used for both purposes. Can you imagine for a moment that power magnifying the strengths of creatures as inherently evil as the Raksasha—or any of the other monsters you have not even met yet, whose evil exceeds that of the Raksasha so greatly, that it is like comparing the strength of a kitten to that of a mountain lion?"

The shard seemed to heat up against his skin with the warning, as if confirming Bastian's words. Tolen was seized with the sudden desire to give the shard back to the Watcher. He looked up to see Bastian watching him closely, and his blue eye started to burn and itch.

"Bastian?"

"Yes?"

"Why does my eye freak out when I look at you? It doesn't do it all the time, just once in a while."

Bastian took a deep breath and his thick eyebrows drew together. The look made Tolen think the Watcher was deciding how much to tell him.

"Remember our conversation about the Dreamers? I told you that when your body feels a strong emotion, your life force reacts through your gifts. Because you have been taught to fear and hide your gifts—"

"I go into sensory overload. My anger channels into my abilities."

"Yes. You have been subconsciously holding your gifts back. Your eye knows what it can do and when it recognizes me as a fellow Watcher, it reacts."

Tolen rubbed his eye. "What is it supposed to do?"

"What does it do for you now?"

"Sometimes it brightens or sharpens images that are far away and sometimes when I look at you, it'll burn and pictures will flash really fast across it, but I can't tell what they are, and in the Lava Beds…I saw—well, I swear I saw Macy—"

"You saw into Macy's future when she was being held by the Phantom tree."

"Yeah."

Bastian stretched his arms above his head. "Macy told you a little about my race, did she not?"

"She said it's a group of ancient men who are responsible for guarding the Radia Shards and finding the Chosen."

"Yes, that is correct. Watchers have abilities no other race has. Our eyes link us to one another, we can see what other Watchers see when the need arises, if we allow each other in. We also have what we call our Second Sight, which allows us to sense the needs, emotions, actions, and thoughts of our Chosen wards. This extra sense gives us deep personal knowledge about our wards. It makes it almost easy to deduce what their next thoughts and actions will be. Second Sight, coupled with the ability of all Hidden kind to sense the shifts in the Balance, whether the cause of the shift is good or evil, can give a Watcher time to plan for what may be coming.

"We are not always correct, the future shifts every second with even the most infinitesimal decisions. Therefore, no one can actually *tell* the future. Watchers simply have more information to *speculate* on future events relating only to those for whom they are responsible," he tipped his head, "with almost complete accuracy." There was no arrogance in his tone.

Tolen sat up straighter. "But I *saw* what was going to happen to Macy. I saw it like a real memory, like it had already happened. It wasn't a guess. I *knew* she was going to be killed."

"That is how Second Sight works, Tolen. You *see* the outcome as it will happen based on the choices and emotions affecting the Balance at the current instant. But your actions shifted that future. Macy was not awake and making decisions. The Phantom was making the decisions. But her life force was aware of what was happening; it could feel what was happening to her body even if her mind was not conscious enough to process it."

Tolen kneaded his forehead. "That's intense."

"Yes, it is."

"You said Watchers only *see* for their wards. Does that mean I'm somehow responsible for Macy?"

"That is a complicated question Tolen, one I am not quite ready to get into yet. For one thing, you are very tired and it is bound to be a very long conversation. You have a lot to learn still. I will help you acquire the skills necessary for you to use and understand your Watcher's eye, but for now, it is more important for you to learn to shield yourself. I can sense your agitation. I think we should continue our conversation when we have both had more rest." Bastian stood and stretched.

Tolen nodded without regret. In truth, he was fine to leave the whole watching the future thing to later. It was a little huge. Instead, he thought of something else he'd like answered before the Watcher left.

"Why is Macy nice to me one minute then bites my head off the next?"

Bastian smiled at the change in conversation. "Macy is an amazing individual, with a rather tragic past. You have already guessed how her parents were murdered. The Shadows killed them the day she was chosen. I did not reach her fast enough—"

"But didn't her parents have gifts? I mean, why couldn't they fight them off?"

Bastian folded his arms across his chest, opened his mouth, closed it, opened it again, and blew out a resigned breath. "Macy is human."

"What?" Irrational disappointment burned through Tolen's chest.

"Macy is not from the Hidden race. The Radia Shards give all the Chosen their unique gifts, the ability to see servants of the Dark, as well as enhance their life force's natural ability to sense the subtle changes in the Balance—"

"Wait. You mean *human* Chosen…"

"The Chosen are *all* human."

Tolen's stomach dropped. "Except for me."

"Yes."

A sick realization pulled Tolen out of his dark thoughts. "Macy's parents couldn't fight off the Raksasha and the Shadows because they couldn't see them."

Bastian shifted his feet. "Yes. Her parents were blind to what was happening around them—paralyzed by the immense Fear they could feel, they could not even *try* to fight back…" He took a shaky breath. "I am certain you can understand how the loss of her parents would make Macy emotionally distant. She does not let people in, she does not trust easily, and she does not forgive."

He nodded at Tolen as he continued. "You, however, are the opposite. You are likeable and naturally kind. Although not ideal, you have had some semblance of family life. You grew up with a mother who loved you and doted on you. You had a loyal and caring friend…"

Bastian paused. Tolen was sure he sensed how difficult it was for him to hear about his mother and Dane. But it was true. He had had a loving mother and an incredible friend.

Macy had not.

"But Macy had you. At least she never had to wonder who or what she is."

"True, but she has not experienced a *normal* human life since her sixth birthday. I love her like she is my own flesh and blood, but I am not a parent—I am not capable of offering the same kind of love that comes from those blessed with that title. I am her Watcher, guardian, caregiver, teacher, and trainer. I have taught her the deep secrets of our origins, the truth of the Light and the evils of the Dark. I have taught her to fight and destroy Dark creatures. I have had to tell her stories and legends that would terrify the strongest of humans. I never read fairy tales with princesses or knights in shining armor to her and then tucked her into bed with a kiss on the forehead. I was never able to sooth her after a nightmare with words like 'it was only a dream.' I had to tell her the truth."

Bastian's regret pierced through every word. Tolen could not doubt the love he felt for Macy—Bastian might not believe he deserved the title *father*, but Tolen disagreed. In this area, he was envious of Macy.

Ironic. She was jealous of him because he had lived the human life, but *she* was the *human*. Macy was human.

They were not the same.

His earlier disappointment turned into an aching sadness. "I didn't know."

"Macy is a human with a pure heart. The Light chose her to protect the human race and the Radia Shard gave her the gifts she would need to do it."

Tolen thought about everything Macy had been subjected to and what his own childhood should have been like. Hot anger bubbled inside him. "Why does this have to happen?"

"You must understand, Tolen, such tragedy is brought upon our races because of the wickedness of the Dark. It is both disgusting and unjust that evil can force such desperate, but necessary, measures. Although not all stories of being Chosen are as tragic as Macy's, or yours, all have required an enormous sacrifice for the grander picture."

Tolen stared across the room, unconsciously fingering the shard around his neck. He could feel it tug him toward Macy even more strongly than it tugged him toward Bastian.

"Something else you should understand, Tolen, is that Macy has never had to relate to humans before. She does not know how to be subtle and tactful. She has led a straightforward life. I am afraid I have not taught her much in the art of diplomacy. However, underneath the harsh facade, she is one of the most incredible people in the world. Be patient with her. One day you will see the whole Macy and it will change your life."

Tolen shifted on the bed. That was a little deep.

"Destiny always is." Bastian rubbed the back of his neck and then his head turned toward Macy's curtains as if she'd called his name. "Excuse me. She is waking up." He turned and rushed back to Macy's hidden bed.

Tolen pulled his knees up and dropped his chin onto his arms. Something about Macy brought on feelings he couldn't understand. The overwhelming desire he felt to protect her and keep her safe was confusing, and a little frightening.

Macy was beautiful, terrifying, and far more equipped to be the one doing the protecting.

○○○

Macy turned on her side and groaned. She hurt everywhere.

Every muscle seemed to be on fire and every bone in her body felt like splinters poking her from the inside.

Bastian ran a huge hand across her forehead. "Would you like some more Soreah for the pain and to help you sleep?"

She bit her lip and frowned. "Maybe?"

Bastian chuckled and shook his head. "You are not admitting weakness *LaUnahi*. You have been through much. Do what your body tells you…" his smile faded. "I am so sorry."

She ignored the pain and lifted her hand to swat his arm lightly. "I told you to stop that. This isn't your fault. If anything, it's my own fault for not being able to deal with the freakin' Shadows."

He placed a finger over her lips. "And I told you no more of that."

"Then we'll both shut up about it and move on. Deal?"

Bastian shook his head again. "All right, deal." He helped her sit up and swallow the vial of Soreah medicine and a sip of water.

"Thanks." She handed him the glass and he helped her lie back down. "So where's the Ninth now?" She tried to sound like she didn't really care, which didn't work, of course, since he knew what she really felt.

Bastian feigned ignorance and answered casually. "*Tolen* is sitting across the room, quite tired after trying to learn to shield himself. Macy, it might be a good idea to start referring to him by his real name. Tolen did save your life after all."

"What?"

Bastian explained the events of her rescue while her face burned scarlet.

When he finished, she opened and closed her mouth several times before any words came out. "But that's…if it had been anything other than the Shadows…I'm still tougher…Crap." She dropped her head and sighed. "Does this mean I have to like him now?"

"Silly *LaUnahi*, you already like him." She glared as Bastian chuckled.

"But you do not have to tell him that. Although, I do believe you owe him a thank you and definitely your respect." His eyes sparkled. "I think with time you will be glad to have him as a friend. He is a good boy."

She rolled her eyes. "So, when will we be leaving?"

"Possibly a week or more. The Shadows are still roaming the coast. Tolen needs training and you are in no shape to travel just yet."

She scowled and he shrugged. It was the truth, but she hated it.

"I will let you rest. I need to see to some arrangements. I will be back to check on you shortly." He squeezed her fingers and left.

Macy stared at the curtains blocking her sight of Tolen's bed. She wasn't sure exactly how she felt about him. Yes, her feelings had softened. She understood him to a degree, at least what he was going through. She knew he was in the denial phase of his grief; that place where you focused on the here and now and didn't think any deeper than that. But it couldn't last long. Eventually, Tolen would have to come to terms with the fact that he would likely never see his mother or best friend again. It wasn't going to be pretty.

She twisted her hands in the sheets. Could she be his friend when that moment came? She had enjoyed talking to him, more than she thought she would. She'd had a freaky reaction to his touch of sympathy in the Jeep. Her Kuna had gone crazy. Heat had flooded to her palms so fast and strong she almost hadn't been able to contain it. Her body had tingled with fierce energy. She'd pulled her hand away for fear that she was about to set the truck on fire.

Helga, the Doogar healer, walked through her curtains holding a tray of food. Following behind her looking nervous was Tolen, holding his own tray. Helga situated the tray on Macy's lap.

She tried to figure out what Tolen might want. Maybe he was looking for Bastian.

"Can I join you?" His voice tripped a little and a hint of red popped on his cheeks.

She felt her own face warm. He wanted to be with her? She wasn't sure if she was ready to try out the friendship thing. She hadn't had enough time to really think about it. "Um, sure. I'm not sure where Bastian went."

"I think he was going to meet with Hander again. How are you feeling?" Tolen sat on the stool beside her bed as Helga bowed to them both and left.

He took a bite of food and looked at the floor while she answered.

Macy shook her head. Weird kid. "I'm fine—those Doogar healers are worriers."

Tolen nodded and glanced around.

The silence became awkward, the only sound chewing and swallowing. Macy wondered if he'd come in just for the company rather than because he actually had something to say.

"Are you okay?" Macy stared at him curiously. "You seem kinda tense."

He chuckled once. "All this stuff is so strange. Chosen, gifts, all of it. And being underground, relying on a crappy old watch to keep my days and nights straight is hard to get used to."

She nodded, that made sense. It took her a long time to get used to the Hidden world and she'd been a gullible kid. "It'll get easier with time. And I guess we're going to have to get used to being underground. At least for a while. Bastian says the Shadows are still roaming up and down the coast waiting for us to surface, so we can't leave anytime soon." She frowned.

Tolen barely raised his eyes to hers for a brief moment, but they were kind and warm. "You ever been to the training camp he wants to take us to?" He asked in between bites.

She blew a strand of hair out of her eye. "Nope, but it sounds awesome."

"Have you ever been to any training camps before?" Tolen bit off another piece of the hard bread.

Macy frowned and shook her head. "Only certain people are allowed." She tried to keep the hardness out of her voice.

"I wonder why I'm allowed."

Macy fidgeted with her blanket.

Tolen chuckled and the awkwardness dissipated. "It's okay. Bastian told me that when I'm ready he'll fill me in on whatever it is about my destiny you guys don't want to tell me."

She smiled, feeling relieved. "Well, that makes things a lot easier. Now when you ask me about something and I can't say, I won't have to lie."

Tolen lifted an eyebrow. "Have you been lying?"

She tilted her head and tapped her chin with her finger. "No. I don't think so."

He clenched his teeth.

"Kidding, dude. You need to lighten up."

"Right." His eyebrows drew together and she could tell she'd hit a nerve.

"Hey, sorry." She started to shift her position on the bed, but quit moving when it sent bolts of pain down her leg. "I'm not very good at this stuff. Conversations with humans…" She trailed off.

"I'm not human remember." He grinned half-heartedly and sighed when she cringed. "You're better than you think. At least you can joke about our situation. I've spent my life living in a fantasy version of a soap opera. There was a lot more drama than comedy in my house."

"Still, I know that lying is a sore spot for you. I should've kept my mouth shut."

He shrugged. "You're forgiven."

She cleared her throat. "I also owe you a thank you…for…saving my life." She felt her face grow warm again and looked away.

"I'd do it again in a heartbeat." She could tell he meant it and it sent funny flutters off in her stomach. She leaned back against the headboard and kept her face averted. How was she supposed to respond to that?

"I guess we're even now. You saved my butt back in the canyon." His tone was back to normal, so she felt comfortable looking back at him.

She smirked. "Oh buddy, we won't be even for a long time. You're not that cool yet."

He grinned, and a trace of warmth surged along her skin—much like it had when they touched in the Jeep—as he smiled. "It's a competition, then. We'll see who's the coolest by the time I finish training."

Macy raised her eyebrows, playing along. "The winner gets to choose the prize?"

"Works for me." He stood up and held out his hand. "Deal?"

Macy bit the side of her lip and slowly took his hand.

When their fingers met she thought her stomach was trying to leave her body. The warmth rushed back, pleasant and confusing.

He held her hand a little longer than necessary.

"Deal," she whispered and pulled her hand free.

CHAPTER EIGHTEEN

THE SHIELD ROOM

FOR THE LAST HOUR, TOLEN HAD PACED IN CIRCLES OUTSIDE THE INFIR-
mary, around and around the tiny antechamber, waiting for Kiad to come
for him. Helga told him after supper last night that he would be starting
his official gift training the next morning at six. Tolen had set his watch to
wake him at five, but had woken up at four-thirty and couldn't get back to
sleep. Around five, he got tired of staring at the ceiling and started pacing
the entrance.

Bastian stepped out of the infirmary and nodded at Tolen. "I will
join you at your training session as soon as I can. Hander wants to have
another meeting this morning." He grasped Tolen's shoulder before heading down the far right hall.

Tolen went back to pacing, checking his watch, and fiddling with the
shard around his neck. It was 6:05 before Kiad showed up.

He grabbed Tolen's arm just above the elbow and shook—Tolen was
beginning to recognize this as the Hidden version of a handshake—and
pointed a chubby finger at the center hall. "Training will always be down
the center hall. That way is the living and eating quarters." He gestured
to the one on the far left. "It branches off in all directions. Don't go there
unless you have someone with you. We take our privacy very serious. It is
against our code to go into the living area uninvited. The two tunnels on
the right are for workers and elders only."

"So, in other words, I can go down the center hall, and the hall on the left—if I'm invited. Other than that, stay put?"

Kiad tilted his head and nodded. "Sounds about right." He motioned for Tolen to walk with him into the hall leading to the living quarters.

"I thought we were training?"

Kiad continued walking. "Breakfast first."

Tolen swallowed back his disappointment. He didn't feel the least bit hungry. Ever since his talks with Bastian he had felt a consuming need growing within him. A need that he wanted to feed, as it overtook his grief for Dane and fueled his hope for his mother's survival. He'd come to two decisions last night as he'd lain in bed and waited for sleep to take him.

One, he *would* listen to his thoughtful heart, as his mother had called it, and his heart told him he didn't hate Bastian or Macy. If he was completely honest with himself, he did trust them. A little. They had protected him and kept their word so far.

Two, he wouldn't be a burden to Dane's people. He would do what they asked of him, work hard, and earn their respect. Dane had sacrificed so much for Tolen, not just his life, but also in their friendship. He owed it to his best friend to learn to shield and get out of here so he wouldn't bring harm to these people. Yes, he wanted their help—needed it even— but he would not be as selfish as to put them in harm's way. He wouldn't stay, at least no longer than he had a choice.

Once these decisions were set in his mind, he could think of nothing else. Even his dreams had been chaotic, filled with images of himself in candlelit rooms trying to fight while surrounded by a pearlescent bubble. He had a purpose and he was ready to start living it.

He barely noticed the room Kiad led them into until he felt eyes on him. He looked around the circular room to see at least a dozen Doogar, ranging in age from very young to very old, watching him from low stone tables carved into the sides of the cave. They seemed to have stopped talking all at once. One man had paused with his spoon halfway to his mouth. Soup dripped slowly back into his bowl.

Kiad cleared his throat and walked to a counter covered with large bowls of food—the coarse bread, yellow soup, chunks of some sort of meat, mashed potatoes—and began filling a tray. He motioned for Tolen to copy him. Tolen's discomfort made his hands shake as he filled the tray. He skipped over the large bowl of mashed potatoes, reminded forcefully of Dane. How many times had he laughed about his best friend's strange preferred breakfast of mashed potatoes on bread? A kind-faced elderly woman behind the counter smiled as she handed him a cup of water. He returned her smile with as much sincerity as he could. She patted his hand as he walked away.

Kiad led them to a table containing two men who looked to be around the same age as Kiad, probably mid-to early-thirties. "This is Deegan and Elryn," he introduced them as Tolen sat down. "They will be helping me train you."

Deegan had dark red hair, a long black beard, and cunning black eyes. Elryn was clean-shaven, his long blond hair waved down his back, and his eyes were gentler, more relaxed than Deegan's or Kiad's.

They nodded at Tolen, their faces impassive. Either they didn't really care who Tolen was, or they were good at hiding it. Whatever their reasoning, Tolen was grateful for their apparent acceptance of his presence as they began chatting with Kiad about menial tasks. Tolen was able to eat and observe without feeling pressure to contribute to the conversation.

He ate quickly, bouncing his knee absentmindedly until the others finally finished and stood up. Kiad motioned with his hand for Tolen to follow and the three Doogar led the way down one of the many tunnels away from the cafeteria, Tolen assumed back toward the training rooms.

The tunnel twisted and turned, and twice they veered down a side tunnel, until Tolen was utterly lost. Finally, after about ten minutes of tunnels that all looked the same, they entered another open area with five tunnels branching in different directions. Above each tunnel entrance, Tolen noticed a symbol with strange writing beneath it. With a start, he realized he could read it.

Beneath a symbol that looked sort of like a crescent moon in the center of a circle it read, *Elemental.* The other symbols he couldn't quite decipher, but the words were fairly clear. Two read *Armaments,* one *Metaphysical,* and one *Assessment.* Although the names were pretty self-explanatory, Tolen was grateful when Kiad explained in more detail.

"While you are here, we will work on different aspects of your gifts. The most important goal, however, being your shield. Our Sphere will always be nearby to shield you as you practice, so the Dark will not sense you when you are increasing your powers, but the sooner you can do this yourself the more effective your training will be." He pointed to the metaphysical room. "In the morning, after breakfast and before lunch, you will work on your shield in here. After lunch you will alternate between the Armaments and Elemental rooms, where you will learn basic sparring techniques and how to recognize and use some of your gifts."

Tolen nodded. "Why only some?"

Kiad stroked his chin. "There are only a few trainers here who know enough about a few other gifts aside from Télora to effectively teach you."

"Okay." Tolen felt the men watching him and cleared his throat. "Sounds good. So, in here first?" He walked toward the Metaphysical room, but Kiad put a hand on his arm to stop him.

Tolen paused and looked at the men's serious faces. "I'm sorry. Am I doing something wrong?"

Kiad shook his head, but it was Elryn who spoke. "We must warn's you before you's begin. Yesterday, you's tested your shield in a normal room so that Kiad could be getting a feels for your strength. Today you's will be in a special room, blessed and created by our people with a specific purpose. You's must clear your mind before you's enter, and only be entering when your purpose is set and in line with what's is to take place within the room. This room can read your heart, just as the door of the Binithan can. It will sense if your purpose is not what it should be and will either trap you's inside or lock you's out."

Tolen looked at the innocent looking doorway and felt the hair on his neck stand up. *Okay, creepy.*

"You must take a moment and prepare your mind before you enter." Deegan spoke in a low gravelly voice.

Tolen nodded and closed his eyes. He needed to learn how to shield himself. That was his purpose, right? He opened his eyes and looked at the men. They raised their eyebrows and motioned him forward. He walked toward the entrance, but the closer he got the more he felt something holding him back, as if invisible hands were grabbing onto him. He paused just outside the door and tried to step through, but his foot met an unseen barrier. His heart sank. What had he done wrong?

He glanced back at the men and shrugged, feeling stupid. "I guess I'm doing it wrong."

Kiad walked around Tolen in a slow circle. "What did you think of when you closed your eyes?"

Tolen swallowed. "I thought about how I need to learn to shield myself."

Elryn shook his head. "You's have to go deeper than that. Think deeper. What's does a shield mean to you? Why's are you's needing it? Why is it important? Your heart must speak to the room, not your mind."

Tolen looked away from the little men. Between what Bastian and these men expected, he was beginning to realize that tapping into this person he was supposed to be was not going to be easy. It was requiring him to delve into a place within himself he had always tried to avoid. For so long he had just been going through the motions, living a fake life, hiding his fears and worries, just existing, not allowing himself to really feel.

Everything Bastian had asked him to do—listen to his heart, feel the pull from his abilities rather than fight it—and now the Doogar, feel, feel, feel…Did any of them realize how difficult this was for him? It seemed that for Hidden kind all they did was feel and follow their emotions. This concept was as foreign to Tolen as playing video games would be to these men.

"Can I get a minute alone?" Tolen asked softly.

They didn't answer, but slowly left the opening and disappeared down the tunnel they'd come from.

Tolen leaned on the wall beside the door he was supposed to enter, slid down to the floor, and pulled his knees to his chest. If he couldn't just think about what he wanted, he had to *feel* it, then it was going to require a lot more focus and a willingness to retrain his way of doing things. He would do it because he had to, but if he understood what the men were saying, he was going to have to do it because he *wanted* to. He had to *desire* it.

How?

He thought back on Elryn's advice. *You's have to go deeper than that. Think deeper. What's does a shield mean to you? Why's are you needing it? Why is it important? Your heart must speak to the room, not your mind.*

He pinched the bridge of his nose. *What does a shield mean to me?* He thought about the purpose of a shield. It protects a life force from detection, but it also protects those around you. Because if you bring the Dark in, no one around you is safe either. *What does a shield mean to me? It means protection from evil for others and myself.*

He felt a subtle shift in the air beside him, as if the barrier were thinning. He focused harder. *Why do I need a shield? Because right now I am a danger to others and myself. I do not want to endanger or burden the people here.*

The dirt floor outside the room stirred slightly.

Why is it important? Because without it I'm a sitting duck.

He felt no change with the air and figured this answer must not have been good enough. He tried for deeper. *Why is it important?* An unwelcome lump tried to force its way into his throat as the truth rose to the surface. *Because without it…I am dangerous.*

A burst of air shot into the anteroom, covering Tolen with dust. He coughed and stood up. Flickers of light danced through the entrance and across his face. All the other rooms remained dark. He paused outside the door and looked inside. The circular room was lit with flaming torches along the walls, but was otherwise empty. The ceiling disappeared into the darkness above the flames.

Tolen glanced over his shoulder, wondering if he should go in or wait for the men to return. His curiosity won out and he lifted his foot to step into the room. For a split second before his foot passed through the barrier, he felt a spasm of fear. What if he ended up locked in here? But once he passed through the door, the fear left and it seemed as if his purpose became more solid. He did want to get stronger. He didn't want to be a danger to anyone—at least not anyone associated with the Light.

He looked around the room to see the walls were painted with fading hieroglyphs and more symbols that matched those above the doors. The room felt warm, comfortable, and safe.

"Good job."

Tolen jumped. Kiad's voice seemed to shatter the gentle calm in the room.

"Thanks. It wasn't as easy as I thought it would be." He cleared his throat. "Thanks for letting me have a minute to figure it out."

Kiad nodded. "I realize I was unfair in my testing of you yesterday. You must forgive me. We are not used to someone your age in the Hidden being so ignorant. Today will be different. I will explain more before I ask you to try something. We will begin as if you are one of our children."

It was an insult, but Tolen knew it was only the truth as the little man saw it, so he tried not to be overly offended. He squared his shoulders. "I'm a fast learner. Let's get started."

Elryn smirked, but the other two remained stoic and only nodded.

"Stand in the center of the room." Kiad explained. "Elryn, Deegan, and I will stand around you in a triangle, creating a circle of power with you at its center. First, we will teach you to recognize our vibrations as they affect the Balance."

"But, doesn't that mean you'll be dropping your shields?"

"Yes, but the Sphere of the Binithan protects us. All those of age who have mastered their shields keep them in place so as not to further burden the Sphere, but she protects the children and visitors who come in need of healing, as well as those who train in this room. We will be safe."

Tolen gave a nervous nod. "Okay."

The three men stood around Tolen about four feet away. Elryn and Deegan closed their eyes and bowed their heads. Kiad waited for Tolen to look at him before he spoke. "Tolen, every life force in this world gives off a vibration, a signal of their inner energy. Each signal is as unique as the person is and so differs slightly. Nevertheless, the strength of the Light or the Dark within the Being is very distinct in the way it affects the signal. This is why, with time, you will be able to tell how many people, or creatures, are in a room before you enter, and how many of them are filled with light or darkness.

"Think back over your life to two people you have been in contact with that have had a lasting impression on you, not because of what you knew about them, but because of what you felt the first moment you met them. Think of one who you knew was good and one you knew was bad—in that first moment."

Tolen thought over his past. His first thought was of Dane and his heart clenched. The first moment Dane showed up at school and took the desk next to his, Tolen could feel his goodness. He radiated kindness. It took him a minute to think of someone who brought on the opposite.

Finally he remembered one man he'd encountered once when he was nine years old. They'd been living in California at the time and they'd stopped at a gas station. He'd been standing beside the rows of candy while she ran to use the bathroom. He distinctly remembered hearing the door chime and seeing a man walk into the store wearing a gray hooded sweatshirt, but it was his eyes that Tolen could remember most. For a split second, he'd glanced Tolen's way with the most hate -filled eyes Tolen had ever seen.

The man laid his money on the counter to pay for his gas, turned, and left. That was all. But Tolen had stood there shaking until his mother returned. He no longer wanted candy and begged his mother to let them leave. She quickly paid for their gas and they left. It took him two days to tell her what had happened, and even then, he felt afraid to even talk about the man who had done nothing. His mother had always used her abilities to sense the character of people they didn't know before she let them in their house, or let them teach Tolen at school, but this was the first time he could remember being grateful she had this ability. For a long time after the incident, he made her check before he would set foot in a public place.

Had he been sensing vibrations all along?

Kiad tilted his head. "I can see you remember. Now, I want you to go beyond the memory, deeper into it. Remember what you felt with the good person. How did you feel?"

Tolen took a deep breath. "I felt happy, safe."

Kiad nodded. "Good. And with the second?"

Tolen shivered involuntarily as he thought again how he'd felt that day. "Afraid, weak—almost helpless."

Kiad nodded gravely this time. "Yes, yes. The Light inspires feelings of peace, contentment, trust. Your life force was drawn to the goodness in the other person. The Dark does the opposite, unless you are dark yourself. It provokes feelings of despair, fear, weakness. The weaker it makes you feel, the more it is drawn to you as prey."

Tolen shivered again. Having it pointed out like that, he could see the reality of it. He could also see, as he thought back over the people he'd met through his life, how everyone had varying degrees of light and darkness in them. Jeff Macro wasn't as dark as the man in the gas station had been, but he hadn't had a lot of light either.

"Now that you recognize how each makes you feel, Light and Dark, you can train yourself to be more aware of the vibes so that you can sense things, Being or creature, before you even see them."

"That makes sense."

Kiad nodded his approval. "Now that you understand, you will test it. Memorize where we stand."

Tolen regarded the men. Kiad stood in front of him. Deegan at his left and Elryn at his right. He nodded. "Okay."

"Close your eyes and keep them closed. Focus on each of us in turn. Sense the light and darkness within us."

Tolen focused first on Kiad, it took a moment, but then he could feel when the little man dropped his shield. Warmth, power, and greatness flowed from him. Not necessarily kindness as he'd felt with Dane, but not cruelty either. More serious than Dane, but wise and good. There was very little darkness in him.

He turned toward Deegan, but Tolen almost opened his eyes when Deegan dropped his shield. There was a more equal balance of darkness and light in Deegan, but he was measured and in control of his darkness. He too was powerful, but much more aware of it. His arrogance fed the darkness within him. Tolen turned away from him quickly. Elryn had to be the closest to what he'd felt with Dane. There was barely a trace of darkness in him. He was humble, kind, and a tiny bit mischievous. Tolen could picture them being friends.

"Keep your eyes closed." Kiad said. "We are going to shield and move. When you feel us again, point to where you believe we are, and say our names. Press your palms together and push your energy out into your hands. Sometimes it helps."

Tolen wasn't sure how to do what he asked, but he put his palms together anyway, and was surprised when it helped him relax and focus. It felt weird when their shields went up, almost as if he was suddenly alone. One by one, their life forces reappeared.

It took him several minutes but eventually he got it right. They put him through the drill four more times and he was surprised how tired he was getting.

"One last exercise and then we will break for lunch." Kiad handed Tolen a water skin and waited while Tolen drank his fill. "It is time you recognize your own vibrations, your own power. Only then can you learn how to hide it from the Balance. Creatures of pure Light or pure Dark cannot hide from the Balance. Their vibrations are too strong. They can be shielded by others—good Spheres or bad—but they themselves cannot shield. As you learn to recognize your own vibrations, you can hide them."

Tolen didn't really like the idea of finding his own darkness.

Kiad seemed to know his train of thought. "We cannot, and should not try, to recognize our own darkness, or our own light for that matter. You will only feel for your body's unique signal. Once you learn to recognize it you can learn to block it from affecting the Balance."

"Block it how?"

Deegan tapped his thick fist on his thigh. "Have you ever noticed how a detailed picture looks different in sunlight versus artificial light?" he asked in his gravelly voice. "How the colors change and you see things you hadn't noticed before?"

Tolen nodded. "Sure."

"Did the picture change or just your perception?"

"Just my perception."

"As you learn your signal, you will learn how to send out other signals, other *pictures* around your own to disguise it. To change the way it *feels*."

"So, it's kind of like I'm hiding behind other pictures?"

Deegan folded his arms and nodded once. "A *shield* of pictures, or *feelings*. But in order for it to work, you have to be able to hold your power inside, only letting it out when you need to use it. No matter how good a shield is, it cannot block strong uses of power."

Tolen's eyes narrowed. "I think I'm starting to get it. My life force is still there affecting the Balance, but if I learn to shield, I can confuse the signal enough to not be detected, unless I'm actually using my abilities."

Kiad's answering smile lifted Tolen's confidence, until the next words left his mouth. "If you thought recognizing vibes was hard, just wait until you try to create false ones to hide behind. You're in for a real test today."

CHAPTER NINETEEN

SPARRING WITH THE ELEMENTS

"It's not going to happen Bastian, so you can stop pestering me." Macy held back a grimace as she tugged on her socks. She wasn't about to let him see how much pain she was in. She probably would have let the Sphere here heal her, but she wasn't healing anyone these days, not since the three of them showed up and she had to focus all her strength to guard this place *and* hide Tolen. But let Tolen heal her? No. It set a bad precedent. He probably already saw her as a wimp after everything that happened. She would show him and Bastian that she could get by just fine. She would even walk to the cafeteria for lunch and prove to Bastian that she was perfectly capable. She just wished she didn't have to use the stupid cane.

"You are being stubborn. Tolen did not understand enough to fully ask your body to heal before. The bones are reset, but they are not completely healed. The muscle tissue is still severely bruised. He knows more now. If you would just let him finish your healing—"

Her glare made him snap his mouth shut, but the exasperated look didn't leave his eyes.

"I'm fine. I'll be good as new in a few days. Besides, you said Tolen needs some time to train anyway. What's the sudden hurry?" She tugged on her boots and had to bite her tongue to keep from groaning. Spots danced in front of her eyes and she knew Bastian wouldn't miss the reformed curses echoing through her mind, but he just shook his head in frustration. He knew her well enough to know no amount of pushing would get her to do something she didn't want to.

"I am not in a hurry."

She raised her eyebrow at him and he amended. "Not exactly. It is important that we not stay too long and endanger the people here unnecessarily, but it is vital that Tolen learn what the Doogar can teach him before we get above ground and face what waits for us."

"Okay, for starters, when you're ready to leave I won't hold us back. I'll be fine, but what exactly is up there waiting for us? I can feel that the Shadows aren't nearby, so what is it?"

He paused and she resisted the urge to pinch his arm, something she hadn't done since she was a small child.

"The DéHool are still hunting. Hander has sent scouts above and they have seen traces of them, but have not been able to find them. There are also indications that small bands of Raksasha and Kinchomen have been lurking about."

Macy tugged her fingers through her tangled hair until Bastian handed her a brush. She absently pulled it through the mess as she thought about what he'd said. DéHool were the biggest concern. The *only* concern as far as she could see. Raksasha were easily dealt with, and Kinchomen were small lizard-like creatures that were more known for causing chaos and disorder than real mayhem. They were probably only there to help disguise the presence of the DéHool. "As long as we exit in an area that the DéHool haven't been seen, we really don't have much to worry about, right?"

"Actually, the fact that it does not seem we have much to worry about is what has me the most worried." He held out a rubber band and watched as Macy tied it in her hair, but his mind was elsewhere. "The Dark knows Tolen is the Ninth. It worked very hard to stop us in the Lava Beds. It knows we came in here, but it has yet to try and destroy the Lava Beds to get to the Binithan."

"Yeah, but with their Sphere blocking Tolen's power, the Dark wouldn't know if he was still here or not. They'd be tipping their hand without all the cards." She snatched the wooden cane from where it sat propped against the bedside table and used it and the bed to stand up. Bastian held out a hand to help, but she shook her head. "It doesn't really make sense for them to attack this place does it? It's too well protected. Unless they know without a doubt that he's still here."

Bastian sighed. "That is Hander's argument as well."

She took a hesitant step forward and pain shot through her thigh. Her breath came out in a whoosh and Bastian grabbed her arm, wrapped it around his waist, and dropped his other arm around her shoulders supporting the majority of her weight.

He continued their conversation as if he hadn't done anything, allowing her to keep her wounded dignity. "He too believes that the Dark has ceased its search for now in this place and has shifted to the known exits of the Binithan. He also believes that if we leave through a secret exit, we should be safe."

Macy looked up at him from under his arm, ignoring the sweat beading on her face and running down her back at the effort to use even this tiny amount of strength. If she didn't get a handle on this, she'd have to eat her words. "Okay, so what is it you know that we don't?"

Bastian shook his head and lifted her so her feet barely touched the ground, giving the illusion that she was still walking, though they both knew she wasn't. She wished she didn't have to go along with it. "It is not knowledge, but confusion that has me worried. It is flashes of a vague future, distorted and impossible to unravel. It is a *feeling.*"

A shiver rolled across Macy's shoulders. If there was one thing she trusted more than anything, it was Bastian's *feelings.* He was never wrong. She took a deep breath as he reached the doorway to the cafeteria. "Well…I guess we'll just have to take it as it comes and prepare for anything."

He squeezed her arm gently and helped her sit at a table nearest the doorway. Two tiny women rushed to fuss over Macy while a third brought her a tray of food. As hungry as she'd been ten minutes ago, her conversation with Bastian had left her stomach feeling hollow. What would they face when they left this place?

Tolen walked toward the cafeteria on shaky legs. Kiad hadn't been kidding when he said it would be a lot harder to recognize his own *signal*. Yesterday he'd told him to focus on the power he felt as he'd healed his hand and bring it back in. The exercises Kiad had him doing today felt nothing like that. He stepped into the cafeteria and got in line behind Deegan. Something made him want to turn and look back at the entrance. He followed the urge and noticed Macy sitting alone, eating. His stomach gave a funny flip and he realized his shard had pulled his attention her way.

A satisfied smile lifted his lips seeing her sitting at the table rather than propped up in bed. He loaded his tray with food and made his way over to her. Her eyes lit up when he approached and his stomach flipped again. She seemed *happy* to see him. The thought warmed him and he felt more relaxed as he pointed to the seat across from her. "Can I join you?"

She nodded and slid her tray closer to her. "Sure."

"Where's Bastian?" He asked as he folded his long legs beneath the table.

Macy lifted her chin toward the other side of the room. Tolen followed the gesture to see Bastian sitting at one of the low tables, his legs stretched out to the side, deep in conversation with a group of fierce looking Doogar.

"Who are they?" He asked, taking in the men's haggard appearances, rough clothing, and tangled hair and beards.

Macy took a sip of water. "Doogar scouts and trackers."

Something triggered in Tolen's memory as he watched the men. Bastian said Hank, or Handrak, Dane's father, was a Doogar tracker. A famous one at that. His appearance definitely matched that of the men with Bastian. Tolen wondered if they liked the alcohol as much as Hank did, or if it was the outdoor life making them appear so rough.

"So, how's training going?" Macy interrupted his musing and he turned back to see her watching him with curiosity as she ate.

Tolen shrugged and picked up a piece of bread. "Okay I guess."

Macy acknowledged this with a perceptive nod. "It's a lot harder than you thought it would be, huh?"

"Oh yeah." He twisted the bread in his hands. "A heck of a lot harder."

"You're working on your shield in the mornings, right?"

Tolen nodded. "Yep."

She looked away and nibbled a piece of meat. "That makes sense. It's going to be the hardest for you to learn, so it'll tax you mentally. Their saving your physical energy for sparring and gift training."

When she spoke, a tiny, barely visible, dimple appeared beside her lip he'd never noticed before. It made her seem even more childlike, innocent—and increased his weird desire to protect her. He cleared his throat and shoved the bread in his mouth. They ate silently for a few minutes until he noticed the cafeteria emptying and his mouth went dry.

He wanted to learn how to use his abilities, so going to the next training session shouldn't be making him nervous. He should be excited. But this morning had taught him that, as much as he wanted it, it was going to be the hardest thing he'd ever done. Harder than calculus. Harder than working part-time and worrying about his sick mother. Harder even than it had been to keep silent about his abilities, and hold them back.

More than ever before, he had something he wanted to succeed at, and was terrified of failing.

Macy slid to the edge of the bench, and grabbed a cane. Tolen slid out and offered a hand. "Can I help you?"

Macy glared at him, but quickly tried to soften the look. "No, I'm good thanks." She cleared her throat. "I wasn't going to leave yet anyway." She tapped the cane against the table and Tolen sat down, holding back a smile at her cover up. She wasn't about to admit she needed help, especially to him.

"What are you going to do this afternoon?" He asked.

She tipped her head. "Sit in the infirmary bored out of my mind, I guess."

"You could come watch me train." He spoke without thinking, then immediately wanted to take it back.

She looked at him with narrowed eyes. "You wouldn't mind?"

Tolen shrugged, but kept his eyes on the table so they wouldn't give him away. "Bastian said he was going to come, so I don't think it's a secret thing." His heart pounded as he waited for her response. She was smart and gifted. She knew what Chosen were supposed to be like. She could help him, but she also intimidated him.

"It does sound a lot more fun than sitting in the infirmary. I've never seen Doogar fight before." She smiled and he found himself getting lost in her tiny moment of joy. Her dimple became more prominent and her eyes danced in anticipation. As nervous as he was, he couldn't stamp on her excitement.

"Okay, cool." He saw Kiad get up and walk their way. "Well, it looks like I've got to go. So…I guess I'll see you in a bit." He gave a small forced smile, and her answering grin turned his own to genuine.

"Great. See you in a few." She waved. "Bye."

Tolen chuckled, feeling happier than he had in days, the guilt was still there, and the need, but for that tiny moment it was balanced. "Bye."

He followed the three men out the door with lighter steps, his earlier weakness forgotten, replaced with a drive to get going. He just hoped that he wouldn't embarrass himself in front of Macy. He thought of her dimpled smile and his stomach flipped again.

He paused outside the entrance to the Elemental room, but it was easier this time to get in. His reasons for wanting to learn these abilities were not much different than needing to learn his shield. He hardly felt the barrier this time. Within seconds of thinking of his desire, the torches flickered on and he stepped inside. Kiad, Deegan, and Elryn followed, conversing silently.

Tolen walked around the room to look at the series of murals on the walls. Unlike the hieroglyphs in the Metaphysical room, which consisted of symbols and words, these depicted the various elemental gifts, the *Eight* that Bastian had told him about. There were illustrations of whirlwinds, growing mountains, blazing fire, great waves of water, shafts of bright light, sprouting vines, running animals of every kind, and a smeared image that must be showing the gift of the unseen. What'd he call them? It was something like dice, but Tolen couldn't remember exactly. It'd been a lot to take in.

"Dicernan." Bastian said from behind, and Tolen turned to see him settling Macy in a tiny chair just inside the entrance. Her cheeks were pink, but Tolen wasn't sure if it was because she was embarrassed about being coddled, or if it was from the effort to walk to the room. She seemed winded, but determined to appear normal.

Tolen met her eye for a moment, but she quickly turned her attention to something in her lap. Her scabbard. She unsheathed her knife and started sharpening it by the glow of the torches.

Bastian moved to Tolen's side and pointed to the mural. Tolen turned his attention back, ignoring the unfamiliar tingle of pleasure he felt at seeing Macy. This Chosen stuff was weird.

"This is the depiction of the Dicernan. The *Unseen.*"

"What does that mean?" Tolen let his curiosity take over.

"The Dicernan have the ability to create a shield so powerful that not only are they hidden from the Balance, but they are hidden from every form of detection, even physical sight."

"Whoa. How is that even possible?"

"That Tolen, is a very good question, and one you will probably have to get answered by another Dicernan. It is a gift I myself have never studied." He gave Tolen an apologetic smile. "But do not worry. You may not learn how to use this gift here, but the time will come when we *will* find someone who can teach you."

Kiad walked over, looked up at Bastian, and held out his arm. "We're all set. Are you ready to begin?"

Bastian shook Kiad's arm. "I am."

"Wait, you're training me?" Tolen didn't mean for it to come out harsh. He really had decided to trust Bastian and let him teach him, he just thought he'd be learning other stuff before he had to learn the Watcher's eye thing.

"We will not be training in your Watcher abilities today, Tolen. That will come later, possibly much later." He added at the relieved look Tolen could feel on his face. "Today the Doogar and I feel there is something more important I can help you with, that relates directly to your feelings toward me."

Tolen swallowed. That didn't sound good.

"We need to address your anger," Kiad said. "If you are to learn how to connect to your gifts the right way."

Tolen frowned. This *really* didn't sound like a good idea.

"You have nothing to fear," Bastian said calmly. "This will be a lesson in understanding and focus. Not a reprimand."

Tolen nodded but still felt uncomfortable. He glanced toward Macy to see she had paused in her sharpening, but kept her head down, obviously trying to listen without appearing to. He looked away and felt his muscles tighten.

Bastian pointed to the center of the room and waited for Tolen to lead the way there before stopping to stand in front of him. The Doogar completed the circle on all sides with Tolen at the center, same as in the shield training. Kiad had said it created a circle of power with Tolen at the center. He didn't have a chance to ask what it meant before Bastian started speaking.

"Anger in itself is not a terrible thing," Bastian lifted his hand at the shock this raised in Tolen's thoughts. "It is true. Anger has its purpose, as does every emotion. Anger is a signal to our mind that something is wrong and is in need of a resolution. How we choose to resolve the problem decides whether our anger can help or hinder us. Anger, Tolen, is always the secondary emotion. It is the reaction to the cause. In order for you to control your anger, you must look deeper and get at its root. This way, when you are faced with anger in the future, you can know how to work through it."

Kiad spoke from Tolen's left. "We will teach you to step back from the moment and channel your feelings the right way."

Tolen pushed his shaky hands into his pockets. "How?"

"Tiny exercises."

"O…kay?" Something about the way Kiad said tiny made him nervous, like he was being sarcastic.

"Tolen," Bastian regained his attention. "The first onslaught of anger lasts but a few seconds, from that point on it is you feeding the anger that keeps it there. Often just taking the time to count to ten, or recite a few preplanned words in your mind, or imagining yourself somewhere else, can defuse the anger and reveal its cause, allowing you to come up with a better solution. Before the Doogar begin, I want you to think of these three things and how you could use them in an intense situation."

Tolen thought about how he used to deal with intense situations; he escaped into the Dreamer's world. He was determined not to do that anymore, so he pondered Bastian's techniques. He knew counting to ten wouldn't work for him, he'd tried that before at his mother's suggestion and it hadn't worked in the slightest.

Recite something? But what? A few words from his mother's favorite poem popped into his mind. *I am the captain of my soul.* Shivers ran down his arms. These words made complete sense. He was the captain of his soul. Bastian told him he had a choice in his fate. Well, if he had a choice in his fate, didn't that also mean he had a choice in his reactions as well?

If he could learn to control them that is.

I am the captain of my soul. He looked up at Bastian to see a hint of a smile on his face. Okay, he was on the right track.

What about an imaginary place? Where would he want to be if he could whisk away to some made-up place? A tiny face with a dimpled smile popped in his head, and he pictured himself sitting at a table chatting with Macy. Not one of the tables here, but like the ones at school. They were talking and laughing like normal teenage kids. The image brought warmth to his fingers and he clenched his fists tighter in his pockets. He peeked at Bastian to see his smile had turned to a look of concern.

He jumped out of this thought and went back to reciting the words. "Okay, I think I know what to do."

Deegan mumbled, "Now comes the hard part."

Elryn chuckled.

Kiad shushed them and met Tolen's gaze. "I need you to go back to a time when your anger caused you to do something with your gifts that you regret. Something..." his eyes were apologetic, "painful."

Tolen felt Macy's eyes on him and he knew she would know this one. It was the time the trees had hurt his mother. Tears burned the back of his throat and he couldn't meet Kiad's eyes.

"Don't focus on the reaction. Try to remember the feeling before the reaction."

"All I remember was anger," Tolen said through his teeth.

"Why were you angry?"

"Because I hated being different." And there it was. He didn't know how he suddenly recognized it, he just did, he could remember perfectly. Before the anger built, he felt a shift in the center of his body, a warming up, a growth of power. Once the anger took over, he unintentionally fed the power *with* the anger, until the two became an unstoppable force—directed at whomever he blamed for making him angry. As the realization flooded over him he felt the warmth in his center growing, but he still didn't know how to control it, or direct it.

Kiad spoke quickly, "Say the word *tin'ruhl*."

"*Tin'ruhl!*" As the word burst from his lips, a wall of dirt shot up from the ground, surrounded him, knocked him off his feet, and then the warmth subsided. "Is everyone okay?" He jumped up and shouted at them through the wall.

He heard Elryn chuckle again.

"Touch the wall and ask it to remove," Kiad called.

As soon as Tolen's fingers brushed the dirt and the thought left his mind, the walls crumbled to his feet. He looked around in awe and excitement. Had he really just done that?

Macy was no longer sharpening her knife but looked as shocked as he felt.

Kiad smiled. "Well, Tolen, I think you just found your signal."

Tolen looked down at his hands in amazement.

"Now that you know what to look for, you can call on it." Kiad lifted both hands. "But, I recommend waiting until we can teach you more words and you practice managing your anger, this way when you are faced with a dangerous situation you will know how to act, instead of react."

"Cool. What do I get to try next?"

Elryn laughed louder with a mischievous glint in his eye. "You's might be wishing you hadn't asked. Now we get to make you's angry."

ooo

"He's is dangerous." Hander filled Bastian's cup before sitting across from him at the tiny table in his living quarters.

Bastian nodded once. "He is the Ninth."

"He's is a child with huge amounts of power he does not know's how to control. The more he learns the more dangerous he's is becoming." Hander sipped from his mug and eyed Bastian with speculation. "Are you sure he's is not better off, not knowing what's he is capable of?"

Bastian set his mug on the table and leveled his eyes with the tiny man in front of him. "We did not choose his destiny, Hander. The Light did. We can choose to honor that choice, and do all we can to remedy the problems created by his parents' choices, or we can go against the Light."

Hander clicked his tongue. "That's is not fair, Watcher."

"It is the truth."

Hander glanced over Bastian's shoulder, his eyes unfocused. "Truth yes, but not's altogether reassuring." He looked back at Bastian and stroked his beard. "Continue's teaching him the simple words only, and elementary sparring. I's afraid if you's teach him too much, our Shield will not be able to block's him. She is struggling all's ready."

Bastian stood and bowed. "I understand. Two weeks at most, and we will leave."

"But the girl is not's healed."

"I have a plan to try and fix that."

Chapter Twenty

Doogar, Daggers, and Decisions

Macy rolled her sucker stick between her teeth, and hobbled into the training room for her usual afternoon pastime, watching Tolen practice.

A pattern had started over the last three days. She exercised in the morning, ate lunch with Tolen—sometimes Bastian joined them, sometimes Elryn, and sometimes they were left alone—then she watched Tolen train in the afternoon.

It didn't feel as awkward to be alone with him as it used to. He'd relaxed quite a bit around her and she found that he actually had an interesting personality. He was a deep thinker. He really believed that his mother was still alive somewhere and he was determined to learn all he could about his gifts, get good enough to try and find her, *and* save his father. He was still in pain over his friend's death, but he'd buried it beneath the drive to save his parents. He asked many questions about the Chosen, and she started to feel that he was beginning to accept his new life, despite not being told everything and even though he still wouldn't admit his abilities were gifts. He was even getting a handle on his anger whenever the Doogar schemed it out of him.

However, something still made her nervous around him and she couldn't quite pinpoint what. Sometimes she would catch him staring at her, and when their eyes met, her insides would do funny things. She felt drawn to him in ways she couldn't understand. She felt anxious to see him whenever they were apart, and she found herself often thinking of the way he looked when they talked, how his weird eyes would sparkle whenever she laughed or smiled, and how her Kuna would sometimes just zing to her fingers when he showed up in the same room as her. None of it made sense and it made her uncomfortable.

She tried ignoring him, focusing on the physical therapy the Doogar healers wanted her to do every morning, and finding things to stay busy in the afternoons. She always found herself hurrying through her mornings to get to lunch at the same time he would be there, and wandering back to wherever he was supposed to be in the afternoon. She'd even caught herself pacing the infirmary after dinner, waiting for him to return from cleaning up so they could chat before Bastian made them go to bed.

She wondered if she was going crazy. Maybe being underground was messing with her head.

Yet once again, here she was, crashing in on his training session, watching his every move, secretly enjoying the way her fingers warmed and her heart picked up when he noticed her entrance and smiled.

She mentally shook herself, pulled the mangled stick out of her mouth and fished in her pocket for a fresh sucker before settling onto her usual spot on the floor.

Tolen called up a wall of dirt in the middle of the floor, and her stomach did a somersault. It looked so cool!

Tolen lifted his hand and the wall collapsed under his touch. The little warriors patted him on the back. Tolen looked over at her and she gave him thumbs up. Heat trickled down her arms and her fingers tingled. Her face burned with the reaction of her Kuna and she looked away.

"Little one?" Kiad walked up beside her. Though it was obvious he'd spent more time among humans by his clearer speech, he obviously hadn't picked up on addressing people the right way. He had been calling her "little one" since they arrived. She thought it was a bit much considering she was still taller than most of the Doogar, including him. Bastian said it wasn't an insult; they were referring to the fact that she was so much smaller than Bastian or Tolen. This didn't stop it from being annoying.

She pulled the sucker from her mouth. "Yeah?"

"Are you feeling well enough to join us?"

She grinned. "Really?"

Kiad nodded. "Bastian wants you to practice. Your healers have given it the okay as long as we take it easy on you." His eyes glittered with suppressed humor.

Macy clenched her teeth and stood up from the floor, ignoring the pain in her leg, and tried not to limp to the center of the room. She stuffed her sucker back in her mouth.

Tolen looked over, raised his eyebrows, and smiled.

Her pulse rose. His smile was really nice. His pale blue eye, something that at first had wigged her out, was actually a perfect contrast to his dark brown eye. Gold from the light of the Binithan streaked his wavy chocolate hair where it touched his collar. Pretty soon he'd need a ponytail like Bastian. She chuckled at the thought.

Tolen's smile turned quizzical and she stopped laughing. She'd totally been staring! She cleared her throat and looked away.

Kiad passed around wooden bows, arrows, and small curved wooden daggers. "A Doogar blade is extremely sharp. As Tolen has never used one before, we have been practicing with these." He handed Macy the piece of wood.

It looked like a toy.

Kiad turned to Tolen. "We will try to improve your accuracy later with the bow and arrow. For now, we will continue with the dagger. By the time you leave you shall know enough of the basics to aid yourself in battle, should the need arise before you reach the camp."

"Why do I need weapons? Wouldn't it be better to use my abilities?" Tolen twisted the wooden dagger in his hands.

Macy snorted. "Dude, haven't you felt what happens to you when you use your gifts? You're exhausted, right?"

Tolen raised his eyebrows. "It does drain me a little bit."

"Well if you're using *only* your gifts in a fight, it's going to drain you *a lot*. Remember how long you slept after we got here?"

His jaw flexed and he nodded.

She was being rude again but what else could she say? She bit hard on her sucker. *It's the truth.*

"Well, you don't have to be so obnoxious about it," Tolen snapped.

Macy's sucker fell out of her mouth. She hadn't said the last comment aloud.

Kiad looked between them with a curious expression. "Little one is right. Your gifts should be your last resort. As we have discussed in your shield lessons, it is almost impossible to keep your life force shielded from the Dark when you are exerting your power. The Balance is affected the most when you are at your peak, which draws more creatures to you. You are much better off trying to deflect, or kill, as many creatures as you can before you resort to your gifts."

Tolen shifted his feet. "Sometimes the trees act without my asking. Does that mean I'm using my ability without realizing it?"

Kiad cocked his head to the side and eyed Tolen shrewdly. "Maybe. It is possible that your connection with nature is strong enough that it is aware of your emotions and needs and reacts of its own free will. For now, I would suggest you try to pay attention to your thoughts as you fight and make sure you are not asking for help from any outside force."

Macy remembered Ardia. Some trees were definitely helping Tolen by their own choice.

"Okay." Tolen ran his hand through his hair and tugged on his collar.

Kiad paired them up. Elryn stood on a table to spar with Tolen. Macy paired up with Deegan. Kiad walked between them giving pointers, showing them specific moves and counter attacks.

Macy was sweating twenty minutes into the mock fight. Her weak body made her angry. Deegan moved in and she tried to slide under his arm, but her knee gave out and she ended up barely rolling out of the way of his strike. Heart pounding, anger building at her weakness, she knew she had one shot to win this fight before she collapsed.

She pushed what remaining strength she had down to her lower body, jumped up off the floor, ran up the wall, and pushed off to come down on Deegan with a kill stroke. Deegan fell to his back and raised his palm in defeat. She stumbled past him, dropped her knife to the dirt, and leaned over with her hands on her knees. Her ribs throbbed with each deep gulp of air.

"You have done too much," Deegan panted. "Rest now. You are very skilled." He bowed and walked away.

She leaned her back against the wall and slid down to the ground. Her left arm and leg were burning and shaking. She looked over to see Tolen still fighting. Sweat soaked every inch of his light blue t-shirt, making it cling to his body. He was more muscled than she'd realized.

He had changed so much since Green River where he tried so hard to be invisible. It was strange to see him standing tall and fighting. It created a whole new picture of him, a picture of him as the real Ninth of legend. Goosebumps rose on her arms and a strange tingling rose from her toes until it filled her entire body. She was a Chosen for crying out loud. She didn't have time for silly things like relationships—besides he was the *Ninth!*

An hour later, they finally stopped when Kiad determined that Tolen had gotten the hang of blocks and parries. Kiad collected the wooden daggers and paused in the center of the room. "Tomorrow we will focus on jabs and kill shots. Deegan will also teach you grappling, in case something gets close enough to grab hold of you." He grinned at Tolen's horrified look, bowed, and the three Doogar left the room laughing.

Tolen walked over to the water drum beside the entrance and dumped a cup of water over his head.

Macy couldn't stop staring as he walked over and sat down beside her.

"Sorry about earlier," she mumbled. "You know…being obnoxious. It's kinda the way I am."

"Just kinda?" He smiled and shook the water from his hair with his fingers. It splattered her face and she slugged his arm.

He chuckled. "It's okay. I'm starting to get used to it."

She considered slugging him again but smirked instead.

He laughed again softly. "How are you feeling? That was a hard workout for someone healing from broken bones."

She bit the inside of her cheek. "I'm great."

The corner of his mouth lifted and he met her eyes with a playful grin. "You're absolutely sure you don't want me to heal you the rest of the way?"

"Yep."

He chuckled again and she pushed her shoulder into him, enjoying the contact more than she knew she should. "You're still not that cool."

He shrugged. "Not yet. I've got plenty of time though." He looked at her from the corner of his eye. "I must admit the competition isn't going to be easy. Even injured you're lethal."

"Just you remember that." She bit back a grin, trying to ignore the tingle of pleasure she felt at his compliment. "You're not doing too bad yourself."

"It's a lot to remember."

Macy traced her finger in the dirt to avoid being distracted by his strange eyes and the feeling in her stomach. "Bastian told me when I was first learning not to focus so much on the 'how' as the 'when'. The *how* is already stored in your brain from your training sessions. The *when* is based on the actions of the enemy you are up against. If you're concentrating on when to act, your brain and your life force work out the how for you."

"Like instinct?"

"Exactly."

He nodded slowly. "When everything happened with the Phantom tree, I think that's what I did. Everything worked the way I needed it to even though I've never been trained to use Nature Speak."

"And you'll never be trained how to use your Nature Speak." Macy lifted her good leg and rested her arm on her knee, her heart fluttering as she remembered the Phantom. She'd never been in so much pain.

"Isn't that what the Doogar have been teaching me?" Tolen waved his hand around the room.

"No, they've just been teaching you a few key Hidden words so you can connect to your gifts. *How* your life force speaks to Nature was born with you. The language itself is ingrained in every neuron of your brain, body, and life force—you just can't remember. What the Doogar are teaching you is how to connect with what is already there. That's why you were able to do what you did in the Lava Beds. Deep within the reaches of that thick head of yours, your brain already knew what had to be done. It worked with the strength of your freakishly strong life force. It pulled out what was embedded in your brain at birth and combined it with your power, sending out what you couldn't because you were focused on the *when* and what you wanted to happen."

"Was that a compliment?" Tolen gave her a sideways look.

Macy shrugged. "Take it however you want to, dude."

He gave a thoughtful half smile. "It sounds crazy impossible."

"Tell me about it. The first time I created fire in my hands, I thought Bastian had slipped me some illicit drugs or something. I totally freaked."

"You didn't know what you could do when you were chosen?"

"Nope."

"Why not?"

"My gift didn't show itself until about a month after Bastian found me. Sometimes a Chosen's shard gives them their power right away. But with dangerous gifts like fire, it comes on slowly—a six year old suddenly creating fire—ever seen the movie *Fire Starter?*" She grinned. "The Light wanted me to learn a little bit more about the new world I was in before I had the responsibility of my gift."

"Sort of what Bastian's doing to me, not telling me everything until he thinks I can take it?"

Macy tucked a piece of hair behind her ear. "Um, yeah." *If you had any idea buddy, you'd totally freak.*

"I might not freak out. I'm not a total pansy. I can handle more than he thinks I can."

Macy jumped. Huh. He clearly didn't realize he was answering comments straight out of her head—well she wasn't about to enlighten him. He was sensing her thoughts more and more, but only the thoughts that directly related to him. He was also obviously sensing her physical well-being. She frowned. She didn't really like it, even if he had no idea what he was doing. "Bastian can be pretty overprotective. Keep practicing and maybe it won't be much longer before he feels like you're ready."

Tolen crossed his long legs beneath him. "I guess I *am* still having a hard time taking everything in. Half the time when I'm alone, I'm pinching myself to see if I'm dreaming."

Macy couldn't stop herself from reaching over and squeezing his hand. "I pinched myself for three years straight after I was Chosen—I still haven't woken up." Her Kuna surged to her fingertips and her stomach flipped, but she didn't want to let his hand go. "I *could* tell you, Tolen, but honestly, I won't do that to you. Bastian is right. Learn everything you can about your new life. I think you'll know when you really are ready to accept it all."

She made to pull her hand away before her Kuna got too strong, but Tolen held on. He laced his fingers through hers and started rubbing the back of her hand with his thumb. His eyes met hers and the look she saw there made her hands start to shake.

It was like seeing fire.

The smell of eucalyptus and roses swirled in the air and Tolen dropped her hand.

"Ouch." He rubbed his hand on his jeans.

Macy's face burned. She focused on calling the heat away from her smoking palms.

"Sorry," she mumbled. What was it with this kid? How did he do that?

His head shot up and he met her eyes with a curious expression. "The next time you want me to stop holding your hand you just have to ask." He chuckled softly, ran his fingers from her elbow to her wrist, and lightly tapped her palm. "Thank you Macy, for talking to me and spending time with me since we've been here, for being my…friend…" He stood up and waved. "See you later."

The fire rolled back to Macy's palms. She closed her eyes and held her breath trying to keep the heat inside. She heard him leave but she couldn't move. Never before had she had to try so hard to hold in her Kuna.

Why? Why did he touch her like that? Maybe that was how they were in his family— really affectionate…*really weird*. It wasn't because he actually *liked* her, like romantically or anything. No, he was nice, like Bastian kept saying. Weird, but nice.

Her heart resumed a normal pace and her Kuna eased to only the slight burn she felt deep in her chest all the time.

Yes, that was definitely it. Tolen was just nice. She'd have to keep him from showing his niceness anymore or she was bound to do something really embarrassing.

She pulled herself off the floor and fervently hoped Bastian had been too preoccupied with his planning to pay attention to what his Chosen wards were doing.

With a shake of her head, she hobbled off in the direction of the kitchens, ignoring the flutter in her stomach at the thought of Tolen's touch.

ooo

Tolen hurried out the door and shook his tingling hand, berating himself with each step. He should have helped her up. He should have offered to walk with her to dinner. She probably would have said no, but it's what a gentleman would have done. He was such an idiot. She had a way of muddling his brain.

Worse was the fact that he had to admit to himself that he'd wanted to touch her for a while. The more time they spent together, the more drawn he was to her, and he was beginning to doubt it had anything to do with the fact that they were both Chosen.

No, it was more just Macy herself that drew him. When the arrogance was off her face, it left a childlike vulnerability in her eyes. When Tolen looked into them, he could see a tiny glimmer of the young girl whose human life had been stolen from her and he felt overwhelming compassion for her loss.

His heart had been broken by what happened in the canyon, Macy's had been shattered ten years ago. She'd learned to put the pieces back together in her own way. How could he begrudge her that, even if she could be annoying sometimes?

She had more depth to her than any girl he'd had the slightest interest in at school. He found himself constantly trying to get her to smile or laugh, just so he could watch her. She was beautiful, but it was more than skin deep. She was good, and fascinating, and so much more than he could ever deserve.

She was human.

And he wasn't.

He shoved his hands in his pockets and walked past the cafeteria toward the bathing area. Suddenly he didn't feel like eating.

Chapter Twenty-One

Nightmares

The next week at the Binithan passed much like the first few days. Tolen trained twice a day. They ate. They slept. The monotony was predictable, safe, and he liked it. He'd learned a lot in a short amount of time and was beginning to feel more confident with his abilities. In fact, the only thing he seemed to be really struggling with was Macy.

They still ate together and talked, but ever since he'd held her hand, she'd been more distant. Careful.

He hadn't meant to scare her off, but maybe it had been for the best, even if he didn't like it. They weren't the same. He was Hidden kind. She was human. They were only meant to be together as Chosen fighters.

So why did it bother him so much?

It had become such a distraction that he'd been having a harder time accessing his abilities. It was ten times as hard to call the warmth than it had been when he'd first healed his hand and discovered his signal. He tried thinking of his empathy for others to bring it out, but it wasn't working as well as he knew it should be.

He didn't want to blame her for it. He knew it wasn't *her* fault, but he couldn't help but feel a little resentful toward her. Did she feel nothing for him at all?

Sometimes, he would catch her looking at him. Sometimes when he was near her, he thought he could smell the strange scent she gave off whenever she was about to use her gift, and he wondered if she also felt that pleasant energy when they were together.

He wanted to talk to her about it, but he felt too stupid. What if he was wrong, and she didn't feel anything for him, and he just embarrassed her with his questions? Instead, he continued the game, talked about simple things, and didn't touch her again.

He shook his head and turned his attention back to the doorway as Macy limped by. She was pacing the hall outside the room the Doogar had set up for the three of them. It was more of a large area, not necessarily a room, with two arched open doorways leading to the other living quarters and the training rooms. Bastian had left again "to council" after breakfast and still hadn't returned. It was driving Macy crazy.

Tolen checked his watch. It was 10:30 p.m.

Obviously, they wouldn't be leaving tonight. Bastian had had them pack up and get ready to leave three nights ago, but they still hadn't left. The Doogar were getting anxious. More and more Dark servants were scouring the Lava Beds, patrolling the known exits and on the lookout for secret ones. Tolen suspected their postponed departure had less to do with Macy's healing, and more with his faulty shield. He just couldn't maintain it for more than a few hours, less if he was practicing with his abilities.

He watched Macy limp by again. She still favored her left arm and leg, but she didn't let it slow her down. Tolen hadn't asked if he could heal her again, but he had considered having Bastian hold her down while he did it anyway. The occasional painful twinges he felt as his weird abilities connected to her well-being only made it that much harder not to think about her.

He tugged off his sneakers and stretched out on his bedroll. Like Bastian, Tolen found that it was a lot more comfortable to stretch out on the floor than to try and fit across three tiny beds.

He watched Macy pace a few more lengths until his eyes began to droop. He turned on his side and drifted off…

Areen Parks stood in front of him, her thin arms crossed over her chest, her white lips pressed into a hard line.

"Mom?" Tolen reached out toward her but the closer he tried to get, the farther away she appeared. "Mom? I'm so sorry, Mom! Wait!"

Her image shimmered and disappeared. What little light there'd been disappeared and the blackness loomed thick and heavy as oil. Cold, bone-aching cold, pushed down on him, paralyzing him. Tolen needed to get out. He could barely breathe. His eyes couldn't focus through the gloom.

An eerie, flickering blue light appeared from somewhere above in the windowless room. He looked up and saw a dripping torch hung high on the wall. The wall seeped with black liquid that trailed down and disappeared somewhere in the darkness.

He had been here before.

He shuddered, his heart pounded, and sweat ran down his face.

"Tolen…" someone whispered hoarsely from beside Tolen's feet.

Tolen's eyes moved toward the sound without his control.

The man was lying on his side, his knees drawn to his chest. The filthy rags he wore barely covered his emaciated body. His elbow length hair, the color of bracken, was wispy and tangled. The skin of his face, stretched tight over his skull, looked bloodless and waxy. If it wasn't for the shallow rise and fall of his chest and the fact that the man had just spoken, Tolen would have believed him dead.

The man's skeletal hands curled into claws as they reached up into the nothingness. His dead eyes fixed on Tolen's face.

"TOLEN!" Bastian shook him roughly.

Tolen bolted upright and vomited on the floor beside him.

Bastian handed him a wet rag and he wiped his mouth.

He looked up to see Macy, white as a sheet, crouched on the floor staring at him.

"Are you all right?" Bastian put a hand on his shoulder.

Tolen nodded, but the image of his father flicked across his vision again and Bastian quickly thrust a bowl towards him. He threw up again and again until there was nothing left in his stomach.

Helga appeared with a glass of water and a fresh cool rag. She put the rag on Tolen's forehead, cleaned up the mess, and then left again quietly.

Tolen lay back down and rolled over to face the wall. Tears leaked out the corners of his eyes.

"Tolen," Bastian whispered.

"Just leave me alone for a while. Okay?" he mumbled.

It was several seconds before he heard them both get up and move to their own beds. He heard the squeak of Macy's mattress and the rustle of Bastian's blanket. He squeezed his eyes more tightly shut and willed the picture to leave his mind.

His mother was gone, along with the only life he'd ever known, and he would never know his father because he was going to die in the Shadow Prison. He was failing them. He wasn't strong enough. Tolen wrapped his arms around his head and tried to curl into a tighter ball as the anguish ripped through him. He should have saved his mother; he shouldn't have left her there. He should be out trying to save them both. But he didn't know how.

Bastian started to sing, low and soft, and the anguish slowly faded to despair so heavy it felt like a lead blanket had been placed over him. Tolen opened his eyes and stared at the wall.

It could have been hours or minutes later that Bastian sat beside him again. Tolen wasn't sure how long he'd been lost in a stupor.

"I will make you a promise." Bastian's deep voice was gentle and soothing.

Tolen continued to stare at the wall.

"The Doogar have determined our route to the Radia Warriors camp, and the leader there is a very powerful and good Sphere. I believe they can offer us the protection we need while you learn to master your shield. Once you do, I will ask the warriors if they will help you try to rescue your father."

Tolen blinked and turned to look at the Watcher.

Bastian's eyes were filled with sadness. "I cannot promise you they will agree to it. But the Radia Warriors are the best qualified for such a mission."

Tolen pulled the damp rag off his head. "Can you understand that I need to at least try?"

Bastian looked at the floor. "Yes, Tolen, I do, but I cannot in good conscience allow you to go there untrained. You simply do not know enough. It would be like sending a lamb to the slaughter. I am sorry."

The despair got heavier. "But you'd be with me and you know plenty." He said without hope.

"Knowledge does not bring limitless power. Sometimes, it just helps you know when to act and when not to."

"I can't let him die, Bastian." His voice cracked and he cleared his throat.

"I will do what I can. I promise. The Radia Warriors can help you train."

"What if it's too late?" He whispered.

Bastian sighed and glanced down at his hands.

"Then that would be his fate," Tolen muttered. "You already told me that. Sorry."

"Do not apologize Tolen, you are in a very unique and difficult position." He patted Tolen on the head and stood up. "Helga left you some Soreah. It will help you have a dreamless sleep. Rest, we shall leave in the morning."

"For sure this time?"

Bastian nodded, but looked worried.

ooo

Macy stared up at the ceiling listening to Tolen's soft snores. Her eyes burned and the lump that had lodged itself in her throat refused to leave. Why did it hurt so much to see Tolen suffering like that? It felt like her heart was going to jump out of her chest when he'd started thrashing around screaming and she couldn't get him to wake up.

She'd run as fast as her leg would let her, screaming for help.

When Bastian couldn't get him to wake up either, she'd been so scared that something Dark had found a way to take him.

So scared it made her angry. For the past week she'd tried not to think about him in any way other than a friend and fellow Chosen. She'd forced down any stupid, romantic thought that tried to enter her head. They were different. They had a job to do. There could never be anything more between them. And she'd felt like she was doing a pretty good job until now.

As she watched him struggle during the nightmare and then again after he woke up, her chest hurt so bad she wished she could light something on fire just to let it go. Deep down, she knew it wasn't her Kuna beating for release from her chest, it was her heart aching for someone else.

She clenched her fists on the bed, gritted her teeth, and squeezed her eyes shut. Bastian touched her arm.

A single traitorous tear broke free and trickled down her face onto her pillow.

ooo

Tolen shivered involuntarily. The hidden Doogar tunnels Kiad, Elryn, and Deegan had been leading them through the last two days were not warm, comfortable, or illuminated with golden light like the Binithan. They were narrow, dark and damp, and reminded him too much of his nightmares.

Bastian told him they were heading toward Klamath National Forest where it met the border between California and Oregon, but underground it was easy to lose your sense of direction. For all Tolen knew, they were going in circles. One cave looked like the next. Sometimes he could hear thunder and knew they were close to the surface, other times the only sounds were their own footfalls and the drip of water somewhere in the darkness.

Kiad said that sometime today they would enter the final tunnel that would take them as close to the camp as they could get. Tolen was grateful. He was exhausted, not only from the trek itself but from the effort of shielding himself. It was so hard. Learning to use the weapons and words of the Hidden had been so much easier than shielding.

He tried to focus on the invisible quivering tug inside his body that said his life force was shifting the Balance. He tried to concentrate on resisting the tug, pulling back the warmth, and holding steady. He tried to distort the signal he sent out, but everything had become more difficult since the nightmare. The hopelessness blanketing him because of his lack of progression in his abilities, fed by the guilt that he wasn't ready to go after his parents, made everything seem heavier and harder.

He started panting and Bastian touched his shoulder from behind.

"You are doing fine. You will not have to hold on very long once we reach the surface."

Tolen nodded but didn't say anything for fear everyone would hear the nervousness in his voice. It was bad enough having Bastian know what was going through his head without making the others think he was a wimp.

"No one believes you are a wimp," Bastian whispered quietly enough that no one could hear.

Tolen shoved his fists into his pockets and walked faster, wanting distance between himself and Bastian. Of course, the Watcher understood and slowed down.

"What's the hold-up?" Macy asked from behind Bastian.

Tolen walked faster.

Macy hadn't said three words to him since his nightmare. Sometimes, he caught her looking at him with what he thought was a sad expression, but she'd quickly looked away so he couldn't be sure. At first, he'd wondered if he'd offended her when he'd asked to be left alone. But it felt more like she didn't *want* to be around him.

His shoulders slumped. He was so tired. Tired of caring what Macy thought. Tired of trying to be good at something he barely understood. Tired of trying to prepare for whatever destiny was waiting for him that no one wanted to tell him. Tired of pretending he didn't miss his mother and Dane like crazy. Tired of waiting for someone to finally say he was grown up enough to hear the truth.

His foot caught on something and he stumbled forward.

"Are you okay?" Macy's voice came from directly behind him.

Stunned, it took Tolen a few seconds to respond. "Yeah, I'm fine." He stood up and dusted his knees off. Macy must have passed up Bastian when he'd backed off. She wasn't letting her sore leg slow her down.

"Tolen?" Kiad's voice echoed back to them.

"I'm coming." Tolen started to walk forward and Macy brushed his back lightly. His skin burned where her fingers touched him.

"Are you really okay, Tolen?"

His jaw flexed, knowing she wasn't talking about his stumble. "Do you really care?"

Macy sucked in a breath but didn't say anything.

He pulled away from her hand and followed the bobbing light of Kiad's torch, ignoring the guilty feeling in the pit of his stomach.

CHAPTER TWENTY-TWO

FIST FULL OF TEARS

MACY'S LEG TREMBLED BENEATH HER. SHE TRIED TO HOLD IT STEADY SO no one but Bastian would notice—unfortunately, she couldn't hide anything from him.

The cavern they were in now was wider and taller. Cold air whistled along the passageway from somewhere she couldn't see, carrying with it the faint sound of rushing water. The Doogar had chosen this place to rest and eat before they made the final leg of their journey. She understood their reasoning, but couldn't help but wish they had picked somewhere a little less cold and creepy.

She glanced at Tolen. He was standing off to the side, barely visible in the torch light, kicking a rock.

As the tunnel widened, Kiad had them walk side-by-side in pairs. Bastian had insisted she be with Tolen.

Tolen didn't look her way once the whole time. She knew she should have tried to talk to him as they'd walked. She *should* try now. She did care how he felt. She did want him safe and happy. So why couldn't she just tell him that?

She bit her lip. Bastian nudged her from behind and she realized Kiad was speaking to her.

"I'm sorry, what?" She hoped the orange light from the torches would disguise her red face.

Kiad's black eyes glittered with irritation. "We are nearing The Fist Full of Tears—an extremely difficult climb. It leads to the surface at a steep incline. I asked if you thought you were able to handle it or if you'd let Tolen complete your healing."

Macy bristled. She had kept up pretty well considering how bad she ached. Bastian had only begged them to stop for her twice, against her wishes, in the last thirteen hours. Kiad was being a putz.

"Lead the way buddy, I can handle it," she growled.

Kiad lifted an eyebrow. "Very well, but if we slow down much more, we will not reach the camp before nightfall. If you *don't* keep up, I will hold you down while the boy heals you. Understood?"

Tolen smirked.

Macy took a step forward and Bastian grabbed her shoulders. "She will be fine Kiad. Continue on."

Kiad shook his head and turned back, beckoning the rest to follow.

After thirty minutes of scaling a nearly vertical wall, Macy was beginning to worry that Kiad might have to make good on his threat. Her legs burned and she was getting a monster of a headache. She knew now why it was called The Fist Full of Tears. The passage began narrow, slowly widening out like a raised fist, and water trickled down the walls from some hidden source, like tears. Or it was the fact that, as she climbed, she started wishing she could punch Kiad so bad it brought angry tears to her eyes.

Bastian kept a hand on her back to help but they were still slowing down. She hoped it wasn't enough for Kiad to comment.

"Bastian?" she asked.

"Yes?"

"I can't feel the Shadows. Do you know where they are?"

"No. I have been trying to see ahead, but I am not getting very far. I am sure they will have had to regroup and, hopefully, will be far away when we surface."

"Think there will be anything else waiting for us?" She thought about the DéHool and Bastian's *feeling*. As weak as she felt, she was really hoping he'd been wrong.

Bastian took several steps before he answered. "I hope not. The secret place where we will exit is far from where the Dark has been concentrating their efforts, but that does not mean they will not have scouts everywhere."

Macy could just see Tolen's back through the darkness. His head turned toward them at Bastian's answer, but he didn't say anything.

Macy's arms and legs were going to fall off. She was sure of it. She'd been clinging to the dry roots sticking out of the rock, dragging her way up the steep incline for the last thirty minutes. It felt like thirty hours. If she wasn't afraid she might need her Kuna once they stepped back into the world above, she'd have used her gifts to help herself out a long time ago.

"Not much farther!" Kiad called down.

Macy looked up to see a tiny dot of light forever above them. Only the Doogar who didn't seem to get tired could call *that* "not much farther."

"They are used to the denser air down here. We are not," Bastian mumbled breathlessly from behind her.

Macy snorted. "Cheaters."

"Bastian?" Tolen's voice drifted down.

"Yes?"

"What are DéHool?"

Macy's grip slipped and Bastian grabbed her waist.

"Why do you ask?" A tremor of fear only Macy would notice laced Bastian's voice.

"Ardia has been traveling above us. She says she has spotted some tracks that look like theirs. She says they're not all together, as if someone tried to hide them, but didn't do a very good job."

"Has she seen any other indication of the creatures' presence?"

"No, but she says the tracks are fresh. She says to be careful."

"Duh," Macy whispered.

Bastian poked her back.

"What? It looks like your feeling was right." Her whisper was fierce. "Crap. Can we stay in the tunnels?"

"No. This tunnel stops where we're going to get out and we don't have enough supplies to turn back."

Suddenly, five thick tree roots shot through the hole above and wrapped around each of them, dragging them up through a shower of rock and dirt.

Macy screamed before she realized this root wasn't squeezing the life out of her. It was cradling her gently, blocking her from the falling debris.

"Tolen?" Bastian shouted as they soared toward the surface.

"The DéHool are about a quarter of a mile from the exit. They're running. I asked Ardia to help us get out faster so we don't climb out to an ambush."

Elryn nodded from his root cocoon. "Good thinking." His black eyes were wide.

Kiad twisted to look at Bastian. "They want you out of the way."

"Weapons ready everyone," Deegan shouted from above.

Macy pulled her dagger from her belt and looked to see the others doing the same.

Tolen's face was white.

Her stomach plummeted. DéHool were one of the fiercest creatures of the Dark. Even the most skilled of warriors rarely ever defeated them in the legends.

Tolen didn't have a chance.

Bastian clenched his teeth. "How far to the camp once we reach the surface?"

Kiad frowned and looked above him. "I'm afraid it's still about 50 miles."

"Macy." Bastian's root was wedged close enough to hers that she could hear him even though he spoke barely above a whisper. "We must protect him. You know what will happen if he is taken. Stay with him no matter what. The two of you should be able to cover that distance more quickly than the rest of us."

"Bastian—"

"Macy. Promise me. Give me your word that you will protect the Ninth. Get him to the Radia Warriors."

"Don't talk like you're not coming with us."

"*Give me your word!*"

They finally broke the surface. The light from the setting sun cast a deathly red glow on the trees.

Macy swallowed as the root lowered her gently to the ground. Bastian stared at her with an unwavering expression.

The sun disappeared beneath the horizon and thick foreboding darkness fell heavily over them.

Macy looked into Bastian's eyes and nodded as the gates of night opened and all Hell broke loose.

CHAPTER TWENTY-THREE

TO THE DEATH

MACY PLANTED HER FEET AND HELD HER KNIFE READY AS THE DéHOOL wolves leapt from the shadows of the trees. The earth shook beneath their monstrous paws. Their evil blood-red eyes danced with wild fury. Saliva dripped from foot-long fangs. They were as horrifying as they were beautiful—standing at least ten-feet tall, five-feet wide, covered in thick, glossy, fur.

Majestic…powerful…mesmerizing… A dozen words filled Macy's thoughts describing them, but two words screamed louder than the rest.

Lethal. Merciless.

The six wolves stalked forward slowly, arrogance in every step. Macy, Tolen, Bastian, and the three Doogar were nothing but parasites to them. Tiny, weak, easily dealt with.

Bastian slowly sidled in front of Tolen. Macy shifted slightly behind and to his other side. Kiad, Elryn, and Deegan created an arrow point in front. Macy's hands shook and her palms tingled.

"Stay together," Bastian whispered. "Protect each other."

A silky, black DéHool with a bloodstained muzzle lunged forward.

Deegan ran up Kiad's back and launched at the creature—his dagger sliced into the wolf's snout and it howled in fury.

The group of DéHool broke apart. Three moved in on the Doogar, snarling and snapping, driving them farther into the forest. The remaining three circled behind closing in on Bastian, Macy, and Tolen.

The wolves paced back and forth. Their red eyes flicked anxiously. Occasionally, a frustrated whimper escaped between growls.

It was easy to tell who they were here to kill and who they had to leave alive. Macy and Bastian were in the way like the flies over a meal; a nuisance that would not be dealt with kindly.

The wolves weren't supposed to hurt Tolen.

Prickles rose on Macy's arms. She felt the blood pulse fast through her veins as she let her Kuna build.

"Macy," Bastian breathed. "Shakra."

Macy nodded once to show she heard. Keeping the dagger held high to disguise her actions, she felt along her belt with her other hand until she found the pouch holding the Shakra.

She lifted out three small silver disks and held them tightly in her palm. She closed her eyes for a half a second and sent her will to the Shakra.

"*Mig'nata!*" She threw the razor sharp discs as hard as she could.

They whizzed through the air with blinding speed. The DéHool didn't notice them until it was too late. Dark red splattered the ground from a gaping wound in the chest of one, the shoulder of another. The wolves howled angrily and began swatting at the disks as they sliced into every inch of fur and flesh they could touch.

Bastian motioned for Tolen and Macy to start backing up but paused in horror as the DéHool soared upward in an eerily synchronized jump out of the way of the Shakra. Unable to change course fast enough, all three of the speeding disks slammed into the trees and embedded themselves in the thick bark.

A dark shadow passed above their heads and a Doogar slammed into the same tree with a sickening thud.

Elryn fell to the ground. Dead.

"No!" Tolen shouted and moved forward, but Bastian threw out his arm to stop him.

Fierce howls of triumph from the DéHool and pain-filled cries of vengeance from the Doogar rang through the darkness.

A deep menacing growl turned Macy's attention back to the wolves in front of them. Their skin twitched beneath their blood soaked wounds.

"Macy!" Tolen shouted as another DéHool leapt forward.

Suddenly, a branch from a huge pine tree wrapped around her waist and tossed her over the heads of the wolves. The needles cut into her skin as she twisted, trying to get free.

The tree dropped her behind the DéHool. She could see Bastian standing in front of Tolen from beneath the wolves' bellies. One of the wolves flipped around to face her; hate burning from his eyes. He took two steps in her direction, saliva spilling from his mouth. This was not going to be a mercy kill. Tolen, in his attempt to save her, had thrown her into an even more dangerous situation.

Macy took a step back, but paused when she felt a shift in the Balance. Something else was coming toward them.

Crap! Raksasha! The Shadows would not be far behind. As if to confirm this thought, lightning lit the sky miles in the distance.

Smoke began to furl from Macy's palms.

The wolf in front of her hurtled forward, his jaws open wide. Macy flipped backwards through the air and landed on her toes five feet back. Her sore leg wobbled beneath her and she concentrated on sending strength down to it without compromising her Kuna. The wolf lunged again. She kicked off the tree behind her and his fang grazed her left arm as it tried to catch her mid jump.

She landed on his neck. Warm blood quickly spread through her ripped sleeve and dripped off her fingers as she clutched its thick fur. The wolf stood on its hind legs and thrashed its head through the air trying to throw her off.

She squeezed her legs as tight as she could against the DéHool's muscled body, kept one hand wrapped in its fur, and lifted her knife in the other—her blood ran down the hilt and off the edge as she called her Kuna. Seconds later, the blade glowed red-hot and she shoved it deep into the soft flesh of the wolf's neck.

It flailed its head side to side furiously.

Macy tugged her knife free of the creatures neck and jumped off, prepared to hit the ground and roll, but a branch from a nearby tree caught her and lifted her out of reach of the thrashing DéHool.

Ardia?

Macy didn't have time to wonder, her arm burned and she gasped for air as she shimmied up the tree. Her hands were smoking and the smell of eucalyptus and roses swirled around her head. She slowed the Kuna, but her heart still thudded in panic.

Where was everybody else?

She ripped the bottom of her shirt with her teeth and wrapped it around her bleeding arm. She looked down and watched the wolf collapse into a puddle of its own blood. She whipped her head around, aiding her sight in the darkness. The Raksasha would be here any second…and the Shadows.

Thunder boomed and her heart stuttered in her throat.

Finally, she saw movement. Kiad and Deegan were still engaging the DéHool. It was too hard to tell who was winning. Frantically, she searched for Bastian and Tolen. They should be right there! Her fight couldn't have taken place far from where they had been, but Bastian, Tolen, and the other two DéHool were nowhere in sight.

o o o

Tolen shifted his feet and the DéHool in front of him marked the movement with its blood-red eyes.

Bastian lifted a hand up behind him. "Don't move," he whispered.

Tolen strained his neck to see the fight between Macy and the DéHool that had gone after her, but he couldn't see around the two monsters in front of him.

Tolen leaned forward and the DéHool growled.

"No, Tolen. Macy is strong enough to handle it. Focus on the now."

Macy's advice came back to him. *Focus on the when, let the how take care of itself.*

Focus on the now. Macy was an amazing fighter, but—

Tolen jumped when the most menacing voice he'd ever heard filled the night air.

"Give us the boy and you can go free." It was more a growl than a voice. Low and horrifying.

The DéHool could speak.

Bastian made a sound in his throat that sounded much like the DéHool's growl followed by a humorless chuckle. The nearest wolf bared his teeth.

They slowly pressed in, forcing Tolen and Bastian backwards into the dark forest. Soon the only thing Tolen could hear was the heavy panting of the DéHool and the pounding of his own heart.

"Tolen, the trees …" Bastian whispered.

Of course! Why hadn't he thought of it before? Wasn't this exactly what the Doogar had been trying to teach him?

Thunder boomed in the distance and an eerily familiar cold moved toward him.

Shadows?

Tolen shook his head and focused on the life forces of the trees he could feel around them. He tried to pull the warmth to his center so he could use the words he'd learned, but it wouldn't come. The blanket of despair was too heavy. He couldn't shake it off.

"Fight it, Tolen. It is your fear of the unknown that causes you to doubt. The Shadows are using your fears against you. Fight it!" Bastian met Tolen's gaze.

Tolen could see his anguish mirrored in the Watcher's eyes.

I can't do this. I'm not strong enough.

His mother was missing, and his father was most likely dead. His best friend died because of him, and now he may have just sent Macy to her death. He'd failed them all. He'd lost everyone he ever cared about. He was alone and it was all his fault.

"You will never be alone." Bastian jumped into the air and swung his machete in a high arc above his head. Blood burst from a deep gash in the nearest DéHool's underbelly and it fell to the ground. The remaining wolf howled and bounded into Bastian, throwing him backwards. Tolen couldn't see where he landed.

"Bastian!" Tolen ran forward, his own pain forgotten, the Shadows' veil rent by the horror of what Bastian had done.

"No!" Heat blazed to Tolen's fingertips and he could feel the life forces surrounding him, their warmth almost tangible. *Please, please help us…* he begged. He called to the earth and the trees, using the words the Doogar had taught him.

Large chunks of earth broke away from the forest floor, gathered into huge clods and flew from the ground into the creature's back. Half a dozen aspen trees ripped free of the dirt, curling their roots through the earth, swatting their branches, but with each swipe of the wolf's massive paws, their branches snapped like toothpicks.

A tortured scream filled the air and Macy broke through the trees with fire trailing from her hands. "NO! NO! BASTIAN! NO!" Tears coursed down her cheeks as she ran to where Bastian had disappeared.

Black skeletal Raksasha suddenly appeared everywhere, running along the ground, jumping from the trees, blocking Macy and the wolf from sight.

Tolen ran into the swarm swinging his knife at everything he could, the trees following him, swatting, stabbing, crushing. Spikes of hardened dirt shot up around him as he pushed forward, knocking aside the Raksasha like randomly stacked dominos.

Block, parry, jab, twist, lunge, jump, run. He visualized his mock fights with the Doogar, letting his instincts take over.

Black and red blood covered everything; the smell of singed fur burned his nostrils.

The remaining three DéHool ran toward him, followed by the screaming Doogar. A Raksasha threw a spear and he barely rolled out of the way. He slammed hard into the base of a tree, his right arm pinned beneath him. Blood dripped from his nose off his chin. He jumped back up and started running again, wiping his face on his sleeve.

More trees joined the battle without him asking as he passed them, his life force connecting to theirs on a subconscious level. They grabbed everything they could reach, lifting the Dark creatures into the air and crushing them. The trees were no match for the DéHool, but the Raksasha were almost too easy.

Tolen finally broke through the center of the mass to see Macy standing in the middle of a ring of fire holding Bastian's huge blade. The Raksasha paced around the flames shrieking, afraid to go through.

Tolen ran forward, stabbed a Raksasha, and used its body to launch himself over the flames. He could hear the trees crashing in behind him.

Macy fell to her knees next to Bastian, dropping the red-hot machete. The Watcher's broken body was covered in blood. A burning, headless DéHool twitched on the ground beside them.

Tolen dropped beside Macy and ran his hand over Bastian's face, willing the heat to come.

"No, Tolen. It is too late." Blood trickled from Bastian's mouth as he spoke. A gash across his chest poured his life onto the ground.

The dirt moved beneath their feet and Macy screamed.

"Night Demons! Bastian! You have to move!" She lifted one of his arms and he groaned.

"No, Macy." He coughed and grabbed both Tolen's and Macy's hands.

"Tolen, remember to trust your thoughtful heart." Bastian stared deep into Tolen's face and his Watcher's eye reacted. The Radia crystal around his neck throbbed with a sadness so deep it brought tears to Tolen's eyes.

Bastian touched Macy's cheek and lifted his Radia shard from around his neck. His hand shook as he held it out to her. "Macy, remember your promise."

"No, Bastian, I won't leave you here. I won't! Please, please!" She pushed her hands under his body and looked up toward the sky. "Please don't take him!"

Bastian squeezed his eyes shut and tears seeped from the corners. "Macy," he said in a choked voice. "You gave me your word." His grip slackened on both their hands and his last breath rattled from his throat. The necklace fell to the blood-drenched earth.

Bastian was gone.

"No! No! Bastian!" Macy's cry seemed to burn her pain into the world around them.

Tolen nearly collapsed from the weight of her sorrow.

He watched in horror as a skinny, scabbed hand broke free of the dirt followed by a grotesque head without eyes. Once both arms were free, it dragged its legless torso from beneath the ground—its decaying flesh covered with maggots and bloody scabs. It began clawing its way along the ground until it reached the side of the dead wolf. It lowered its fanged mouth and began sucking at the blood on the ground.

"Help me!" Macy was trying to heft Bastian's lifeless body upright.

More hands and heads were rising from the ground. The Night Demons were coming for Bastian.

Ardia!

A bough lowered to the ground and wrapped around Bastian. Ardia gently lifted him high in her branches.

No creature will touch him. She promised.

Thank you.

Go Tolen! Run now while the wolves are distracted by the Doogar. The camp is not far. Look for the rainbow in the east. It will appear with the rising sun—you do not have much time.

Macy tugged a pouch from her belt with shaking fingers. She pulled open the strings and poured a handful of dried leaves into her palm. "*Minradak Siadras,*" she sobbed while tossing the herbs on the ground surrounding Ardia. The Night Demons who headed toward them screeched and turned away.

"What did you do?" Tolen watched the Demons shriek angrily—confined by the flames but restricted from their food.

Macy turned to Tolen with a haunted, dead look in her eyes. "I made this spot burial ground. Night Demons can't enter sacred places." She reached down, and curled her fist around Bastian's shard, picked up the discarded machete and backpack and tossed them over her shoulder.

She looked once more into Ardia's branches before grabbing Tolen's arm and digging her fingers into his skin. "Run, Tolen. Run as fast as you can."

"What about the Doogar?"

"GO!" She shoved him hard and took off running straight through the fire.

He looked between where Macy disappeared and the still fighting Doogar.

Protect each other. Bastian's voice echoed through his mind.

Ardia, stay with Bastian. He concentrated on the life forces of the other trees. *If you can hear me, please help the Doogar.* He watched the trees surrounding the fight start swinging at wolves, Raksasha, and Night Demons. He clenched his fists, and took off after Macy. He felt more than saw a group of Raksasha pursuing them. He quickened his pace until he caught up to her and they settled into a fast-paced run. Guilt, horror, grief, and anger, coursed through him like poison.

ooo

Run.

No, I can't anymore.

RUN!

It was the first time Macy had ever heard Bastian's voice so clearly in her head, echoing through every part of her body. She could feel the pull of Bastian's life force leaving her. Only his body remained in Ardia's branches, the part that made him who he was, the part she had loved as a father, no longer stayed with her.

Macy's heart felt like a lead weight in her chest.

She ran from Bastian's lifeless body. She ran from the Raksasha, the wolves, the Shadows. She ran from the Dark. She ran from the despair that tried to engulf her. Every last bit of energy she had she pushed to her legs, relishing the pain that burned through her still healing leg—it took the focus off the other pain that threatened to stop her heart.

She was alone. For the first time in her life she was truly alone.

She glanced at Tolen as he matched her stride for stride, and a sick sort of hatred filled her. It was his fault. If he hadn't thrown her behind the wolves, if he just knew who he was and what he was capable of—he could have saved them all. They wouldn't be in this mess. Bastian would still be here. He wouldn't have had to give his life to save the Ninth.

Protect the Ninth… Bastian's voice echoed.

I will take him to the Radia Warriors, Bastian. I won't fail the Light. But then I'm done. I never want to see his face again.

The trees blurred as she ran, but Macy didn't notice their color. The world around was gray and lifeless—just like Bastian. Her breath caught and she stumbled. Tolen grabbed her arm but she tugged out of his grasp.

The Raksasha tailing them shrieked in defeat and gave up the moment the sky began to lighten on the horizon. A bright rainbow illuminated the eastern sky a half-mile ahead, slowly beginning to fade as the sun made its appearance in the sky.

"There." Tolen pointed and slowed down. "Ardia said that's where the camp is."

Macy turned toward the hazy lines of the vanishing rainbow.

Light was warmth—light was peace. Macy knew this but felt neither. Empty, hollow—that's how she felt.

She fell to her knees and everything went black.

Chapter Twenty-Four

The Followers of Light

"Macy!" Tolen dropped to Macy's side. She looked terrible, her face ashen and covered with dirt and dried tears, her arm wrapped in a blood soaked piece of her shirt. His stomach clenched. He hadn't even known she was injured.

The sound of crunching bracken met his ears—someone or something, was coming. Tolen whirled around and his heart stopped.

A group of seven huge men emerged from the trees. Their silky dark hair fell in long, colorfully beaded, thick braids down their backs. Strange, beaded, leather headdresses crossed low on their foreheads, and wove gracefully back into their hair.

Their clothing was an array of dyed animal skins pieced into leggings. They wore vests that hung open, exposing intricate breastplates of bright crystals that glowed softly. Over each shoulder they carried an intricately carved long bow, and a quiver of arrows hung on their backs. A gleaming curved dagger dangled from sheaths strapped to their thighs.

Tolen jumped to his feet, blocking Macy from view. The closer the men got the taller they seemed. They towered over Tolen's 6 foot 2 inch frame, making him feel like a child as he looked up into their intense brown eyes.

Within a few seconds, calm filled him, and he felt safer than he ever had in his life. These men radiated goodness. Their eyes, though fierce and serious, held no malice. There was no thirst for violence in their countenances. They were powerful, but deep in Tolen's heart he knew these men did not use their power the way the Dark did. In every way they were the opposite of the creatures he had encountered since he first learned who he was.

Radia Warriors?

"Is she all right?" A man with blue beads in his headdress stepped forward, holding his hands behind his back. His deep voice held no cruelty, but the power behind it still made Tolen nervous.

"I—I think so. She's hurt and she passed out."

"We'll take her to camp. We have a Sphere there who can help her."

"Can—Can I just do it now?"

"What do you mean?"

"Heal her. I sort of know how."

The man's eyebrows nearly disappeared into his headdress. "You are a Sphere?"

"My mother is."

The man bowed and motioned for Tolen to proceed, his eyebrows still raised.

Tolen knelt down beside Macy again, held his hand above her arm, and called for the warmth. He looked at her face and his heart ached for her loss. His fingers blazed and he ran them across her injury. Her face twisted as the skin pulled together, but she didn't wake up. As an afterthought, he ran his fingers over her weak leg—asleep she couldn't argue with him. He felt the bone finish knitting together and the bruising within the muscle disappear. It was easier this time, now that he knew what to look for, just like Bastian had said. Tolen swallowed back the guilt that wanted to consume him for the role he'd played in his Watcher's death, and touched Macy's cheek to try to get her to wake up.

"She will wake when she is ready." The man held out his hand with a strange look on his face, almost wary. "I am Incrah, captain of this band of Radia Warriors."

Tolen stood up and shook Incrah's massive arm.

Incrah ended the handshake quickly and waved his hand toward the others, pointing them out in turn. "Jéno, Kapha, Rada, Denhon, Sernad, and Beyn."

Tolen knew he'd never get their names right. "I'm Tolen…and this is Macy."

Incrah looked Tolen up and down. "You have entered the Unastra training camp. We will take you to Jonas—he is our Sphere and leader. He will know what to do with you." He knelt beside Macy. "I will carry the girl. You look near to death yourself." He lifted Macy into his huge arms.

Tolen glanced down at his bloodstained shirt and the cuts on his arms. His watch was so badly damaged from his crash into the tree he could barely read it through the scratches. He felt a pang of anxiety as the strange men surrounded and herded him through a gap in the trees. He could barely get his achy body and tired feet to keep moving.

"How did you find us, young one?" A warrior with tawny beads in his headdress spoke up.

Tolen shook his head, trying to clear the sleepy fog that had settled over his brain. He had no idea what he was allowed to say. "Uh, we were in the Binithan with the Doogar and we left…we got in a fight with some Dark creatures and then…then we ran here."

The men gave him curious looks but didn't say anything after that.

The trees soon thinned to reveal a huge open space. A river flickered lazily in the distance. Row upon row of tents rimmed the area. Everywhere fires burned in pits, and people of every kind milled about doing the most extraordinary things. Some stood in makeshift arenas sparring with swords or knives, some practiced with the long bows, shooting at stuffed targets painted black like Raksasha.

In front of one tent a young girl, probably no more than seven or eight years old, sat with a deep look of concentration, twisting her fingers as she manipulated a tuft of wildflowers to lace around her feet until it looked like she was wearing pretty grass sandals.

A few feet down the line a group of nine or ten teenagers stood facing a row of makeshift targets. Exhausted and nervous as he was, Tolen couldn't stop himself from pausing to watch.

Two young girls were calling up rocks and with only their minds, sending them screaming toward their targets. One young man with a waist-length braid literally disappeared, then reappeared right at the target, and slammed a knife into its center. Two others, a boy and a girl, standing near the river, called up thick ribbons of water and shot it, not at the targets, but rather doused the entire line of youth, sending them all into shrieks of laughter. Suddenly there was too much mud, wind, and water, to see what they were doing. Tolen turned away and moved to catch up with Incrah just as he stopped in front of another tent.

"Wait here." Incrah carried Macy into the tent. When he returned, she was no longer in his arms. "She is in the care of our Houseman. He will see that she is safe. You will follow me."

Tolen swallowed and looked at the tent, his stomach knotting up. It didn't feel right leaving her, even if he couldn't doubt the man's honesty. His Radia shard warmed against his chest, comforting him with the knowledge that wherever they took him, he'd still be able to sense her, and he pushed his heavy feet on.

The rest of the warriors parted company as Incrah led Tolen to the shade of an enormous tree. Beneath it, sitting on a carved wooden chair, a very old, very bent man, with white wispy hair that brushed his shoulders, watched them walk forward expectantly. His brown eyes were cobwebbed with white, but still perceptive. In his gnarled hands, he held a chunk of wood that he appeared to be whittling into some type of animal.

"Ah, I have been waiting for you Tolen."

Tolen jumped and the old man's lips curled into a half smile. He looked up at Incrah. "Thank you, Incrah. You may go. Tell the Houseman to bring McLacy to me once she wakes, will you?"

McLacy? "Um, you mean Macy?"

Jonas' white eyes focused on Tolen once more. He looked amused. "Is that what you call her? Hmm. Interesting."

"Certainly, Jonas." Incrah bowed slightly and gave Tolen barely a passing glance.

Tolen watched the warrior walk away until Jonas cleared his throat.

He looked back to find the old man staring at him. His eyes were creepy. Tolen shifted his feet and Jonas put the wood down.

"Eight there are, and the Ninth shall lead them," he whispered.

Tolen's shard pulsed with strange warmth and a strong feeling of deja vu came over him, as if he should know what the crazy old man was talking about.

The man leaned forward. "You are not what I expected…but still, whatever *is* what one expects, hmm? I am Jonas, Sphere and leader of this camp."

Tolen's exhausted, grief-muddled brain could barely process what was going on around him, but he managed to ask, "H-how do you know who we are?"

"Forrest Bastian is a great Watcher." Jonas laced his knobby fingers under his chin.

Tolen's heart swelled with sadness at the mention of Bastian. "Yes he was—"

"*Is*," Jonas interrupted.

Tolen tried to swallow the golf ball sized lump rising in his throat. "I'm sorry. He…he's dead. The DéHool…they…they killed him." *Because I screwed up.* The thought burned a hole through his chest.

Jonas tilted his head. "And you believe that duty ends with death, do you?"

Tolen rubbed his eyes. "Huh?" He just wanted to forget this whole day ever happened. Couldn't the guy just let someone take him back to Macy's tent or any tent for that matter? The adrenaline had long since worn off, and now that he knew they weren't about to be attacked, it was taking all he had to keep his eyes open.

Jonas leaned on the armrest, dropped his chin into his hand, and tapped his temple. "There is much to be done and little time in which to do it. The Dark is plotting something; something as implausible as it is terrifying. The shift in the Balance, though unnoticed by most, is there. Darsapean is gaining strength."

"Dar—who?" Tolen rubbed his temples. This guy made no sense.

Jonas ignored him. He seemed to be talking more to himself than Tolen. "Fate is intervening. Your arrival has changed the course. The Dominants will be here tomorrow. You and McLacy will have time to regenerate while we wait. There is much you must do." He took a deep breath and slapped his hands on his knees. "I will have a tent prepared for you to rest. We will begin the ceremony as soon as McLacy wakes." He turned his cobwebbed eyes to the forest and dismissed Tolen with a wave of his hand.

What?

Someone tapped him on the shoulder and he turned to see Incrah standing there.

"This way." He led Tolen away from Jonas, away from the camp, and away from Macy. He no longer felt in control of his body, more like his limbs were working of their own accord, his mind was too exhausted, his thoughts too painful to try to think.

He barely acknowledged Incrah as he held open the flap to a small canvas tent. "Macy?" His lips felt numb and difficult to move.

"She's fine. She's resting. Sleep, Tolen. We'll be back for you as soon as she wakes."

Tolen could barely nod as he tripped forward and collapsed onto a low, blanket covered cot.

Tolen tossed pebbles into the small stream and watched the ripples roll across the glassy surface. This place was surreal in its beauty, the atmosphere so different from the intense and frightening world he'd been in the last few weeks.

He'd slept through the rest of the day yesterday and all last night. Tolen tried to decipher the time beneath the deep scratches on his watch. About 6:30 in the morning was his guess.

He'd considered walking back into camp and looking for Incrah, or even the weird guy Jonas, but as soon as he stepped out of the tent the quiet stillness of the morning had felt too peaceful, and he'd only made it as far as the stream fifty feet from his tent. He knew there was a bigger reason he didn't want to face anyone—Macy in particular. He could never take back what happened. If she knew Bastian had died to save Tolen, she'd never forgive him, and how could he even expect her to? His petty anger toward her the past few days only added another rock to his guilt-riddled gut. First, he'd scared her off with his touchy-feely stuff, and then been mad at *her* for not being interested. Of course she wasn't interested in him. He was as dangerous as he'd always feared, and now not only did he have Dane's blood on his hands, but Bastian's as well.

If he could, he would stay in this spot and never face anyone again. Even the drive to save his parents couldn't penetrate the despair he felt. He'd failed so many times, how could he possibly believe he could actually save his parents? Even Bastian hadn't believed he could do it. He was stupid and naïve.

He threw another rock into the water, eyes stinging, and then dug his fists into the dirt, teeth clenched to hold back the emotion. It did no good to cry.

He stood up, whirled around, and smacked right into someone. "Oh, excuse me. Sorry." He stepped back to see a beautiful young woman with wavy black hair and odd, bright violet eyes. The tips of her ears were slightly pointed.

"You're an elf." He blurted and snapped his mouth shut.

The young woman smiled, showing perfect white teeth. "I'm a Lafar. Our kind inspired the elf legends, but it isn't our true name. I'm called Nova." She held out a delicate hand.

Tolen shook her arm, realizing afterwards that he'd just been digging in the dirt. "Tolen."

"I'm sorry, Tolen, about intruding on you." She dusted off her arm. "I didn't know you were here. I come to the stream to collect Kornikye for the Houseman. Lafar are the only ones who can coax them out of the water."

"It's no problem." He only understood half of what she said.

She smiled again and Tolen's stomach gave a funny flip despite the war going on inside him.

"Nova!" A squat old man in a dirty apron waddled toward them.

Nova's face reddened.

"I thought I told you to fish for the Kornikye downstream. You know you are not supposed to interfere with the boy's Solitude."

"Sorry," she mumbled and quickly darted back into the trees.

The squat man bowed. "I am sorry, young one. Nova has a tendency to let her curiosity overrun her good sense. Forgive us, please."

"Oh, it's really no problem—"

"Everyone calls me Dirt."

"Dirt?"

"Yep." He held out a small covered basket. Tolen thought he could smell fresh bread. "Breakfast. I'll leave you alone now." He bowed again and followed Nova into the trees.

Tolen debated on following, but instead dropped back down to rinse his hands in the stream, embarrassed that he hadn't realized how dirty he was before shaking Nova's arm.

He wondered if Incrah would really come and get him when Macy woke up, or maybe she already had and didn't want to see him. He dried his hands on his pants, stood up, and stared in the direction of the camp, feeling no desire to go and find out.

He walked into his tent, set the basket on the floor, dropped face down on the cot, and squeezed his eyes shut against the pain.

CHAPTER TWENTY-FIVE

A WATCHER'S FAREWELL

MACY STARED UP AT THE DIRTY CANVAS ROOF OF THE TENT, TRYING TO ignore the emptiness in her heart. She'd known she would have to lose Bastian one day. She'd known it would be hard. She had no idea it would be this hard.

She looked down at her healed arm, perfectly strong leg, and wished she could punch Tolen. Heck, she wished she could punch anyone.

She bit her lip in frustration. It was hot enough, and light enough, that the sun had to be fully up, but she hadn't gone outside yet. Why bother? She didn't want to see anyone.

She heard someone approaching but made no move to sit up. The tent flap opened but she didn't bother to look over. It was probably just the Houseman. When she woke up, he'd been sitting by her head sprinkling smelly herbs all over her face. He'd nodded once with a grim smile and left.

"Time to get moving McLacy Allicandra."

Macy shot upright. Some old fart stood in the tent door leaning on his cane.

"How do you know my real name?"

"Forrest Bastian is a good Watcher."

"Was—"

"*Is.*" The old guy sighed and shook his head. "You and the boy share the same misunderstanding. Death does not stop duty."

Macy clenched her teeth.

"My name is Jonas, Sphere and leader of this camp. It is time for you to join us." Jonas's cobwebbed brown eyes bored into her face. "The ceremony is about to begin."

"No, it's time for me to leave. I did what Bastian asked. I brought the kid to the Radia Warriors."

"That is not what your Watcher asked of you. He told you to protect the Ninth. If you leave now, you would be breaking your promise. Tolen needs you. The Balance put you together for a reason."

Macy's face burned. "Oh yeah? Well I'm sick of the Balance messing with my life. Why the crap did the Light have to choose me anyway?"

"That is a very good question, and only you can find the answer."

Macy sat back on the cot and dropped her head into her hands.

Jonas shuffled over and put a hand on her shoulder. She tried to shrug him off, but for an old guy he had a pretty firm grip. She gave up and settled for glaring at the floor.

"The Balance can feel the depth in every life force on this planet. It is made up of both good and evil, touchable matter and untouchable energy. It shifts and sways like the wind. The Light within the Balance finds those souls that are pure and good, just as souls filled with evil are sought by the Dark. The Light chose you because there is something within you that shifted the Balance so much that it knew it needed you. You have a purpose McLacy—a purpose far greater than being a Chosen protector for humankind. You need to find your purpose, you mustn't let your parents' or Bastian's loving sacrifices be for naught." He paused as if waiting for her to speak. When she refused to take her eyes off the floor, he continued.

"You understand that selfishness is for the Dark. You have felt for yourself the joy that comes from realizing that your life, though a sacrifice, saves countless others. You, although you deny it, care more for the lives of others than you do for yourself, and you know that this is the way it should be. If the people of the world did not love themselves more than everything and everyone else, there would be no darkness. If so much of humankind and Hidden kind did not believe that life is about the fulfillment of selfish and wicked desires, even at the expense of those around them, darkness would fade and light and truth would take its place.

"McLacy Allicandra, you are pure in heart, even though you do not yet see it. You have a great purpose. You must find it. You are too important." Jonas lifted his hand. "Now, get up and come with me. It is time to give Forrest Bastian a proper farewell." He turned and shuffled out of the tent.

Macy rubbed her hands across her face. Jonas's words pounded through her head. If Tolen had been what he was supposed to be, Bastian would still be alive. If he hadn't separated her from the fight, Bastian would still be alive. Every way she looked at it, Tolen's weaknesses had caused Bastian's death.

She shoved off from the cot, pushed her hands into her pockets, clenched her teeth, and followed the old geezer through the tent door.

A tug in her stomach, that was becoming more and more familiar, made her glance up from the ground as she neared the camp. Tolen sat on a log about fifty feet in front of her, head down, staring at his watch. He looked up, their eyes met, and he jumped up so fast he almost fell over. Macy looked away, pulled a sucker out of her pocket, ripped off the wrapper, and shoved it in her mouth.

"Macy?" Tolen asked softly.

She allowed him half a glance.

"Macy, I'm so sorry about Bastian. I—"

She waved him off, fighting the stab of pain at the mention of Bastian, and turned to Jonas. "So, where are you doing the ceremony?"

Tolen sighed and shoved his hands into his back pockets.

Jonas swung his head side to side. "Time, place, truth, lies, love, and hate; all things that make life what it is, also make it what it shouldn't be."

Macy looked at the ground and rolled her eyes.

"Come." Jonas pointed deeper into camp. "The ceremonial hut is this way."

They followed Jonas to a low wooden shanty. Macy kept tight to Jonas's opposite side, as far from Tolen as the small walkway between tents would allow, trying to pretend he wasn't there or, better yet, that he didn't even exist.

She felt him slow down, allowing the space she put between them, and fought against the glimmer of pity trying to worm its way into her thoughts. The corrosive hatred toward him she'd been feeding writhed and twisted in her stomach. She clenched her teeth. Her feelings were justified.

Tolen was dangerous. Everyone he cared about ended up dead or taken by the Dark.

Jonas ducked under the low open doorway of the shanty. Macy dropped her sucker into a patch of bushes and followed in behind. Tolen nearly had to bend in half to fit. At the front of the tiny room, a small gathering of six people sat on logs in a circle with three spaces left. Jonas took the head, leaving two for Tolen and Macy. Macy hurried to the empty seat between two crotchety looking old women. Tolen sat next to a middle-aged man and an ancient looking woman. They both acknowledged him with a nod. He folded his arms on top of his knees, and stared at the floor.

Macy looked away, squared her shoulders, and turned her attention to Jonas as he started to speak.

"For thousands of years the Beings of this world have tried to make sense of mortality. What factors determine how long we should be allowed to live? Why do some who seem so young, healthy, and filled with potential, die without reason, while many aged souls live on? But only one truth explains what cannot be explained. This life is not the end. Once we pass through Light's door, we enter into a far more glorious state—shedding mortality for immortality in the form we began in."

All thoughts of Tolen fled Macy's mind and suddenly the room seemed too small for all these people. Her pulse raced and sweat pooled on her upper lip. She wiped it away, fighting the urge to run.

"Those of us left behind have the greatest struggle. It is us who must learn to exist without *them*, go on without them. Too often we mistakenly believe we can go back to who we were before our loss, but this is not possible. We can heal, we can be strong again, but we will not be the same.

We can choose to allow our loss to fill us with bitterness and anger, or we can take all those things we gained from our association with our loved one and let them mold us, help us grow into our own potential, forever grateful for the time we had."

She had to get out of here. It hurt too much!

Jonas started to sing in the language of the Hidden. Soft, melodic, poignant, devastatingly beautiful. The desire to flee disappeared as the pain in her heart nearly dropped her to the floor. Her head fell onto her arms and she pressed her eyes shut, but she couldn't stop the tears from pushing out the corners.

The tiny room filled with warm light that Macy could see through her closed lids. She sensed Bastian's presence and a gentle breeze ruffled her hair, almost like a gentle touch on the top of her head. Her breath caught, she had to bite back a sob, and then the feeling disappeared. She didn't know how much time passed before she finally looked up, but when she did, there were only three people left in the room. Jonas, herself, and Tolen.

Tolen's eyes were fixed on the dirt floor, his elbows on his knees, his hands clasped between his legs. He seemed to be barely holding himself together. She could see it in the way he hunched his shoulders, the shallow breaths he took, and the despair that radiated from him.

She gritted her teeth and looked away from his pain, sorrow shoved away as the anger returned. He barely knew Bastian. The only excuse he had for being upset was because he felt guilty. As he should. She looked over to see Jonas staring at her, shaking his head slowly, his hands wrapped around his spindly cane. She took a deep breath and stood up.

"Tolen, it is time for you to speak to the Guardians," Jonas said softly.

Macy started toward the door but Jonas held up his hand. "McLacy. Stay."

"Why—" Jonas raised an eyebrow and she took a deep breath, closed her eyes, and sat back down, her hands tingling.

The room was suddenly bathed in darkness. Small pinpricks of multi-colored lights began to appear on the ceiling, walls, and floor until the entire room looked like the night sky.

"There is no beginning of Light and Dark." The deep voice—no *voices*, synchronized voices—seemed to come from nowhere and everywhere at the same time.

"They have always been. Worlds have been formed and destroyed. Lives have been created and obliterated. Alliances have been made and broken. Always the Light inspires. Always the Dark enslaves. You have been chosen by the Balance to fight for the Light. Two choices lie ahead for you with the greater call. Follow the road that will save *both* worlds, or ignore your destiny and watch them fall.

"You have been chosen, Tolen Daedal Téloran. Will you accept your destiny?" The voices faded.

"You must answer, Tolen," Jonas whispered.

"Yes." Tolen's voice cracked. "I-I accept."

Wind rushed through the room. Macy felt the joy from her Radia Shard pulse through her and she clenched her fists. *We need him…or at least they think we do. Accept it.* But her internal pep talk didn't stop her hands from shaking.

"Your sacrifice has been accepted." The deep voices echoed. "You are now truly a member of the Chosen Ones. The Light will guide you so long as you seek it out. Learn your purpose—ask for what you need with a pure heart and the Light will give it to you."

The stars disappeared and sunlight filtered in through the doorway.

"What was that?" Tolen looked up at the wooden ceiling that moments ago had been covered with stars.

"A communication link to the citadel. You just spoke to the Guardians."

"I did?"

"Yes." Jonas tapped his arm. "Wait here. Incrah will be coming to take you to meet the Dominants."

He gave Macy a significant look and she glared back.

Jonas sighed and left.

Macy got up to leave but Tolen blocked her path. "Macy, wait. Please."

She tried to step around him, but hunched over he completely blocked the door.

She took a deep breath. "Move."

"Macy, please?"

She stepped to within an inch of his face—their eyes level with him bent low—anger, pain, and fear feeding the hate-monster growing inside her. "Look Tolen, just because Bastian and I found you does not mean we were ever meant to be anything but mutual acquaintances. That's it. If it weren't for the fact that the Light can't win without you, I never would have put up with your crap!"

Tolen flinched and clenched his teeth, but didn't back down. "I don't expect you to ever forgive me for what happened and I don't expect you to want to have anything to do with me ever again, but don't," he ran his hand through his hair, "don't let your anger ruin your life." He pointed out the door. "Jonas was right. Don't be bitter. You had a great life with Bastian. He loved you. He'd want you to be happy."

That's it! "Don't give me advice about what Bastian would want," she spat. "You hated him, even after everything he tried to do for you. He'd still be here if you weren't so weak!" A sliver of vicious satisfaction slithered in her gut as Tolen's face fell.

His eyes hardened, the blue eye dilating so wide it became almost black as he lashed back. "I don't know what I'm talking about? You are so selfish! You really think you're the only person in the world to have ever suffered? Fine, your story is tragic and terrible, but taking it out on everyone else is b—"

Macy's fist connected with Tolen's jaw, all her anger driving the punch. He flew sideways into a wood beam that cracked on impact. The ceiling started to crumble over him as Macy fled, the heat building inside her no longer containable. Flames shot out of her palms and she couldn't even care what she lit on fire as she ran into the secluded forest.

As the heat faded from her hands, Macy scrubbed the tears from her face as she ran to the seclusion of the trees. Jonas's earlier words pounded through her head. She felt like her insides had been scooped out and all that was left was hollow space. Bastian would be disappointed in her behavior, but as much as she didn't like the idea of disappointing him, she couldn't stop the anger that threatened to consume her. But the thought returned that if Tolen had been what he was supposed to be, Bastian would still be alive. He would still be here fulfilling whatever mission the Light had for him.

A tiny voice in the back of her mind whispered that maybe, just maybe if they'd told Tolen his destiny he would have been prepared for what waited for them in the forest above the Binithan. That maybe it wasn't all his fault. Maybe he really was sorry and wanted to help her face her grief.

She clenched her fists and pushed her way deeper into the trees. So what? It didn't matter either way. Bastian was still dead and nothing could change that. The world might need the Ninth, but she personally didn't. She'd make sure they had what they needed to train him. She would fulfill her promise and make sure he was protected, and then she would go back out and fight the Dark, *on her own.*

oOo

Tolen crawled out from under the pile of timbers and stood up rubbing his jaw.

"That girl's got a nasty temper."

Tolen turned to see Nova standing beside the remains of the shanty, holding a basket in one hand and pointing to a string of grass fires leading into the forest with the other. A handful of people were rushing around with buckets of water to douse the flames.

"Here." Nova held out the basket. "Dirt said you didn't eat the breakfast he left in your tent and thought you'd need some food before you start training."

"Oh. Thanks." Tolen took the basket, but he had even less of an appetite now. His heart pounded painfully in his chest and his hands shook with anger.

"So you get to meet the Dominants today, huh?" Nova watched him with her head tilted to the side, her eyes wide and curious. Either oblivious or not caring about the waves of anger flowing off of him.

Tolen passed a hunk of cheese between his hands and tried to slow his breathing. "Yeah, I guess." He couldn't really focus on Nova and he wasn't in the mood for chitchat. A part of him wanted to go after Macy and force her to listen to reason, but the other part kept repeating her words. *He'd still be here if you weren't so weak!*

"Aren't you excited? I mean you're being trained by the Dominants. I'd be on the ninth cloud."

Tolen's neck prickled. His anger quickly replaced with a strange sense of anticipation mixed with apprehension. "I think you mean cloud nine," he choked out. *Ninth… The Ninth shall lead them.* The strange feeling of déjà vu he'd felt when Jonas said those words came back stronger than ever. What did it mean? He looked out the corner of his eye to see Nova watching him with her eyebrows raised. Could she know something? If she did, would she even tell him? Should he even ask her to tell him?

Be careful Tolen… Bastian's warning in his head was so loud Tolen jumped.

"Are you okay?" Nova touched his arm. Tolen's skin burned beneath her fingers and his Watcher's eye dilated, pulling in her features. Her eyes were concerned, but there was something else in them, something elusive. She blinked and it was gone.

"I'm…not sure." He walked over to sit on a log marking the path. "I think I need a second."

"Should I go get the Houseman?" she asked, looking toward camp.

"No, I'm fine. I just want to sit for a minute." Should he ask her?

Bastian's voice echoed in his head again. *Be careful.*

Why? Why did he need to be careful? It was just a random comment. Wasn't it?

And then he knew, knew from the pounding in his heart, the warmth of his shard against his chest, the growing need to know what this tiny little sentence meant. This was it. This was the big secret that Bastian said he wasn't ready to know.

Tolen clenched his teeth as a surge of reckless frustration passed through him—imagined warnings or not, he *was* ready to know, despite what anyone else thought.

He ran his hand through his hair. "Nova, can I ask you something?" His heart pounded out a nervous rhythm in his chest.

She raised her eyebrows. "Sure."

He took a deep breath and faltered. Nova was a follower of Light. She was beautiful and kind, but he didn't know her. Maybe this was why he could ask her though. She would have no idea he wasn't *supposed* to know....

Suddenly the idea of going against Bastian's wishes made him break out in a sweat.

"Tolen?" She was starting to look nervous. "Are you sure you're okay?"

He chuckled anxiously and started kicking the ground with the toe of his shoe. He took a deep breath and swallowed. He needed to hurry, Incrah could show up any minute, but he wasn't even sure how to ask for what he wanted. "Can you...can you tell me about—what the Ninth is?"

Her eyebrows jumped to her hairline. "You mean *you* don't know the legend?"

"No."

"W-O-W." She mouthed the word. "Um, if *you* don't know then... maybe...you're not supposed to."

Tolen squeezed his eyes shut. "I figured you'd say something like that." He glanced up to see her studying his face. He looked away and she touched his chin, forcing him to look at her—his stomach gave an uncomfortable flip when their eyes met.

She sighed. "The Ninth Chosen is a really old legend. I don't know it word for word, but I can give you the basics. My brother used to tell it to scare me when I was little." She dropped her hand from his chin but grabbed his hand. His heart thudded in his chest. It felt weird letting her hold his hand, but also strangely comforting.

"I'm sure you've been told about Light and Dark?" she whispered.

He nodded.

"The Balance?"

He nodded again.

"Good. Well, thousands of years ago during the Radia Revolution," she glanced over, and satisfied that he didn't look confused, went on, "before each Watcher set off after the Chosen ones, a prophecy was made by the oldest Guardian. The day would come when more Beings, including humans, would choose the ways of the Dark over Light. The Dark would become so powerful in both worlds that it would cause a collapse in the Balance. The dimensional barrier between our worlds would break down and the strength of the Light that has kept the worst of the creatures of the Dark imprisoned would cease.

"You've fought Raksasha and DéHool; now try to imagine something far worse, worse than every nightmare you've ever had, and every horror you've ever possibly imagined, running rampant, killing, and destroying everything they meet that stands in their way.

"The earth as we know it would no longer exist. The human race would be exterminated, the followers of Light eradicated."

Tolen swallowed.

Nova twisted her hair around her fingers. "The Guardians had to find a way—some last chance for the good in the world. They begged and pleaded with the Light, they held council after council with the Radia Warriors, Protectors, and the Watchers.

"At a point when they feared there was no hope, the Light set one last Radia shard free. It went to the oldest Watcher in the Hidden. His name was Eamun Woodlore. Through the Last Shard, Eamun was given the prophecy of the Ninth. As the Dark grew and the Balance tipped more in their favor, the Last would select a Watcher and send its power to his Chosen shard. The gifted shard would then find a life force so pure and good that the Dark could not influence it. The Shard would then give this child a piece of every Hidden gift. These *unlimited* gifts would give them the strength and ability needed to unite the Chosen, as well as all fighters for Light, in a Final Battle against the Dark, for the hope of all Beings.

"The Guardians sent Eamun into hiding to protect the Last Shard. They have been waiting for the arrival of the Ninth Chosen ever since."

"The Ninth *Chosen?*" Tolen whispered.

"Yes."

"It's not a group? It's just one person?"

Nova squeezed Tolen's hand tighter. "Yes."

"Are you two through?" Incrah stood over them his eyes livid, his nostrils flared.

A look of terror flashed across Nova's face and she almost fell over in her hurry to leave. She didn't even give Tolen a parting glance as she scurried away, leaving her basket behind.

Tolen looked up into the eyes of the Radia Warrior, not knowing what to say, how to take what he'd just learned.

Incrah's eyes softened to a look of pity. "Put it out of your mind for now Tolen. It is time to train. The Dominants are waiting."

Tolen stood up and shook his head. "Incrah, I'm sorry I can't. I-I just—" He turned on his heel and staggered back toward his tent; shame, guilt, worry, fear, and anger all vying for the biggest spot in the storm cloud of emotions swirling over him. He passed people, but saw no faces as he stumbled along the dusty trail. A tiny part of him was surprised Incrah hadn't tried to stop him, but the bigger part couldn't care. He barely made it through the tent door before he dropped to his knees.

For years he'd wanted to know who he was, what he was. And when Bastian and Macy showed up at his door, he felt sure he was going to get some answers. But the Watcher said he wasn't ready to know everything. He'd determined to learn, train, prove himself ready to know the full truth. He'd thought he'd found a friend and ally in Macy. But as the full weight of the Legend of the Ninth settled over Tolen, he knew just as he'd been wrong about Macy, he'd been wrong not to accept Bastian's plan. Even though he didn't fully understand what it meant, he felt no comfort, no relief in this new knowledge, only rising dread as the thought pressed down on his mind and heart.

I am the Ninth Chosen.

And he was not ready.

ACKNOWLEDGEMENTS

With the second edition of *The Shadow Prison*, now called *The Chosen Chronicles: A Chosen Life*, I have several incredible new people to thank, along with all those who have been with me since the beginning.

First, I must thank Heather Godfrey, Kirk Edwards, and all the amazing people at Snowy Peaks Media who loved this story from the beginning, and stood behind me with their encouragement and support as we took it to the next level. Thank you for this opportunity. You guys are fabulous!

I also want to thank my husband, Brent, and my two awesome kids for all the excitement, love, and super cool ideas; my parents, Jan and Jacy, for always being my biggest fans; my sisters-in-law, Staci and Tricia, for cheering me on and taking care of my social media needs; and all my remarkable friends for the love and encouragement when I need it most. I am truly blessed.

Big hugs and immense gratitude go out to my first edition beta readers and reviewers for all your advice, support, heart-warming and encouraging comments, and *positive* criticism that kept me writing and trying harder. I hope you find what you asked for in this edition.

Big thanks also to my second edition helpers: Dawn, Lisa, Angie, Suzie, Heather, and Laura for your character insights, and my new beta readers KayLynn, Kirk, TayLyn, Andrea, and Shannon.

Thank you David P. King, amazing author and ultimate blogger, for such a stellar review.

Thanks to Deborah Bradseth of Tugboat Design for her incredible talent designing the cover for this second edition, and to KayLynn for the gorgeous interior. You both are truly gems. Love ya!

And finally, I once again want to thank all the incredible youth I've had the privilege to work with over the years. This is all because of you.

THE CHOSEN CHRONICLES

SHADOW

THE

PRISON

K.A. PARKINSON

THE SHADOW PRISON

He wasn't alone.

The feeling that someone was watching him pulled Tolen from his restless sleep. He opened his eyes to see Jonas—the ancient guardian for the Radia Warrior camp that Tolen temporarily called home—sitting beside the cot, knobby hands folded across his cane, focused intently on Tolen's face.

Tolen sat up quickly and the blood rushed from his head, making Jonas appear blurry. He rubbed his eyes and cleared his scratchy throat. He'd slept terribly, his mind spinning like a carousel all night, tossing garbled images and sounds around and around, while his subconscious tried, and failed, to make sense of it all.

"Good morning Tolen," Jonas whispered.

"Is it?" Tolen mumbled while rubbing his temples.

Jonas shrugged his thin shoulders. "I suppose that is up to you."

Tolen knew why Jonas was in his tent watching him sleep, but figured he'd let the old guy bring it up, since honestly, he really didn't want to talk about it, but knew he'd have no choice. He leaned over, tugged on his sneakers, walked over to the metal basin, and splashed some of the cool water onto his face. The icy water dripped on his bare shoulders. He tugged a faded green shirt over his head and ran his fingers through his damp chocolate colored hair—all while trying to ignore that he had an audience.

Jonas waited until Tolen had sat back down on his cot, propped his elbows on his knees, and met the old man's eyes, before speaking.

"You had a difficult day yesterday."

Tolen looked at his clasped hands and shrugged. "I didn't do anything hard."

"I said difficult, not hard."

Tolen raised an eyebrow at the strange old man.

"Gift and weapon training is hard, *difficult* is accepting what you do not understand."

"How can you accept something you don't understand?" Tolen shook his head in frustration.

Jonas tapped his fingers on his cane. "Truth is truth whether it makes sense or not. That's why you couldn't deny what you learned, even if you didn't fully understand it. Yet."

Tolen thought back to what Nova told him about the Legend of the Ninth Chosen, how he'd known it was him, even though it made no sense. He looked into Jonas's strange eyes and saw a hint of a twinkle behind the cobwebbed surface.

He looked back at his hands and kept his eyes down as he asked, "Bastian told me I wasn't ready to know my destiny yet, that it wasn't the right time." He heard Jonas shift on his seat. "But, yesterday, Nova… I…she said some things, some things that…"

"She said some things that got your heart pounding and your mind working," Jonas prompted.

Tolen nodded.

Jonas took a noisy breath. "That was your body's response to truth." He waved his hand. Tolen could just see the tips of his fingers from his bowed position as they swished by. "Go on."

"There are only eight gifts."

"Yes."

"You said something along the lines of 'the Ninth shall lead them' when I first met you."

"Yes."

"I can do a combination of things that no other Hidden or Chosen can do."

"Yes. Yes you can."

"So, my destiny…" Tolen gulped. "I-I'm supposed to be some sort of leader?"

Jonas leaned forward and Tolen looked up to see his expression was very grave. "That is a crucial *piece* of your destiny, yes, Tolen. But it encompasses far, far more than that."

Tolen met the old man's gaze and tried for confidence, but his insides were wriggling. How could he, a consistently dangerous failure, lead anyone? "Can you tell me—?"

Jonas was shaking his head before the question had completely left Tolen's lips. "No, Tolen. The Watcher is right. There is much you still need to learn before you are ready to accept the grander part of your destiny."

Tolen's stomach twisted. More secrets. His hands closed into fists in his lap. How much worse could it be? He wasn't running away from it even if he wasn't ready. He'd been doing things beyond what was expected of him for years. Didn't that count for something? He'd been making decisions that would have qualified him as a man in the human world since he was twelve years old, caring for his sick mother, responsible for their food and bills.

A glimmer of fear quelled his inner argument. What if all this secrecy was because he was as dangerous as he feared? He shook off the thought and leaned back until his shoulders brushed the side of the tent. "How am I supposed to fulfill a destiny I don't even know?" he tried to keep his tone calm, but his frustration leaked through.

Jonas shook his head. "Your desires are fueled by anger and guilt, neither of which are good sources of energy to drive your intentions. Until you want to know for the right reasons, the knowledge will only hurt you, and slow your progress toward the ultimate purpose of your destiny."

Tolen bit back a retort that would just prove the old man right, and instead pushed on to something else. "Bastian said that the Light wanted me to try to save my dad from the Shadow Prison. I really think that the Dark might have my mom there too." He took a deep breath and plowed on, ignoring the regretful look forming on Jonas's face. "Bastian said he would ask the warriors here to help me, but since h-he's gone, I…I'm asking you. Will you help me?"

Jonas stared back until Tolen's hands started to shake and he had to look away. "Tolen, when is your eighteenth birthday?"

This question was so far off base that Tolen's hands stopped shaking and he glanced back into Jonas's lined face. "July tenth."

Jonas nodded slowly and ran his thumb across his crinkly chin, his eyes deep in thought. Calculating. "Less than a month away."

Tolen swallowed and nodded, not daring to hope that this weird twist in conversation had something to do with helping him.

"Has anyone told you of Transcendence?"

"Transcendence?" Tolen shook his head.

Jonas nodded as if unsurprised. "Transcendence is the point at which the physical body and the metaphysical gifts of the Light fully intersect and become one. It is the time when your powers, your *gifts*, reach their peak, their strongest. This always takes place on the eighteenth birthday." He leaned forward and the gravity of his next words sent a thrill of fear over Tolen. "At your Transcendence, Tolen, not even the Spheres of the citadel will be able to shield you if you don't learn enough. If you don't exercise patience, learn all you can, and master your anger, when you transcend, the Dark will take you for their own." He tapped his temple. "Work hard, Tolen, focus, discover the right fuel for your desires, and then we will help you. The journey to save your father, and possibly your mother, will be fraught with danger and much difficulty. It is not an idle task. If you are not ready to face the darkness of the Shadow Prison, if you are too close to the time of your Transcendence and your gifts are too erratic, it would be a mission destined to fail, no matter the amount of warriors who went with you."

Tolen bit his lip as the truth settled over him. He was dangerous. He knew this. Could he really expect others to follow him on a quest to save his parents when he could be the very reason they would fail? "Maybe…Maybe the Radia Warriors can go without me? Maybe they can find a way to save him—them?"

Jonas narrowed his eyes. "Tolen, there is something you need to understand about your Watcher gift. You saw your father because *you* are meant to watch over him. In your visions, did you see anyone besides yourself in there with him?"

Tolen shook his head as the nightmare filled his mind—his father on the floor, Tolen standing above him, helpless to do anything. "No. It was just the two of us."

"A Watcher sees flashes of present, possibility, and set future." Jonas pointed to Tolen's eye. "If the vision you beheld showed only yourself, then it is very likely that you are the only one who holds the key to his rescue. Other unseen factors *may* have played a role, but ultimately, no matter how many warriors I send, you may be the only one with the tools to succeed. I do not want to send my family into a losing battle. Tell me if your visions change, but until then, Tolen, I suggest you work to make yourself ready to achieve what your visions are urging you to attempt. When I feel you are ready, when I feel you are strong enough, and in control, I will ask my warriors to go with you."

ABOUT THE AUTHOR

K.A. Parkinson was raised in a small suburb where she spent most of her time hiding under her bed with a book, a bag of cookies, and a flashlight. She currently resides in Utah with her husband and two children. If you would like to learn more about K.A., and the world of the Hidden, please visit www.kaparkinson.com.

To learn more about Snowy Peaks Media, please visit
www.snowypeaksmedia.com

If you enjoyed this book, please review it on
Amazon or Goodreads.

CHARACTER INDEX

FOLLOWERS OF LIGHT (BY ORDER OF APPEARANCE)

McLacy (Macy) Allicandra Burdow—Chosen (human)

    Parents: Max and Alli Burdow

Forrest Bastian—Watcher

Tolen (Parks) Téloran—The Ninth Chosen (Hidden kind)

    Parents: Daedal Téloran (Protector) Areen Téloran (Sphere)

Dane Smithy—Doogar

    Father: Hank Smithy—Doogar

Hander—Doogar

Kiad—Doogar Warrior

Deegan—Doogar Warrior

Elryn—Doogar Warrior

Incrah—Radia Warrior Captain

Jeno—Radia Warrior

Kapha—Radia Warrior

Rada—Radia Warrior

Denhon—Radia Warrior

Sernad—Radia Warrior

Beyn—Radia Warrior

Jonas—Sphere and shield to the Unastra training camp

Lafar—Light elves

SERVANTS OF THE DARK (BY ORDER OF APPEARANCE):

Shadow Wraiths—Thick, black, oily, mist-like creatures who hide in storm clouds

Raksasha—Blood trackers. Main purpose is to track and kill the Chosen

Night Demons—Blood drinking demons who pull themselves up from the ground to feed on the death of the battlefield. Their decaying flesh is covered with maggots and bloody scabs. They are bald, have no eyes, or legs. Night Demons are one of the most grotesque creatures born of darkness

Divinators (crows)—Their eyes have been replaced by Oracle stones. Whatever they see, their masters see

Reconn—Chameleon type creatures used mostly as scouts

Phantoms—These mist-like creatures are placed within the dead or dying to reanimate and control them

Ookra—Demon servants

DéHool—Giant demonic wolves. Their sole purpose is to hunt and destroy Watchers

Darsapean—Lord of the Dark, currently imprisoned in Misery

Daemon—Demon Master and High Captain of the Dark

Daklafar—Once Lafar-Light Elves, but now serve the Dark

Tormentors—Tall women with gray skin, lifeless black eyes, and floor length orange hair. Their screams cause unbearable pain. The dark uses them to extract information from their prisoners

Kreydawn—Mindless creatures controlled by Suppressors

Suppressors—Single-eyed creatures with the Dreamer ability, they control the services of the Kreydawn

Chosen Groups/Abilities:

Honitahai—Nature speakers: have the ability to speak with all plant life and ask for aid

Kunamin—Fire wielders: can create, manipulate, throw, and snuff fire with their hands

Télora—Earth Movers: can ask the dirt to do their bidding

Arwah—Wind Shifters: can use the power of wind to aid them

Dicernan—Unseens: can become invisible

Leenwa—Water Callers: can call water from anywhere and ask it to help

Animashta—Listeners: they understand animal's thoughts and communicate with them. They can project their own thoughts and desires into the animal's minds, as if they are sharing thought. It enables them to work together as a flawless team—so long as the animal is listening and willing. The animal always has a choice—it is not forced the way the DéHool are

Lóklana—Radiance: they can call light in darkness from within the life
that stores it

Hidden Language Dictionary:
Ladonradi—The Light
Degani—The Dark
Liosladon—May the Light lead and protect you wherever you may go
Ladon—Light. Light come forth is Radi
Tò'—The
Y'na—I am
Hai—Here
Mindra—Chosen
Vast—Fight
Pench Ni'yā àlo—Be still
Lon'adras—Heal
Dón—For
Y' takra—Take me
Da'bay—Friend
Ke'ay—Help
Mea—Me
Chan'ta—Please
Mah'ne—Journey
I'kashti—Summon
Walkarna—Servants come
Minradak-con-siadras—This ground is sacred and protected. The words
spoken to bless the earth and make it burial ground, protecting those
buried from the Night Demons
To'conchla serith hune doocrah—The Ninth shall lead them.

Chosen Terms:
Mi'no ha—Life to fire
Vin'akra—Life to wind

Ma'sha—Hear me animal

Win'tashta—Water hear my call

Tin'ruhl—Earth hear my call

Radi'non—Light come forth

Los'lon—Nature hear me

Vel'don—Veil me within

To'Conchla—The Ninth

Mindra—Chosen

Words said to increase the body's natural abilities. Each word when said with intent has the power to speak to the life force and ask it to enhance that body part:

Konsh'la—Makes your hearing stronger. "The ears"

Inreedo—Makes your eyesight stronger. "The eyes"

Mig'nata—Increases strength. "The body"

To'—The

Lon'adras—heal, repair, return